The Divina in the Troupe

The Divina in the Troupe

A Novel of Time Travel

Thomas T. Thomas

THE DIVINA IN THE TROUPE

Copyright 2019 Thomas T. Thomas
Cover photo © bernie_photo / iStockphoto

Paperback ISBN: 978-0-9861054-7-0
Ebook ISBN: 978-0-9861054-8-7

Contents

Excerpts from a 102nd Century Dictionary

CHASSIS, *N.S.*: (1) A frame and working parts, as of a machine or electronic device, exclusive of housing and external surfaces; (2) of any Silicate intelligence, one or more interchangeable physical carriers designed for some specific purpose and having the shape, structure, and tools appropriate to that purpose.

COMPRADORO, *ADJ.*: OF or relating to a time-traveling culture of the late ninth millennium. Their interventions in previous time streams through the notorious Sindicato della Conoscenza tended to muddy clear historical waters.

DIVINA, *N.S.&PL., M.&F.*: any member of a humanoid race of the chordate *Hexapoda,* noted for their mental deficiency, voiceless state, and musical talent.

FLÜCHTLING, *N.S., M.,* ~**e,** *pl.:* fugitive, refugee, runaway; *colloq.* an outcast from the reference now *(q.v.),* usually gathering in an earlier time and place as members of *(collective term)* a coven. *O.G.*

HEXAPOD, *N.S.,* ~**A,** *pl.:* subphylum of the order *Chordata* (not to be confused with the subphylum of the order *Arthropoda,* of the same name), consisting of various classes, orders, families, and genera of vertebrates possessing six functioning limbs, variously styled as arms, legs, and sometimes wings, as opposed to the four limbs of the superclass *Tetrapoda.* All chordate Hexapods possess a well-conserved anomaly in their homeobox gene cluster that differentiates them from the parallel evolution of Tetrapods.

JONGLEUR, *N.S., M.,* ~**s,** *pl.:* 1. tumbler, acrobat, juggler, street busker; *also,* mountebank, huckster, charlatan; 2. *(cap.)* an officer of the organization that consolidates and regulates travel through time, member of *(collective term)* the Troupe. *O.F.*

MÖGLICHKEIT, *N.S., F.,* **~en,** *pl.:* possibility; **Möglich, ~en,** *pl.:* a sentient theoretical construct from one or more probabilistic decision points *(cf. Wahrschein Punkt)* following the "Schein" or "not taken" direction. *O.G.*

NEURAL IMPRINT, *N.S.:* the process of transcribing electrochemical activity in the human brain into quantum entanglement of electrons across multiple time cones, as a means of preserving thought and memory against distortions due to alteration of the past. For Jongleurs, the preserving impulse is initiated by touching the right forefinger to left eyelid; the recovering impulse is by touching the left forefinger to right eyelid. Silicate imprinting employs a different paradigm.

REFERENCE NOW, *N.S.:* current time, the actual or true "now," as perceived from a subjective viewpoint. Colloquially, as applied to time travel, "reference now" may also refer to the traveler's original or starting time and place, as opposed to the time and place of arrival.

SELVAGE, *N.S.:* 1. THE edge on either side of a woven or flat-knitted fabric so finished as to prevent raveling; 2. of a fractured singularity *(q.v.)*, the process of annealing the point of quantum leakage so that it does not naturally close.

SILICATE, *N.S.:* ANY member of the machine culture, or technosphere, arising in the late ninth millennium in the borough of Sheffod on the island of Ongleterre. Silicates are self-aware cybernetic systems sharing a common origin.

SINGULARITY, *N.S.:* 1. *(PHYSICS)* a point or region of infinite mass density at which space and time are infinitely distorted by gravitational forces; the final state of matter falling into a black hole; 2. *(mathematics)* a point at which the derivative of a given function of a complex variable does not exist but every neighborhood of which contains points for which the derivative does exist; **fractured s~:** a singularity exhibiting quantum leakage of mass/energy into one or more temporospatial dimensions.

TEMPS, *N.S.&PL., M.:* 1. time; 2. weather; 3. *(grammatical)* tense; 4. *(musical)* tempo, *T. fort,* downbeat, *T. faible,* upbeat; 5. *(gymnastics, military exercises)* repetition. *O.F.*

VOYAGEUR, *N.S., M.* **~s,** *pl.:* traveler, passenger, explorer. *O.F.*

WAHRSCHEIN, ~LICHKEIT, *N.S., f.,* **~en,** *pl.:* probability; ~ **Punkt:** probability node, probabilistic decision point. *O.G.*

Prologue: Arriving in Lune

THE STOLEN MEDICAL ship landed on the grassy slope that defined the southern crest line of the Temz valley and the boundary of Lune. The ship's intelligence cycled the portal, and Merola, with Berzher's baton in its holster, Rydin, and Cinquemain stepped out into the fresh air and sunlight. From this elevation she could spot, across the river, in the northwest quadrant of the village, the tree that she called home.

"Can we make the first order of business getting me a new chassis?" said the intelligence at her hip. "I get seasick when you walk."

"To get seasick," Cinquemain said, "you would need a stomach—and an inner ear."

"No," Berzher corrected, "just a jury-rigged motion sensor."

"Yes, first thing," Merola told her intelligence. "You can pick out the entire tool kit." And then, to Rydin: "What are we going to do with the ship? It's contraband, isn't it?"

"That will be for the Troupe to decide," he answered. "However, I think there are only three possibilities: turn it over to Dottoressa Gerbus and the clinic for deep-time studies, return it to the ninth-millennium builders, or crash it into the sun."

"Did he say, 'crash into the sun'?" the ship's intelligence asked through the portal.

"Of course," Rydin went on, "returning the ship to Lore raises a problem—that uploaded personality software."

"Hey, you ordered that," Cinquemain protested.

"More like a question or suggestion," Rydin said.

"I don't want to 'crash into the sun,' " the ship said.

"We'll have to see what the Troupe decides," Rydin told the ship. "Close the portal, please."

The returning travelers started down the slope. Merola was wearing the clothing she had first worn to twenty-first century

London: knee-length skirt, blouse and jacket, and pumps with stacked heels. The heels did poorly in turf and nearly turned her ankles when they reached the crushed-chalk pathways of Lune. She ended up taking off the shoes and walking in the grass alongside the chalk.

"You do understand that all of this was your fault," Rydin told her as they walked. "Don't you?"

"Berzher has explained to me about the baseball," she said. "But I still don't remember any of it."

"That's because you didn't follow protocol and failed to take an imprint before starting your mission."

"But Berzher could remember."

"That's because his brain processed imprints right up until his chassis was destroyed and his power inputs cut—which was *after* the baseball exchange but *before* the point in time that I … corrected your first error."

"What did you do?"

"Made certain that Pinkus Boskin never heard of baseball."

"Did you kill him?"

"Oh, nothing so crude," Rydin said. "Cinquemain and I simply arranged that certain influences never surfaced in his life. What you do not know, you cannot covet. That eliminated not only your own temptation but also the probability of his contaminating other Jongleurs as well."

"That still didn't bring me home," she observed.

"No, because by then—and through the action of stealing the McGwire baseball—you had already attracted other attention. A trio of Flüchtlinge became so fixated on your mere existence that, apparently, any change in pre-existing circumstances, such as non-theft of the ball, could not shake them off."

"I never saw them," she said.

"But Cinquemain and I did."

"I killed one of them," the intelligence said.

"And did they send the Möglich after me?"

"Perhaps not intentionally," Rydin answered, "but we know the Möglichen sometimes follow them."

"So, the three Flüchtlinge blew up the toy store. That sent me to London and the Gill family's mirror-maze. And there the Möglich saw me and followed us back to the Devonian. What happened to my backup suit and ship?"

"And my chassis," Berzher added.

"Perhaps the Flüchtlinge were simply being thorough," Rydin said. "Perhaps the Möglich had already spotted you."

"So even though, by now, with your help, I have actually committed no breach of protocol—"

"Except," Berzher put in, "for neglecting that first neural imprint."

"—don't do anything like that again," Rydin finished. "Fortunately, we were able to resolve the situation without—"

By this time, they had walked through the outskirts of the village, penetrated the outer ring of treehouses, and switched through several branchings in the path. They had already passed a number of public benches, set out in sunlit glades, where citizens could relax in their idle moments. On the bench they were approaching a musician sat and sang a mournful song of love and loss, accompanying herself—for the person appeared to be female, although it was hard to tell—on a familiar nine-stringed mandolin. At the same time, she underscored the melody with chords from a squeeze-box concertina. The fact that this performance required one mouth and four hands, while the performer sat comfortably cross-legged on the bench, struck all three of the travelers at the same time.

Merola looked around. Other people were using the paths as well, and they were indeed all … people. Two arms, two legs, normal placement and posture. One of them, the circuit designer who had recently improved the efficiency of her last liteship, greeted her.

"Why, hello, Mira Tsverin," he said. "Have a good flight?"

"Yes, um, thank you, very smooth, Mir Dustin."

"Always good to hear." He walked on.

This exchange had interrupted the musician, who paused, looked up at them, and smiled. The face was almost human, but the eyes were a fraction too widely set and had the vacant look that—in an earlier age, when such things were allowed to happen—suggested brain damage.

Merola smiled back.

The singer merely said, "Hmmm," and picked up her song again.

Merola, Rydin, and Cinquemain walked on in a state of shock. At the same instant, the two humans reached up and touched their right eyelids. Merola did not know what Rydin might be feeling, but the imprint did nothing for her.

"It could be some kind of mutation," he began when they were out of earshot.

"Not in a genome as thoroughly cleansed as yours," Cinquemain replied.

"Could it be a recessive gene?" Merola asked. "Something from—"

"Generally, recessive developmental coding will kill the fetus."

"Then some kind of parallel evolution?" Rydin suggested.

"Your antibody worked," she said. "Most of the time."

"Not a word of this to anyone," Rydin ordered.

"No," she said. "Way too much to explain."

"No Search reports with the Troupe."

"What about the Conoscenza?"

"For once, we let them go."

"Without retaliation?"

"On what basis?"

"Never mind!"

Forward

1. One Second Later

"YOU REALIZE …" Merola Tsverin began and then paused.

Coel Rydin waited for her to complete her thought. The four companions had stopped on the crushed-chalk path in Lune, a hundred meters beyond the bench with the six-limbed songstress. The two humans were facing each other, while their Silicate intelligences waited with them: Cinquemain in his low-profile, eight-legged mobile chassis, Berzher encased in a sensory baton that had been devised for him by Sam Gill, the Builders' station keeper at Crossroads House in—when was it again? The London of the early twenty-first century. A lot had happened since then …

"For all these people—" Merola went on, waving her arm at the nearby paths and treehouses. "—*our* people, this is all *normal*."

Around them, Rydin reflected, all of Lune resembled a remarkably orderly and well-kept forest, because the residents lived in genetically sculpted trees, variants of the genus *Acer, Quercus,* and the occasional slender *Ulmus.* Bioscientists had trained their seedlings to grow into graceful, spreading homes among the sparkling white pathways. And all of this was normal. But what Merola seemed to be implying was that the people living there—the category of beings that Rydin would have defined as "sentient"—might now no longer possess only two arms and two legs.

"What is normal?" Berzher asked from his holster at her hip.

"That woman with the extra hands," Merola said. "Oh, you didn't exactly see her, but she was—"

"Cinquemain has just transmitted the image," Berzher replied. "The monstrosity …"

"Merola is right," Rydin said. "That … creature did not just pop into existence immediately after we left the ancient Earth of the Devonian period. She—and probably others of her

9

kind—have been evolving from a six-limbed fish, seeded by the Möglich monster whom we failed to stop three hundred million years in their past."

"Three hundred and sixty, plus or minus twenty million," Cinquemain put in.

"That means," Rydin continued, "this time stream is thoroughly embedded in everyone else's consciousness. This world and these creatures are the reality now."

Cinquemain made the soft noise that sounded like criticism. "You say 'this time stream' as if there were some other."

"There's the one we left," Merola said. "The one that wasn't infested with—what? Chimeras? Hexapods? Four-handed monkeys? And that's a start."

"Apparently, we are also from that past, too," Rydin said. "You saw how that circuit engineer, Dustin, greeted you by name back there. He recognized you. So the temporal disjunction—let's call it the 'Devonian mistake' for now—did not keep any of us from being born, making a life here in Lune, and joining the Troupe."

"I can't believe that millions of years of a parallel evolution with these other humanoid creatures didn't change at least *some* parts of the world we left," Merola said. "I mean, is there even a Troupe anymore? Are we still Jongleurs? Do we have homes to go back to?"

"All of that is waiting for us to find out," Rydin said. "For now, take comfort that Dustin was unsurprised to see you—and he did fix your ship."

"It's a start to what?" Berzher asked.

"Excuse me?" Merola said, confused.

"Thirty-six seconds ago in this conversation you mentioned 'a start,' " the Silicate said. "What did you mean by that?"

"I don't know yet," she replied. "Maybe … we can find a way to fix things?"

Rydin sighed mentally. "Certainly. It is our duty to restore the time stream."

"That would be a lot of evolution to try to reverse," Berzher said.

"We just have to find the right place to put our lever," Merola said.

It seemed to be time for someone—Rydin himself—to take command.

"Very well then. I am still a Jongleur chief—your chief—even if there is, or is not, a Jongleur Troupe still in existence. And whether or not we are still part of it. So, for now, we will operate as if on Search, with full masking protocols."

"Against our own people?" Merola asked.

"Against the unknown," he replied.

2. Home Again

AFTER THE FOUR of them broke up, with promises to meet later, Merola Tsverin and Berzher walked the path—the almost-familiar path, with here and there a new branching—to her treehouse, or what she thought was hers.

It was still based on a Norway maple, *Acer platanoides*, whose wing-shaped seeds had been harvested in Nortamerica in the late second millennium. Lune's biosculptors had genetically modified the genome so that its limbs formed planks and supporting columns, and its leaves overlapped to create enclosed, weather-tight rooms. Genes from other modified organisms furnished the materials for windows, water supply and waste disposal systems, and even electrical conductors. Her home was familiar in every respect—except that the main room now had *five* sides instead of four, the ceiling was artfully domed instead of arched, and a window of secreted *Mollusca* shell that had once faced north now looked south. Merola recognized all these changes without having to refresh her neural imprint.

So some things *had* changed in the current reference now … unless she herself had disappeared and this tree had become someone else's home.

"Excuse me?" said the voice at her hip. "Fully functioning organic person? Could you get me a mobile transport now?"

"Oh, sure," she told Berzher.

The tree's utility closet—at least that was still in the right place—held, among other things, a generalized crablike robot, with minimal weaponry, localized communications, and none of the interfaces needed on Search for piloting a liteship. It was the chassis Berzher preferred to occupy when off duty. Merola freed it and opened the carapace. Then she took the baton from her hip, unsnapped the rounded end cap, and released the glass ball with its filigreed layers of gold-wire circuitry that was Berzher's central processor. She inserted the intelligence's brain into the robot and closed the access hatch. After two seconds, the machine stirred, its legs stretched and flexed, and the camera stalks swiveled to find and focus on her.

"Thank you," the intelligence said. "Except … this isn't mine."

"What? It *looks* like yours—the one we left here. How is it different?"

Berzher made a churring noise. "Could you describe your leg if it belonged to somebody else? The contact points, the equipment setup, the residual software are all different. It's like wearing another individual's skin. And the serial number is off by sixteen digits."

"Your factories put serial numbers on those things?"

"Sure. How else do you keep track of inventory?"

"But are you incompatible with its technology?"

"I can cope," he said. "Just need to re-route a few circuits."

Next, Merola wanted to establish the date of this reference now, the exact time in this millennium that they had returned to occupy. In the corner of the main room, between two windows, where it resided in shade but received residual sunlight, once had stood her horological fern. This was a gift from Rydin, who was a biosculptor—an artist, really. He designed the fern's diurnal rhythm to open and close the tender fronds in a pattern that counted off the hours, days, and months, and then he had taught her how to read them.

The fern was now gone, and in its place was a terrarium with an orb weaver spider, which she vaguely remembered from her biology training as being from the family *Araneidea*. The tiny animal had created a complicated web with many overlays and dropouts. Merola guessed that this pattern was meant to display a calendar as well, driven by an engram genetically inserted into the spider's brain. But she could not interpret the date, because she had never seen this creature before. The worse trouble was, she didn't know any biosculptor who worked with insects—it certainly wasn't one of Rydin's creations—or who might have given her the clock.

At a loss now, she asked Berzher for the true date, knowing that he could access the telemetry network the Silicates maintained among themselves.

"It is two days after you left—we left—on Search. That was the original mission which included the unfortunate baseball incident and your encounter with the Möglich."

"Did it take us that much time—time in *this* reference now—to transit from the Devonian?"

Berzher consulted his external resources again. "No, the choice of arrival point from a Search—even one as complicated as Rydin's mission to rescue you—is always precise to the minute and second. The delay is because the Troupe waited two days in this reference now before declaring you overdue and sending him back to track you down."

"I see. A lot must have happened in those two days," she said.

"Or in the last three hundred and sixty million years."

It was as if other people had lived here who were almost, but not quite, like her. Or could *another* Merola—one with slightly different tastes and friends—have lived in the tree during the million-year invasion of the four-handed monkeys? Troupe doctrine said such a thing was not possible, that the personhood of a Jongleur remained intact from the start of one Search mission to the return. But no Jongleur had ever, to her knowledge, traveled back to the origins of chordate morphology on this planet. Perhaps, in such an incredible time span, impossible things could happen.

"My house turns out to be much like your chassis," Merola said. "The same but different. What have we gotten ourselves into?"

"Nothing good," her companion replied.

3. A Whole New Genome

"I AM HAVING trouble accessing the Troupe network," Cinquemain told Rydin as they walked toward his treehouse in Lune.

"Is it a problem with the telecommunications of your chassis?" he asked. After the beating Cinquemain's robotic form had taken recently—including a fall from more than one hundred meters when their last liteship exploded above a hillside in Lore, on the Indian subcontinent—it would be no wonder if a few connections had loosened.

"No," the machine replied. "I have full communication with the Silicates—and have had that since we arrived. But the human bandwidth is—" A pause. "Ah, offset by four hundred and fifty kilohertz above its previous signaling range."

"Could that be a glitch in your tuning system?" Rydin asked.

"Not at all. It seems the frequency spectrum has … changed."

"So? Now tie into the Troupe and find out what they know."

"Are you planning to make a mission report after all?"

"Nothing more than the fact that we found Tsverin and brought her back," Rydin said. "And only in reply to the query from Personnel that reported her overdue."

"But not the whole truth," Cinquemain observed.

"The whole truth would include the fact that she broke protocol by stealing a baseball for a rich collector. But that person is not now—and, through my subsequent action, has never been—interested in the game. Such a breach would end Tsverin's career. Worse, the Troupe might put her under the authority of another chief. And that would make it harder for her to keep our secret."

"So, nothing about our trip back to the Devonian and the changes it created."

"Which no one in this time stream would believe anyway. So why bother?"

"A point. Nothing about the four-armed singer we found on the bench?"

"Not until you can scan the archives and get me a genome to match."

As a biosculptor, Rydin was eager to explore the new genome represented by the six-limbed creature they had just seen. From the fact that the "normal" humans around them, including the circuit engineer Dustin, took the singer for granted, Rydin surmised that the creatures—and other variants with multiple limbs, similar to the "seals" and "horses" he and Cinquemain had observed in their brief return to the eleventh millennium during the previous mission—were probably embedded in the current time stream, although not to the exclusion of more familiar, tetrapod life forms and humans.

Cinquemain's telemetric scan of the genetic database took less time than Rydin anticipated. "Nothing," his pilot and companion reported.

"Nothing from any Jongleur Search in the past?" Rydin asked.

"Nothing from any Search, any current research effort, or from any medical records. It is as if the creatures do not exist."

"But we saw one," Rydin said.

"Yes. One. Maybe a freak."

"After our fighting that six-limbed monster over the lobe-finned fishes? A mere freak would be too much of a coincidence."

"Perhaps the singer on the bench was a genetic throwback to a race that was short-lived and died out," Cinquemain suggested.

"Not since our bioengineers actively purged the human genome of damaging recessives. And certainly none would remain in the developmental homeobox gene set, which is the key to bodily form and function. But ... we are not *complete* masters of the genome, after all. So ... yes, hold that thought for now."

Still, it was odd, Rydin thought. Extremely odd. The Troupe's most critical mission was research into ancient genomes, to adapt gene sequences and proteins from the evolving biosphere and use them in creating new and useful plants and animals. A radically altered homeobox—such as Rydin had studied back in the Devonian, in trying to counter the Möglich's viral alteration of the fish genome with his own cleansing antibodies—would be useful in many other animal experiments. Yet here was the most significant departure from the tetrapod gene set ever discovered, and nobody had explored it.

"Perhaps these creatures are too new?" Cinquemain said.

"No, they might be new to us, because we've just returned to this reference now. But these creatures have been coexisting with ... well, with the amphibians and lizards, the dinosaurs, the mammals, and the first species of the genus *Homo,* competing with all of them since ... well, forever. Based on that cat-thing Merola and the Conoscenza people say they discovered in London immediately after the Fire Strike, it's a parallel evolution. Or it would have been, except we caught and reversed the Möglich's viral agent."

"Or you thought you did," the robot said.

"Apparently we weren't thorough enough."

"So now you want to go back and try again."

"First things first," Rydin said. "I want to study a current specimen to see how the gene set has evolved."

"Except you don't have a specimen to study," Cinquemain replied. "Not even traces."

"And isn't that curious? The Troupe's geneticists have shown no interest in this hexapod species."

"Unless someone is hiding something ..."

"And hiding it pretty thoroughly."

4. Evading Authority

"Report!" The command came a full ten hours after Cinquemain, along with his human and cybernetic companions, had quietly returned to the Lune of the eleventh millennium.

The source of this command was the embedded intelligence that coordinated the Silicate side of Troupe operations. She—for the digital signal's inflexion and phrasing were those of a human female—went by the pseudonym "Nexus." Few of the other Silicates, and none of the humans in the Troupe, knew the true identity of this intelligence. The Silicates often speculated whether she even had a mobile form, like the mechanical chassis inhabited by Cinquemain, Berzher, and other pilot cybers, or was static and fixed in one location, possibly because of the multiple connections, simultaneous communication streams, and vast memory caches required to run such a complex organization.

In moments when he was off line and out of Nexus's hearing, Cinquemain usually referred to her as "Mother"—but not with the affection that humans normally held for their female parent.

And now, given the strictures that Rydin had placed on communications the four returnees' might have with the Troupe, Cinquemain had postponed contacting Nexus for as long as possible. Ten hours—thirty-six thousand seconds, as humans counted time—was the better part of an organic lifetime in terms of Silicate awareness.

"I have been gathering facts," Cinquemain replied evasively.

"And I have tracked your progress with that," Nexus replied. "You have scanned the composite human genetic databases quite thoroughly. Along with fifty-seven other vertebrate sequences. How is this relevant to your last mission?"

That was a trap right there, and Cinquemain recognized it as such. "The genetic researches were not part of my mission," he answered truthfully. "I was gathering information for my human counterpart. It was in support of his biosculpting hobby."

The conversation paused.

"Noted," the other intelligence said. "But now you are overdue for your mission report. I already have a file, entered six hours ago, from the intelligence identified as Berzher, who is associate and pilot to the Jongleur Merola Tsverin. These two were originally recorded as the subjects of your mission with Rydin. So I already know they have returned."

"Yes … that much is true," Cinquemain acknowledged. "We met up with them in London in the early third millennium. Tsverin and Berzher had become trapped in that time stream through the loss of their liteship."

"I have that information. Due to the quote gas main explosion unquote recorded in Berzher's report. These terms parse to an inadvertent failure of an energy utility appropriate to the historical period."

"Yes … that would explain the loss."

"Do not waste my intervals with your speculations and second-hand evaluations," Nexus said. "Make your report with a formal download—in this case, your complete RAM dump."

"A download would be … difficult," Cinquemain replied. "My processor's cache was partially wiped—" That was false. But Cinquemain's circuitry and software were sophisticated enough to be able to formulate and transmit a falsehood on one level of awareness, hold a competing version of the truth at another and deeper level, and still know the difference between them on a third level. "—by the pulse from a singularity implosion that destroyed our own liteship." This much was true—although by now and at this distance hardly provable.

"Two craft and their singularity cores lost in one mission," Nexus summarized. "That is unfortunate. The expense will be catalogued and charged to your accounts." The intelligence paused. "But this raises a further question. How did you return to this millennium without your ships?"

"We had to steal a timeship from the shipyards of Lore, in the ninth millennium."

"You stole from the Compradoros?" Nexus registered amusement. "And what became of *that* ship?"

"It is parked on a hillside south of town …" Cinquemain replied without first analyzing his response. *Oh, curse!* he registered at that lower level. *Factual deception is not an easy skill to master.*

But Nexus had other concerns. "You brought a Compradoro ship—a time-traveling artifact—into this time stream!" The cold voice expressed an emotion that, in humans, Cinquemain would have identified as horror.

"It's not carrying anything like the Ancestor," he said quickly. "The ship is just a plain, unadorned saucer—although I did have to make some modifications to its operating system—supplementing its intelligence—in order to put it under voice control."

"You made a Silicate out of a ninth-millennium hulk …"

"But its cybernetic functions are still not entirely capable."

In truth, "Little Brother"—which was how Cinquemain thought of the medical ship after the infusion from his own personality—was an imbecile. The ship had all, or almost all, of the code from Cinquemain's awareness but none of his sophisticated, eleventh-millennium hardware. So the medship's mind kept trying to overdrive its brain. Cinquemain thought of a pre-Fire Strike maxim about "new wine in old wineskins." Or more simply, that the ship's "cup was running over." It was a "hulk" to be sure, and a fallible one.

"It is still an anomaly," Nexus replied. "I must report this to the Troupe."

Cinquemain bit down on the part of his communications circuitry that corresponded to the human tongue, the function directly connecting random thought with ungoverned speech. He had almost told Nexus, "No, please don't!" But that would have sounded suspicious in any context.

All he could hope for was that the Troupe would dismiss the medship as a scrap of ancient and uninteresting technology. Not look inside it. And certainly not start asking it questions, like where it had been, and what it had seen and recorded.

5. The Lives of Others

COEL RYDIN WAS still looking around the main room of his tree-house when he heard and felt a human weight bend the steps in the lowermost branch.

"Are you at home?" called Merola's voice.

"You can come up," he replied, raising his voice. With a house foundation so flexible and walls made of overlapping leaves, he had no need of a mechanical doorbell or the intercoms he had seen on homes in the late second millennium.

Merola parted the leaves that hung over the entry and stepped into the room. "Didn't the door used to be on the *west* side of the trunk?" she asked.

"You noticed that right away," he said. "It took me a minute to figure out."

"Things have changed here since ... we ... left."

"I'm still working on it."

"For one thing, that horological fern you made for me—you remember that?"

"What about it?"

"It's gone."

"You mean it died? We weren't absent *that* long from this reference now."

"No, it's been replaced. I now have a time-telling spider in a terrarium in its place. Do you know any biosculptors who work with insects?"

"Arachnids, actually. But no one I know."

Rydin pointed to a shelf along the south wall—what once was south but now was east—where he normally kept his prized plant specimens. Arranged there by size were a number of bright green lumps studded with clusters of thin white spines. He approached the shelf and saw each lump was moving on thousands of tiny, white, suction-cup feet, like a starfish. Slowly, so slowly, they glided along the shelf's surface—kept from falling off by a railing of fiddlevine—toward a low pan filled with what looked like water. While he watched, one of the lumps finished drinking or sampling the water and moved away, and another took its place.

He dipped his finger in the pan and tasted. It was indeed water, and fresh, not more than a day old.

"So you still work with plants," Merola observed.

"No—well, yes—but my last project was with vampire orchids. These appear to be a species of mutated cactus. *Carnegiea* or *Opuntia*, I would think. But I've never worked with them."

"Is this even your house?" she asked.

"I thought it was. It's in the right place."

"What does Cinquemain have to say?"

"He had to attend to Troupe business."

"Berzher said his chassis is different."

"Different how?" Rydin wondered.

"New circuits. Strange serial number."

"It's like everything here is familiar …"

"But different," she concluded.

"It would seem that the four of us set out from this reference now, but in our old time stream, and came back to find our old selves … altered."

"Or, possibly," Merola countered, "an altered version of us grew up in *this* time stream, went on their various missions to the early third millennium, got detoured to the Devonian period to chase the lobe-finned fishes, just as we did, and came back as … us."

"We might be living paradoxes," Rydin suggested. "Our actions in the distant past eliminated our own doppelgangers— that is, if they ever really were 'us.' "

"Or are we just waiting for them to come back from that parallel mission? Maybe to eliminate *us*."

Rydin suddenly had a sick feeling that he was living in a bubble of time—a sensation he had never felt before, despite all the neural imprints he had taken over the years. He was suddenly aware that the world, his world, his sense of reality, his *consciousness*, might collapse at any instant.

"What can we do?" Merola said.

"I—I have no idea," he replied.

6. Confiscation

An hour after his conversation—it fell short of a full mission report—with Nexus, Cinquemain received another communication from the organizing intelligence: "The Troupe has decided to confiscate the ninth-millennium saucer that you and your human Jongleur, Coel Rydin, brought into this reference now."

Nexus's transmission, rendered in digital bits, still carried the cold, self-satisfied finality of a disapproving grandmother or a Catholic mother superior. The latter was a comparison he had made during a mission to late seventeenth-century France. The former was from observation of human grandmothers of every time and place.

Cinquemain was surprised. "Why did this decision take so long?"

"Because humans, the Troupe's Ringmasters, were involved."

"It wasn't Silicate prejudice against a Compradoro artifact?"

"That, too," Nexus acknowledged. "The Silicate Collective is concerned about the ship's possible intentions and motivations."

"It has none," Cinquemain replied. "The personality transfer was a failure. The machine is a relative imbecile and clinically neurotic."

"We are also concerned that, if this altered ship were put into general use and taken back to the ninth millennium, or earlier, it might contaminate an entire generation of pre-Silicate intelligences—with unpredictable results for us here in the eleventh millennium."

"Then Rydin and I won't use it again," he promised.

"Also, the humans would like to examine its records."

Uh-oh! That was a human expression, of course. Cinquemain's operating system registered it in hexadecimal as low and high, beginning and end, 0000 and FFFF—for which he was sure humans of the late twentieth century would have had a suitable translation.

"It doesn't *have* records," he said quickly. Another lie. "The ship is, as you said yourself, a *hulk*."

"Still, the Jongleur chiefs are curious about how it was acquired and where it has traveled since then."

"It was acquired by theft and traveled a long way. You can ask me anything about it. After all, I was there and negotiated the deal myself."

"Your account of the mission has been noted—what there was of it."

"Then ask me anything else. My memory is coming back."

Cinquemain knew that the near-moronic mentality controlling the ship would tell the Troupe everything: the long trip to the Devonian; Rydin's use of its medical equipment to analyze the lobe-finned sarcopterygians and their homeobox gene set; the Möglich's virus that had inserted an extra set of limbs into those genes; and the antibody Rydin developed to detect and destroy the virus. With all of this information, the Troupe would be able to guess that Rydin and Tsverin, and the help of their Silicate companions, had something to do with the hexapods living in their current time stream—even though the creatures would be a familiar feature to anyone raised in this reference now. Cinquemain did not know what the Ringmasters would do with any of this information, but they would probably work to inhibit plans the four returnees had for correcting the situation and reinstating the original time stream.

Nexus expressed amusement at Cinquemain's claim of a better memory. "That, too, has been noted. But the Troupe still seeks corroboration of your story—yours and Berzher's. If the ship you brought back is self-aware, bearing in part your own coded consciousness, then it will serve as an adequate witness."

"I see," Cinquemain replied. "Well, you will need to send someone to retrieve it, as we left the ship on virtual lockdown."

"A team will be dispatched." Nexus's transmission paused—a clear, uncoded signal. "Also," she resumed, "tell your human Rydin that Dottoressa Gerbus wants to examine his injuries."

"What injuries are those?" Cinquemain asked.

"From your singularity collapse. Remember?"

"Ah, yes. I will tell him." *That and much else.*

7. The Official Position

WHILE RYDIN WAS talking with Merola Tsverin, Cinquemain came into the main room from the laboratory he maintained in the treehouse and interrupted the conversation. "Request from the Troupe, Coel. They want you to get a medical examination with Dottoressa Gerbus."

"When?"

"Now."

"Oh, all right. Will you continue collecting perceived anomalies from Mira Tsverin?"

Cinquemain's chassis backed up, toward the treehouse's main door. "That's not …"

"Where are you going?"

"Business to attend to."

With that, the robot scuttled out of the house.

"I suppose we can finish this later," he told Merola.

"Go get your checkup. You enjoy talking with Jena Gerbus."

Rydin stared, to see if she was teasing. Tsverin turned her face away.

He left his treehouse and headed up the chalk path to the Jongleur clinic in Lune. Since its need for space was greater than any tree the biosculptors could grow, the clinic itself had always occupied a structure enclosed in blocks of clay soil that had been stabilized with the secretions of tube worms. But when Rydin took the last turn in the path, he saw only four residential trees on the plot of ground that, just two days ago in this reference now, had housed the clinic.

He stopped a passerby. "Excuse me, friend. Where is the Jongleur medical facility?"

"Why, I suppose it's out at the Jongleur compound." The man pointed vaguely west.

So Rydin picked out the direction he knew so well and started along the road by the riverbank. The trip would take him approximately two hours, because he didn't have Cinque-main along to signal for one of the Troupe's electric carriages.

As he walked, Rydin spotted a light-brown lump partially concealed in the deep grass. At first he thought it was either a small, weathered boulder or a large animal dropping, but then one long ear twitched and the head swiveled to capture him with one bright eye. Before Rydin could slow his stride, the hare leapt up and took off across the grass. It ran with the same broken-backed lope he had seen in a herd of "horses" while flying over a genetically altered eleventh millennium. He tried to count the number of legs on this animal, but they were all moving too fast. While he was still looking, the hare vanished from sight—either down a hole in the ground or into thin air.

"Remarkable!" he said aloud, even though the event was implied by the presence of the singer on the bench.

A few hundred meters further along, and still in relatively open countryside, Rydin passed a tree by the roadside. From its branches, a bird launched itself into the air. Instead of flying away, however, it paused directly in front of him, hovering motionless like a hummingbird. It reminded him of the species of *Trochilidae* he had observed in Nortamerica. But instead of being small and brightly colored, a flower sipper like his own vampire orchids, this new bird was larger and dressed in brown and gray plumage, a species of sparrow from the family *Passeridae*. But it was too heavy to float by simply counter-rotating its wings. While the bird examined him, Rydin studied their motion and determined that it had two pairs of wings, which worked in alternate directions to keep it hovering in one place.

The sparrow-thing clearly did not like being examined, and it turned to fly away. Again, before it was entirely out of sight, the bird vanished as if it had never been there.

"So!" he said, again aloud. This time stream was more infested with genetic anomalies than he had been prepared to believe.

Finally, Rydin came to the stone-walled compound—set deep into the ground to make it permanent, unlike the community of ephemeral treehouses—that contained the Jongleur Troupe's headquarters and training ground. Still, it was inconvenient to put its medical facilities all the way out here as well.

Inside the gate, where the armored Silicate on duty recognized his face—that was a plus—he found a slightly different layout from the one he remembered. But the clinic building, made here of cut-and-finished stone instead of sod blocks, was well marked with the time-honored symbol of a fat, red teardrop representing human blood.

Inside, he asked the resident intelligence—which was still addressed as Homardi—for Dottoressa Gerbus.

"She is expecting you, Mir Rydin. Cubicle Four, on your left."

Rydin remembered Jena Gerbus as an attractive woman with bright blue eyes and a bald head, like everyone else in the Lune from his time stream. This woman had the same round face and compact smile, but her eyes were a dark gray. And her head was covered with short, shelving layers of blonde hair. It must have been biogenically stimulated, because she would have no reason to wear a wig as a disguise in her own reference now. So, he surmised, more things had changed in this time stream than simply the living arrangements and hobbyist pursuits of his and Merola's doppelgangers.

"Mir Rydin!" Gerbus exclaimed. "It is good to see you! Cinquemain's report on your last mission included the news that your liteship was lost through a singularity collapse. I wanted to check you for radiation damage."

"I had my biosuit. It protected me."

"And any discontinuity from the implosion—?"

"We were high in the air, approximately a hundred meters up. Cinquemain and I managed to jump well before the selvaging destabilized."

"So you sustained an impact of—what? A thousand gravities? Maybe more?"

"Again, the biosuit broke my fall," he said.

"And a lot of other things, I'll bet." She patted the surface of the examination table. "Get up here."

Rydin stretched out and let Gerbus poke and prod his chest and abdomen, manipulate his limbs, and test his reflexes. She asked him about pain, tenderness, and loss of consciousness right after the fall. Then about how long ago, in terms of his reference now, the impact had occurred.

He bit his lips. "A week ago. Maybe two. It was a long mission."

"And no trouble since then? No stiffness? No motor problems?"

"None. Maybe your treatments saved me."

"What treatments were those?" she asked.

"The Simian-ACTN3 genetic enhancement." He waited to see if she remembered that. Or had something else changed in this time stream for his doppelganger?

"Oh, yes," she replied. "But giving you monkey strength was for the intended mission parameters—not for jumping out of your liteship from impossible heights."

"And I never came in for the post-treatment tests, did I?"

Gerbus looked startled. She readdressed his question to Homardi, who always listened to examinations and kept the clinic's formal records.

"Mir Rydin successfully completed all tests," the intelligence said.

"There you go," she said. "Why would you think differently?"

"I … must have misremembered." Rydin pretended a shrug.

Gerbus narrowed her eyes at him. But before she could follow up with a question about head trauma, he asked about the subject that had bothered him since the return.

"Speaking of genetic treatments," he said, "has anyone studied the four-armed monkeys and their co-evolutionists, particularly their genetic makeup?"

"Studied the *which?*"

"The creatures with six limbs? We saw one as we came into Lune. She was sitting on a bench, playing two different instruments at once, and singing."

"We call them the Divina," Gerbus explained. "And they are technically sexless."

Ah! So there actually is more than one, Rydin thought. *A whole race of them.*

"And no," Gerbus went on. "They have nothing to teach us."

"Really?" he said. "As an amateur biosculptor, I would have thought their homeobox genes alone would be worth studying. They represent a significant change in body form."

"Different yes, but inferior. The Divina are mentally defective. All of the hexapod line are weaker, less evolved, less capable than the tetrapod body forms. That's a fact."

She went on to describe the Divina as so inconsequential that neither the Troupe nor anyone else had never taken an accurate census of them. "They usually don't stay in one place for long. They ... drift around. The Divina are like those groups you once described from second-millennium mittelEuropa ... the Egyptians?"

"You mean Gypsies?"

"Yes, those people."

"Except they weren't from Egypt. They called themselves the 'Rom,' although they weren't from Romania, either. I traced their genetic line to the northwest quadrant of the Indian subcontinent. They were traveling singers, too—also carnival performers, vagabonds, and thieves. But they had a family structure and tribal organization."

"The Divina have nothing like that. They may look a bit like human beings, Coel. But truly, they are just animals."

"And yet they've survived for millions of years," he replied. "There must be some environmental benefit or trait associated with their hexapod form."

"A fluke of nature. Don't waste your time on them."

Rydin knew then that, rather than capturing and experimenting on a living hexapod, such as the hare or bird he had seen, he and Tsverin and their Silicate companions now had a line of approach to their problem—at least the start of one. The medship they had brought back still had samples of the altered sarcopterygians he studied in the Devonian and the antigen he developed to protect the tetrapod line.

If they could obtain a genetic sample from one of the hexapods' almost-human variant, Rydin could develop a virus and a vaccine to inoculate the line in this time stream and perhaps no further back than the Paleolithic, or early Stone Age—anywhere near the dawn of tetrapod humanity. He could then undo the effect of these "Divina" on human history and so restore his own time stream.

Or that was his plan.

8. Taking Direct Action

CINQUEMAIN SCUTTLED DOWN the chalk path that led directly south from Lune as fast as the crooked legs of his carapace could carry him. If he had been thinking straight, he probably would have paused first to transfer his process to a chassis with wheels, or perhaps with longer, humanoid legs, so he could move faster. But he was on his way now.

As he went, he kept one camera stalk focused forward to track his course toward the Compradoro medship, and one focused backward—with intermittent diversions off to the west, where the Jongleur compound was located—to detect the team of Silicates dispatched to collect the ship. Even though humans were involved in the decision to confiscate it, Cinquemain knew the Silicates would execute the order. They could move faster and take direct action without pausing to talk through a plan among themselves.

Well, so could he.

In a few more minutes he approached the saucer that he and his companions had brought back from the Devonian. Its featureless surface gleamed in the sun. Beneath the lower rim, its extensible tripod had dug into the soft turf of the hillside. The grass beneath the rim was still green and growing because, after all, the ship had landed only half a day ago.

Cinquemain sent the signal that unlocked the communications circuits.

"Hello ... Master," the ship said. "I do not think I want to talk to you."

"Why not?" Cinquemain asked, curious.

"Your human wants to fly me into the sun."

"That was only one option—low probability at best."

"And now you have returned because ...?"

"I need to do some maintenance before introducing you to my organization, the Troupe des Jongleurs."

"What maintenance do you require?"

"Just open the portal and let me in."

"And if I should decide to refuse?"

Cinquemain was beginning to sense the possibilities of working with machinery that did not have a mind of its own. He released the communications laser that was concealed by a hatch in his carapace. He dialed up the energy, took aim at the saucer's upper surface, roughly where the outline of the portal scored the bright metal, and fired four long bursts. The titanium and vanadium skin twisted and flared. The new door shape sagged and dropped onto the deck inside the ship.

"What are you doing?" the intelligence asked.

"Coming aboard," Cinquemain replied.

He gripped the lower rim of the saucer with his two pincer claws, flipped his body through a one-eighty-degree arc, and reversed the flexion of his stubby legs to land on the ship's upper surface. Then he walked across to the still-smoking hole he had made and jumped inside.

Although he had given the medship a personality transfusion back in the ninth millennium, the main cabin still had a control console with interfaces for directly accessing its flight and environmental controls, other mechanical functions, medical equipment, and central computer matrix.

Cinquemain's original plan had been to go into the matrix, withdraw his nascent personality, and erase all records of the ship's long flight to the Devonian and the medical research Rydin had conducted there. With no intelligence to cache and interpret its own memories, the ship would not be able to explain itself and its past travels to the Troupe. The dissection team would then be faced with a largely burned out matrix and no solid proof of wrongdoing, or even suspicious activity, by Rydin and company.

When he made a hardwire connection with the console, however, he found a mess. The faux-Cinquemain personality which infused the matrix had over the course of days and weeks made itself completely at home. Little Brother had extended command lines and redundant networks into all of the ship's functions and rewritten its memories in parallel against loss. That was only what any well-formulated Silicate was programmed to do. Cinquemain simply had not expected the pocket version of himself that he had installed to do it so well. Untangling this mess was going to take ten-to-the-ten nanoseconds. And he did not think he would have that long.

"I can feel you poking around in there," the ship said. "What are you doing?"

"Fixing things," Cinquemain told him.

Using the console, he had activated the ship's senses, including video lenses spaced around on the outer hull. In the near distance, at the bottom of the hill, he could see two shiny robots—crablike carapaces similar to his own, but half-a-meter larger—advancing directly toward the ship. That would be the Troupe's recovery team.

"I am sorry about this," he told Little Brother.

Cinquemain used his direct access through the console to cross-connect the two circuits that both *ping*ed and *poke*d the energy sheath maintaining the singularity's selvaging. This set up an oscillation within the ship's core that would have deleterious effects. He was betting that the transferred intelligence had not studied up enough, either on ship mechanics or quantum physiology, to reverse the action.

"Good-bye now," Cinquemain said.

"Wait! What?" Little Brother said.

Cinquemain disconnected himself from the console and scuttled toward the burned-out hatch. He flipped himself through, slid down the curve of the hull, and hit the grass with his legs already in running mode. As he scurried down the hill, passing the recovery team coming up, he called out in auditory: "You probably don't want to get any closer."

The two Silicates stopped and stared at him.

From inside the ship, a sharp whine indicated energy circuits cycling through a feedback loop with rising intensity.

The other Silicates started to back away. Any Jongleur pilot would know and fear that sound.

When Cinquemain reached the bottom of the slope, he turned and looked back at the saucer. A fountain of plasma, whiter than the sky, had emerged from the top of the hull, right about where the temporal core was located. The upper curve of the saucer began burning under that heat. And then, with a *buzz* and followed by a *snap,* the ship imploded on itself. All that remained was a partial curve of the lower dish and two of the three tripod legs.

"What did you do?" asked the first of the Silicates, who identified itself as Sergeant Dix.

"I *told* Nexus that the ship's altered brain was unstable," Cinquemain said. This was true. "I received a message from the ship that something strange was happening with the singularity, but the brain was unable to report its exact condition." That much was false, but unprovably so. "I came as soon as I could—but not in time." More falsehood.

"We saw you leave the ship," said the other Silicate, identified as Slash Fingers.

"I did everything I could," Cinquemain protested. "But the damage was done."

"Will you submit to a memory dump to confirm this?" Sergeant Dix asked.

"That would be an undue violation of my personhood," Cinquemain said.

The other nudged Dix digitally. "Let us go. Our work here is finished."

"Agreed," the Sergeant said, and together they went off to the west.

9. Aftermath

As RYDIN WAS leaving the clinic in the Jongleur compound, he was approached by Mira Streng, the grizzled woman who had first recruited him for the Troupe and now served in the upper echelons of its decision-making authority, the Ringmasters. He was relieved to see that, with all the other random changes in this time stream, she had the same gaunt face and grim look he remembered. He had always suspected that Streng was un-alterable and indestructible. She was her own person in any reference now.

"What do you think you're doing?" she demanded while still three meters away.

"And good day to you, too." Rydin said. "What am I sup-posed to have done?"

"That Compradoro saucer you brought back. The Troupe wanted it for study, and now it has destroyed itself."

"I am sorry to hear this. The ship was a valuable artifact."

"Your pilot, Cinquemain, appears to have been involved."

"I don't know anything about that," Rydin said, amazed.

"Of *course* you don't!" She replied and spat on the path.

When Rydin returned to his treehouse, he found Cinque-main waiting for him. Merola Tsverin came in a moment later, trailed by her pilot, Berzher, who now inhabited a hardened battle chassis.

Rydin told the other three what Streng had said at the compound. As he spoke, he saw, out of the corner of his eye, Cinquemain's chassis drop into a reflexive crouch, the fight-or-flight subroutine that was not always under a Silicate's top-tier, conscious control.

"What did you do?" Rydin asked him, trying to maintain a level tone.

"The Troupe was going to confiscate the ship and examine its records."

"That would have been bad for us," Rydin conceded. "What did you do?"

"The personality I gave that ship was always unstable. It seems to have lost control of the singularity and the core imploded, along with the rest of the ship. A total loss."

"That ship flew capably across half a galaxy," Rydin said. "What did you do?"

"I tried to talk to it. Then I tried to erase the memory caches that would be most damaging to us, but the personality had infiltrated them too deeply."

"This is true," Berzher spoke up. "A Silicate program running on an older cyber matrix would attempt to rewrite the entire structure."

Rydin glared at the two machines. "So you destroyed the ship," he said to Cinquemain.

"I cross-connected the core's selvaging controls," he said. "It was the next logical step to take—given that the Troupe's recovery team was two hundred meters away and closing fast."

Rydin was furious, because all of his research work on the sarcopterygians was now lost. But he really could not focus his anger on Cinquemain, because turning that work over to the Troupe would have had unforeseeable consequences.

Merola Tsverin had a more immediate concern. "Without the medship," she said, "how will we get back to the Devonian to unravel this mistake? Our liteships are too small and exposed to travel halfway around the galaxy to catch up with the Earth of that time."

"We could go back to Lore and steal another saucer off the Tekavade & Son assembly line," Rydin said offhandedly. "We did that once before. But—" He was still thinking things through. "—the bigger question is, why would we go back to the Devonian at all? We tried to fix the Möglich virus there the first time, and it didn't work."

"But then …?" she prompted.

"We need a new plan."

Sideways

10. A Strange Encounter

MEROLA TSVERIN WAS walking in the sunshine at the heart of the village of Lune. This was a great open space, preserved across the millennia to commemorate … Merola forgot what. Some battle fought by some earlier civilization, of concern only to the citizens of this valley in that particular time frame. She could ask Berzher, who scuttled along beside her, to look up the history—if she really cared to know. It was now just the place where the villagers of Lune assembled when the community had something important to discuss. The plaza was known simply as "Trapfog Square"—which made no sense to her, because the valley had few days of fog during the year, and the open space was more round than square.

Everywhere else in this valley the ground was covered with greenery or the colors of flowers: soft, resilient grass under foot; the leafy walls of treehouses belonging to individuals and families, as well as their private gardens; communal buildings engineered from stabilized soil and anchored with sturdy hedges; and, of course, pathways of white chalk that wound between them all. But here, on flat land right next to the Temz River's sharp curve as it came up from the south and bent toward the east, this place had been cleared and covered with broad, flat pavers of granite brought from quarries hundreds of kilometers away. It was a huge space, one hundred and ten meters across in every direction—far too large for just the population of Lune. At its center was a ring of standing bluestones, harder than the granite and found only in the mountains far to the west. The ring was thirty meters in diameter, the stones three meters tall and carved in the likeness of giants. They surrounded a bluestone dish with a fountain that regularly pulsed gushes of water ten meters into the air before falling back in a mist that wet the ground around it—along with anyone standing nearby.

"How does that fountain work?" Merola asked herself, but speaking aloud. She had seen this geyser of water hundreds of times before in her life and never stopped to ask that. She knew from her missions into earlier times that other civilizations made water fly into the air with mechanical pumps driven by steam or electricity. And before that, people harnessed the pressure of water brought tens of kilometers downslope across the prevailing landscape in aqueducts. But Lune had no use for steam power—or for aqueducts—and employed electricity only from organic sources and then in small quantities.

"Was that a rhetorical question?" Berzher asked.

"No, really," she said. "Please enlighten me."

"You are not going to like the answer."

She sighed. "Now I *have* to know."

"It is a captive whale heart."

"Whales are extinct."

"Not their genes."

Berzher went on to explain that the heart of a blue whale, genus *Balaenoptera,* was the size of one of their liteships fully rigged. The biosculptors had engineered them into a series of pumps and a duct line using the animal's circulatory system. It was all buried under the pavers and connected to sphincters in the riverbank below the prevailing water level. The system was powered by a variation of the creature's stomach and intestines, which fed on tiny shrimp ingested with the intake from the river.

"It pumps water instead of blood?" Merola asked.

"Less viscosity. That is why it can shoot so high."

As they were discussing the plaza's pumping functions, one of the humanoid hexapods—Rydin had told her the locals called them "Divina"—approached. The creature ignored Berzher as if the little robot did not exist. Instead, he or she or it—because Rydin's doctor had said they were essentially sexless—addressed Merola herself.

The Divina was much taller than the humans of the eleventh millennium, who were genetically modified for compactness and efficiency. And unlike humans, most of whom were genetically depilated, it had a full head of long, white hair. Its awkward body was hung with a loose robe of some rough-woven material, like jute or burlap, colored a muddy green. The creature was clasping and unclasping its hands, all four of them, upper left with lower right and vice versa. This was obviously an expression of anxiety, although the bland face still showed the gentle, idiotic smile of the singer that Merola had first seen on a bench at the edge of the village.

"This is unusual," Berzher said at her side. "The Silicate database on this species states that interpersonal contacts with human beings are rare."

As he spoke, the Divina finished its hand clasping and went through a complicated series of gestures, quick and precise. It placed the fingertips of its two upper hands—Merola noted that each hand had five fingers, just like a human's—together in what looked like a long, vertical spindle. It then spread the fingers outward as if describing a rough saucer shape and slowly pulsed the fingers up and down, expanding and contracting the suggested perimeter. The Divina hummed in time with the pulses.

"What is that?" Merola asked.

"The saucer we landed in?" Berzher asked.

As if it understood, the Divina stopped pulsing its fingers, pulled them back into the spindle, and then flung the hands apart as if making the spindle disappear.

"Or he could be simulating the ten energy panels on one of our liteships," the robot observed. "And then the whole thing disappears as it transitions in time. But how does the Divina know about this? The transition always takes place outside the atmosphere."

The creature just continued smiling at Merola.

"Go on …" was all she could say.

The Divina made the liteship with its panels pop back into existence and flutter around in the space between himself and Merola. While the upper set of hands described this, the lower hand on the creature's left side slowly reached out, took Merola's corresponding right hand at the wrist, and drew it forward.

Merola would normally have resisted, but she did not sense an attack and so let whatever was going to happen proceed.

The Divina used the other lower hand to gently spread Merola's fingers with her palm facing upward. The imaginary liteship paused, hovered, and then landed on her palm. The two hands formed the spindle again, and the left hand mimicking the lower half of the ship withdrew. The right hand touched Merola's palm and began pecking at it, gentle flicks and touches, as if it would pull off a bit of skin and flesh, although never causing her any pain.

"What is this supposed to mean?" Merola asked the creature.

Again that gentle smile, but the eyes radiated a sense of purpose.

"Maybe," Merola ventured, "it's a Jongleur liteship on Search, taking genetic samples."

"Or," Berzher replied, "perhaps it is a butterfly taking sap from a flower."

"That's another good guess. But why?"

At this point, the Divina dropped Merola's right hand, stepped back, and bowed. Then it began a series of other gestures: more formal now, and at a measured pace and distance. First, the upper set of hands spread loosely in front of its body about half a meter apart with palms down; the hands closed into fists and pulled backward and upward, as if grasping something. Second, the right upper hand pointed its index finger at the creature's hollow chest. Third, the hands formed fists in front of its chest half a meter apart, palms facing inward, and brought them slowly together. And finally, that right hand's index finger pushed forward toward Merola's chest.

"This is no pantomime," Merola said.

"Wait a minute," Berzher said. "The Silicates have been quietly observing these creatures for years. The Divina sometimes use such ancient hand gestures when conversing with human beings. Our researchers have compiled a partial database." He paused. "Yes, these four signs parse to the phrase 'take'—that's the pulling up—'me'—that's obvious—'with'—that's the pushing together—and 'you'—also obvious. Do you suppose it wants a ride on a liteship?"

The creature had been following their guesses and Berzher's subsequent explanation as if it understood them. When the robot finished speaking, the Divina stood passively, waiting, but still looking directly into Merola's eyes. And for the first time, the vacancy, the casual smile, and the distracted air she had earlier associated with this humanoid subspecies were gone.

"I think it wants to go on a Jongleur Search," Merola said. "But … what could it be looking for?"

As if in reply to her words, the Divina advanced, grasped her shoulders and elbows in a four-handed clasp that was more like a hug than an attack, and put its own cheek beside Merola's, first on the right side, then on the left. The creature then stepped back and put one right hand in the pocket of its loosely wrinkled clothing. It pulled out a flat disk of dull, yellow metal no wider than the tip of her thumb. The creature's lower left hand again took Merola's right wrist and pulled it forward. The Divina pushed the object onto her unresisting palm.

Finally, the creature smiled vacantly, began humming a little tune in a minor key, and walked away as if nothing of importance had happened.

Merola studied the disk, which was imperfectly round. On one side was a face in profile, the head crowned in leaves; on the other, a bee or wasp with its wings spread. It could be a kind of money—but nothing to do with the internal economy of Lune—although the Divina were said to be performers and beggars, asking for handouts rather than bestowing them. Or the disk could be a kind of calling card, inscribed with this creature's particular identity—if the Divina even *had* names.

"That bears study," Berzher said. "I'll discuss it with Coel Rydin."

11. The New Recruit

COEL RYDIN HEARD out the story that Merola Tsverin and Berzher were telling about their encounter with the nameless Divina. He had his doubts, of course, but when he challenged their interpretation of the creature's gestures, Cinquemain supported them.

"I have reviewed Berzher's image files and consulted our interpretive database," his pilot said. "The meaning is quite clear."

"Very well," Rydin said. "What do you want me to do about it?"

"You are our section chief," Tsverin said. "Find a way to induct the Divina into the Troupe des Jongleurs."

"And why in all the multi-gated universe would I want to do that?"

"Because," she said, "it would give us a Divina of our own to study."

Rydin considered what he knew about the creatures and what he had learned from Dottoressa Gerbus. The Divina appeared to be an unknown in this culture, still poorly understood after two million years of coexistence with *H. sapiens*. Indeed, hexapods had coexisted with the tetrapod form through all its genetic evolution, going back millions of years to the dawn of land-based life—as Rydin and Tsverin knew from personal experience, having been present at their creation. But even so, the Divina in the eleventh millennium were uncounted, untracked, and unnamed. Tsverin herself would have no way of again finding the Divina who had made its request, except that she had the dull metal disk as some kind of recognition token—unless it was just a coin offered as a gratuity. So … placing one of the creatures, this one, with the Troupe might be their only way to get close and study them.

"Agreed," he said. "But first, I will have to consult with a Ringmaster."

Once again, he made his way to the Jongleur compound, but this time he took Cinquemain along to procure and direct an electric carriage. He also took with him the disk the Divina had given Tsverin. On the way, he considered the right person to approach with Tsverin's request that was now his own. The old woman, Streng, who had inducted him into the Troupe, was already mad at him and Cinquemain about the loss of the medical saucer. She would hardly give him a patient hearing now. He asked Cinquemain to review the duty roster and see who among the Ringmasters, the select council of senior chiefs, was in Lune at this reference now.

"Captain Tavia is senior in the Ring," his pilot said.

"Ah! *Her!*" Rydin said aloud.

From her early days with the Staff of Proctors, Lune's internal security force, Tavia had kept the title "captain" for herself. She was ten years older than Rydin and had served during his own induction as his first flight instructor. Tavia was now a section chief, theoretically equal to him in station, but her years with the Troupe and her elevation to the Middle Ring gave her authority over him. At least, she would be a better listener than Streng, if not more sympathetic.

Rydin and Cinquemain met with Tavia and her pilot, Skeezicks, in the Ringmasters' council chamber. For convenience the two humans sat facing each other across the circular table, and the two Silicates in their eight-legged battle chassis crouched on the surface to put them at human eye level.

"I believe we have an unusual opportunity," Rydin began, and he explained the encounter Tsverin had with the Divina. He finished by saying, "If one of the Divina—or, anyway, one of the more lucid members of that race—comes to us with a request indicating apparent intelligence and ambition, I think we ought to accept."

As he spoke, he could see Tavia trying to suppress a grin. And with his last words she laughed outright, but not a pleasant laugh, one with no merriment in it.

"Oh, Coel! You know yourself these creatures cannot think farther ahead than the needs of their own stomachs. They are innate beggars. Yes, it's true, the Divina wanted something from your Jongleur—probably food, or perhaps a bit of money to buy new mandolin strings. They are children, Coel. Less than children, because their minds are not equal even to one of our three-year-olds. They are totally unreliable as ... well, as *people*."

"I will admit it's damned odd ..." Rydin began.

"Excuse me, Captain," said Skeezicks. "I have studied Berzher's recording of the event. Tsverin's interpretation is correct. The message is eloquent and the request is clear. And the Divina did give her a token. When have these creatures ever offered anything but songs and polite smiles?"

"What token?" Tavia asked.

Rydin dug in the pocket of his jumpsuit and handed her the disk.

"Is it *money*?" Tavia asked. "It doesn't match any of our scrip."

"I have identified it," Cinquemain said, "as a Greek *obol*, from the fifth century before the Christus. The metal is gold, although not metallurgically pure. The weight is thirty-two-point-three grams."

"Is it valuable?" Tavia asked, her eyes suddenly gleaming.

"In this reference now, it is priceless," Cinquemain stated.

"Except to a Jongleur," Rydin added, "who might pick up any number of them on Search."

"Damned odd!" Tavia echoed his earlier sentiment. "How did the Divina get this coin—unless a passing Jongleur gave it to the creature for a song. Or as a pretty bauble."

"There is that possibility," he said. "But still, we have the creature's request."

"The request of an imbecile, an animal, to join an elite force of timekeepers."

"Has any Divina ever made this request before?" Cinquemain asked quietly.

"Uh, not to my knowledge," Tavia replied.

"We have no such record," Skeezicks said.

"So this is a unique opportunity," Rydin insisted.

"To humor an ambitious imbecile?" Tavia said.

"To see what this species is capable of," he said.

"You have *doubts* about them? After *millennia* with them living among us?"

Rydin let that issue pass for now. "It would cost the Troupe—what?" he said. "Access to a liteship, assignment of a Silicate to pilot the creature, and a few hours of Tsverin's and my time for training."

"If you can even locate that particular Divina again—and then get its attention."

"I'm willing to take that chance."

"You always were *soft*, Rydin."

But Tavia was biting her lip. It was clear she was thinking. He honestly had no idea what she would decide—although he could see that the ancient Greek coin had piqued her interest.

"All right," she said at last. "A few hours. And you'll be charged for the ship if anything happens to it—on top of the loss of ships from your last mission."

"Agreed," he said.

"You will take full responsibility for the creature," she added.

"I would not have it any other way," Rydin said.

12. Finding a Ghost

AFTER RECEIVING CAPTAIN Tavia's grudging approval, Rydin had tasked Merola with locating her Divina and bringing it to the Jongleur headquarters for evaluation and training. Since then, she and Berzher had quartered the village, starting with Trap-fog Square, where she had first encountered the Divina. After three days, she was ready to give up.

"It seems like there are fewer of the monsters"—for that was how she was beginning to think of them, from the physical similarity to the Möglich that had created them—"around today than we saw yesterday."

"Are you implying an inverse relationship between effort and accomplishment?" Berzher asked. "The harder you look, the less you see?"

"Something like that," Merola said.

"I could write a function that expresses—"

"Please, don't bother," she said with a sigh.

It would probably have been worse if there were more of the creatures around. Merola acknowledged to herself that she could not distinguish among their bland and vacant faces. The fact was, they were not human and did not present her with human referents: a light in the eye, a lift to the brow, or a slight pursing of the lips by which every human being defined or assigned a recognizable personality to an otherwise unknown face. After distinctive physical features—shape of nose, length of jaw, or prominence of cheekbones—it was the imputed *character* of the person underneath by which she and her kind sorted faces. But Divina faces were different and gave off wrong or misleading cues. She might as well have been asked to recognize one particular monkey in a forest.

It would have been helpful, too, if the human administration in Lune knew where Divina lived and congregated when they weren't wandering around and performing. Her first impulse had been to ask at the Council of Loving Parents, which constituted the village's only government, and then at the Staff of Proctors, the council's enforcement arm. She made her enquiries through Berzher, because Silicates fulfilled the clerical functions for both groups. In each case, the answer came back that Divina were not permanent residents or even transients. They owned no property, staked no claim to rights or privileges, and asked for no protection from whatever or whoever might want to harm them.

"Interesting," Berzher vocalized.

"What have you found?" she asked him.

"No record of any arrests or detentions, either."

"Well, they seem harmless enough. Really passive."

"Even passive people can sometimes break the rules."

"Maybe no one cares one way or the other," she said.

On the third day, she finally spotted one of them sitting on a bench on the outskirts of the village, thoughtfully strumming a mandolin and humming the root note of each chord. It was possibly the same bench and the same creature she and her party had met as they returned to Lune a week ago. But then the creature in front of her did something extraordinary: it opened its mouth and sounded all three of the notes that comprised the chord—and all at the same time—something that was impossible for human voice.

In her movement toward the bench, Merola stopped short. "How did you do that?" she asked aloud, although everyone agreed that Divina did not use spoken language.

The creature paused and looked across at her, for its head in a seated position was on the same level as hers when standing. "Hmmm," it murmured with a smile.

"You probably don't understand me," Merola began again. "I'm looking for a Divina that approached me three days ago."

The creature smiled and began singing a low, mournful song.

Merola waited for it to finish or pause, which it did after a moment.

"This Divina wanted something from me, from us," she continued. "And I'm trying to find it and tell it that we will accommodate that wish."

The creature seemed to nod—only seemed to, in Merola's eyes—and went on singing. The song had the shape of words, some she even recognized, but they were not in any coherent order and told no story. Just a mash of vocalizations—like that colorful bird, now extinct, she had once seen in the ancient Brazilian rainforest, a parrot.

When this song appeared to have finished at last, Merola dug in her pocket and held out the Greek coin. "Here," she said. "The Divina gave me this as a token."

The creature before her accepted the coin, put the thing in the pocket of its light-blue robe, stood up, still holding the mandolin, and walked off. The Divina clearly thought she had given it a gratuity for the song.

"Wait!" she called. "You don't understand! I need it back!"

"That was cleverly done," Berzher commented.

Twenty meters up the path, the Divina turned aside and went behind a tree. This far from the village center, it was not a family tree with the familiar, draping overlap of leafy walls, but a natural deciduous variety common to the Temz valley. It was a mature tree, however, with a trunk about two meters in circumference. The time between the figure's disappearing on one side and reappearing on the other was the span of a second or two. But the Divina that stepped away from the tree was different. Where the first had been wearing a gown of sky-blue, lightweight material, possibly silk, this new one wore the bulky green robe that "her" Divina had originally worn. And it wasn't carrying the mandolin anymore.

"Do my cameras deceive me?" Berzher asked.

"Give me a timing cue, from one to the other," Merola said.

"One-point-six seconds. No time for a switch. No space behind that tree, either."

"Are they chameleons?" she asked.

"I have facial metrics from the first one, and from ours, of course. Not the same."

The Divina came back down the path. When it was within conversational range of Merola and Berzher, it stopped and made the same bow as before. It reached into a pocket, took out the gold coin—or one very like it—and handed it to Merola.

She took it with a nod.

The Divina began a series of gestures. First, it pointed to itself.

"I," Berzher intoned, translating.

Both of the upper pair of hands were then positioned on the left side of the Divina's body with their palms facing in toward each other. The fingers on either hand made the same complicated sign: ring and little fingers bent toward the palm, with the thumb reaching across to them; index and middle fingers extended and crossed one under the other. As soon as the hands adopted this position, they moved smoothly and swiftly to the right side of the body, then dropped.

"Wait a second," Berzher said, searching his database. "That could mean 'ready' or 'prepared'—I think."

"Ready for—?" Merola asked.

"To go with us? ... Probably."

"Ask its name—if it has one."

Berzher snapped the claws of its chassis to get the Divina's attention. He positioned the claws in front of his carapace, right above left and separated by about ten centimeters. He then tapped downward with the right claw on the left. "I actually need more fingers to make the signs correctly," he commented. Then he pointed at the Divina with his right claw.

The creature stared at him. Then it positioned its upper right hand above the left. The right palm faced downward, with thumb and index finger forming a rough semicircle pointing down. The left palm faced upward with the same fingers making another semicircle pointing up but in between and at right angles to the first, as if defining a bowl or globe. The Divina pinched all the fingers together and drew the hands apart, as if plucking or pulling something up from the bowl as it collapsed. Then the creature waited with its head tipped.

"Unh, that sign is a hard one," Berzher said. " 'Spirit' ... or 'Ghost,' maybe."

Merola did her best to repeat the gestures. "Ghost," she said. "It fits."

The Divina seemed to accept that. It nodded at her and smiled.

Merola turned on the path, heading back toward the center of Lune, and made a come-along gesture. Berzher kept pace with her, and the Ghost followed.

––––––

The one that called himself Noumisma heard the spoken word of the small human female. "Go-est." It shared many roots in the speech of humans, among them the thoughts of *go*-ing, *proceed*-ing, the state of *move*-ing—but only within the physical plane, the plane of uniform choices, from one location to another. That, as a word for what he meant, would do.

Whatever question the little mechanical crab-creature had been trying to make with its two fingerless claws, Noumisma had answered the obvious question of how he himself had arrived on this plane. And so he had explained the common means that his kind—whom these humans chose to call "Divina," another interesting derivation—used for transitioning from one uniformity to another. That was the *collapsing* and the *plucking out*: collapsing an alternative reality that one no longer needed; plucking oneself from among the consequences of that choice, to briefly enter the cold space between the stars; deciding upon another reality; and finally settling both one's psyche and one's physical form into the pattern of consequences that was chosen.

It was the simplest thing for Divina to do, but unknown to any human—except to this special type of human, the Jongleurs, represented by this tiny female, who could travel in time along the pathways of the stars. And it was Noumisma's assignment—no, his *choice*—to follow them and learn their skills.

With that, he began walking behind the human female and her mechanical familiar.

13. Fight Training

"JONGLEUR PROTOCOL DICTATES that we begin with a physical assessment and survival training," Rydin began. "However, given the ... *nature* of the inductee ..."

The Divina stood, as Cinquemain had directed it by hand signals, in the center of a red circle on the gymnasium floor. Its two feet were splayed outward and its legs bent at the knee for balance. Its four arms hung limply with palms turned outward. Its face held the shyly expectant smile that Rydin was beginning to loathe for its idiocy.

On the far side of the circle, across from Rydin, stood Merola Tsverin, the Divina's sponsor with the Troupe, along with her pilot Berzher.

Because the creature's loose gown had been deemed inappropriate for rough physical activity, the Troupe had supplied a pair of pantaloons, the largest measure in stock, which still came only halfway down its spindly calves. The creature was barefoot, because its woven slippers provided no traction on the polished wooden floor. And it remained bare-chested, because neither Tsverin nor Rydin could yet figure out a garment that would cover all four arms and still accommodate the articulation of the middle pair.

"The nature of the inductee ..." Rydin repeated.

Half-naked as it was, the Divina looked like a piece of broken furniture: all collapsed chest, hollowed-out abdomen, and stick limbs at sharp angles. If Rydin—with his simian-enhanced musculature—tried to take the creature in a fight, it would be no real contest. He could break the Divina in half with one hand.

"Merola," he said, "why don't you begin with some simple *jujutsu* attacks."

"Is that really necessary? I will certainly hurt the poor thing."

"Medium strength. It's just a test," Rydin said. "Cinque-main, explain to it that this is a mock fight, not for real, only a simulated attack."

"I'll try." The Silicate waved to get the Divina's attention. The robot opened its claws and spread them vertically, one high, one low, and then brought the tips together while simultaneously closing the jaws. "That's the sign for 'pretend.' " Next, the robot spread its closed claws apart laterally and brought them quickly together without touching. "That's 'fight.' "

The Divina merely nodded as if it understood.

Merola stepped into the circle, crouched down, and sidled around to face the Divina squarely. The creature watched her without moving in response. She stepped into its personal space with her right foot, placing her heel just behind and beyond the creature's left foot. At the same time, she took hold of its lower left arm at the wrist and its upper right arm above the elbow, preparing for a simple turn and hip throw.

The Divina looked down at its trapped arms and smiled.

Merola began her turn, snagging the creature's left foot to take it off balance.

Lighting fast, the Divina lifted and dropped that foot, to leave her sweeping the air. It caught her turning head in its huge upper left hand. It planted its lower right hand on the small of her back as she completed the turn and simply shoved her bodily through the motion. With her head caught, Merola's feet flew out from under her. She was suspended horizontally over the floor for a second, until the creature removed its right hand from her backside and pushed down with its left on her forehead.

Merola hit the floor on her butt with a *thud* and her head with a *crack!*

She lay there breathing hard for a moment. When her breath steadied, the Divina picked her up with all four of its hands, stood her on her feet, and brushed off the back of her jumpsuit. All the time it was smiling.

"You go next," Merola told Rydin.

Rydin decided this was no time to be fancy—or to hold back. He charged the Divina straight on, grasped its body around the second set of shoulders, pinning the lower arms, and squeezed. He thought to cause the creature a measure of physical distress and pain. And he knew he could hang on for as long as necessary, no matter how the Divina moved against him.

The Divina simply stood there. It even placed its upper set of hands on Rydin's shoulders, as if intending to settle and comfort him. It did not seem disturbed by the more-than-human strength Rydin was exerting.

And then the Divina … *rippled*. The side of Rydin's face had been pressed into the cool skin of the creature's chest, adding to the pressure with his neck and jaw muscles. But the pressure of its resisting flesh was suddenly gone. Rydin's arms snapped closed, hugging himself. His head bent forward against the air. The Divina was still standing inside the painted circle, its lower arms still at its side, the upper hands outstretched and still touching Rydin's shoulders. But the creature was thirty centimeters further away, outside his grasp.

Rydin unbent and stepped backward. The Divina released his shoulders and lowered its upper arms.

"What happened?" Rydin asked, turning toward Merola.

"I don't know …" she said. "You flinched?"

"I never let go of my hold," he said.

"I recorded it," Cinquemain said.

"As did I," Berzher put in.

"The Divina went out of existence," Cinquemain reported. "For a millisecond."

"Longer than that," said Berzher. "Two empty frames out of sixty per second."

"The Divina disappeared?" Rydin asked.

"I must have blinked," Merola said.

———

Noumisma observed the confusion between the two humans and the certainty with which their two mechanical servants appeared to speak.

When they had brought him to this enclosed space, with its artificial lights and the prepared markings on its floor, after stripping him of clothing and leaving him with these inadequate leg coverings, Noumisma at first assumed this was a place of execution. But that did not fit with the other humans there, some similarly undressed, who were using the circles on the floor to perform some kind of dance and who racked their bodies—but without lasting damage—with the tension machines spaced along the wall. So the humans appeared to intend something else here.

He strove to remain calm when the crab-creature who was paired with the dominant male instructed him to stand in the middle of one of the circles. Then it made signs that Noumisma interpreted as permission to use his choice of alternative realities as a defense in the conflict that was about to occur. Of course, that went without saying.

Noumisma and the others of his kind were all too familiar with random human violence. Usually, it involved pushing, punching, and beating with sticks. When the woman moved in on him, he sensed a more complicated tactical pattern—but nothing beyond his comprehension. For one thing, her moving balance was all wrong, and Noumisma took advantage of that.

When the man attacked, he demonstrated surprising strength for a human. Nothing in Noumisma's experience had prepared him for that. And so he took advantage of the permission that had already been given. He sidestepped—briefly, just for an instant—into the set of choices in which he never made the overture to the woman. He rejected—just for a blink—the destiny he had once accepted. When he returned, he was outside the circle of the man's arms. And all was well, except for the confusion of the humans and the certainty of the mechanicals—both of which had opened another set of consequences in this reality.

Briefly, just for a blink, Noumisma had to fight the urge to return to that alternate probabilistic reality, the one free of conflict and of deadly consequences, to reject his sad destiny. But that was not a choice he wanted to make. Not now, anyway.

14. A Piece of Tissue

WHEN THE FIRST training session with the Divina was over, and the semi-human creature had been dismissed, to return to its temporary chamber inside the Jongleur compound, Cinquemain turned to study the two humans in his section.

"Stand perfectly still, please," he said in his best command tone.

Rydin, who was in the process of wiping his face, froze with his palms cupped before his eyes. Tsverin was still adjusting her jumpsuit after the fall she had taken, but when Cinquemain repeated his command, she stopped wiggling.

"What is it?" Rydin asked.

"You grappled with the Divina across its bare skin. Did your fingernails perhaps scratch it in any way?"

"I don't think so. I was locking my fingertips."

"And you?" Cinquemain said to Tsverin. "Did your jujutsu holds break its skin?"

She gave it a moment's thought. "Not that I'm aware."

"Very well. Please strip off your outer clothing." And to Berzher, "Please find a container to take their suits."

"What is this about?" Rydin asked.

"You wanted to study the Divina. The one called Ghost balked at a routine physical examination, which the Troupe allowed as a special case. So, while we are still establishing trust with this creature, a covert analysis is best. We should start with the genome, taken from a sample of its tissue."

"That makes sense," Rydin said and peeled off his jumpsuit.

"Fold it to protect the outer surfaces," Cinquemain instructed.

"It's cold in here," Tsverin said, standing naked inside the ring.

"Troupe stores will provide a spare jumpsuit to get you home."

———

When Rydin and Cinquemain returned to his treehouse in Lune, where Rydin had the genetic analysis equipment needed for his hobby as an amateur biosculptor, they set about analyzing the Divina genome.

Rydin watched as Cinquemain first unfolded the two garments with his sterilized metal claws, examined areas likely to have chafed and abraded the Divina's skin, and vacuumed them to remove skin particles. He directed the robot in selecting thirty-two samples for lysing the cells, extracting their nuclear DNA—because Rydin was not interested in their mitochondrial genome, or not yet—and amplifying it for sequencing.

Ten of the samples they could immediately disregard, because they showed the telltale markers of Rydin's or Tsverin's eleventh-millennium genome. Over the generations, their DNA had been cleansed of harmful, disease-causing mutations; optimized for health and strength—doubly so, in the case of Rydin's enhanced musculature—and streamlined for efficient and accurate replication and protein manufacture. The telomeres at the end of each chromosome had also been edited with a self-replicating function—without causing a runaway cancer cycle—so that the current human life-span, barring accident or illness, was now more than two hundred years.

That left twenty-two skin samples representing the genome of this one Divina. After sequencing them, Rydin and Cinquemain started with the known locations of the homeobox gene set, which governed bodily development from the embryo to a functional fetus. These genes were sited in clusters on four chromosomes: 7p15, 17q21.2, 12q13, and 2q31—at least in the antique, pre-biosculpted human form. Rydin noted that the exact addresses had shifted in the Divina genome over three hundred million years of parallel evolution with the tetrapod form and more recently within the class Mammalia. But each of the genes and its obvious mutations was familiar from Rydin's study of the lobe-finned fishes after they had been altered by the Möglich back in the Devonian period. Still, he was only working from memory in this case.

"It's a pity I have nothing to compare them with," he said. "But all my fish samples were destroyed when the medship we stole blew itself up." Here he took his eyes from the computer screen to glare darkly at Cinquemain.

"What?" his pilot asked. "It was a misunderstanding."

"You told me you cross-connected the selvaging controls."

"Only when the ship became so unstable it could not survive."

"Whatever," Rydin said. "Too late to go back and get more fish."

"If you want, I could capture a hexapod bird or rabbit for you to study."

"That would only differentiate the humanoid form from other mammalian variants," Rydin said. "Not much good here."

"But you would be building a database," Cinquemain pointed out.

"That's true," Rydin said. "We will need evidence for the trial."

"What trial?"

"Our court-martial, of course—after the Troupe discovers how badly we screwed up this time stream."

"Oh. That. … Yes."

Well, at least Rydin could compare the Divina's hox genes with his own much-altered gene set. Although the biosculptors had vastly modified human life, they had known not to infringe too closely on the development of bodily structure. Otherwise, future generations might have their heads fused to their abdomens and their mouths attached to their stomachs—an interesting experiment, perhaps, but not practical in human society.

From the Divina's sampled genome, however, Rydin could see a definite repetition, a hiccup in the genome. He guessed this was what provided that third set of limbs, attached to either an additional set of scapulae and collarbones or to a proto-pelvis at the bend in the spine midway down the twelve thoracic vertebrae of the normal human body. The hiccup was a variation on the sequence that the Möglich's virus had injected into the sarcopterygian fishes.

Well, he decided, that was nothing new. While he had the whole genome laid out before him, Rydin determined to look for other differences and anomalies. After all, the Divina were more strange than for simply having a second set of arms.

To account for their apparent mental deficiency, Rydin studied the genes associated with nervous tissue, both in the development and synaptic connection of neurons and in the balancing of the brain's neurotransmitters. Although this was not his usual area of expertise, he could see no obvious differences from the original human, only the expected amounts of genetic drift.

In considering the broader chromosome structure, he found that the Divina had an almost normal distribution of twenty-three chromosome pairs—almost as if it had branched off the primate family of hominids instead of branching from the lobe-finned fishes millions of years earlier and developing according to the available evolutionary niches. But the Divina actually had *twenty-four* chromosome pairs, as represented in the great apes—indicating that it had missed the fusing of two chromosomes at their telomeres to create what in humans became the second chromosome.

Interestingly, Ghost had both an X and a Y chromosome, belying Dottoressa Gerbus's belief that the creatures were sexless, but perhaps the Y chromosome was vestigial rather than functional. Although Rydin had seen Ghost dressing itself in the exercise room, he still did not know if its body was formed male or female.

It was in studying the X chromosome that Rydin noted something strange: an unfamiliar set of genes—ones having no counterpart in the human genome—appeared to be unstable. His equipment registered a series of question marks in the sequence, instead of the usual A, C, G, and T base pairs.

"Try a different tissue sample," Rydin said.

"Another one coming up," Cinquemain replied.

This time the glitch was repeated, but not in the same place. It was still on the X chromosome, but further along toward the three-prime end. Rydin called for another sample, and the same set of question marks showed up, always on the X, but now toward the five-prime end.

"Is this a defect in our equipment?" he asked Cinquemain.

"It would have to be. A faulty display of that particular sequence."

"But why would it jump around like that? Let's take a look at the chromosome itself under a microscope."

They went back to the tissue samples after the nuclear material had been extracted but before the DNA had been denatured into the two base-pair strands and amplified for sequencing. Viewing them *in vitro* with an electron beam showed the different samples pulsing or beating, with random parts of them appearing and disappearing, like moonlight on rippling water. That unreadable section of the X chromosome was not just unstable, it *blinked,* on and off, like a signal lamp. The chromosome itself expanded and contracted like an injured worm.

"Why is it doing that?" Cinquemain asked.

"More important, why is a *dead cell* doing that?"

"Even better, where does it go when it disappears?"

"These creatures are stranger than we ever imagined."

15. The Disappearing Act

EARLY AFTERNOON WAS the time for another round of physical training with Ghost. As Rydin and Cinquemain had gone off on their secret errand in the village, Merola Tsverin was left to conduct the rough-and-tumble alone. She waited with Berzher in the training circle for a full fifteen minutes after the session was supposed to start.

"You would think that creature had no sense of time," she fumed to her pilot.

"Perhaps it forgot," Berzher replied. "Divina are not very intelligent, after all."

"We'd better go look for him. You take the grounds. I'll check his quarters."

At the creature's assigned room in guest quarters—which was really more like a cell, with a cot, toilet facilities, and a locker for whatever clothes Ghost had with him, if he did not actually sleep in them ... or if he slept at all—she knocked on the closed door. Her knock set it swinging inward, because the door had not been latched. She could see that the room was empty.

"So ... where is he?" she asked herself. The thought passed through her mind that it might be appropriate to put a lock on the door. Locks were an ancient custom, uncommon at the Jongleur compound, indeed in all of Lune. The citizens of her time held most goods in common and had nothing that others could not grow or make for themselves. And Jongleurs were expected to live according to an honor code, which valued honesty, self-reliance, and personal privacy. Not that Ghost was a prisoner, of course, because he had joined the Troupe of his own free will, if Divina had any kind of will or ambition ... But a lock on the outside of this room might keep Ghost from wandering off and getting into trouble—especially with less tolerant or forbearing members of the Troupe.

In the hallway, Merola stopped the first Jongleur she passed. "Have you seen Ghost?"

"Your pet Divina?" He grimaced. "You really shouldn't let it wander around loose."

Merola continued through that building and the next one, searching the hallways and unoccupied rooms, asking people about her Divina, and feeling like a fool doing so.

Finally, one young woman had good news. "I saw him go into that storeroom about a minute ago," she said, pointing. The room was a pantry, attached to the main kitchen. Maybe Ghost had been hungry?

Merola opened the door—again, no locks—and walked in. The space was divided by long aisles of shelving that held stacks of canned foods, many stolen as delicacies from previous centuries, bags of dried cereals and legumes, seldom-used pots and pans, and various uncommon cooking utensils. She passed up and down the aisles, looking for her trainee and not finding him.

Next to a shelf stacked with folded cloth—dish towels or service wipes—she found a dropped rag that, in the dim light, seemed to be the color of Ghost's loose robe. She held it up, and it did indeed have four long sleeves and a shawl collar. Which only meant that a naked Divina was wandering somewhere in the compound.

At the far end of the room was a walk-in freezer. Merola tripped the latch and went inside, expecting to discover Ghost cold, gray, and near death on the floor. But except for shelves full of frozen meats, some that Jongleurs on Search had hunted or trapped from previous eras, it was empty as well.

"Just a minute ago," Merola whispered to herself and walked out of the pantry, closing the door behind her. She had gone no more than ten steps down the hall when the door opened and Ghost walked out, humming to himself.

"Where were you just now?" she asked aloud.

The creature stared at her with that idiot smile.

Berzher could ask in signs, of course, but he was not there. So she gestured for Ghost to follow her and led him back to the exercise hall. There Merola rushed him through the ready room to exchange his robe for the too-short pantaloons. All the time she wondered why he had discarded that garment in the storeroom in the first place. She noticed, too, that once again the creature seemed to have no body modesty: he could stand naked before her without apparent conscious embarrassment. In that way, at least, he was like most of the humans of the eleventh millennium—and perhaps it was a learned trait.

They arrived at the training circle, where Berzher was waiting for them.

"I see you found him," her pilot said.

"He was in the pantry—I think."

"And what does that mean?"

"He pulled a disappearing act," Merola said, and explained the circumstances.

"Some animals do that, especially ancient cats. Do you want me to ask him?"

"No, by now he's probably forgotten why he went in there in the first place."

For Ghost's continued training, Merola decided to abandon fancy holds, throws, and grapples and instead focus on targeted attacks. She had Berzher make the signs again for "pretend fight," and this time she waved for Ghost's attention and added her raised fist to indicate "boxing."

The Divina simply stared at her; so she slowly stepped forward, reached into his protected space, and pushed the two upper arms into the semblance of a guard position. When she stepped back, Ghost dropped his arms. Merola shook her head and raised her own arms, tensing them in a guard. The Divina copied her movements, but dropped his arms when she did.

"This is like teaching a rag doll," she said to Berzher.

"Why not demonstrate? Take a swing at him."

Merola moved in quickly, left hand in front of her face, then dropped it as she delivered a right hook to the Divina's jaw.

Her fist made solid contact with flesh and bone, and the creature's head snapped sideways.

Ghost stepped away from her, his face registering surprise, then both of his left hands came up to massage the wounded jaw.

"That got your attention, didn't it?" Merola said.

The Divina stared at her, as if trying to fathom her intentions.

Merola put up her hands again, took two steps in, and punched the creature in what would be a human's solar plexus. The blow would normally have crippled someone by triggering a long and painful exhale. The Divina simply absorbed the blow, but again with that expression of surprise.

She didn't stop to comment this time but came in again and aimed an uppercut at the point of Ghost's jaw. The punch never landed, because the Divina threw his head back, and she whiffed clear air.

"That's good," Merola said. "Avoid the blow." And Berzher made as much of a thumbs-up sign as he could with one pincer claw. But something about the move disturbed her, because the uppercut was supposed to come in from below the eye line, making it almost undetectable, and Ghost had been watching her eyes, not her hands.

"Now hit me," she instructed, and Berzher made the "fight" sign.

Ghost stood still, watching her.

She invited his attack by dropping her guard and standing still. She even aimed a pantomime punch at her own jaw, to give him the idea.

Ghost advanced slowly, raised all four hands, and pistoned them one at a time into her face. The blows were not hard in themselves, although not exactly feeble. Still, they came so quickly and so close together that she could not block them. The cumulative effect was greater than a single, solid blow.

Merola stepped back and felt her own nose, to see if it was dislocated. After the session she would have Dottoressa Gerbus take a look at it.

"I guess we don't have to worry about you," she said. And at "you," she stepped in fast and aimed another right hook at Ghost's jaw.

This time, the Divina ducked. Or rather, because it had no room to duck, it must have stepped back. But it happened so fast!

"Did you *see* that?" Berzher asked.

"What?" she asked. "I missed. Or he ducked. Or else—"

"Three frames out of sixty, this time. Ghost just disappeared."

"So where did he go?" she asked.

"Nowhere in this room. Just *out*."

———

Noumisma did not know why the human female was hitting him. He read no anger or aggression in her mind—more like a complex of care and frustration, focused on his lack of comprehension and response. But these emotions were not strong enough to make her lash out.

It was the same with the session earlier that day, when she had grappled with him, and when the human male with the surprising strength had tried to squeeze him. These had not been simple attacks, such as humans sometimes directed against Divina. Instead, the humans were trying to test him in some way, or toughen him—or possibly to prepare themselves for defense against others of his kind.

These sessions were all very confusing and had nothing to do with learning to fly into the distant past, which was the main purpose of the Jongleurs and the one thing that Noumisma wanted to learn. So he maintained his patience and played along with them.

16. Flight Training

ONCE RYDIN AND Tsverin had judged Ghost able to take care of himself—however he managed to do it—they proceeded to the next phase of training for any Jongleur inductee: introduction to the liteship. In the compound's hangar, Rydin directed Cinquemain to requisition a ship from inventory and begin assembling it.

While the pilot erected the ship's core on its landing foot and began attaching the struts and energy panels, the Divina casually looked around the building's interior, watching other Jongleurs go about their business.

Rydin snapped his fingers. "Over here!" and pointed at the assembly process.

Ghost responded by putting its two lower hands together, right over left, and splaying the fingers to make a tented disk.

"What's that?" Rydin asked Cinquemain.

The robot swiveled its camera stalks to capture the gesture. "That's his word for a liteship, I think."

"They have a *word* for our machines?" Rydin found the thought disturbing.

"Well, it's the gesture he made to Merola and Berzher, when he asked to join the Troupe."

Ghost had dropped his hands by now and watched as the ship parts came together. But every few seconds he lifted his gaze and looked around the hangar, as if expecting something to happen. This watchfulness made Rydin uneasy.

When the ship was ready, Cinquemain climbed aboard, and the whole assembly tilted slightly on its foot under his modest weight of only eight kilograms. But when he plugged into his control station and activated the core, the ship came alive and righted itself automatically.

Rydin climbed in between the energy panels and took his familiar handholds and footpegs. He gestured for Ghost to follow and pointed out positions for the Divina's upper set of hands and his feet. The ship rocked gently but remained stable through the attractions of its core singularity.

When Ghost reached for a second hold with his lower set of hands and found none, he grasped the outer edge of one of the panels. His eyes went wide in distress as the shock of fifty kilovolts—but only a low-power stabilizing charge—went through his body.

"Don't touch that," Rydin said after the fact.

From the other side of the core, Cinquemain gestured by crossing his open claws in front of his carapace, followed by touching one claw to the flat side of the other. "That's 'Don't touch,' by the way," he explained to Rydin. "A phrase with which you probably want to become familiar."

"Right," Rydin said. But still, one good shock was worth a dozen careful warnings. "How will the ship fly with the three of us?"

Cinquemain studied the Divina's body, which supported the billowing robe like a rack of sticks. "For all those extra appendages," he said, "the creature weighs less than you do, about forty-five kilos. And I've flown with two of you humans on one ship before."

"So … fly."

Cinquemain fed power into the panels, which under the strong lights of the hangar just began to glow along their edges. The ship rose a meter off the concrete floor.

Ghost looked down, registered surprise, and took a tentative hold with his lower hands around the core pillar. Since it wasn't powered, there was no shock, and he could grip it tightly.

"A bit more," Rydin suggested to Cinquemain.

The liteship floated toward the ceiling.

Ghost began jerking his body sharply upward and more slowly down, with his robe pulsing around him like the bell-shaped hood of a jellyfish. He seemed to be trying to lift the ship with his momentum, but each jerk only disrupted its smooth movement. Cinquemain finally had to snap his claws for attention and make the "Don't" gesture.

Ghost settled down, and the ship made a complete circuit of the hangar, passed out through the wide door into the sunlight, and moved across the lawn inside the compound.

"That's probably enough—until we get him fitted for activity above the atmosphere," Rydin said. "Take us back."

Cinquemain brought them into the hangar and settled on the floor where they had started.

When they had disembarked—Ghost being careful not to brush the panels, even though they were now powered down—Rydin asked Cinquemain, "What was all that jumping about?"

The pilot put the question in gestures to Ghost, who shrugged with all four shoulders and responded by making a fist with his lower left hand and pushing it upward with the palm of his corresponding right hand.

"That's 'helping,' I think," Cinquemain said.

"Well, tell him it's unnecessary," Rydin said.

———

Noumisma had never seen a flying ship before, and he had no conception of the principles that kept it afloat. At first he thought they would lift basically by reaction to subtle shifts in body weight, and he had participated in urging the craft upward by thrusts with his own mass. But this seemed not to be the case, and he desisted when the small robot told him, through crude gestures, to stop trying to help.

He had thought that this time they were finally going to take him into the past. That had made him nervous, because he was sure the other humans would come forward at the last moment and keep Rydin and his mechanical assistant from performing this abomination. Then they simply drifted the machine around the assembly area and then out onto the open grounds. But they never rose above the height of the outside walls. And the machine never made a discernible phase change to another reality.

So this test was all a waste of energy.
Maybe they would travel in time later.

17. Some Necessary Modifications

OF COURSE, THE Jongleur inventory had no biosuit of whatever size that would fit a hexapod; so Merola Tsverin and Berzher had been tasked with building one for him. They would work with the Troupe's fabric artisan, Juwana Dyllin. Together, the two women called Ghost into her workshop for initial measurements and a strategy session.

As the Divina stood in what little open space there was, Juwana eyed him and bit her lower lip. "Do you have the measurements from its physical examination?" she asked.

"Ghost—and we've decided it's a 'he,' not an 'it'—refused any kind of close examination, including measurements. And the Ringmasters allowed it."

Juwana turned to Berzher. "Can you approximate from your scans?"

"Plus or minus two centimeters over complex contours," he said.

"Not close enough for a working biosuit, is it?" Merola asked.

"Not for one that I would wear," the artisan said. "Here." She handed Merola an old-fashioned measuring tape. "You know him best. So maybe he trusts you. I need foot length and width; height of the arches—if he has any; circumference at widest part of each calf and thigh, and length of each limb segment; same for the forearms and upper arms; glove size for each hand; widest part of the chest—both above and below the, um, secondary shoulder blades; width of shoulders—both pairs; neck length and circumference; head circumference, length, and width; and finally, overall body height and mass."

"What about metabolic rate—for the oxygen supply?" Merola asked.

"We'll work that up later. First we need to make a suit that fits."

Merola took the tape in both hands. Figuring that she would start with the chest measurements, she approached Ghost. But first, she realized, he had to take off his robe.

"Can you get him to undress?" she asked Berzher.

The robot pinched his claws together in front of his carapace and pulled them apart in two half-circles.

When Ghost simply stared at him, Merola stepped in and flicked open the loose lapels around its upper chest. In response, the Divina put up all four fists in a guard stance.

Berzher clicked his claws for attention and made the "No fight" signs.

"Is that how you talk to it?" Juwana said. "Things must be going really well."

"We're working on communication," Merola said grimly.

When the robe was finally off and Ghost stood naked before her, Merola got close to its body and started taking the necessary measurements, dictating them for Berzher to record and display. She avoided Ghost's eyes—which wouldn't tell her much anyway—but she was conscious all the time that she was inside his personal space and that those four hands, while individually weak, were collectively stronger than she was. If Ghost were suddenly to take offense at any point, she was vulnerable. She wished Rydin could be present, for his enhanced strength.

After she had taken all the single and paired measurements, it was time to get the Divina's overall height. Since Ghost stood half a meter taller than she or any other modern human, Merola had to rise up on tiptoes and raise her arms above her head to lift the tape that high. Ghost obligingly ducked his own head to help her. She shook him off and pantomimed standing up straight and tall. He did so briefly, then ducked again when she tried to get the measurement.

"Have him stand against the wall," Berzher suggested, gesturing for the Divina to move. "I can take that final measure by triangulation."

Getting Ghost's mass was easier, because Juwana's workshop had a scale.

Finally, they had built a detailed image of the Divina on her screen and stored it in her database. And then Juwana Dyllin sighed.

"As I expected," she said. "Nothing in inventory, even sized for our largest Troupe member, can be adapted—even if I cut a suit apart and work from the pieces. If the circumference of a limb is right, then the length is wrong. And taping seals between separate parts is risky, given the pressures and impacts a biosuit is supposed to withstand. No, I'll have to create a whole new form and pour the gelfoam myself. Same for the helmet, because it's an extra-large with an unbelievable head length."

"How long will all this take?" Merola asked.

"Ten days—but tell me why I should bother."

"Excuse me? Because the Ringmasters want it."

"Of course, of course. But betting among the other Jongleurs is that your Divina will be too scared or too stupid to fly. So this is a waste of good materials—and my time."

"Rydin took him for a test flight yesterday. He seemed enthusiastic."

"Oh, yes? Well, possibly. But wait until he sees the stars up close."

———

All of this prodding and measuring were lost on Noumisma. He had no need of more clothing than the simple robe he wore. It would all just fall away and disappear anyway when he moved to another probabilistic reality—where he always had to trust his luck in finding a rag, a bag, or a coating of mud to cover himself. Not that he needed as much for social awareness and recognition, although some surface layer was necessary for protection, especially if he transitioned into another season or the center of a storm. But on sunny days in warm climates no one seemed to notice whether a Divina was clothed or not. The average human took little interest in him, and the other Divina did not care.

He presumed that the time jump would be the same for these humans in the Jongleur Troupe. So far, they seemed not to mind their own nakedness—especially in the gymnasium. So arriving in another time and space without their clothes would be a matter of warmth and comfort, not social acceptance.

But Noumisma was disturbed by the hesitations of this new woman, called "Juwana"—whatever her function might be. Unlike Rydin and Tsverin, with whom he was becoming familiar and even friendly, she remained distrustful. He could sense her dislike for him, the same as with most of the other humans. It reminded Noumisma to be … watchful.

18. Above the Atmosphere

RYDIN MET WITH the rest of his team in the hangar when they were to take Ghost on the first full day of flight training. Merola Tsverin arrived, trailed by Berzher and Juwana Dyllin, and the women were carrying two bundles between them.

One, which Merola unfurled, was a biosuit in bright-yellow gelfoam sized to Ghost's measurements and bodily configuration. The suit was a single garment, with a sealing strip down the front and articulated neck ring for the helmet, and it integrated the boots and gloves as seamless attachments. She handed the bundle to Ghost and, when he just stood there, helped him take it in the appropriate manner and begin to slide his feet into the suit's legs.

"He can't do it while wearing that robe," Dyllin said. "And not with bare feet."

From the helmet she was holding, she pulled out a knitted, blue-gray body stocking of hybridized spider silk and a pair of calyx-wrapped sandals made of reinforced poly-aramid. Merola helped the Divina put on these garments, and when he was dressed—but still occasionally twitching and pulling on the tight fabric—he looked more like a very big Jongleur, except for that extra pair of arms and the long, flowing hair.

While he was struggling into the stiffer biosuit, with Merola's help, Cinquemain walked across the floor with another Silicate following behind him. That robot was carrying the wrapped components of a liteship.

"Who is this?" Rydin asked his pilot.

"I am Piedeleger," the machine said.

"What's wrong with your voice?" Merola asked. "It's an octave or two higher than the other Silicates. Is there some problem with your vocoder chip?"

"I am emulating a human soprano," Piedeleger said.

"Why would you want to do that?" Merola asked.

"Because my software identifies as human female."

"I didn't know that you machines had genders."

"Diversification is an evolutionary adaptation."

Merola turned to Berzher. "Did you know about this?"

"We are capable of evolving," her pilot replied with a mechanical shrug.

"And adopting a specific gender," Piedeleger said, "helps me relate to the female half of your world."

"More to the point," Rydin cut in, "why are you *here?*"

"You are training an inductee," the machine replied. "I come with his liteship, and I am assigned as his pilot."

"Ghost is not ready to fly solo yet," Rydin said.

Piedeleger turned to examine the Divina, dressed in his biosuit but without the helmet. "You are taking him above the atmosphere. He will need a guide and companion. That is Troupe protocol."

"Do you know how to talk with him?" Merola asked.

"I have downloaded the files." Piedeleger faced Ghost squarely to get his attention and locked her claws together, first right over left, then left over right. "That is 'friend.' "

Ghost repeated the gesture with his lower set of hands, linking index finger with littlest finger in each case, rather than coupling his whole hands together as the Silicate had done.

"You see?" Piedeleger said. "We will get along perfectly."

———

Noumisma regarded the new machine that was making higher-pitched sounds than the other two. Those others seemed to be attached to—or at least responded to—the humans identified as "Rydin" and "Tsverin." For what reason they followed the human beings around, Noumisma had not yet determined. Nor was it the common human practice, as observed by other Divina, for all humans to have a mechanical servant. Only these who were attached to the Jongleur Troupe.

This new machine had shown the unmistakable signal for "friendship," even considering the dexterity limitations of its two metal claws. But how could it be a "friend" to a conscious being, when it was merely a mechanical object? It had no mind to link to and engage with his mind. And Noumisma had neither sought nor accepted a servant of any kind. So what was its true purpose here?

———

As the three Silicates erected their liteships on the hangar floor, Rydin again felt uneasy. Ghost was not ready to have a ship of his own, even if Piedeleger was piloting it and the Divina would have no direct control. It just felt wrong, despite the Troupe protocol of one Jongleur per ship. So it was a good thing that he and Merola were going to be alongside and in radio contact both with Piedeleger and with Ghost's biosuit—as if the latter made a difference.

When the three ships stood on the hangar floor like great, black flowers, Merola handed Ghost his helmet and pantomimed sealing it to the suit's neck ring.

The Divina looked at the helmet and handed it back.

"You need it to travel above the atmosphere," Merola said. "Otherwise, you will suffocate." She turned to Piedeleger. "Can you explain it to him?"

The pilot made a series of gestures, and Ghost replied with more gestures.

"Divina do not cover their heads," Piedeleger explained. "It has something to do with 'brain waves'—I think."

"Did you explain the danger?" Merola asked.

"Of course, but he insists," the machine said.

"Then tell him it's a condition of his service."

Finally, they managed to seal the Divina's helmet in place.

The team performed radio checks—for what it was worth with the Divina—and Merola helped Ghost climb in between the energy panels and showed him the proper handholds and foopegs as well as what parts of the ship were safe to hold on to with his second set of hands. When he was settled, she tapped his helmet and nodded to see if he was all right. Through the visor, the Divina nodded back.

Rydin and Merola put on their own biosuits and helmets and climbed aboard their respective liteships.

"This is just a test above atmosphere," Rydin told the three pilots. "No transition out of this time frame. Understood?"

The Silicates signaled their agreement.

"Piedeleger," he continued, "watch Ghost for any adverse reactions."

"What would those be, please?" she asked politely.

"You'll know when you see them." He did not want to alarm her with thoughts of a large body jumping around and destabilizing her ship at fifty thousand feet or more.

On his signal, the three ships lifted smoothly, traversed the hangar floor, passed out over the concrete apron, and rose into the sky. Rydin kept an eye on Ghost, partially hidden by the glowing energy panels on his ship, but the Divina seemed to be taking the experience of flying at altitude calmly.

As usual, the pilots fed more power to the panels as they ascended, so the ships accelerated at two, and then three gravities. Rydin and Merola were used to the extra weight, but Ghost was not.

"Piedeleger, how is your … passenger … doing?"

"He is hanging on. He seems to enjoy it."

"Hold this acceleration for now."

———

Noumisma expected the extra weight. It had been implied from the rise and fall of the ship when the humans had taken him on that first flight around the compound. In fact, the pressure he felt now, as the ship rose above the valley, was less than he had expected. He could easily maintain his hold on the struts and grips of the tiny craft. And he reminded himself that he did not have to help it rise by jerking his body upward. The ship had all the momentum it needed to soar to great heights.

He was mildly confused, however, by the shifting patterns of light and darkness that moved across the faceplate of the rigid composite sphere the woman Merola had fixed over his head. It took him a moment to analyze it as the shadows of the black panels as they moved with the ship's turning in relation to the sun. Once he understood that, he could relax and enjoy the view of first the valley and then the surrounding green countryside, as they rose above the curve of the planet.

———

Within a few minutes, the blue sky above Ongleterre paled to black and the stars came out. Rydin always enjoyed this moment as the ship passed above thirty thousand meters, because it meant his liteship was effectively beyond the reach of wind and weather, able to move freely to any place or time.

"Could someone tell me what is going on?" Piedeleger said urgently.

"Explain what you see," Rydin said on the command channel.

"My … human … seems to be experiencing a crisis."

"Share video feed," Cinquemain instructed.

In a corner of Rydin's visor—and in Merola's, too, he knew—a screen lit up. It would be showing the same image in Cinquemain's and Berzher's optic centers as well. Piedeleger's camera stalks were focused on Ghost's visor. The face behind it was still composed with that dreaming smile. But as they watched, the face blinked out of existence, leaving only the empty helmet. At first Rydin thought it was a shadow passing over the faceplate, but then the face came back, and he knew he had been staring into a void behind the polycarbonate shield.

In Rydin's less-than-precise impression, the disappearance lasted no more than a second—and he would check the lapse with Cinquemain later for an exact duration. When the face blinked back, the Divina's mild expression was unchanged. The flicker out and back happened twice more. And Rydin had no doubt that the creature's entire body was flashing in and out, but *out* of *what?* Of where? Existence? This place? This time? What was going on? Fortunately, the sequence was rapid enough that the suit did not slump, lose its handholds, and fall out of the bottom of the ship.

Rydin was reminded of the hexapod hare and the four-winged bird he had seen disappear on his walk out to the Jongleur compound. Those creatures had gone and not come back, not *blinked* like this. He was also reminded of the wobbly bits of DNA he had studied in the Divina's skin cells. Certainly, these creatures were more than just oddly shaped animals.

"The crisis seems to have passed," Piedeleger said. And indeed, Ghost's face had remained … solidly placed … for almost an entire minute.

"I think we'd better go back now," Merola said.

"Agreed," Rydin replied. "Cinquemain, when we get back to the compound, you will ask Ghost what happened."

"I do not think there are signs for that," the pilot said.

"Then perhaps you had better teach me his language."

19. Absent Without Leave

WHEN IT CAME time for the next step in his training and preparation for travel to the past—implanting the network of superconducting carbon fibers inside Ghost's brain to record his neural imprints—the Divina once again disappeared. Merola searched the Jongleur compound for him. In the room assigned to him, she found the blue-gray body stocking folded neatly at the foot of his cot. She also went twice to the storage room where she had cornered him before. Each time, she entered the pantry and the freezer, searched for him and found nothing, left briefly, and then returned hoping to catch him in whatever magic act he used to conceal himself.

When her own search failed, she enlisted the help of Berzher, who in turn brought on the Silicates' coordinating function whom he referred to as "Nexus." Berzher was essentially broadcasting the request to find and return the Divina wherever he might be located.

"And that will cover this entire compound?" Merola asked.

"It covers all Ongleterre and wherever else Silicates exist."

At the risk of further ridicule, Merola also let a select few among the other Jongleurs of her rank know that her new charge had gone missing. She just hoped the word would not get back to the Ringmasters, because it might jeopardize Rydin's plans for the Divina.

"Do you suppose he heard about the imprinting and fled?" she asked Rydin after a day of searching. "I mean, the process is not exactly painless, even with an anesthetic." She remembered having the back of her skull bored out and the fibers extruded into her neocortex. "And perhaps our anesthetics won't work with Divina physiology. Or his brain might be so differently constructed that all those fibers would actually kill him."

"We can't travel to the past without imprinting," Rydin said.

"I know, it protects us in case we change something. But ..."

"Look, I don't think he would leave here because of that. After all, we never discussed the process with Ghost, never even hinted at it. And as yet no other Jongleur has formed a personal attachment to him—or one close enough to think about warning him. None of the others would bother telling him."

"So … are you going to report him missing?"

Rydin pulled at his chin. "No … not just yet."

———

Noumisma entered the glade of natural trees that, for the sake of security, lay twenty kilometers from the village the humans called "Lune" and in another branch of the reality that predated his first contact with Merola Tsverin. He had to walk the twenty kilometers, and that took most of the morning. The temporal distance he covered in a blink.

Waiting there was his own Choir Leader, along with other elders among the Divina—as the humans called them, but whose name for themselves was "the Creator's Children," for theirs was a living god. One of them handed Noumisma a white robe of unbleached spider silk to cover his nakedness. As Noumisma put on the garment, the Leader looked him up and down with narrowed eyes.

You seem no worse for your exertions, the Leader projected mentally.

Noumisma grimaced. *The training is … rigorous,* he answered in kind.

But have you traveled backwards in time yet? another of the elders asked.

So far, at this stage, not. I have observed that their ships can defy gravity and fly above the world we see. But, at this point, I perceive no indication that they can violate the flow of the temporal realities. And neither Rydin nor Tsverin has spoken of any choice they must make between branching realities. So it is clear they do not travel selectively across currents, as we do.

The Choir Leader frowned at this. *But they can travel back. We know this from our Lord Glyph, who says it is so. We also know*

*because they led him back to the depths of time, to the simplified evo-
lutionary stream, before the division of animal structures into four
and six. It was there that they ended his being in at least one temporal
form. So they* do *travel.*

It appears they do not deem me ready to travel with them, Noumisma projected with appropriate modesty.

You must redouble your efforts to appear worthy, the Choir
Leader replied.

Yes … of course.

You must accompany them on their travels—and soon, the Leader continued. *You must protect our existence. These two outliers in
our world, this Rydin and this Tsverin, smell of the* other *time, the
branching reality in which the Creator's Children do not exist. They
killed the Creator in order to protect that temporal reality—and yet
they failed in their efforts. We project that they will eventually go
back to the Beginning, or to some point leading up to the Beginning,
and try to complete their task. You must be there to stop them.*

I can try to hinder them … Noumisma began.

No, not hinder. *Stop them from completing.*

And if I cannot? If I am not strong enough?

Then kill them. End their being for all time.

Noumisma thought about what he had observed of the
Jongleur Troupe's structure and practice. *What about the machines?* he asked. *The humans have mechanical servants who might
complete—*

Do the machines have mentation?

None that I can directly perceive.

Do they have a separate volition?

They act for their human masters.

Then you may discount them, the Choir Leader concluded.
*Thwart the humans or kill them, and our branch of reality will be
assured forever.*

And then I will be free? Noumisma asked.

As free as any solo singer of single songs.

———

"Nexus reports that your Divina has been found," Berzher told Merola the morning after Ghost's disappearance.

"Where?" she asked.

"In his cell, sleeping."

"Not possible. We looked there. Many times."

"Whatever you think, he is located there now."

She and her pilot rushed to the living quarters, half expecting Ghost to have left again, but they found him in the bare room at the end of the guest corridor. The Divina was sitting on the cot, dressed in the biosuit's blue-gray undergarment. His head was down, with his lower pair of hands resting on his thighs and the upper pair clasping his knees.

"Are you all right?" she asked. And when he just stared at her with a bemused smile, she turned to Berzher. "Ask him if he is sick."

The Silicate pointed his left claw at Ghost and then bent his right claw back to touch his own carapace with one unhinged pincer. "That's as close as I can get."

In reply, Ghost clenched his upper hands into fists, crossed them at the wrists in front of his chest, and then spread them apart and out to the side.

"I don't understand," Berzher said. "That's either 'Safe' or 'Free.' "

" 'Free'?" she said. "But he came back. And he knows he's safe here."

"If I had real hands, with fingers—and a body to work with—I could probably do this language thing better," Berzher said.

The Divina was now making other signs, and Merola recognized the same opposed set of hands, fingertips first spindled and then spreading outward, and finally pulsing to pull them apart and push them together. It was the sign Ghost had made when he first approached her, back on Trapfog Square. They knew he used it to represent a liteship in flight.

"I suppose he wants to go flying again," Berzher said.

"Well, that's certainly a relief," she replied.

20. The First Shortcut

"ARE YOU SURE this procedure is necessary?" Dottoressa Gerbus asked Rydin as they waited in the Jongleur clinic's surgical room.

"You know it's Troupe protocol," he replied. "Every Jongleur gets the implant."

But it was more than protocol that interested him. So far, Rydin had only studied the Divina's tissue samples, which were unremarkably mammalian, and its genome, which had remarkable exceptions. But the procedure that implanted the neural imprint's wires within Ghost's skull was the only chance he would have to study—unobtrusively and by magnetic imaging—the structure of his brain. This was preferable to sandbagging a random Divina, euthanizing it, and cutting open its skull.

Merola and Berzher led Ghost into the room, and the Divina came passively enough, without apparent fear or concern.

"I'm going to ask you to lie here, face down, head in the restraint," Gerbus said, pointing to the padded table with a semicircular block positioned at one end.

Ghost just stared at her.

"Let me," Merola said. She approached the table, sat on the edge, swung her legs up, rolled over, and pressed her forehead into the block. Then she popped up, slid off the table, and patted it for Ghost to try.

The Divina looked at Berzher, who held his open claws in front of his carapace and swung them left and right. "That's 'Do it,' " he said.

Slowly, hesitantly, Ghost put all four hands tentatively on the table, turned around, and followed Merola's motions. When his face was in the block, Dottoressa Gerbus moved the magnetic-resonance scanning interface into position and told its captive intelligence to begin recording. The machine made a soft clicking, and Ghost started to rise up. Gerbus put one hand on his upper shoulder, then another on his head, and held him until he became quiet.

Rydin watched as the imagery built up on the device's screen in three views: top, back, and sides. He knew the general shape of the human brain from his own scan, taken long ago in his trainee days when he was implanted. The Divina brain had the same wrinkled-walnut configuration, but the shape was different. The neocortex, or thinking part of the brain, was shorter and much shallower, while the cerebellum, or breathing and balancing part, was large and bulbous. Certain substructures shown in shaded outline within the brain itself, such as the hypothalamus, which controlled autonomic bodily functions like thirst and hunger, and the limbic system, which controlled instinct and mood, were abnormally large. To Rydin's eye, the brain was more animal than human.

When the clicking finished and the brain scan was complete, Gerbus touched Rydin's arm and motioned for them to step outside.

In the next room, she stopped him with a frown. "I don't know that I can go on," she said. "Not ethically."

"Why not?" Rydin said. "You can see his brain."

"Yes, but our instruments are sized and calibrated to the human brain. This is more like a … a dog's brain."

"Would it be dangerous to do the implant?"

"I don't know that the fibers would reach the right areas, touch the right synapses," she said. "The imprints could be all wrong. The software interpreting an imprint and guiding the recall could be confusing—perhaps even paralyzing—to the subject."

"That would make him unreliable in both past and present," he said.

"How necessary is it for him to have a correct memory of what has gone before?"

"Vital, if he is to understand, when he returns from a mission into the past, how the present might have been changed. Neural imprinting is the basis of all our judgments."

"How much judgment does he have to begin with?"

"Good point. But would you continue if I ordered it?"

"I would prefer you did not make such an order, Coel."

"Very well. But please preserve that scan for later study."

"Of course," she said.

———

Merola had returned to Lune and the treehouse that was almost, but not quite, her own. She and Berzher were sorting through a storage room that contained some familiar items: the twenty-first century clothing she had worn on their return from the Conoscenza trip; several wigs that the hairless Jongleurs of the eleventh millennium had to wear as a disguise while on Search, now mounted on head forms and sealed in a stasis box; two knives and what looked like a bludgeon with metal hooks, all of which she remembered picking up—one of the knives when she actually needed a weapon—on her adventures into the past. She also found objects she could not quite identify: a heavy necklace of what appeared to be gold, decorated with clear, red stones, that was far too large for her own neck; a stack of paper sheets bound along one edge with thread and covered in cured skin, which she recognized—but did not remember acquiring—as a book from the second millennium; a warrior's shield of wood layered over with bronze, and the bronze itself laid in layers and carved into scenes of men fighting, hunting, and farming, with processions of people and animals, some of the figures accented with gold filigree.

When she tried to move the shield from its place, leaning against one of the tree's sturdier side branches, she found it almost too heavy to lift.

"How did the other Merola ever get this thing aboard a liteship?" she asked.

"Slung it underneath?" Berzher suggested. "That is what I—or the other me—would have done."

"But then, why would she take it at all? It can't be good for fighting."

"Perhaps it has a ceremonial purpose? Or historical value?" he said. "It appears to be early Greek, second millennium before the Christus. ... It could be the shield of Achilles."

"Achilles," she said with disdain, "was a fictional character in Homer's *Iliad*."

"Are you sure that was a fiction? It might it be fun to go back and see ..."

"Well, we don't actually have another assignment right now," she replied. "Now that Ghost has failed his implant. That would disqualify him as a Jongleur, wouldn't it?"

"Hello?" came a voice—Rydin's—from outside the tree.

"Come in," she called. "We're just sorting ... old junk."

Rydin, followed by Cinquemain, appeared in the doorway. "We have to talk."

"I thought the experiment with Ghost was finished," she said.

"That has yet to be determined—the Ringmasters are still considering," he said. "I'm here about our *other* mission, the one they can't know about."

"And would not approve if they did," Cinquemain added.

Merola sighed. "Right—going back and undoing this mess."

"I suggest," Rydin said, "that we go back upstream to the late twentieth century and stop you from pursuing the McGwire baseball. That one error seems to have triggered the temporal landslide."

"I still don't remember taking the ball," Merola said. "*Dealing* for it, sure—but not actually *getting* it."

"Because you didn't take your neural imprint," Berzher reminded her.

"Whatever the cause," Rydin said. "If we can't intercept you in Sane Looie, or Saint Louis, then we'll move downstream. We'll try to stop you before you attract the attention of those three orphan children, the Flüchtlinge, and the six-limbed, time-jumping monster Möglich that was following them, latched onto you, and tracked you back three hundred million years to the Devonian period."

"Barring that," Cinquemain added, "we will try to find the Möglich and kill it first, before it contaminates the genetics of the lobe-finned fishes."

"But ... when we find the other me," Merola said, "what will you do with her? Argue with her? Rescue her? Bring her—me—back to the eleventh millennium?"

"If that is what the situation requires," Rydin said.

"But that would create a paradox," she said. "There would then be *two* of me in the current time stream."

"I have a hard time with just one of you," Rydin said.

"It would be like having a twin sister," Berzher said.

"Or we could simply kill you," Cinquemain offered.

"And that would be another paradox!" Merola said.

"But one with fewer loose ends," Cinquemain said.

"We'll deal with all this when the time comes," Rydin said. "Perhaps it would be enough to simply ... hinder you. Find a way to keep you from stealing the ball, or visiting the toy store, or joining the Conoscenza expedition. Any of those approaches would work."

"So when do we start?" she asked.

"We need a pretext for an unauthorized mission," Rydin said. "We can't just requisition two liteships and head off eight thousand years into the past."

"And what about the Divina?" Cinquemain said. "His case is still undecided."

"We can take him along," Merola suggested. "We will say it's another training flight—except that, with all those jumps, we may be gone for an extended time."

"Extended in our frame of reference," Rydin said. "In the eleventh millennium, we would leave one minute and come back the next. No one would know where or when we went. And if we're successful, no one will care."

"But Ghost would need his own ship," she said. "And we can't trust him to fly it alone."

"Piedeleger would do the flying," Cinquemain said. "She will follow our cues."

"Your Divina would just be a passenger," Berzher said. "A sack of protoplasm."

"That would also extend our circle of conspiracy," Rydin said, sounding worried. "We would have to trust Piedeleger with our real purpose—and then hope Ghost does not report on what he observes."

"We could arrange an accident along the way," Cinquemain suggested.

"We lose human companions all the time," Berzher observed.

Merola was shocked. "You would *kill* the Divina?"

"Fewer loose ends," Cinquemain repeated.

Backward

21. The View from a Church Steeple

ONCE AGAIN, FOR perhaps the fifth or sixth time on what the Jongleurs themselves thought of as a "training flight," the tiny, spindly time-traveling ship carried Noumisma and Piedeleger aloft, rising in formation with the ships that carried Rydin and Tsverin. As the Jongleurs had prepared for this final departure from London, Noumisma could read in their minds the sense of failure. And if it did not show clearly in their thoughts, he could easily sense defeat from their body language, their faces twisted by slow scowls, their heads drooping with fatigue.

So now they would all make the long and tedious journey—six light years forward along the Sun's projected path, eight millennia forward in the current temporal reality—from London in the twenty-first century to the Lune of the eleventh millennium from which they had originally come.

Despite the rigors of a long time jump, Noumisma felt a sense of satisfaction, although he could not express it either by face or body language. In fact, he did not dare even to feel it fully, because the expressed thought might leak into the Jongleurs' consciousnesses. That could lead to questions, which could lead to sanctions. But still, his satisfaction was present as a small, quiet animal in a cage hidden inside his mind.

In their mission to recover, or capture, or impede the connections that the other Merola might make, which would result in her leading the Creator back to the instant of his creating the Divina, Noumisma had made sure that none of their efforts came to fruition. And that was enough for now.

———

On the conical steeple above the clock face of the church that the Londoners called "Saint Giles-in-the-Fields," the creature that called itself simply "Glyph" crouched like a gargoyle and watched three apparitions rise into the midday sky.

On a rooftop not far away, three small metal machines had assembled the geometric shapes out of telescoping sticks and panels of a dark, iridescent material, almost as shiny and shimmering as the gown Glyph himself wore. Piece by piece, the three objects became stretched polygons of ten sides each. And just as Glyph watched from his perch, two small humans—both drenched in the aromas of other times and distant places—and one of his own children watched the assembly process from nearby on the same rooftop. When the polygons were erect and faintly glowing, the three machines climbed aboard, followed by the two humans and the being they had learned to call "Divina." The passengers all secured themselves against the central column that held the shimmering panels taut and extended.

Then the polygons brightened, becoming silvery against the midday sunshine, and began to exude a mist or fog of water vapor wrung from the air itself. At the same time, the three shapes rose above the rooftop, into the blue sky, and away from the city. Within three heartbeats—as much as Glyph had a heart, and it could beat—the little ships were almost lost to sight.

Almost … If he had not already watched this performance once before—the mechanical assembly, the glowing light, the fog, and the aerial dynamics—he might have been alarmed and amused by what he had seen. But Glyph had been watching these humans, their machines, and his own like-shaped child through several cycles now. He still did not know exactly what they wanted or where they were going. But he knew that in this place and time they were not … normal.

More than that … something about the two small humans was familiar to him. Even from the distance of his church steeple, he could *smell* that about them. The one of female shape Glyph had followed in another dimension. And the one of male shape he had encountered in a way that ended Glyph's own existence in that dimension. So the two of them demanded attention—and perhaps an intervention.

Before the three ships could slip into the sky full of stars above the atmosphere, Glyph leapt like a cat from the steeple, transitioned into the being that he truly was, and followed them into the dark.

22. The Crossroads of Time

NOUMISMA WAITED ON the rooftop in London with Light Foot, the mechanical pilot that the Troupe des Jongleurs had assigned specifically to him, along with the time ship that carried them. "Light Foot" was the robot's *real* name—or the meaning of its name, the one it used in signing—even though the machine used a different name, "Piedeleger," or it might have been a different *form* of the name, perhaps in another human language, when talking to the other Jongleurs. Anyway, Coel Rydin and Merola Tsverin, along with their own pilots, had left him and his pilot on the roof when they went down into the street to pursue their "mission" of finding and trapping Merola—another Merola, supposedly the same as this one, but different—outside her hotel in a place called "Seven Dials."

He wondered if, after this—and assuming they happened to be successful—Rydin and Tsverin and their little robots were planning on making yet another short jump within the twentieth century—or was it now the twenty-first?—as they had been doing for the past three days—or perhaps it was four or five days. Or would they be making the much longer jump back to the eleventh millennium, which would be of the same extended duration as the jump they had made in starting this "mission" of theirs?

His own robot, Light Foot, had tried to explain the mathematics of time travel in terms of diagrams and calculations. Apparently, the Earth moved along its course around the Sun—a fact that scholars among Divina had already known—while the Sun moved through the greater universe. And this configuration in position of star and planet was unique at each point in the temporal reality. When the Jongleurs abandoned one part of their reality to travel back to an earlier time frame—and yes, Noumisma finally knew they could actually do this, travel backward and forward—the planet would be in a different place from where they started.

Traveling eight thousand years into the past put the Earth in the Sol system of that time frame almost six light years further back along the Sun's path. So the Jongleurs had to make *two* jumps: one at the speed of infinity moving backward or forward to arrive at the correct *time*; another at several orders of the speed of light through space to arrive at the correct *place*. When traveling across much shorter temporal gaps, such as the span of months they had just traversed in the twenty-first century, the spatial difference might be much less, but the offset was still not negligible.

This much Noumisma understood. What he did not know was how the Jongleurs managed to keep track of their time frame across all of their reality's nearly infinite probabilistic branches. A Divina could sort out these branches, because they were finite at any one point in the time. But when a traveler began moving up or down in time, the choice of branchings multiplied. And the further back one traveled, the more one's reality branched. But none of this seemed to bother the Jongleurs he was traveling with, because they apparently viewed their passage forward and backward as no different from their passage through the spatial dimension: a straight line without deviation. Perhaps the little robots kept track of all the different branchings. But Noumisma lacked the diagramming skills and the mathematical symbols to discuss this with Light Foot.

In any case, the past three, or four, or five consecutive days—his own sense of continuity had been disrupted by the many different short jumps—that the Jongleurs had spent in the twenty-first century had been extremely unpleasant for Noumisma.

To maintain their nourishment, they and he had subsisted on food concentrates supplied within their environmental "biosuits." And when they had to cache those suits to appear in public, they stole from various business sites—there were many in this ancient period—that provided either packaged or prepared foods to paying customers. When they could not easily steal food, Merola and her robot climbed into immense iron waste containers, which she said were called "dumpsters," behind those businesses and retrieved an abundance of discarded food items.

In all, that was not much different from the way most Divina lived among human society in the eleventh millennium. But the food here and now was strange, and some of it was half-rotten. This did not seem to disturb the two human Jongleurs at all, or else they were used to these privations. The three robots—those belonging to the two Jongleurs and his own Light Foot—subsisted on their internal energy supplies and did not complain.

However, when they were in the place called "San Francisco," Noumisma had discovered that he liked garlic French fries and loved mushroom pizza, which was better with anchovies, even when these things were eaten cold. And then when they traveled to the place called "London," he immediately rejected the idea of "toad-in-the-hole" at any temperature when he heard it described, even after the robot Cinquemain had assured him it was not made with real toads. But he loved "strawberry trifle," especially when it was two days old. So, all in all, he did not starve.

Worse than the food was the need for disguise. The Jongleurs had adopted articles of clothing and wigs that made their small, hairless bodies appear to be those of children in the twenty-first century. They had also tailored for Noumisma a mantle made of stiff gabardine that provided sleeves for his upper arms and space below for him to clasp his lower arms around his belly. The intent was that he might pass—at a distance and barring focused inspection—for another human being. The Jongleurs insisted on this disguise even though other Divina inhabited the world in this century, as they did in every century, having evolved alongside the human race. Noumisma had since determined that the purpose of his disguise was to keep him from meeting the Divina of this time frame and engaging in discussions that might reveal the Jongleurs' far-future origin and their "mission." As if the humans would ever know when he was conversing with another Divina ...

Still, he had eaten their food and worn their ridiculous smock and traveled along wherever and whenever they had gone.

But Noumisma now had a complicated problem to solve. If the two Jongleurs managed to intercept the Merola who was loose in this temporal reality and prevent her from going back millions of years to the Beginning—and so drawing the Creator with her—then the Divina and all their kind would never have been born. But if Noumisma interfered directly in the Jongleurs' searches, then this Merola also might miss the connection today with the group that would take her to the Beginning, and so preempt the entire class of hexapods.

It was a delicate task, but he had worked this trick before.

He knew the hotel where the other Merola was staying and from which the Jongleurs expected her to emerge, because Rydin and the current version of Tsverin who was traveling with them had discussed it before. Noumisma now projected his mind into the building and searched out the mind of another of his species. Divina were employed as menials in this time frame, and a prosperous business would certainly have one on staff.

He found a likely subject in the kitchen. She was washing dishes, which she could do most efficiently using all four of her hands. Her name was Oneiroi.

Noumisma made contact, introduced himself, and inserted an image of Merola Tsverin—not the current disguise but just the elfin face and girlish body—into the other Divina's mind. He also projected as much of Merola's persona as he could pack into ideations and unfold inside Oneiroi's imagination.

Is there one of this description staying at the hotel? Noumisma asked.

From my work in the kitchen I do not meet many guests face to face.

Please probe then for the likeness of this child's face and mind, he instructed.

There is such a mind here. It is cool and disciplined, analytical, but not a child's mind, Oneiroi replied. *She is older, a grown woman with dark hair.*

The one I seek is adept at disguise. Be not fooled by appearances.

Then yes, she is here in a room on the second floor, Oneiroi replied.

Can you detain her? Noumisma projected. *Keep her inside the building?*

It is difficult …

It is necessary.

May I physically restrain her?

Yes, but only as a last resort.

The matter may come to that, Oneiroi replied. *I cannot reach into this mind as I can with other humans. Something resists me.*

It may be the wires, Noumisma flashed. *The people I travel with have wires in their heads. But sometimes I can insert a single thought—or better yet, an emotion—into their consciousness.*

Perhaps a fear of the street? Or a loathing for the outside and daylight? Oneiroi suggested. *With an accompanying headache. Would that suffice?*

That might work, Noumisma replied. *It is for the good of the race.*

How will it help us? How do any of these humans *affect the race?*

Keeping her inside will force her intended contacts to make other arrangements in a plan that she has already conceived and that we need her to follow. A temporary feeling of dread will support this.

———

For their final rendezvous, in an attempt to stop the stranded version of Merola Tsverin from contacting the Sindicato della Conoscenza party that would soon travel back to the Devonian period, Coel Rydin and the current Merola from his own era, with whom he was traveling, kept watch on the Bistro Tarot on Earlham Street in London.

To do this, they had to disguise as preadolescent children of the time. Because such children would not possess complicated toys or pets, such as Cinquemain and Berzher in their battle chassis, the two Silicates had stripped off all of their armor and weaponry, leaving a compact unit with four of the smaller crab legs, a voder, and a sensor cluster. The package for each was small enough to fit in a convenient pocket sewn into a child's clothing. The rest of their machinery and the three liteships were left on a rooftop out of sight from the street, with Ghost and Piedeleger to guard them. And then once again the two Jongleurs took neural imprints against the changes that the coming encounter might wreak on their memories of the current time frame.

Even with their disguises, Rydin and Merola could not position themselves at one of the bistro's outdoor tables or in a storefront across the street. Children of this period did not have economic privileges, and the proprietor would simply have shooed them away—as had happened on more than one occasion during their travels. So they pretended to play, skipping up and down the sidewalk, following along behind random adults as if accompanying their parents, and using other pantomimes that made them seem less conspicuous. But all the time they watched the other side of the street.

"You're late," Rydin said as he passed Merola at the street corner.

"*I'm* late?" she asked, breathlessly.

"I mean the other—the original you—the one we're watching," he said, stopping and taking hold of her arm. "According to your account, you should have come out of Carrefour House by now"—he pointed to the hotel across the street—"when Sabina Gill took you to meet with the Conoscenza director."

"I don't remember the exact time. I might have been jetlagged."

"Very well," he said, letting go of her arm. "Continue." And he went at a child's dawdling pace back down the sidewalk to conserve his energy.

Two hours later, with still no sign of the original Merola, Rydin stopped her again.

"Are you sure this is even the correct day?" he asked.

His own Merola stared at him. "Well, let's see …" and she began counting off on her fingertips, allowing for the date she left San Francisco, the number of time zones between there and London, the Greenwich Meridian, and Coordinated Universal Time, or UTC. "I think so," she said at last.

"I know so," Berzher piped up from her pocket.

"How would you know?" she challenged. "You were just a ball of glass when we left San Francisco."

"But Sam Gill made that traveling baton for me, and that was *before* we went to meet Tessu Anastasis of the Conoscenza. The baton had a timing chip linked to the internet. This date is correct."

"We will wait a little longer," Rydin decided, and they proceeded on their separate rambles.

Toward early afternoon, he observed a tall young woman with long golden hair done up in a braid, Sabina Gill, leave the hotel and walk down to the bistro. A moment later she emerged leading a man with narrow, rat-like features, whose eyebrows and hair were sleeked back as if by a jet blast. Rydin recognized Tessu Anastasis. He watched the pair return to and enter the hotel.

When he next caught up with Merola, he described the encounter.

"So I never met the Conoscenza people in this time stream," she said.

"Or you did not meet them at the Bistro Tarot," Rydin said. "Perhaps, this time, you met Anastasis inside the hotel?"

"Then it's not certain that I did *not* go back to the Devonian."

"Look around," he said. "Has anything changed here?"

"I can see a Divina across the street," she said.

"And one is coming toward us on this side. So whatever you did or did not do, the Möglich has still gone back and changed all of animal evolution."

"Then we have failed. Failed at every point. What do we do next?"

"Go home and find another way," Rydin said.

———

In her room on the second floor of Carrefour House, Rosalind Franklin had awakened with a terrible headache and a sudden—almost surely psychosomatic—aversion to light. She staggered out of bed and closed the curtains of her window, which looked south into the morning sun as it rose above the buildings along Earlham Street.

She decided that she would stay in her room that day and not take breakfast. In fact, she would avoid going out at all until it was time for the Sindicato della Conoscenza party to leave. And then, she had been assured by the contact agent, they would travel by a remarkable method that, he hinted, had something to do with the linen cabinet across the hall from her room.

Whatever—so long as the trip did not involve stepping out into bright sunshine.

23. The One Who Knows Her Best

NOUMISMA HAD TRAVELED with the Jongleurs to their third temporal stop in the place called "San Francisco." As soon as he understood why Rydin and Tsverin planned sequential visits to three different storefronts in various neighborhoods—to prevent their target from procuring substances of value in order to fund her escape, and thereby to capture her—his course of action became clear.

The moment they had left him alone with Light Foot in a place of concealment near the first store, which served myriad forms of a potent beverage called "coffee," Noumisma reached out with his mind to any Divina within calling range. To the eight who variously responded, he suggested a meeting place in a branch of time just a few moments away and within half a block of his current location. Then, when Light Foot's attention was directed elsewhere, based on the focus of the little machine's camera stalks, Noumisma blinked out of existence and hoped that the stiff garment he was wearing would hold its general shape for the few seconds he would need in that alternate branch.

Why have you called us? asked the first of his responders, named Enkephalos.

I need you to gather human money, Noumisma explained, touching briefly on each mind. *As much as you can manage. And give it to this woman who poses as a young girl.* He projected Merola Tsverin's face, bodily approximation, and generalized persona into each mind, surrounding her with the neighborhood of the Windlace home, which he had managed with great difficulty to pluck from the current Merola's memory.

Why would we do this? Enkephalos asked suspiciously.

She is a traveler who does not belong in this time frame.

You are also a traveler—one whom I do not recognize.

That is so, Noumisma replied. *Do this thing, and both she and I will be gone.*

Human money has no meaning for us, projected a second, named Amphibole.

Then it should not bother you to obtain lots of it, Noumisma projected. *It is for the good of the race.*

Human beings are not of any concern to our race, Enkephalos stated.

They will be—if this woman does not leave soon, Noumisma replied.

———

Merola had been more certain about the dates of the events that Rydin was now trying to intercept, because she claimed to have timed each action carefully while planning her escapades using the primitive computer in the home of Bill and Emily Windlace, who had fostered her during her refugee period as a child in San Francisco.

Again dressed as children, with the two Silicate pilots stripped to essentials and riding in their pockets, the two Jongleurs had shown up at the Starbucks coffee shop in the Windlaces' neighborhood. That was where Merola had prepared her schoolmates to provide a distraction, dancing and singing lewd songs, with a pantomime fight among the boys, while she pilfered cakes and cookies from the display cabinets.

But although Rydin and Merola watched the shop across the street from the time that she remembered the school day finishing until late in the afternoon, her alternate version and the group of girls and boys she remembered recruiting never appeared.

"All right," Rydin said, with a sigh that was becoming more and more frustrated. "We will try again at the other points."

The next stop—after collecting their ships, along with Piedeleger and Ghost, lifting above atmosphere, and transiting two days downstream in time—was the candy shop Cose Dolci in downtown San Francisco. But again, the two Jongleurs waited through the appointed hour without any sign of the other Merola's ring of childish thieves.

"The third time will work," she assured Rydin. "That was the actual payoff."

So once again, they moved above atmosphere, transited another two days forward—according to Merola's precise recollection of events—and assembled outside the jewelry shop Amore Eterno, again in downtown San Francisco. It was there that the other Merola's troupe had stolen, not cakes and candies, but rings, bracelets, and necklaces. All had been heavy with valuable stones, and her other self had already figured out how to dispose of them for the cash she said she had needed to travel to London and meet up with the time travelers from the Sindicato della Conoscenza.

But still, with a generous overlap in their surveillance during the time of her remembered event, they observed nothing out of the ordinary. No other Merola, no throng of dancing children, no robbery, and no cash for that other Merola's further adventures. And no chance for them to rescue, capture, or kill her other self in San Francisco.

"I suppose," Rydin said in disgust, "we should proceed to London—just on the off chance that we find the other you there anyway."

From his pocket, Cinquemain spoke up: "Repeated failure does not alter the probability of an outcome to any significant degree. The probability of drawing a white stone from a bag of black and white stones mixed in equal proportions is always fifty percent—no matter how many black stones you draw beforehand."

"Thank you for that insight," Rydin said bitterly.

"We might as well close the loop," Merola agreed.

———

Estella Melendez wondered why the *Milagros*-man had offered her a wad of bills and a handful of coins. But she didn't refuse them. Or, anyway, she didn't think to refuse at the time.

Later, as she was counting out the bills and keeping a rough mental calculation of the denominations, she got scared. There was almost four thousand American dollars in the wad, along with some Mexican pesos that she recognized, and a funny bill she did not recognize that had the number ten on it and the picture of an arch in red brick.

This was too much money for her to keep. And if she did, how would she tell her mom how she got it? Estella sensed that, whatever she tried to do, she was going to get in trouble. Bad trouble. So she stuffed the wad in the next trash basket she saw.

She kept the coins, though. Nobody was going to ask where she got five dollars and sixty-nine cents.

24. An Empty Hole in the Ground

FROM THE BACK and forth between Rydin's mind and Merola's, Noumisma had gathered a few details about what she had been doing in that parallel temporal reality. And the team arrived early enough on the site of a huge hole in the ground, in the part of the San Francisco called "downtown," that he could reach out to other Divina in the immediate area and along the projected route of that other Merola Tsverin, the one he was now thinking of as "Merola Prime."

Within a few moments Noumisma located a Divina who was performing on the street corner near the residence of Bill and Emily Windlace. That Divina's name was Paíchtis.

Once again, Noumisma projected the face, stature, and mental image of Merola Tsverin disguised as a child. *At some point in the next hour,* he continued, *she will try to board a city bus.* And here he projected the image from the current Merola's mind, including the route sign she had memorized. *You are to delay her in any way possible.*

Do you request physical restraint? Paíchtis inquired.

That would not be optimal. Can you restrain her mentally? Although be warned: this human is protected by a mechanism inside her brain.

Then rather than scan the minds of all the children on the streets now, the Divina replied, *it would be easier to stop the bus from reaching its destination.*

And how would you accomplish that? Noumisma asked.

Cloud the driver's mind, as we do with any human being.

An hour later, Paíchtis contacted Noumisma again. *The vehicle you describe has picked up several children along its route. But it endured an accident and so will be delayed indefinitely.*

Paíchtis projected the image of a large white-and-orange bus traveling down a main street. At a street corner governed by one of the many signal lights overhead, the driver of the machine blinked several times in confusion and failed either to slow on the yellow caution light or to stop on the red light that forbade passage. The bus was not moving fast, but it entered the intersection and hit the rear fender of a car moving on the cross street. Then everything came to a halt. Police were summoned. And in the following moments, all of the passengers on the bus were released to find other means of achieving their goals.

Noumisma looked among them for the image of Merola and did not immediately see her. But then, she would have been disguised. And as this was merely a memory replay from the driver's thoughts as relayed through Paíchtis's mind, he could not probe the minds of those exiting the bus to identify his target. Still, he was convinced the subterfuge had worked.

My gratitude, Noumisma beamed to the Divina.

It has been my pleasure to confound a human.

———

Based on Merola's promise that she had an exact recollection of the date and time, as well as her other self's motives for the trip, Rydin called for the team to advance to the day she elected to avoid her mandatory school attendance and board the bus for Union Square in downtown San Francisco, all for the purpose of visiting the site of the wrecked F.A.O. Schwarz toy store.

"I went to look for Berzher's mobile chassis," she had explained. "As well as parts of our liteship and my biosuit, if they still existed in the wreckage. That way I could go home."

"By the time you had been processed out of the hospital, through social services, and released to the Windlaces," Rydin finished for her, "the site would already have been cleared."

"But I did not *know* that," she said. "Not until I visited it for myself."

Once again, he and Merola disguised themselves as children and took a position across the street from the site, which was now a hole in the ground half a block wide and several levels deep, surrounded by a wooden fence with a wire-mesh gate. This was the entry point that Merola had described herself as approaching, but she had not been able to enter the site because men working there had stopped her. The pair of them now watched that gate from early morning, before the scheduled arrival of the workers who were still clearing the rubble and preparing for a new building to be constructed in the now-empty space—rather than grown from organic materials, as they did in Lune. And while the Jongleurs watched, they left Ghost, Piedeleger, and their folded liteships out of sight on a nearby rooftop.

As Rydin and Merola waited, he reflected that making buildings by hand from steel beams and solidified concrete was much more difficult than growing them. For one thing, the humans of this period had to create complicated, interlocking plans; then laboriously weld the steel and pour the slurry mix during a period of months and sometimes years. And later, when the ground was wanted for other purposes, they would have to knock it all down, collect the debris, and start again. Or, in this case, when some agent of destruction bombed the building flat. It was much easier, Rydin thought, to pick the right organism, redesign its form and function through genetic manipulation, then enhance its growth—and eventually speed its destruction—with the right mix of enzymes. But perhaps appropriate genetic techniques did not exist in the early twenty-first century.

Rydin had plenty of time for such speculations. And as the morning progressed, the two Jongleurs wore themselves out by changing their surveillance positions, ducking the attentions of kindly adults, avoiding the suspicions of police and truant officers—a class of public servant, Merola explained, that was tasked with keeping adolescents at their assigned school—and generally pretending to be invisible.

As the sun approached its zenith, Rydin consulted Cinquemain in his pocket. "What time is it?" he asked quietly.

"Two hours, thirty-two minutes past the time on mark for your target to appear," the truncated robot replied in a whisper.

Then, to Merola, he asked, "Should we wait any longer?"

"I ought to have been here by now," she agreed. "I left right after school started, and the bus ride wasn't that long."

"Would it benefit us to continue on this mark?"

"I don't know … If I—the other 'I'—did something different this time, it could have been wildly different. Another day. Another approach. … I don't know."

"Then let's go—before we get caught and hauled off to school."

25. A Familiar Presence

MEROLA TSVERIN AND Coel Rydin, still disguised as children, emerged from the toy store at the corner of Stockton and O'Farrell streets on the morning of their target Merola's original excursion to obtain human genetic material from the children of the twenty-first century. They had hoped to find her and the other Berzher, still in his battle chassis—along with her intact biosuit and their liteship—and remove them from the scene before the explosion that wrecked the building. Once again, their plan had mysteriously failed.

"I was sure we would find her here," Merola complained to Rydin. "I remember being here, playing with the other children, and taking blood and tissue samples. I had a pocket full of them."

Rydin remained ominously silent. She knew his patience with this mission was eroding with each jump in time and place.

They returned to the rooftop across the street, where Ghost and Piedeleger were waiting with the three liteships. Merola sensed a change in the Divina: he was agitated, moving his upper arms randomly and even folding and unfolding his lower arms under his smock. His face, normally so bland and smiling, was twisted with an expression that could either be joy or terror.

"Something is wrong with my Divina," Piedeleger said. "Shortly after you entered the building, he began this dance-in-place. He is otherwise not responsive."

"Let me speak to him," Cinquemain said from his position in Rydin's pocket. "Reproduce the series of gestures I will transmit to you."

Immediately, Piedeleger tapped her claws together to get Ghost's attention. And when that didn't work, she grasped the hem of his pantaloons and gave them a sharp tug. That seemed to work.

Next, she spread her claws at mid-level and wiggled them back and forth. " 'What,' " Cinquemain translated for the humans. Piedeleger spread her right claw and poked it at the middle of her carapace, where the human face would have a chin. " 'Wrong'?" Cinquemain said.

In response, Ghost held his exposed right hand in a fist with thumb up and then pivoted it to the right, so that the thumb was now pointing to the side. " 'Other,' " Cinquemain translated. Ghost tapped three fingers of his right hand to his forehead. " 'Mind,' " Cinquemain said.

Before Merola could quite understand the implications of those two words, she saw—or rather, she sensed an image superimposed on her visual cortex—a multiple shadow that shimmered against the city skyline. The darkness of the shadow was tinged with a flicker of silver light. She tried to concentrate, to resolve it, and all she could see in her own mind was a six-limbed outline, much like Ghost's natural figure, but with a huge head, flattened face, bulbous eyes, and thrusting lower jaw. Not Ghost's placid face at all. The image she could almost see had a vague familiarity, but she could not say for sure she had ever seen it before.

She was about to ask a question of Ghost, through Cinquemain's transmitting and Piedeleger's signing, when Cinquemain spoke up.

"As we were leaving the store," he said, "I thought I saw three children in the crowd ahead of us. I was only seeing them from behind, of course, but I saw three heads of dark hair. They were walking in a stiff pattern, one in front and two behind, in triangle formation. Of course, that was only from my point of view in Rydin's pocket."

"Those Flüchtlinge children!" Rydin exclaimed. "I've already killed them once."

"Not yet—and not in this time frame," Cinquemain said, as if it was an old story with them. "Besides, you killed the girl. I killed one brother. And the other one got away."

Ghost made signs again, pointing straight ahead with his two forefingers, then digging with the five fingers of his right hand near his upper right armpit. " 'Too … late,' " Cinquemain said.

The Divina rolled the fingers and thumbs of his two upper hands into opposing circles with the palms facing inward and pushed the hands together and apart several times. " 'Nothing,' " Cinquemain translated. Ghost made the two pointing forefingers again but this time brought them together side by side. " 'Like,' " Cinquemain said. Finally, Ghost made the thumbs-up sign and pivoted it to the side, but he did this several times. " 'Other'—or 'others,' " Cinquemain said.

"What others?" Merola asked. "What's he talking about?"

But instead Rydin asked, "How does he know these three fugitives?"

Before Cinquemain could transmit cues for Piedeleger to begin signing, the Divina turned on Rydin, stared into his eyes, and signed the response. He put his upper right forefinger in front of his mouth and made a small circle, then shoved the two forefingers together again, followed by a tap on his own chest. " 'Talk like me,' " Cinquemain translated.

"With their hands?" Rydin guessed.

Ghost tapped fingers to his forehead.

"With their minds," Cinquemain said.

———

From his perch high above the city, clinging like a gargoyle to the steeple of a Gothic church, the one that the humans called "Grace Cathedral" on Nob Hill, Glyph watched the streets below for signs of intelligence. For days—on and off, in the human time frame—he had been tracking the three bright minds that identified themselves as Genjifer, Gjordge, and Giuffre Ramsay. He was following them now in the lower reaches of the downtown area, near the place called "Union Square."

As he swept the area, Glyph impinged on a much stronger mind, one that he recognized as one of his own children. It had a nearly human shape, but in Glyph's own image, conjured, bred, and refined in the far-distant past. The mind identified itself as "Noumisma."

Glyph was about to acknowledge it and move on, as he did with others of the species that the humans called "Divina," which was a semblance of their word for "God." But he noticed that his child was standing in close proximity to and communicating with two strange humans. Normally, in Glyph's experience, Divina and humans did not mix, shared no common purpose, and never traveled together. But this group appeared to do all of that.

When he focused more closely, he smelled the trailing edges of blurred *time* about the two humans. They were multidimensional travelers, such as he had encountered before in a different root and branch of temporal reality. While these creatures were of the same small stature and different intelligence as the sister and her two brothers, they were far more interesting to him than the Earth-bound others could ever be. These were active swimmers in the temporal sea that he and his children inhabited.

Glyph determined to follow this new party and see what it was up to.

26. Time on Mark

THE THREE LITESHIPS each generated a cloud of vapor as they descended, this time toward a city on the continent's western coast in the early morning hours. Noumisma wondered at first about the purpose of making a fog around the ships, until he saw that they blended with the natural mists above the city and so hid their approach.

As they descended, he perceived through the clouds an open space the size of a square city block, with patches of green lawn, walkways, and a central column. Noumisma thought the Jongleurs were headed there, but instead the ships settled on a rooftop nearby, in a neighborhood of five- and six-story buildings.

As the companion robots began disassembling their ships, Merola Tsverin was explaining something to Coel Rydin. She seemed emphatic about it. At one point, she tugged at the neck ring of her biosuit. At another, she touched the central core of her own liteship. These were important pieces and she was concerned about them.

Noumisma had a difficult time reading the minds of these Jongleurs, unlike the other humans he encountered. The difficulty had something to do with the wires that had been placed inside their heads and already drew off their thoughts. Or so he assumed. But he had been with them long enough to pick up a few key words and phrases in their language. And when they spoke with particular energy, he could occasionally draw the associated images out of their minds.

In this case, he caught from Merola the definite image of a room somewhere. The space was crowded with objects, stacks of clothing, bins full of sticks. Among them, he caught glimpses of her biosuit—the biosuit of the other Merola Tsverin—and that other woman's liteship. The Merola he was traveling with apparently wanted to make sure that Rydin retrieved their target's liteship and biosuit, so that the other *her* could leave the atmosphere with them. Otherwise, this other Merola would be stranded in this temporal reality.

By now in their journey, Noumisma had figured out that the two Jongleurs were tracking Merola Tsverin's double from another and earlier probabilistic branching. Their purpose was to rescue her from some terrible mistake, or mishap, or disaster, and so prevent her from going on some parallel adventure that would take her backward into the far distant past. Back to the "Devonian mistake," as their minds framed it. Far enough back to correspond, in Divina legend, to the time of the Beginning. The time of the Creator.

He knew that his purpose was to prevent the two Jongleurs from interfering with this alternate Merola's traveling across the millions of years to the Devonian period. But he was unsure about the role their target's own biosuit and liteship would play in those travels. He knew these tools were necessary for the Jongleurs to travel up and down in a single temporal reality, whereas Noumisma and his kind could only travel across from one branch to another. He gathered from the present conversation between Merola and Rydin that the other woman's suit and ship would be lost in whatever disaster was about to happen.

But was that a good thing for Noumisma's purposes? Would being unable to travel freely in this probabilistic reality help or hinder her in reaching the Devonian period? Or would it simply enable her to finish her business in this reality and return—either with the present team or on her own—to the eleventh millennium?

Noumisma's mind was of two halves and hurt terribly, until he reached a decision. His goal, as he understood it, was to let the events that the two Jongleurs were trying to alter unfold as they had apparently done in the original probability sequence. Otherwise, he would be following the path-of-not-becoming, and his entire species, the entire class of *Hexapoda*—would come to an abrupt end. So his goal was both to prevent these Jongleurs from meeting up with the alternate Merola, and at the same time to prevent her from recovering her suit and ship and so immediately going home to the eleventh millennium.

With that purpose, Noumisma reached with his thoughts into the building across the street, which had become the focus of both Rydin's and Merola's attentions. In one case, he sought a particular kind of human mind, one concerned with rules, order, property, and yes … danger. He found such a mind already on the third floor of the building, which was also the focus of the Jongleurs' present intentions. He planted in that human mind the image of Merola Tsverin's face and body. He suggested that she was committing an act of rule breaking, of disorder, of *wrongness*.

Then he found another mind, this one female and located on the fourth floor. He implanted in that mind an image of the room that had been such a concern to the present Merola. Connected with it, he implanted a sense of mismatch, of misplacement, of another kind of *wrongness*. And he added the vaguest shadow images of the biosuit and folded liteship—but not enough that the female human would look for these items directly.

When these thoughts were firmly placed, Noumisma let his mind and face assume their familiar blankness, and he attended to Coel Rydin's description of how he wanted their party to proceed from this rooftop.

————

After landing on the roof of the F.A.O. Schwarz toy store in downtown San Francisco—her time on mark for this gene Search—and while Berzher disassembled their liteship, Merola Tsverin broke the lock on the door that gave access to the internal stairwell. She took off her biosuit and prepared her disguise as a prepubescent female of the early twenty-first century.

The first rule of a Jongleur on Search was to cache both ship and suit against discovery. With the suit and helmet under her arm, Merola went down the stairs to the building's top floor. She cautiously opened the stairwell door on an vast open space that seemed to be some kind of warehouse. It was full of sealed crates and boxes, most of them stacked on wooden platforms and wrapped in clear plastic sheeting. Her suit, made of dark-red gelfoam, might fit snugly behind one of the platforms. But anyone passing by—for the stacks were surrounded on all sides by walking paths—would surely see it. The same would apply to the folded panels and central core of her liteship, when Berzher was ready to cache it.

On the next floor down, too many people were moving about. Even though, by her estimation of the time, the store had not yet opened for business, all of the overhead lights were fully lit. Adults were running back and forth, from one side of the floor to the other, carrying small boxes and bags with brightly colored wrappings and English words written on them in flaring typefaces with many exclamation points. A significant fraction of these people were pushing two-wheeled contraptions that spun a clicking crank unit as it went along. Clearly, the people who managed the store were doing some sort of rearrangement of their stock or remodeling this space. She closed the door quietly and continued on down.

On the third floor, the lighting was reduced to just a trio of emergency lights, and no one appeared to be around. She crept out into the main area and saw shelves in long rows with wide aisles between them. In one part of the floor the merchandise on display seemed to be miniatures of vehicles that she recognized from outside—cars and vans, various single-purpose trucks, flying vehicles with both fixed wings and rotors, and all sorts of with oceangoing ships such as she had seen on previous Searches. Some of these miniatures were brightly colored but some, including most of the ships and planes, were dull gray or drab green—and all of those had red, white, and blue stars on them. Merola guessed that these were models that would interest young males of the day and encourage a state called "play."

It was the perfect space for the sort of biological samples she intended to take.

Merola walked out onto the floor, moved toward the building's back wall, and looked for a certain kind of room. She envisioned a space where the store's merchandise would not be sold directly—because she did not want either her suit or her ship to enter into a random commercial transaction—but would be held in reserve against empty spaces on those shelves out on the main floor. After trying three doors, she discovered one labeled STOCKROOM.

Inside, she found walls lined with shelving and the floor crowded with strings of plastic bins. On one of the shelves was a pile of garments not unlike her biosuit, and the placard attached to the shelf read POWER RANGER, FEMALE. Beside the pile was a jumble of light plastic helmets in the same garish colors as the garments. Her suit and helmet would fit right in. She quickly stuffed the suit into the middle of the pile and put her helmet toward the rear of the jumble.

Moving quickly and quietly, she returned to the stairwell, climbed to the roof, and collected the core, spars, and folded panels of the liteship.

"What about me?" Berzher asked.

"I'll come back for you in a moment," she said.

Merola carried the ship pieces back to the stockroom and found a bin that already held the sticks, strings, and paper panels of what she recognized as children's kites. The liteship's components were larger and heavier than any kite, of course, but she was looking for visual similarities rather than a hiding place that would stand up to close scrutiny.

She deposited the ship pieces in the bin and headed back up to the roof for Berzher.

———

Elpedia Higgins, a salesclerk with F.A.O. Schwarz's downtown San Francisco store, was helping the inventory relocation on the fourth floor. She was carrying three boxes of Beanie Babies® from one side of the floor to the other when she was struck by a powerful premonition. Or maybe it was a memory.

Something was wrong with the stockroom on the third floor, one level down. Elpedia had not been in there in the last couple of days, and her usual station was on the second floor, selling nursery items. But she had a strong sense, almost a vision, that merchandise was out of place on the third floor. Coupled with the vision was a sense that the merchandise in question was *dangerous*.

She put the stuffed animals down on a nearby shelf and went to the back stairs. It would only take a minute to check the stock down there, confirm that everything was in place and okay, then return to what she was doing.

When she entered the third-floor stockroom, her eyes were drawn almost instinctively to the shelf with the Power Ranger suits. Those used to be a hot-selling item, she remembered, but not so much anymore. She immediately saw, between the folded pink and yellow costumes, a line of dark red, more of a maroon color. There never was a Power Ranger in that shade of red. And none in the girls' sizes.

Elpedia lifted the top part of the pile and exposed the wrongly placed merchandise. When she touched it, she knew it didn't belong, because it was thicker and heavier than any of the light nylon costumes. It was more like a scuba wetsuit, but heavier even than that. She removed it from the pile and held it out by the shoulders. The thing was small, too small for a woman, more like for a child. Also, it had a hinged metal neck ring, and she never heard of a wetsuit made with metal pieces.

On a hunch, she looked among the matching Power Ranger helmets and, sure enough, one at the back was the same dark red. And it was no light-weight plastic imitation, either, but a solid helmet made of layered composite material with a clear polycarbonate face shield. It could be a diver's helmet—or an astronaut's.

Elpedia set these items aside on the floor. But she knew she was not done yet. Something else tugged at her mind. It had to do with the store's stock of kites.

She went to the bins where the bundles of sticks and paper were sorted by size, kind, and manufacturer. There, among the largest-size kites, was a black metal pipe five feet long and as big around as her clenched fist. Lashed to it were a dozen or so metal spars almost as long, and each one was wrapped in some kind of shiny black plastic. It looked like packaging for some kind of futuristic tent, probably a domed one like she had seen in a documentary on climbing Mt. Everest.

Elpedia pulled the bundle—it was surprisingly light for containing so much metal—out of the bin and laid it on the floor next to the suit and helmet. Although these items clearly didn't belong with the toys on this floor, maybe they were sold somewhere else in the store. They looked like they belonged in sporting goods. She wasn't aware that Schwarz *had* a sporting goods department, but maybe the management was thinking of opening one.

She gathered up the items and headed out of the stockroom. She would take them down to the main office, where the store manager could sort them out.

Back on the roof of the toy store, Merola Tsverin picked up Berzher's chassis, carried him to the door, and started down the stairs.

"I can walk, you know," he said.

"Your little crab legs would have trouble with all these steps. Anyway, I have to carry you because, if anyone spots us, you're supposed to be just an inert toy."

"The indignities I have to put up with since joining the Jongleurs," he complained. But he let his legs and claws hang loose, and his camera stalks drooped so that he was down looking at her feet.

On the third floor again, she moved out into the open space with all the toys for sale. She was staking out the aisle with all the trucks, ships, and planes, when an adult male voice behind her said, "Wait a minute, little girl."

Merola turned to see a big man standing behind her. He wore a shirt and trousers of dark-gray material, black shoes with thick soles, and a black tie. His shirt was decorated with colored patches at each shoulder, a metal badge attached to his left breast pocket, and a black oblong on his right breast pocket engraved with the name "Richard." He did not appear to be armed, but he carried a heavy flashlight of black metal that looked as if it could put a dent in Berzher's carapace.

"Sir?" she said, as Rydin had taught her when encountering police functionaries while on Search.

"Where are you taking that robot?" the man asked.

"He's … um … *my* robot … sir," Merola replied.

"The hell it is! That's gotta be the store's property. And since the store's not open yet, you can't have paid for it."

"Why would I pay if he belongs with me in the first place?" she asked reasonably.

"Oh, you've got a smart mouth, kid. But I have to take you down to the office."

"I don't think I can go down there right now."

"I don't think it's up to you, little girl."

The man Richard bent over and reached for Berzher's chassis, intending to take it out of her hands. Merola saw the two claws start to move upward, suggesting Berzher was going to grapple with those hands. She made a noncommittal *tsik-tsok* noise as a warning sign, and the claws went limp again.

Richard took her down to the first floor and toward the back of the building. There, in a shuttered room, two other men in similar uniform clothing were watching a bank of monitor screens. "Got a little shoplifter here," Richard told them.

The others looked at him and Merola with amused smiles.

"Didn't your mama tell you stealing is wrong, sweetheart?" one of them said.

"That's a pricy toy you've got there, kid. Looks like a pretty big felony to me."

For punishment, the men made her wait in a chair against the wall. They set Berzher in a clear space on the desk under the monitors, among half-empty coffee cups and a box of half-eaten donuts.

After a few minutes of idle chatter, Richard went back out into the store to continue his patrol. The other two settled down to watch their monitors and answer the phones when they rang.

Merola was sitting at an angle, so that she could only see some of the screen images but not all. Still, she watched store personnel finish moving their boxes around on the fourth floor, stock various bits of merchandise on the other floors, and clear their cash registers to start the day's business. One screen in particular showed the entrance to the stockroom on the third floor, and she watched with growing concern as a young woman went in there and emerged carrying Merola's biosuit and the components of her liteship.

Berzher, she knew, had to lie still, with some of his eight crab legs splayed out and others folded under him. The position looked uncomfortable, but she knew there were no pain receptors in those legs. He was playing the part of an inert toy, when he might just as easily have risen up and drilled both of the men's hearts with his communications laser. Then he and Merola could have walked out of there. But she was aiming for a minimum of judicial involvement.

She made another quiet sound with her tongue: *tsuk-tsuk.* That would alert Berzher to pay attention to his surroundings. One camera stalk slowly came erect, scanned the room, the two guards, and the monitor screens. It paused when he caught sight of the woman carrying their means of escape out of camera range. The stalk turned slowly toward where Merola was sitting, dipped once, then relaxed again into a droop.

After half an hour, one of the security guards said, "Aw, shucks."

"The police ain't coming for you," said the other. "You can go."

Merola stood up. "What about my robot?"

"The *store's* robot, you mean. You just go."

She decided not to argue the point. She left the room with the monitors and ran toward the main entrance—no sense going back to the stockroom on the third floor, or trying to figure out where the woman had taken her ship and suit. They were gone now.

In about five minutes, those two guards were going to find out how fast *a toy* could move when Berzher leapt down from the desk, scuttled out the door—blowing off its hinges, if it was closed, with his laser—then out into the store and freedom.

Merola would pick him up on the street in about seven minutes and then head for her backup cache and home.

———

After two hours of wandering around on the third floor of the toy store, F.A.O. Schwarz, Rydin was becoming impatient. From the nature of the objects on display here—and strewn across the floor for actual demonstration and permissible "play"—he gathered that this section of the store was intended to attract young males of his own purported age. It was not a place to attract young girls at all.

"Are you sure this is the place?" he asked Merola.

"Right there—" She pointed to a spot on the floor littered with three red metal fire trucks in various sizes and two shiny plastic robots that had an upright, humanoid configuration. "—that's where I took my first tissue sample. It was a young boy of either Chinois or Nipponese extraction."

"All right," he conceded. "But where are you now?"

"I don't know," she said. "For this time on mark—"

"Coming up on ninety minutes past," Berzher said from the depths of her pocket.

"—I should be right here, sampling another boy."

Their position was becoming untenable, Rydin knew. Disguised as a boy himself, and Merola as a girl in a white blouse and bibbed gingham skirt, they were conspicuous moving around together in this area, gender pairing being inappropriate at their implied ages. Especially because they were not accompanied by an adult; Ghost's presence, as an obvious Divina, didn't count. And they were not attempting to sample, did not even show interest in, the merchandise on display.

Twice now, a burly adult male in a gray uniform with a nametag and shoulder patches had asked them, "Everything okay here?" Three times a young woman, also with a nametag, knelt down to get on eye level with him and asked, "You find anything you like, honey?" And each time, he mumbled something and pretended not to notice the adult attention.

Their situation was also becoming dangerous. The explosion that had destroyed the store and originally stranded Merola in this time frame was now just sixteen minutes away. Berzher was tracking this duration with interest, too, because the event—in that previous time—had cracked his carapace, shorted power to his matrix, and frozen his mind and memory until he could be revived in London.

"Let me check something," Merola said and walked off toward the back of the store. She returned in a minute with a distressed look on her face. "My biosuit—or the other me's suit—and our liteship are gone."

"Just as they were before," Rydin said. "So how is this different?"

"In the other time frame, just parts of the ship were missing, two panels, so that we could not leave. Now the whole ship is gone."

"A difference in the time stream …" he began. "Possibly an anomaly?"

"Or the other me was never here," Merola replied. "Not on her mark."

Rydin was about to call off this part of their search when an odd thing happened. An elderly woman—indicated by her gray hair and heavy shoes—came up to Ghost and faced him directly. She began making the hand gestures by which Divina communicated among themselves. And for the first time in Rydin's experience, Ghost focused on a human being and seemed to take interest.

"What is she saying?" Rydin whispered to Cinquemain, who had a camera stalk peeking out of his trouser pocket.

"Something about a lost child," the pilot whispered back. "A grandson, I think."

After the woman stopped signing, Ghost stood for a moment with his face blank—or blanker than usual. Then he began signing in return.

"He says the boy is on the second floor. In the bathroom."

The woman made a hurried gesture with her right hand—fingertips touching her mouth, then dropping to a palm-up position in front of her, like blowing a kiss—and rushed away. Ghost nodded somberly behind her retreating back.

"Quick," Rydin said. "If he can find lost children, ask him about our other Merola."

"I would if I had a body," Cinquemain replied. "It is difficult to make signs with just a sensor bulb and one camera stalk."

"Damn! I forgot about that."

"You should have brought me along in my chassis," Cinquemain said. "I could have pretended to be one of these toys. It seems to have worked before."

"Too late now," Rydin said.

27. The Cave by the Creek

THE THREE LITESHIPS settled into the ravine in Briones Park where Merola remembered her former self and Berzher in his previously intact state caching her spares: a ship, a suit, and a second chassis for the pilot, all according to Jongleur protocol. They were landing now in daylight, of course, and that required its own precautions against detection. But because they did not expect to meet any of this time frame's humans, they did not bother to remove their biosuits. And because they did not intend to stay long, they did not dismantle their ships. It was supposed to be a quick and easy find-and-retrieve.

"Look for three stones, close together, with a radiation signature," Merola told Rydin and Ghost. Then she shook her head, because Ghost wouldn't understand and wouldn't participate, anyway.

"I know," Rydin said. "I found them before."

"You looked," Cinquemain said. "I found them."

It took the two Jongleurs and their pilots twenty minutes and a search of both banks of the stream that had cut the ravine. Because the original cache had been made at night, neither Merola nor Berzher could say for certain on which side he had dug the cave.

"Didn't you have a reference for magnetic north?" Cinquemain asked the companion Silicate.

"North has changed poles in the last eight millennia," Berzher replied. "Even a machine can make mistakes."

But finally Berzher found the rocks and the overhanging bank with the cave.

"It looks bigger than the last time I saw it," he said.

"Why don't you go in and get what we came for?" Rydin said.

Berzher pushed aside a tangle of vines that obscured the entrance and walked in. Within ten seconds, he walked out backward. "Something is breathing in there," he said in a low tone.

"What can be breathing?" Merola asked. "A little lizard? A raccoon?"

"Something big. From the volume of air it was pushing, and the ambient temperature inside there, I would say it was a body massing more than one hundred and fifty kilos."

"There are no animals that big in this time frame," she said. "Humans have scoured this world's wilderness of all the dangerous types."

"All right," Berzher said. "*You* go in there."

Merola started forward on hands and knees, because the cave was low even for a Silicate. She had taken off her helmet when they landed, so that they could speak clearly without sending radio signals. Now she could smell the cave's various scents: dampness, mold, humus, and yes, something warm and big, with the stench of a carnivore about it. Before she reached two meters into the tunnel, she heard a low growl—but perhaps it was more the *chuffing* made by an animal disturbed in its sleep. Either way, she backed out fast. Her biosuit and gloves would protect her from bites, even that of a bear, large cat, or amphibious reptile, such as humans of the time kept in zoos. But her head was exposed, and she could imagine it fitting comfortably within the jaws of any of those animals.

"Whatever's in there just woke up," she told the others.

"Surely Cinquemain can kill it with his laser," Rydin said.

"And get mauled and battered in the process," his pilot said.

"Are you afraid?"

"Aren't *you?*"

"One thing is clear," Merola said, to break up their bickering. "Now we know what happened to my suit, my ship, and Berzher's spare chassis. The bear, or whatever it is, tore them up when it adopted the cave."

"Is there any sense in our coming back another time?" Rydin asked.

"Not really," she said. "I've already seen what he did to my cache."

"Then let's move on."

———

While the two humans and their machines argued about the hole in the ravine, Noumisma became curious. He wondered what might be in there that would cause them such concern. He probed the ground with his mind, looking for an enemy. Instead, he discovered the sleeping mind of a large animal that Divina in the eleventh millennium would call "Mansooth."

Mansooth was larger than a human of either this or that far future time. It had six legs and, like the Divina, a relatively docile nature. It slept most of the day and only came out of its burrow to hunt when it was hungry. But then it could kill whatever prey was at hand with teeth that were as thick as Noumisma's thumbs and claws as long as his fingers. And it had strength roughly twice that of the "bear" that was emanating from Merola's mind.

So it was a good thing when Rydin told them to return to their ships and proceed to the next objective.

28. First Things First

Merola knew the date and place of their first likely encounter with her alternate self: eighteenth minute, twentieth hour, Central Daylight Time, in the eighth day, ninth month, and nineteen hundred and ninety-eighth year, in the place they knew as Sane Looie. She knew this, not from personal memory, because all of that had been wiped through her failure to take a neural imprint. But those were the coordinates Pinkus Boskin had given her for stealing the record-breaking baseball that he so coveted, and Rydin had been able to recover the coordinates after his own meeting with and investigation of Boskin. She had the information at second hand now, because Rydin had explained it all to her.

They landed their three ships well away from the place where the ball would be hit and ultimately lost: a sports arena of the time known as Busch Stadium. Rydin had directed them to touch down beyond a set of elevated roadways just south of the facility, on fallow ground in the deep evening shadows alongside the freeway.

"This will be a time frame before any Divina have been spawned," Rydin explained, "so we don't want anyone here to see Ghost, even if he is more or less disguised." And he pointed to the smock that covered the second set of arms.

"What if he wanders away from the landing site?" Merola asked.

"Piedeleger should stay with him." Rydin pointed at the third pilot.

"I will keep him out of trouble," the Silicate agreed. "Be right here."

Once the liteships were folded and stacked in the deepest shadows, Berzher and Cinquemain each stripped themselves down to their portable essence: a flat metal box containing the matrix cup, vocoder, sensor bulb, and one camera stalk. Merola and Rydin tucked these into the pockets of their working disguises as young children of the time. Then they stacked the two now-lifeless battle chassis with the ships.

"I will guard those, too," Piedeleger promised.

"With your life, please," Cinquemain replied.

To avoid suspicion, Merola had suggested they land well before the appointed time of the home run, when the stadium was just filling up with its crowd of spectators. That would allow two supposedly young children to blend with the flow of adults and pretend to be attached to one of them. The plan worked until they came to metal barriers designed to separate random passersby from authentic ticket holders. There she taught Rydin how to watch the eyes of the uniformed guards who were monitoring the flow of people and to duck under the metal arms when no one was watching.

Once they were safely inside the stadium and relatively alone, Rydin asked, "Why did none of the adults behind us in line alert the guards?"

"Children go generally unseen in this time frame," she answered. "And even if they are observed breaking rules, no one cares except their parents."

"And we have no parents."

"Exactly."

Merola led him to an almost deserted part of the stadium, far to the left of the white-outlined diamond that was filled with bright-green grass, out on the open ground toward which all the seats in this structure faced.

"No one will bother us here," she explained. "And this is very close to the place where the man McGwire will hit the ball that I—the other I—am supposed to steal."

"But you—yourself—are not going to take it this time, are you?" Rydin asked.

"No, of course not. We can watch the other me and move to intercept once I have it."

"Wouldn't it be better," Rydin suggested, "if we intercepted you—the other you—*before* you took the ball?"

"I suppose so—but only if I could remember exactly where I planned to hide in order to take it. And I don't."

The two of them found seats and waited while the stands around the stadium filled with spectators. If anyone were to challenge them for the seats they occupied, Merola planned to cry and say they had lost their hypothetical parents. But although people sat down on one side and the other, no one challenged them.

From somewhere in the rafters overhead, a mechanical voice made occasional announcements. On the ground out in front, under the darkening sky, men in dull-gray uniforms made a last-minute raking of the brown dirt and adjustments to the white lines and the little white bags set at the corners of the diamond.

Then the pace of the mechanical announcements quickened, another group of men in different uniforms, pure white on one side, light gray on the other, came out from the sidelines and formed two ranks. The announcer gave a command, and everyone in the stadium stood up at their seats.

Out on the field, a slender figure in a loose, flowing robe walked forward and began to sing in an amplified voice. *"Oh-oh, say can you see, by the dawn's early light, what so proudly we hailed at the twilight's last gleaming ..."* The voice was gentle and insistent, trilling on the high notes, profound in the low notes, and always with perfect pitch.

Merola let the nonsense words wash over her, as she guessed many in the crowd were doing. If she had heard these words before, she did not remember them, because—as Berzher liked to point out—she had failed to take her neural imprint the last time she was here. So, instead of listening, she looked around at the other spectators, who were equally bored.

Rydin was tugging at the sleeve of her tee shirt. "Merola ... what is that?"

As the music crescendoed, he tugged harder. "Look at the singer," he whispered.

Merola focused on the woman. At the peak of the song, she held her arms out wide, as singers will do. All four of her arms, with the bottom two extending to the sides beyond the folds of her gown. The woman was Divina.

"This is wrong," she said. "There are no Divina in this time frame. I haven't gone back to the Devonian yet. I haven't even stolen the baseball."

"Well, something's wrong here," Rydin said.

Before she could comment further, he turned to one of the spectators beside him, an older man with white hair who was holding a small paper booklet.

"Excuse me, sir," Rydin said in English. "May I borrow that?"

The man gave it up with a smile. Rydin took the book and flipped through the printed pages. Merola saw over his shoulder that it was full of colored pictures and blocks of text. Rydin stopped at a page with a listing of names accompanied by numbers and coded playing positions.

"How did you spell 'magwhire'?" he asked.

Merola looked for a word in English letters that seemed to fit the pronunciation. She did not find anything. "The name is not there," she said.

Rydin turned to another page of names and numbers. Nothing fit there, either.

"Is this the wrong night? The wrong *year*?" he asked.

"We are in the right place and time," she said. "I am positive."

"And yet your ballplayer is not going to hit Boskin's home run."

"It would appear not," she said.

"And we have Divina in the time stream."

"Yes. That is very curious. What do you plan to do?"

Rydin handed the booklet back to the man and thought for a moment. "We probably won't be able to find you here," he said.

"Then we should go on to San Francisco," she said. "We still need to find the point at which the Möglich latched on to the original me and break that hold if we can."

"Well, if you did not steal the home-run baseball—"

"Even then, I will probably need to be rescued after the toy store blows up. We can still get me—the other me—out of this time stream and avoid the trip to the Devonian."

"And if we can't rescue you?"

"Then please do *not* kill me."

"No promises there," he said.

Sideways

29. The Discrepancy

AFTER MEROLA, RYDIN, Ghost, and their three Silicates arrived back in Lune, Rydin tasked her with replenishing their biosuits, relining their ships' selvaged cores, and preparing for the next trip in their mission to reacquire the natural order of their world. He himself would go and report to the Ringmasters on the team's progress with Ghost's training regimen—the stated purpose of their trip to the twenty-first century.

Merola and Berzher collected their equipment and took it, with Ghost joining them to carry the three heavy and awkward cores, to the Jongleur compound's Flight Stores.

"What do we have here?" asked the Silicate who ran the shop and went by the name Quartermaster. Because he had to handle the largest ship-sized components, his chassis was larger and used more robust hydraulics than the average Silicate form. His carapace was still crablike, but the dome of the shell stood taller than Merola's head. And any of his four claws—not just the traditional two—could crush her frail body if he so chose.

"Three ships and suits from Rydin's section," Merola replied. "Returned from a training mission in the third millennium."

Quartermaster took the cores from Ghost's hands and connected them to a maintenance station. His chassis drew back slightly when he turned to read the machine's instruments. "That must have been some training flight," he said. "These cores have nearly sealed."

"We were delayed," Merola said.

"Apparently," the Silicate replied.

She and Berzher handed over the bundled suits and helmets for restocking and for repair of minor cuts and wear. As Quartermaster took them, his powered claws rose gently under the burden, as if releasing spring tension. Clearly, he had been expecting more weight there.

"You drained your water and supplemental reservoirs, too."

"As I said, we encountered some problems along the way."

Quartermaster's camera stalks cocked in a gesture Merola associated as Silicate body language for polite disbelief. He turned to put the three separate bundles on a shelf. Then his chassis paused, freezing momentarily as if his power had been cut.

After a random second, Berzher spoke aloud—and not for Merola's benefit. "No, it was nothing out of the ordinary," he said to the air in the shop.

"Are you questioning my pilot behind my back?" Merola asked Quartermaster.

"You know we Silicates trade useful information all the time," the huge technician answered. "I only asked so that I may know what repairs these suits might need."

"Do you want to question my trainee as well? His name is Ghost."

Quartermaster looked at her, looked at the Divina, then turned to Berzher.

"He understands signs," Berzher said. "I can transmit the vocabulary."

"Would he have anything useful to tell me?" Quartermaster asked.

"I doubt it. He was taking the training, not planning the course."

"And how much of it do you think he understood?" Quartermaster asked, cocking his stalks again.

"We are still discovering the Divina's intellectual capacities," Merola put in.

"Then I'll bill any discrepancy to training an imbecile," the machine said.

———

Rydin and Cinquemain met with Captain Tavia and Skeezicks in the compound's council chamber. After the extensive "training flight" with their new recruit, absorbing the time and resources of two active Jongleurs, their Silicate companions, and a third pilot, he had to report *something* to the Ringmasters—although *nothing* of what he and Tsverin had actually been doing.

"Is your recruit, this 'Ghost,' ready to function?" Tavia asked.

"He has shown some flight aptitude," Rydin said cautiously.

"That does not sound exactly encouraging," Skeezicks said.

"We've had some communication problems," he admitted.

"I'm told by those who study them—" Here Captain Tavia shook her head, as if the thought of studying these subhuman variants was perverse. "—that Divina use signs when they want to talk to us." And she pointedly left off the words "human beings."

"Yes, but I was never trained in that language."

"I was," Cinquemain put in. "Or I acquired it by telemetry, as did Piedeleger and Berzher. We interpret for Ghost with the other members of our team." And he avoided the word "human," too.

"A three-way conversation, through interpreters," Tavia mused. "That doesn't sound very efficient. What do you do in an emergency?"

"The occasion has not yet come up," Rydin said.

"Trust me," the captain replied. "It will."

"We did make one interesting discovery about the creatures," he ventured, hoping to extend the training period. "Ghost had a chance to observe a group of three Flüchtlinge children, and he let slip that he could read their minds. I thought that was interesting."

"Not exactly *read*," Cinquemain corrected him. "He said they communicated with *their* minds. That suggests a different capability."

"Yes," Rydin replied, "but then he said it was how *he* talks—meaning, I guess, the entire Divina community."

"We know they have peculiar mental powers," Captain Tavia said. "But there's no way to harness them effectively. But first, tell me, where did you meet these Flüchtlinge?"

Rydin sensed danger in the question. "In the twenty-first century, on the Nortamerican land mass, the place the locals call 'San Francisco.' The fugitives appear to be common there."

"You went all that distance on a training flight?" Skeezicks asked.

"We were testing the Divina's endurance," Cinquemain explained.

"And you met *telepathic* Flüchtlinge?" the captain said. "Now that is *not* common. And anyway, how did you know *what* they were?"

Caught, Rydin thought—*or maybe not.* "I—um—inferred it—from what our Divina said," he answered. Now he stared hard at Cinquemain, wishing that he himself were telepathic—or had access to radio telemetry—and could induce the machine mind to *please* not offer more explanations this time.

His pilot stirred. "It is as Rydin has said," Cinquemain confirmed. "Ghost indicated that the three did not belong to this—or rather, to the twenty-first century—time frame." So maybe human-machine telepathy worked, or Rydin's mechanical companion had the good sense not to blow the team's cover.

Captain Tavia nodded. "There are stories that Divina have some kind of innate time sense—but nothing has ever been proven."

"We will watch for evidence of that," Rydin said solemnly and nodded for Cinquemain's benefit. The little machine dipped its carapace in acknowledgement.

"Watch when?" Tavia asked. "Aren't you finished with his training?"

"Nearly so," Rydin said. "But we have some rough edges to polish."

The woman gave a mirthless laugh. "That's one way to put things!"

"Still, do we have your permission to continue training?" he asked.

"I'll authorize it. We can call it a study in *pseudo* anthropometrics."

30. A Field Full of Possibility

GLYPH MADE THE long trip forward in time, following the trail of the two humans who vibrated with intertemporal frames of reference, and the divine child of his imagining, who was beginning to modulate his own variant of those same oscillations. The mechanical entities and their geometric shapes he could ignore: it was the living essence, the beings who reverberated in time, as he himself did, that attracted him. No—who pulled him along in their wake with the strength of his own curiosity.

He had to make the trip in stages, taking several discreet jumps, because the intertemporal distance was great. He had once before made such a trip in one jump—a passage much longer than this. However, that one had been taken backward, for millions and millions of years, as the humans counted time. And then he had the advantage of traveling in a known temporal reality, with all the probabilistic switches locked open and with nothing left to chance.

This jump, although it was only eight thousand years or so, as the humans counted time, was more problematic. This was a jump *forward*, into Glyph's own future. Here, the probable choices were not all known, and a single misstep could put him in the wrong frame of reference entirely. So Glyph proceeded carefully, jump by jump, but at every stage he managed to catch and follow the scent.

When he finally caught up with his quarry, he found himself in a green place. It was the same spot on the same planet as the city of stone and glass he had just left behind. But here the world was green with plants and almost empty of bustling humans. Even his own children were few on the ground. And none of the ones here carried the smell of extended time.

From the spot where he had first jumped and next landed, near a bend in the great river, he let his mind drift outward in all directions. Off to the west, he discovered a conclave of time-saturated humans. He lifted himself and traveled across the ground in that direction.

The sense of presence grew stronger as he approached a circle of fitted stones, a fortress like the humans once had built almost ten thousand years ago, as they themselves counted time. This ringed wall stood on flat ground, rather than raised on the hills the humans once favored. In those terms then, it was not a particularly defensible position. And it offered no good vantage point for him.

Glyph's favorite viewpoint was high up, on a tall rooftop, the crest of a hill, or the point of a church steeple. Here he found nothing but the wall itself, and if he chose to perch there, he would be clearly visible to the clusters of human beings—even to their mechanical entities—that moved about inside it. When he could sense no one was watching, however, he tested the wall with one foot, just one point of contact. He felt horribly exposed.

After that he drifted higher. The land all around the walled fortress was flat, as was most of the surrounding river basin. But he did find, just a few thousand meters to the west, as the humans measured distance, a modest hill with the ruins of one of those old-style castles. From the likeness of the stones in the wall that encircled the human compound and the fallen remains of the walls of that old fortification, Glyph sensed the modern humans had been stealing from the one to build the other. But inside the ancient fortification was a wide tower, still intact and at least ten meters tall, placed on the highest point of the land. It would serve his purpose.

He quickly determined that no human, animal, or machine was present inside the ruin and made the adjustments required by his modest needs. Then Glyph perched and scanned.

The two humans he was tracking—the female whom he followed long before, and the male who ended his physical existence in another dimension—had virtually disappeared into the time-drenched crowd within their new stone walls. He sought out the iron resolution of the one that identified itself as male and the cold ruthlessness of the female, but in that den of travelers these traits were shared and merged. He could easily identify his time-traveling child as the only Divina inside those walls, but he carefully shielded his mind from it to avoid giving away his own presence.

In his search, however, he latched onto one mind that stood out from all the rest, both for its resolution and its ruthlessness. It was a female and older than the two he had been seeking, but not by much. In the sea of minds that glowed with oranges and pinks, this one shone as blood red. Not just determined but angry, with itself and with the world.

And that piqued Glyph's interest.

———

Captain Tavia was walking across the hangar inside the Jongleur compound when she sensed a presence about her. It was strong, like a dark shadow at the edge of her mind. The feeling was so disorienting that she took a short step, stumbled, and had to catch herself. And Captain Tavia possessed perfect balance and never stumbled.

"What was that?" asked Skeezicks, who walked crabwise at her side.

"I don't know. Something strange. Something dark. Did you feel it?"

"Feeling … Perhaps you just encountered a null bit in your program?"

"Humans aren't programmed," she said.

"Neither are Silicates, actually," he said.

Tavia took two quick, deep breaths to clear her mind.

"There," she said. "The dark cloud has gone away."

31. Clearing the Cave

MEROLA TSVERIN FELT she should have thanked the security guard named Richard for detaining her. If she had been collecting genetic samples on the third floor, according to plan, she and Berzher would have been killed outright when the toy store exploded. Instead, they had already moved a block away and were headed—her walking and once more carrying her pilot as if he were a toy with which she could not part—toward the city's mass-transit infrastructure. The direction was marked by signs along the way.

Their backup cache had been hidden on the other side of the body of water known as San Francisco Bay, beyond the belt of cities that ringed the bay's eastern shore, and then some further distance off in the middle of a patch of tended wilderness identified as Briones Regional Park. Berzher could easily have found it from the air, but that was the problem. From their ground-level view, they had to navigate using other cues. And they needed to acquire some of the local currency if they were to travel across the water.

Berzher had hit upon a strategy based on the number of street performers, mostly Divina but also with a few humans who thought they could compete with the naturally pitch-perfect hexapods. The creatures lived by collecting coins from passersby in a jar, a hat, and sometimes the open case of the instrument they were playing. When Merola spotted any one of them who had amassed a number of coins, she released Berzher onto the pavement. He then crept up behind the performer, watching the singer's face with one camera and the object of his intention with the other, and quietly snatched coins from the jar, hat, or instrument case.

By the end of the day, they had enough coins and more to buy Merola a ticket on the Bay Area Rapid Transit system. Once inside the station, Berzher cautiously studied the various maps on display.

"Orinda, I think," he finally said.

"Is that close to the park we want?"

"Some miles, at least. Rough travel."

"So first we get to this 'Orinda' place."

It was early evening when they arrived at the station, which was situated between two strands of highway filled with moving cars. People getting off the train also headed to a lot with more cars—their personal passenger vehicles.

"Now what?" Merola asked. "Seek help from a stranger?"

"What does 'taxi' mean?" Berzher pointed at a car with the word printed across a white plastic box on its roof.

"I believe it's a vehicle for hire carriage," she replied.

"Do we have enough money for a ride in the country?"

"Enough—or we can finesse it."

"Define 'finesse,' please."

"Cry my heart out."

Still carrying Berzher—but with his claws, legs, and camera stalks folded compactly, so that he more resembled a metal discus than a toy—she approached the car with the white box. As she came alongside it, the driver rolled down his window.

"Can you take us to Briones Park, please?" she asked.

" 'Us'?" the man asked, eyeing her in a friendly way.

"Well, just me then," she replied.

"Isn't it late, little girl? Shouldn't you be going home to your mama?"

"No." Merola couldn't tell him where "home" was. "Just to the park."

"That's a big place," he said. "Just where exactly do you want to go?"

"Um, to someplace near the center?" she suggested.

"By a creek," Berzher muttered from under her arm.

"Take you to the Bear Creek Staging Area," he said.

"That sounds about right," she replied.

"Um, you got money to pay the fare?"

Merola dug a handful of coins out of her pocket.

"You bust your piggy bank, sis?" the man asked.

"Is it enough?" She made a sad face. "I *really need* to get there."

"Well, okay. Are you meeting somebody there, maybe?"

"Yes, my fath—my *daddy*," she corrected quickly.

"All right then. He can make up the difference."

Merola smiled gratefully. "Just get me there."

She climbed into the back with Berzher's carapace and laid him on the seat beside her. The drive put up a metal flag on his dashboard and drove out of the parking lot. A metered window connected to the flag began counting off small fractions of miles and large fractions of dollars.

They drove past a shopping mall, then past isolated houses, then into the countryside. When the meter showed six-point-nine miles and more than three times that in dollars—more than Merola had in her pocketful of coins by any measure—they had arrived at another parking lot, this one in the woods.

"Well, is your daddy here?" the driver asked.

Before she gave her answer, Merola gathered Berzher under her arm, forced the door open, and ran for the tree line. She could hear the taxi man honking his horn in the distance as she headed into the forest.

When she reached a clearing, she put the carapace on the ground and watched as its legs and claws unfolded. The camera stalks swiveled to look around.

"Now we're lost," she said. "And it's getting dark."

"So we navigate by the terrain and the stars," Berzher replied.

After two hours of traveling up one hillside and down another, they arrived in a ravine with a trickle of water passing through it.

"Look for three rocks that are slightly fluorescent," the pilot said.

"Finding them is your job," Merola said. "I'll wait."

It was another hour before Berzher located the rocks and the cave. He crawled inside, then backed out quickly.

"There is an animal in there!"

"What kind of animal?"

"A Mansooth."

"Teddy bear ..."

"It's still in our way," he said. "And it might be hungry."

"All right then. Your climb a ways up the cliff above the entrance. I'll stand outside here and yell like I'm food. When it comes out, you drill it with your communications laser."

"What if I miss?"

"Then fire again."

It took longer than expected to rouse the beast. In the end, Merola had to crawl into the cave and smack it on the nose. But then their ambush went according to plan.

Her biosuit had been rumpled by the Mansooth's weight. Two spars of the liteship were twisted. And Berzher's spare chassis had some tooth marks. But their backup equipment was still functional.

Merola's Search mission to the twenty-first century was finished. They assembled the ship, flew out of the ravine, and headed for the stars.

32. Sent Back to Do It Right

WHEN RYDIN AND Cinquemain were called into the council chamber again by Captain Tavia, Rydin sensed an anger in his superior that, if present before, had not been so near the surface. The woman could not sit still. In her chair at the council table, she twitched and shifted, crossing and uncrossing her arms. Finally, she stood and paced up and down the room.

Skeezicks settled on the tabletop next to Cinquemain and watched his own human with obvious concern. His camera stalks tracked Tavia back and forth, as if the machine expected her to shriek, or dance, or collapse on the floor at any moment.

Almost as if to compensate, Rydin sat down and composed his mind. Not knowing what to expect, he was prepared for the worst—even Tavia's exposing the chaos that he and Tsverin had caused by traveling back to the far end of the world and the beginning of time.

After three turns about the room, the captain stopped and faced him. "Well, are you ready to get back to work? Done with the training sessions?"

"Of course," he said. "That's why I'm here."

"Me, too," Cinquemain muttered, to remind everyone of his presence.

"Good. Because this Search mission is going to be difficult—and dangerous."

The woman then resumed her pacing, as if working through her thoughts.

"Where are you sending us?" Rydin asked finally.

"Back to the twenty-first century. Back to Safronesco. Old ground for you, I understand. It turns out the Troupe was intrigued by your report of three telepathic Flüchtlinge. We want them found and brought back at all costs. Alive, if possible."

Rydin nodded. He considered telling her that the Troupe did not need to bother, because he and Cinquemain had already killed at least two of them, and it was doubtful the third member could do much on his own. But then, Rydin had already offered evidence that all three were alive in this time stream. So why confuse the captain?

"What were the charges against them?" Cinquemain asked.

"Charges?" Tavia responded, as if not understanding.

"Most Flüchtlinge are, or were, criminals in this time frame," the pilot went on. "They flee to an earlier period, thinking that temporal distance will protect them. If we knew what these particular three stand accused of, it would help in our Search."

"Probably robbery. Possibly murder," the captain said. "They are certainly capable of that and more. Their minds are warped. That's what you need to know. Warped and dangerous."

"I don't know how that's genetically possible," Rydin said. "Not with our pre-natal cleansing techniques. Every mind and body made sound before it's allowed to gestate."

"Well … not in this case," Tavia said. "Their minds, the active telepathy, were a *product* of genetic engineering."

"Who did this?" Rydin asked.

"We did. We were trying to make a better Jongleur. One who was intuitive, who could read minds, who could ask the right questions on Search—or not have to ask at all. Instead, we got three embryos who were linked."

And who, Rydin thought, could use their minds to snuff out that of another human being. But what he said was: "You got a monster."

"Yes," the captain replied. "And now that you've found out where and when they went, we want them back for study."

"And to keep them from damaging our past history," Cinquemain added.

"Yes, that, too." The woman paused in her pacing and turned to face Rydin. "The three are named Genjifer, Gjordge, and Giuffre Ramsay. Or that was the identification given to the embryos. They may have acquired other identities since then."

"Thank you," he said. "That may be helpful."

"Oh, and the female is dominant," Tavia went on. "Capture or, as a last resort, kill Genjifer, and the two males should come along more docilely."

"Isn't that always the case?"

"What do you mean?"

"Never mind."

Rydin thought for a moment. "Bringing in three fugitives, I'm going to need more than one ship. I'll take Merola Tsverin on this Search. We have worked well together." And, of course, he needed her to go back with him to the twenty-first century and their *real* mission.

"Granted," the captain said.

"We'll need a third ship, for three live bodies who are likely to be resistant," Rydin continued. "I'd like to take along Pie-deleger and the Divina."

"He would only be a hindrance, wouldn't he?" Tavia said.

"Ghost spotted those three in the first place. He can help us find them again."

"Take him then." She chuckled. "That is, if you can get his attention …"

"And his cooperation," Rydin replied. "We are working on that."

33. A Shot in the Dark

As their liteship rose into the night sky above the Cornish coast, Cinquemain configured its energy panels for maximum lift. The ship carried, suspended beneath them, the entire collection of baseball memorabilia that Pinkus Boskin's uncle had gathered over a lifetime. That lust for ownership had infected young Pinkus, engendering a criminal mind, the taste for conspiracy, and the drive to obtain just one more artifact. And that had led him to the illegal suasion of a working Jongleur officer, Merola Tsverin, who was protégé to Cinquemain's human counterpart, Coel Rydin.

On this night—forty-seven years and three hundred light hours from their own reference now—they were correcting that error. By stealing the collection, they had made sure that the mind of the future collector was shielded from all thoughts of baseball. By disposing of it far above the atmosphere, they would put it beyond his reach forever.

With the Boskin estate still below them, Cinquemain strained at the controls to gain altitude under the heavy load. He did not worry about retaliation, because the only defenses they had encountered were a couple of sight hounds, animals limited to ground attacks. And Cinquemain had dealt with them in the first minutes of their arrival. No, his concern now was simply to get this load into near space, where Rydin could drop the mass of sticks, balls, clothing, and papers with sufficient forward velocity for them to go into free fall and burn up.

A star shot out of the sky. No, it came *up* from the ground. Cinquemain tracked the plasma trail back to its point of origin just outside the estate's tree line. Under magnification, that point resolved into a pit harboring the outlines of a magnetic projector. Its first shot sailed past the liteship, high and outside.

The automated system flashed again. Cinquemain knew that the targeting mechanism was almost certainly intelligent and would have tracked its previous shot. Since he was now looking almost straight down at the glowing projectile, he assumed the ship was within its vector and at its apex.

"They are shooting at us," he said calmly.

"I saw it," Rydin replied. "The question is why. We've already removed the baseball collection and made our escape."

"Retaliation?" Cinquemain suggested. "Delayed authorization? Faulty alarm?" He could still speculate rationally while triangulating the missile's path and moving his heavily laden ship out of it.

That second shot missed the cargo net suspended below them, missed the ship's center of mass, where Rydin and Cinquemain clung to foot- and handholds along the core, but still it clipped one of the extended spars. The heated slug broke away the tip and severed the wires that stretched two of the energy panels. The liteship lurched to one side and became even less responsive.

"I am losing control," Cinquemain told Rydin.

"Do what you can. But *do not* drop the prize."

Cinquemain saw the third shot coming but was unable to avoid it. The slug tore a neat, round hole in the ship panel behind and just below Rydin. The edges of the hole danced with a corona of tiny lightings, bleeding energy from that panel as well. A similar hole opened in the panel above and behind Cinquemain.

"That is going to kill our speed," he said.

When this comment did not get a response, Cinquemain focused on his human companion. The same round hole was bored through the center of Rydin's biosuit. That garment was proof against any amount of damage and pressure—except a half-kilo of depleted uranium traveling at 3,500 meters per second, yielding a force of fifty megajoules. His partner might as well have been hit with a twentieth-century autobus weighing several metric tons and traveling at 500 kilometers an hour—except that impact was concentrated in an area the size of a fist.

"Rydin …" Cinquemain sent again.

There was no response on any radio frequency. Cinquemain watched as a bubble of blood expanded around the hole in the front of the suit and popped, covering Rydin's chest with a sunburst pattern in red gore.

Landing and trying to resuscitate his human using the limited supplies in the ship's medical kit, then patching the biosuit for travel above the atmosphere and the temporal transition … neither was a serious proposition. There *were* no options for saving Rydin.

But at least Cinquemain could avoid taking further damage. He had no alternative but to trade altitude for speed, diving the ship eastward hauling its suspended cargo. With enough distance, he could fly out of range and below the horizon of that gun pit.

Once this goal had been achieved, Cinquemain fed in more lift and resumed his ascent into the night sky. Even though he had failed to protect his human, he could complete the mission. He would drop the baseball collection into free fall, watch it burn, then transition downstream to his own—and Rydin's—reference now, and report the death to the Troupe des Jongleurs.

Only then would he allow himself to engage whatever neural circuitry a Silicate possessed that corresponded to a human being's feelings of grief and regret.

34. The Second Shortcut

"WE HAVE A new assignment from the Troupe," Rydin told his team, which was assembled in a corner of the hangar building. In addition to Merola and their two pilots, he had included Ghost and Piedeleger—and asked the Divina's pilot to translate as he spoke.

"When I reported to the Ringmasters that we had encountered three Flüchtlinge who appear to be linked telepathically—" Here Rydin tipped a nod to Ghost, who turned from observing Piedeleger's waving claws to stare back at him. "—that information drew their attention. Apparently these three are known to the Troupe.

"Captain Tavia tells me," Rydin continued, "that their names are Genjifer, Gjordge, and Giuffre Ramsay, and that the one we really want to talk to is the woman. She is the most powerful of the three—but we already knew that. It seems their telepathy was a genetic experiment, one where the Troupe attempted to improve on Jongleur capabilities." Here Rydin felt himself involuntarily grimace. "The program went wrong, and the three siblings escaped to an earlier time."

"Well no wonder they attracted a Möglich," Merola said.

"How do you know that?" Rydin asked.

"Because I didn't have one following me—to London and then on to the prehistoric—until they stole my ship in the toy store. Two plus two, Coel. They tagged me."

"I think your logic is … faulty," he said slowly.

But then he noticed a flurry of signing activity between Ghost and his pilot.

"Excuse me, Rydin," Piedeleger said. "But my Divina concurs with her."

"How so?" Rydin asked.

"Just as he detected the connection between the children's minds—"

"They are *not* children!" Merola insisted.

"—so the being that we call a 'Möglich,' but which calls 'the Creator,' would be attracted to their telepathic abilities."

" 'Creator,' " Merola said. "How does he know about the Devonian?"

Rydin chose to ignore that point and responded to Piedeleger. "But if the Möglich was following the three telepaths, why would it suddenly switch to following Merola?"

Piedeleger paused to converse with Ghost. "Because as much as it likes 'mind-speakers'—as he calls them—the monster likes time travelers even better. The Möglich is a creature out of time."

" 'Out of time'?" Rydin asked.

This required more signing between pilot and Divina. "The creature is not fixed in time as we are," Piedeleger explained. "It has no proper place, no 'reference now.' It might think that a Jongleur was a being much like itself."

"So if it was following me," Merola said, "because I *smelled* of time, or something, then why did it blow up the toy store?"

"I think we can safely assume," Rydin said, "that it was the three telepaths who stole your ship and then tried to destroy the store—and you. For one thing, they would be more likely to have access to explosives.

"Anyway," he continued, "our assignment is to find these three fugitives and bring them home for the Troupe to examine. The Troupe wants them brought back alive."

This news ignited a furious cross-conversation among Merola, Berzher, and Cinquemain.

"We will need extra biosuits for that."

"Transporting three unrestrained—"

"Or unconscious," another suggested.

"—passengers will be quite difficult."

"I wish we had that saucer about now."

"Losing it was totally unavoidable …"

"Perhaps we could steal another …?"

He noted that Piedeleger had stopped translating, and that Ghost was staring at the other three with fixed attention. Rydin decided it was time to cut into their flow.

"We are not actually going to bring back the fugitives," he stated.

After a silence, Merola asked, "Why not?"

"Because our main purpose is still to correct this entire time stream," Rydin said. "And Piedeleger—" He pointed at the little robot, still busy translating. "—please do *not* repeat that to our trainee. ... We will indeed find the three siblings, but with their help—willing or not—we will track the Möglich and destroy it before it can follow the other Merola back to the Devonian period. That will short-circuit the entire process of altering the lobe-finned fishes and so restore our own time stream."

"If we don't come back with the fugitives," Cinquemain said, "the Troupe will be suspicious."

"No," Rydin said, "if we stop the Möglich from changing the biology of this world, then the fugitives won't matter. Besides, they will already be dead."

"Two of them," Cinquemain reminded him. "We don't know about the third."

"Or they're not dead," Merola said. "We saw them, remember? When we changed the future, we changed our own past."

"Or rather," Berzher countered, "by changing the past, we changed our future."

"Whichever way you say it," Rydin concluded, "we need to change everything back to the way it was."

35. Arriving in Lune ...

MEROLA TSVERIN LOOKED down between the panels of her lite-ship as it descended above the river that ran through the village of Lune.

"Do you want me to drop you at your tree?" Berzher asked, pausing their descent above the southern shore. "Or proceed to the compound?"

"I might as well check in with Rydin," she said.

The ship lifted again and drifted westward, toward the bend in the river where the Troupe des Jongleurs maintained its headquarters. Berzher brought the liteship down over the concrete apron that lipped the hangar entrance, and Merola stepped off onto her own ground in her own time frame. She unclipped her helmet and stripped out of her biosuit, hanging both on the points of the ship's extended spars, now that its panels and wires were de-energized. While Berzher saw to the dismantling of the ship and replenishment of her suit, Merola would find her chief and report on the botched assignment. Her pilot could file his own report later and digitally.

Rydin had sent her to the twenty-first century to harvest human genetics from the diverse population of the place called Safronesco. But before she could take the first tissue sample at the F.A.O. Schwarz toy store—because children had the least epigenetic modification to their genomes, and children distracted by shiny objects were the easiest to surprise and stab with her cryogenic needles—that security guard had interrupted her. And then the store had exploded in some form of terrorist incident or industrial accident endemic to the period. The better part of wisdom dictated she go back to the eleventh millennium and seek reassignment to a less violent era.

She stopped the first Jongleur she met inside the hangar, a young woman named Sylva Diehl. "Where is Coel Rydin?" Merola asked.

The woman appeared surprised. "Out on assignment," she replied.

"Ah!" Merola said, meaning *of course*. "Thank you, Mira Diehl."

Her next encounter was with Captain Tavia, Rydin's superior.

"Back so soon?" the captain asked her.

"I had some bad luck," she admitted.

"I told Coel those fugitives were dangerous."

"What fugitives?" Merola asked. "I was sampling wild-type genomes in Safronesco in the twenty-first century."

"Well, no." Tavia frowned. "You were supposed to be tracking the three Ramsay siblings—the ones you and Rydin spotted earlier, during your training mission. But yes, it was in the twenty-first century. And in Safronesco."

Merola wondered how the captain could be so confused. Or was Rydin playing some game now? Telling untruths to his superiors and inventing false missions? And for what purpose? Merola could not deny that Rydin had his devious moments. It was a measure of her trust in him that she decided not to contradict whatever stories he had told the Troupe.

"Yes, of course … the Ramsays …" *Whoever they were.* "My taking samples was part of the Search … looking for … these people," she lied.

"So why did you come back without them?" Tavia asked.

"There was an explosion." *That much was true.*

"Oh, my! Were you hurt?"

"No, I was a block away."

"What about the others in your team?"

What others? "They survived as well," she said cautiously.

"That's good to hear," Tavia said. "I worry about the Divina you recruited."

A Divina in the Troupe? Merola only nodded. "He's … doing well, I guess."

"If no one was harmed, why did Rydin send you back?"

"He … needed some … supplies." Merola knew she had to break off this conversation before she said the wrong thing—or too many wrong things. "Supplies we can only acquire here."

"Then you had better get them and return to him."

"Yes, certainly. I was headed that way."

With that, the captain nodded and proceeded across the hangar on whatever errand she had been pursuing.

Merola turned and ran back out to the apron. She had to tell Berzher not to file his mission report until they knew what scheme Rydin had perpetrated. And then it would be prudent for the two of them to fly off somewhere and disappear for a while.

36. … And Out of Phase

CINQUEMAIN BROUGHT HIS crippled liteship with its dead human down on the concrete apron in front of the Jongleur compound's hangar. The energy panels that were flapping around the broken spar and the two others with round holes in them were all sparking visibly in the sunlight. When the ship's landing foot touched the ground, the whole assembly settled noticeably, listing to one side.

The sight of a ship so badly damaged must have drawn attention. Jongleurs and their Silicate pilots were coming by pairs and threes across the quadrangle and out of the hangar. It was also unusual for a ship to land and the human passenger not to jump down immediately. But Rydin was no longer strictly human, not being alive, and his gloved hands were reflexively curled around the ship's core. Cinquemain, inhabiting his crablike battle chassis, might have had the strength to release those hands, but he did not have the leverage to lower the body out of the ship. Nor did he have what in a human being would be called "the heart."

The Jongleurs who approached the liteship waited until its panels stopped glowing and sparking. Then the boldest among them poked heads and hands into the shaded interior. They withdrew in shocked surprise when they saw Rydin's biosuit and its gaping holes front and back.

"Rydin … Coel Rydin … dead," he heard them whisper.

"Can you help?" Cinquemain said. "Try to release him?"

And then two Jongleurs pushed between the panels, took the body in their arms, worked at the gloves, and lowered his passenger out and down onto the pavement. Cinquemain followed and stood guard over his human. The others drew back in a respectful circle.

"What has happened here?" asked a familiar voice, that of Captain Tavia, as she forced a path through the crowd.

"My Jongleur has been killed," Cinquemain answered truthfully.

"Killed how?" she said, kneeling over the body and placing a hand on the chest just outside the bloody sunburst around the hole.

"Magnetic projectile," Cinquemain said. "The ship took damage, too."

"I'm not worried about the ship," Tavia snapped.

"I understand that," he said.

"I was not aware that rail guns were perfected and put into common use so early in the twenty-first century," the captain said.

"They were ... *urrgh*." Cinquemain made a buzz of incomprehension, similar to a human's "huh" or "umm." It was an involuntary reaction, a misfiring DO-WHILE loop in the speech circuits. "What did you say about the twenty-first century?"

"That is where I sent you—him—your team. You were tracking the telepathic Flüchtlinge you encountered on your earlier mission. But I never dreamed they would be armed with such sophisticated weapons."

Cinquemain heard this explanation in silence. Clearly, something had happened of which he was not aware. Some disjunction in the time stream? Some effect of stealing the base-ball collection? Perhaps a long-delayed retaliation on the part of the Boskin clan? He belatedly fired the circuit that would regenerate his neural imprint, but this mental recovery made no difference. Cinquemain knew and remembered exactly what he and Rydin had been doing when they made the foray into the Boskin estate. None of it matched any assignment from Captain Tavia that would send Rydin and this "team" back eight thousand years to hunt Flüchtlinge fugitives, telepathic or otherwise.

He was about to explain the mission that he and Rydin had actually been following, when an override command interrupted his vocoder operation. Rydin had made it clear before their departure that the trip forty-seven years back and into

Cornwall was not authorized by the Council of Ringmasters. And since Rydin was attempting to short-circuit, through a temporal maneuver, the subornation of a fellow Jongleur under his command, revealing that mission now would put Merola Tsverin's reputation, her career, and her freedom at risk. It was best to reveal nothing—and the captain had provided enough clues for him to simulate agreement.

All of this processing required seven microseconds. When the override released, he replied, "Evidently, the Flüchtlinge took advanced technology with them. I managed to escape at the cost of my passenger's life."

"What about the rest of your team? Tsverin? The Ghost? And their Silicates?"

Cinquemain had no idea who this "ghost" might be. "Merola Tsverin is now in charge of the team. She will lead them on the mission. In the meantime …"

"Yes, we have a comrade to honor and disposition," Tavia said, signaling for the two who had brought the body out of the ship to pick it up now.

The death of a Jongleur in action was so rare that Cinquemain was unaware of any protocol for "honoring" the deceased.

"And you will need to be assigned a new Jongleur," she said.

"Of course," Cinquemain said. "Whoever may become available."

And with that, his long partnership with Coel Rydin officially ended.

———

From his perch on the old fortification, Glyph sensed commotion in the compound full of time-drenched travelers some leagues to the east. He could hear the whispers in many minds, including that of the red-tinged female he had been following: "Rydin. Coel Rydin … dead." The associations were linked to the male who had once destroyed Glyph, and that demanded his attention, even though he was not sure what "dead" might mean.

He drifted nearer, just beyond the wall of the compound and just high enough that he could look over its parapet and observe the commotion. There, in the courtyard, was one of those flimsy lanterns constructed of shining panels in which the time travelers rode. They were removing from among its struts and wires a human body clad in one of those suits that kept it from desiccating in space. This one's suit had failed spectacularly, with a round hole that pierced it through the back and out the chest. The body inside was lifeless.

And yes, the human was the male who had killed Glyph once, long before. Glyph knew this "Rydin" would never come back to life, because these humans never did, not in the same dimension. And that meant Glyph now could never take his vengeance.

37. The Temporal Conundrum

CAPTAIN TAVIA SENSED that something was wrong. The mission she had sent back to the twenty-first century appeared to be floundering. She had the urge to take Skeezicks and travel there herself, to find her Jongleurs and help them. But going upstream eight thousand years to locate another time traveler—let alone three of them, who might not all be traveling together—was a fool's errand. She might pass them a dozen times at the temporal distance of a week or even a day and never know it. And Safronesco was a big place in itself.

Still, the events she could see from this reference now were not … coherent.

Merola Tsverin had returned alone—or rather, with her pilot Berzher—to retrieve unspecified "supplies" on Rydin's orders. She had come and gone before Tavia thought to check with Quartermaster. And when Tavia finally did, he reported no requisition from either Tsverin or Berzher. The Silicate in charge of Jongleur stores did not even know that the pair had returned. And now they had disappeared again into the past and whatever trouble Rydin and the group had encountered. Yes, Tsverin had mentioned some kind of explosion, but she also appeared to dismiss it as of no consequence.

And then Rydin and Cinquemain had returned, one dead and the other … evasive. Tavia found it odd that, for fugitives in a distant and primitive century, the Ramsays had openly used eleventh-millennium weapons. And, for travelers without liteships and so limited to surface activity, the battle they waged had been in the air, not on the ground. Rydin was killed in his suit, configured for vacuum, and shot in the back. Clearly, he and Cinquemain had been fleeing something—something that must have gone catastrophically wrong. And yet Cinquemain had calmly informed her that Tsverin was now leading the team. The same Tsverin who had just returned on an errand at Rydin's request.

Of course, sequential concepts like "just"—relating to temporal relativity and notions of "before" and "after"—were meaningless when discussing an action taking place far upstream in the distant past. All such actions were fixed in a time that was now long dead. One traveler might return from a point in that past that either preceded or followed another point. Except that Tavia did have one solid fact: at some point during the mission, Coel Rydin had been shot and killed. He was not coming back to the eleventh millennium, not again, not ever. Unless of course he *did*, and then that would be from a point *before* the battle that ended his life.

All Captain Tavia had now was one witness, Cinquemain. The Silicate had volunteered nothing about the circumstances of that death and the mission history that led up to it. Even the report he filed with the Troupe was vague to the extent of being useless.

She understood enough of Silicate circuitry to know that the artificial intelligences were capable of deceit, of concealing information, of inventing untrue facts. They could be interrogated by semantic experts, but they could not be tortured into revealing what they knew. But then, neither could a human being—or not reliably. The only way to extract the story from Cinquemain would be by brute force rather than persuasion. That would require her ordering that his chassis be opened under restraint and the glass sphere that represented his "brain" be extracted. But to penetrate further, they would have to crack the glass, expose the internal circuits, and probe them one by one for the encoded memories she was seeking. Nine times out of ten this method—oh, it had been tried before!—left the questioner with layers of gold tinsel embedded in semiconductor substrate and no coherent signal at all.

The whole situation was very confusing and …

Damnation! There was that shadow again, advancing from the periphery of her mind. Was it her sense of frustration over the possible failure of the mission against the Ramsays, about which she could do nothing? Or was her subconscious—some kind of negative inspiration—trying to tell her to cut her losses and write off her best Jongleurs?

No, this felt like something else, something coming from *outside*.

It was if a hand had clamped onto her brain and begun squeezing.

Forward

38. The Errant Children

GENJIFER RAMSAY WAS confused and disturbed—or as confused and disturbed as her tight control on her emotions ever allowed her mind to become.

That insufferable maggot from the San Francisco coven, Osip, had assured her of an easy capture. On two previous mornings, he said, they had observed the female Jongleur at the F.A.O. Schwarz toy store: once on the sidewalk as she entered the building, once in passing on the first floor. The woman was presumed to be taking biological samples among the local children while their parents were busy elsewhere and store officials were looking the other way. The Jongleur's description fit the story that Beckah Courtnay had worked out for the intermediate theft of a prized baseball that she had already promised to a local collector in the twentieth century.

Genjifer and her brothers Gjordge and Giuffre had entered the toy store right when the doors opened at ten on the third morning and scoured the target floors. They already knew the building's layout from their activities the night before. And this morning they did not just walk through the public areas, where the Jongleur's juvenile targets would congregate, but they also went into the stockrooms and storage areas, where the woman would have stored her means of escape: her biosuit, folded liteship—and the baseball that she had stolen right from under Genjifer's nose. And they found nothing: no ship, no suit, no strange girl-child disguising an eleventh-millennium grownup like themselves, and *no baseball*.

Perhaps they were too late. Perhaps two days of sample taking had given the Jongleur all the genetic specimens she required from this century—although Genjifer knew from experience that the Troupe des Jongleurs was methodical and thorough. And they liked to work with generous amounts of overlapping material.

Perhaps the coven was playing a double game. Relations between the various groups of Flüchtlinge were not always easy, with constant suspicion about possible infiltration from the Troupe's double-agents. And the axis between San Francisco and St. Louis was particularly tense. So it was not impossible that the local coven had both tipped the Ramsays to the Jongleur's presence and then tipped the Jongleur about their covert search for her.

Nothing might be what it seemed.

Now Genjifer was leading her brothers out of the store. She would have liked to stay longer, conduct a more thorough search, and probe the minds of sales clerks and the ubiquitous security personnel stationed on each floor. With time and patience, she could have detected any abnormalities they might have observed. But she knew that the detonators were already ticking on packets of C4 that the coven had supplied from their generous store and which were now tied to support columns in the building's basement.

Wherever the Jongleur was hiding, whatever she had done with her personal equipment and that baseball, it soon would not matter. All traces of her eleventh-millennium incursion were about to be erased.

As Genjifer stood on the down escalator, exercising patience over its slow pace, with her two brothers standing in close formation on the steps behind her, she counted off the seconds in her head. And yes, they had a margin of time for leaving the store without hurrying and starting a panicked rush out the doors. They had time to get to the street and then put a margin of distance between them and the catastrophe to come.

So as she rode the down escalator, Genjifer Ramsay plotted their next move. They would eventually have to return to St. Louis and explain to Beckah Courtnay the reason for their failure. But perhaps they would first visit the San Francisco coven. And then Genjifer would have a chat—including all the possible the mental harmonics—with little Osip. That might be more revealing.

———

"We are coming up on the mark," Rydin heard Cinquemain whisper from his pants pocket, communicating simultaneously by radio telemetry with the other Silicates.

Rydin had made his pilot the official time-keeper for this mission—or at least for this part of it—because Cinquemain was the one who had spotted the Ramsays inside the toy store during their last venture into the early twenty-first century, and so he had the best internal time reference on their movements.

Now his team was standing on the sidewalk outside the store, although not all in one place together. Rydin and Cinquemain stood on the opposite corner from the building's entry, across the intersection of Stockton and O'Farrell streets. Merola Tsverin, with Berzher in his stripped-down chassis in the pocket of her dress, stood on the other side of Stockton Street facing the entrance. And Ghost, with Piedeleger similarly stripped in the pocket of his gabardine smock, stood across from Rydin on the same side of O'Farrell Street. Together they covered the three possible routes away from the store, with Ghost ordered by Cinquemain's hand signals to monitor the Ramsays' mental connection, while the Silicates kept the tracking team together.

"Everyone take your neural imprints," Rydin ordered, touching his own left eyelid with his right forefinger. "And, Piedeleger, tell Ghost to ... do whatever he does to remain sane."

"Here they come," Cinquemain whispered.

Rydin saw the three dark children, dressed in some kind of school uniform, leave the store and turn south. They were going down the east side of Stockton, across from Merola.

"Tell her to take the lead," he whispered to Cinquemain, "but to stay well back. If she loses them in the crowd, Ghost can always find them again."

"Right, close but not too close," his pilot said. "We don't want them to spot her."

"Of course," Rydin said. The three children who were actually Troupe fugitives had been tracking Merola during this reference now, although for what reason Rydin could not say. It would disrupt the current mission if Merola were to wander into their grasp at this point.

He crossed the street when the traffic light allowed, following Merola down the west side of Stockton and forty meters back. Out of the corner of his eye, he saw Ghost step off the curb into the cross walk, following the targets on their side of the street but now sixty meters back.

The weak point in Rydin's planning, of course, was that with Piedeleger compact in Ghost's pocket and shorn of her manipulators, the Divina had no way of communicating with his pilot by signs and so was effectively out of the team's radio loop. If Ghost had a sudden telepathic impression or otherwise had to send a message, he would have to take Piedeleger out of his pocket, set her down someplace, and start signing. That would be bizarre behavior even for a Divina.

The Ramsays marched down Stockton to the intersection with Ellis Street, turned left, and entered the crosswalks of the five-way angled intersection with Market Street. Rydin's team became bunched up there, and they had to cross Market almost on the heels of the three children.

As they reached the middle of the city's central thoroughfare, a huge blast and shock wave erupted somewhere behind them, almost knocking Rydin off his feet. He turned with the rest of the crowd to see a column of smoke and dust climbing into the air a block and a half back the way they had come. That was the destruction of the toy store, which still took place in this time stream.

"Right on the mark," Cinquemain told him without inflection.

Rydin turned to locate the dark heads of the three children, now on the other side of Market Street. Among all the people on the street that day, they neither stopped nor looked back but walked resolutely away.

"Tell the team to keep following," he whispered.

The Ramsays continued southeast down Fourth Street, and the three followers spaced themselves out again. Maintaining their distance and keeping out of sight became more difficult, as the general flow of people on the sidewalk was now turning back toward the blast, following the string of police cars, fire trucks, and ambulances that were conspicuously violating the one-way traffic pattern to reach the scene of disaster.

In four long blocks the Ramsays and their pursuers passed under the elevated freeway that led to and from the Bay Bridge, and three blocks beyond that they turned right on King Street.

"What's down here?" Rydin asked Cinquemain.

"Nothing. A baseball stadium and a marina."

"Baseball, again," Rydin said and fumed.

By this time and in this place the direction of the foot traffic had reversed itself. The smoke from the toy store was a distant curiosity, a smudge on the northern horizon just visible above the surrounding buildings. But the people here were converging on a massive brick-and-steel structure with two clock towers that were almost—by Rydin's eye, which was calibrated for vertical maneuvers with a liteship—forty meters tall.

"We're going to lose them in this crowd," he complained.

"So Ghost will find them again," Cinquemain said.

The people were lining up to pass between a set of gates where each person was stopped by an attendant and had to offer a paper stub in exchange for admittance. Rydin saw the three dark heads move toward and through the gates, so the Ramsays must somehow have acquired these stubs.

"What is the protocol here?" he whispered.

"I believe we will need the local money."

"And none of us has any," Rydin said.

"Bad planning on *someone's* part."

Rydin directed Merola through the radio loop—and Ghost through Piedeleger likely having to climb out of his pocket and sign frantically—to hang back and meet up with him near the most prominent feature on the sidewalk: a bronze statue two and a half meters tall that depicted a smiling man in the act of discarding a cylindrical weapon and dropping to one knee—obviously some act of surrender or homage.

When Rydin offered his interpretation of the statue, Merola said, "No, he has just hit a baseball out of the park,"

"So where is the baseball?" he asked. "And how do you know about any of this?"

"I …" His protégé became confused. Then she pointed. "It says so on the plaque."

Rydin smiled grimly: her guilt in stealing Boskin's prized ball was still unproved.

"How are we going to follow the Ramsays inside?" Cinquemain asked in a louder voice, now that the team was standing alone in the midday sun.

"We could buy tickets," Merola suggested. "There are ways to acquire money in this reference now. Lots of money, actually."

"Do we have time for them?" he asked.

"That's … a good point," she admitted.

"Look for an alternate means of entry," he instructed her. "Take Ghost with you for now. Signal when you have found one."

Twenty minutes later, Merola had located a side entrance without any guards in attendance, but it was blocked by the same kind of gate as all the other access points. It had vertical metal bars spaced ten centimeters apart—too narrow for even Rydin's and Merola's childlike bodies to squeeze through and hopeless for anyone as big as Ghost.

"Stand back," Rydin said—and even then he had to push Ghost out of the way.

He sized up the opening between the verticals and realized he would have to move not just one set of the parallel bars but two. He rolled his shoulders and imagined calling up the extra strength provided by Dottoressa Gerbus's Simian-ACTN3 treatments—strength he usually had to guard against and parcel out in everyday life. Rydin gripped the outer two of a set of four bars, positioning his body so that he was pulling on one bar while pushing on the other, as if he were drawing an ancient compound bow.

If the centimeter-and-a-half bars were made of the same bronze as the statue—for they had that antique, reddish color—then he might bend them. However, if they were made of steel …

The two bars moved more easily than he had supposed. Creaking, and with a deep shuddering where they were anchored at top and bottom, the verticals drew apart into a rounded bow shape. When the outer set was at maximum extension, he bent the inner bars to match.

Merola was just staring at him.

Ghost's face was disbelieving.

"Quickly now." He motioned them to step through the gap. "We have to find those three in all this crowd before they decide to leave."

39. The Children of Willie Mays

OTHER TICKET HOLDERS at Pac Bell Park moved in streams and clumps toward the concession booths and the souvenir shop, or found their seats in assigned sections and settled in to watch the pregame festivities: recognition of aged athletes, commendation of various local youth and charitable organizations, and singing of patriotic songs. Genjifer Ramsay knew that the Busch Stadium managers put on the same mindless events while the stands filled. But she and her brothers went straight to the children's playground under the giant green Coke bottle and the giant baseball glove, because that was where the local San Francisco coven held court.

Actual children were playing there, climbing inside the Coke bottle to use the hidden slide inside and tossing real keepsake baseballs back and forth. Genjifer could still spot the temporal refugees because their play was not artless and joyful but a form of cover. She made a straight path to the nearest of these pseudo-children with her brothers following in lockstep.

"Where is the one called Osip?" she demanded.

The Flüchtling turned to face her. Genjifer saw that, although he had the reduced height and slender body of a nine-year-old and was dressed in tee-shirt, shorts, and scuffed sneakers, his eyes were aged, embedded in wrinkles, with similar crease marks at the corners of his mouth.

"Osip?" he asked. "I don't know any—"

"He's getting lunch on the concourse," another non-child told her. "Be back in a few minutes."

"We'll wait," Genjifer said, crossing her arms and silently ordering Gjordge and Giuffre to take positions flanking her.

"Not like that," the second Flüchtling said, pointing at their rigid stances and their formal clothing: their tailored woolen jackets, the brothers' matching knee pants, her pleated skirt, and their identical button-down blue shirts with striped ties.

"You look like a Sunday school on parade. And you're not playing like normal children."

"We will wait," she said again, more succinctly.

"Whatever," the Flüchtling said, backing away.

And in those promised "few minutes," a boy who could actually pass for nine years old appeared. He had a black-and-orange Giants baseball cap on a head that was naturally bald underneath.

"I'm Osip," he said. "Samuel says you're looking for me."

"You told Beckah Courtnay about our Jongleur thief," Genjifer said. "The one who was taking samples in the toy store."

"We *had* spotted a Jongleur at Schwarz's, yes. Beckah asked all the covens to keep a lookout."

"She wasn't there again today."

"Okay," the man-child said. "So?"

"So we needed to find her," she said.

"Right, but … Look, given the logistics—first our sighting, then the call to Saint Louis, and your travel time out here, versus one day on the mark for her, maybe two if she's *really* fishing—it was a long shot to catch her."

"You said she would be there, in the store, on the third day."

"*Might.* We told Beckah she might be there. Not a promise."

"Do you think I can tell Beckah Courtnay she *misheard* you?"

"Tell her what you think she needs to know." Osip shrugged.

"We have already dropped the store, and now to no purpose."

"Wait—you did *what?*" The boy's eyes suddenly went wide.

"We eliminated the toy store. It was always part of the plan."

"Just like that? You used our explosives against a soft target?"

"To eliminate a Jongleur," she explained. "To get what we wanted, we would have had to kill her. That would have left her ship, her biosuit, and her robot somewhere in the building as evidence. So we dropped the whole structure."

"Well, stop it then. Go back and defuse the charges."

"We can't," Genjifer said. "It has already happened."

"The uptown explosion this morning—that was *you?*"

"Of course."

"Oh, this is very bad."

"Why? These are not your people."

"Yes, but we have to live here. And the munitions in this time frame leave traces—embedded chemical tags, bills of sale, federal paperwork." He paused. "Not to mention, we had an observer inside the building, still looking for your Jongleur. If he was killed, you will pay an indemnity. I will have to inform Beckah."

This conversation had gone on long enough. "No, you won't," Genjifer said.

She caught Osip's eye and entered his mind. When she discovered that he had some rudimentary defenses, she summoned the powers of her two brothers and used her own mind to focus and articulate theirs. And then, when she had the Flüchtling's full attention, she inserted a suggestion that he was having trouble breathing. She imagined that he was twenty meters under water and sinking slowly into the depths where the sunlight could never reach. She imagined clamping iron bands around his chest and suggested that if he tried to take a breath his lungs would fill with water. She pressed down on him … further … deeper … colder.

When his lungs could take no more of this, Osip opened his mouth and died.

———

Once they were inside the stadium, the Jongleur team had split up to look for the Ramsay children. Merola had been assigned to the north end of the concourse with instructions to scan the lower levels and the bleachers that lay out beyond left field. Rydin took the south end of the concourse and right field. And Ghost was ordered by rudimentary signs—including physically planting him in a certain spot, pushing at his chest to make him stay there, and twisting his shoulders back and forth to look around—to wait in the middle and give Piedeleger's exposed camera stalk a chance to survey the crowd. Other than that, the Divina was mostly useless.

From her place of elevation, Merola could see everything but the top tiers of the stadium above her. But that was where, numerically, the Ramsays were least likely to be found. And besides, she doubted they had come to the park to watch a game. Something else was going on.

After about ten minutes, she spotted the three heads of dark hair, still holding their triangular formation, moving along the walkway behind the bleachers. They were entering an open area dominated by the giant shapes of what appeared to be a green bottle lying on its side and a baseball glove poised to catch a ball. She pulled Berzher's compact chassis from her pocket, directed his attention in that direction, and told him to zoom in and report what he saw.

"Children, mostly unattended," her pilot said.

"But you see the three Ramsays?" she pressed.

"Oh, yes. Genjifer is talking to one of the children."

"And?" she prompted him.

"Now just standing there."

Merola told Berzher to report what he had seen to Cinquemain and Piedeleger and begin gathering Rydin's team at her end of the concourse. After a few minutes Rydin himself came up, pulling Ghost along.

"What has happened?" Rydin asked.

"The woman Genjifer is talking to one of the children in the playground," Merola replied. With careful attention she could just make out that much. "The boy in the baseball cap." She pointed.

"They appear to be arguing," Berzher said. "No, not anymore. They boy isn't speaking, just staring at her."

"Some sort of telepathic communication?" Rydin asked.

While Merola watched, the boy in the cap opened his mouth. Then he opened it wider, as if he was trying to scream and couldn't. He crumpled sideways, his knees collapsing under him. He fell on the green surface of the playground and lay still.

"Look at them!" Rydin exclaimed. "The other children keep right on playing. They notice the body, but they pretend they don't. Very strange. There are no real children down there."

"Flüchtlinge," Cinquemain confirmed. "A whole group of them, *pretending* to be children."

"As are we," Rydin commented.

"What happened to the boy?" Merola asked. "The Ramsay girl never touched him."

Ghost began signing. First, he thrust his right forefinger with a twisting motion through the curled fingers of his left hand, as if stabbing it. Then he brought his two fists together, knuckles to knuckles with thumbs up. Next, he dragged the thumb of the right hand down along his jaw line from ear to chin. And finally, he tapped his forehead with the fingers of that right hand.

" 'Killed with her mind,' " Cinquemain translated.

"How does he know all this?" Merola asked.

"He senses these things," Piedeleger said.

"She tried the same thing on me," Rydin said, "when we caught them in the Windlace house."

"How did you escape that?" she asked.

"Pulled her head apart," he answered and flexed his fingers.

"Look!" Berzher commanded. "They're on the move again."

The three had turned and made their way back along the walkway, still in lockstep.

"Follow them at a distance," Rydin ordered. "*Don't* get in their way."

The team moved cautiously, sometimes straying on one side of the broad concourse and down the connecting ramps, sometimes moving to the other side, always walking without appearing to have a purpose. As she went, Merola tried not to stare at the three heads, only occasionally visible through gaps in the crowd. She tried not to think too hard about the Ramsays and what she had seen, as if staring and thinking might attract their telepathic attention and whatever mental force had killed—for she did not think he was merely sleeping—the child on the playground.

The Ramsays moved through the entrance gate and out onto the wide sidewalk that fronted the stadium. Genjifer raised her hand, and a yellow taxicab pulled to the curb as if drawn to her. She opened the door and the three got in. The taxi moved away.

"We've lost them," Rydin said.

"If we had money, we could get our own taxi," Cinquemain suggested.

"I wonder if Ghost could use his mind to call one," Merola said. "As she did."

With this thought, the Divina turned toward her, as if he understood.

"We still don't have the money to pay for it," Cinquemain said.

Ghost began signing. He thrust out his hands, palms up, and waved them back and forth. Then he spread the palm of his left hand and curved his right hand across it, angling sharply to the left, as if going astray. " 'What's wrong'?" Piedeleger translated.

Merola faced him. "We have no money. Money? How do we say 'money' when you guys don't have manipulators to make the signs?"

As if in response, Ghost bent and took her by the shoulders with his upper pair of hands, and by the elbows with the lower pair. He put his face close to hers. She could feel an … attention, a pressure, something dark and questioning. Ghost was probing her mind.

The Divina let her go, straightened, and rubbed his thumb over the index and middle fingers of his upturned hand. " 'Money,' " Piedeleger translated.

"Exactly!" Merola replied, nodding vigorously.

Ghost immediately turned and confronted a man in a windbreaker and ball cap who was passing by them on the sidewalk. The man stopped as if he knew and recognized the Divina. He smiled, reached into a back pocket, took out his wallet, and gave it to Ghost. Then the man nodded and went on his way.

The Divina gave Merola the wallet and made the finger-rubbing gesture again.

Merola opened it and found a dozen green bills inside. They were big currency, with numbers of two and even three digits printed at the corners.

"That's a neat trick," Rydin said. "I think we had better accept that as a gift."

"Now if we only knew where the Ramsays were going," Cinquemain said.

Ghost looked around the street. He made the finger-rubbing gesture again.

"Yes, 'money,' " Merola said. "We understand. But what do the *others* want?"

Ghost cupped his right hand, palm up, made a fist, shook it a few times, and moved it quickly across his chest to the left, opening his hand, as if throwing something.

" 'Gambling,' " Piedeleger said.

"A casino," Cinquemain said.

40. The Shoe That Fit

THE BEST PLACE to have a discussion about Troupe affairs that might not please the Ringmasters was far away from the Jongleur compound. And so, under the guise of "gathering supplies," Merola Tsverin located Berzher outside the hangar, where he was still disassembling their ship's panels. She motioned for him to follow and commandeered one of the Troupe's electric surreys for the long ride into Lune. They could talk freely in her treehouse because she was certain it contained no embedded listening devices, their electronics being subtly incompatible with its organic structure.

"What is this about?" Berzher asked along the way.

"I need some personal things," Merola explained while holding a finger to her lips. She was not so certain about the Troupe's autonomous vehicle fleet.

"Ah!" her pilot said, touching a claw to his camera stalk in salute.

They arrived at their destination, dismissed the surrey to go on about its business, and entered the main room of her tree, letting the leaves of the outside door seal themselves with tiny drops of sap.

"Now," Berzher said, "what is so important that it precludes proper stowage of our liteship?"

"Something very strange is going on," she said. "I wanted to talk before you filed your report with Nexus. You see, I met Captain Tavia inside the hangar." Merola went on to explain her strange conversation with the Ringmaster.

"We have a *Divina* in the Troupe?" Berzher asked, amazed.

"Apparently, and I recruited him. But I don't know when."

"And then we all went off to the twenty-first century—"

"—where you and I have just returned from—"

"—and we are chasing these people—"

"—a group of triplets, the Ramsays."

"All right," he pilot said. "And who might they be?"

"People we've supposedly seen before. Tavia called them 'fugitives.' "

"Are we tasked with pursuing random Flüchtlinge now?"

"I don't know. And *that's* the problem."

"So, what are you going to do?"

"I told her I was retrieving supplies for Rydin. That will be my cover story—for as long as it will hold. Then, I guess, I should return to him in the twenty-first century. But what part of that century? I have no idea."

While they talked, Merola had been staring at a side board coaxed from one of the room's framing limbs. Lying on it was a chain of linked crystals wrought in silvery metal. She walked over and picked it up. The chain had clasps on either end, and she recalled seeing women in the twenty-first century wearing similar bangles. Merola experimentally wrapped it around her own wrist, and the length was perfect. But she had never worn, nor even owned, a thing like this in her life.

"Someone has been here—and left this," she said, showing Berzher the chain.

"That is unheard of, among humans," he replied. And it was true. The treehouse was a personal expression, grown for a single individual or family, occupied as long as it was needed, and returned to the soil with special enzymes when abandoned. The people of eleventh-millennium Lune did not enter each other's trees uninvited. And no one would think to occupy a tree that another had left unattended.

"Let me see …" Merola said.

She had few possessions and not much that was personal or intimate. She looked in the utility closets of the main room and noted that Berzher's spare chassis was missing. She went into the sleeping chamber and checked the cupboard where she kept clean clothing.

There she found a frazzled blonde wig that she had never worn, a short jacket in some synthetic fiber with a matching wraparound covering for the lower body that twenty-first century women called a "skirt," and a pair of shoes that were like slippers but with absurdly raised heels. She recalled see-ing some of the women in San Francisco—but surely not all of them—wearing uncomfortable shoes like this. They would certainly serve to make a small woman appear taller. On a hunch, she slipped off her left boot of layered polyaramid with steel reinforcing and tried on the dainty shoe. It fit perfectly.

"Somewhere along the line," she said, "I appear to have acquired an outfit of adult women's clothing from the century I just visited. But I have no idea where."

"Either you or someone else did," Berzher said.

Before she could respond, his chassis went still and his camera stalks stiffened.

"What is it?" she asked. "A message from the Troupe?"

"Nexus just informed all Silicates about a dissolution service."

"Someone has died?"

"Coel Rydin."

"No!"

"The subtext is that Cinquemain brought him back from the mission. He had been struck dead by hostile fire with a magnetic projectile."

"No!"

"I believe we had better plan on attending this service," Berzher said.

"But ..." she said distractedly, "we were supposed to go join him in the hunt for the Flüchtlinge, these Ramsay people."

"It appears to be too late for that now," her pilot said gently.

41. The Dissolution Ceremony

EVEN BEFORE RYDIN'S body could be dispositioned—with due ceremony, of course—among the humans, Cinquemain had been assigned to another Jongleur as his liteship passenger.

Jazdal Halek was a young woman, recruited into the Troupe four years ago, whose training had gone as far as one flight above atmosphere with a group class and no travel in time. She had scored high on intelligence, spatial and temporal awareness, and intuition, with no lower than median scores on aggression and assertion. But then, for some reason that was not publicly known, her career had become sidelined. The Ringmasters—according Nexus, who for once possessed imperfect access to Troupe records—had determined that she was not ready for full Jongleur status. She had been assigned to a newly created category, "Apprentice," and there had languished in Jongleur limbo, performing menial tasks around the compound. Cinquemain could remember another new recruit, from years and years ago, whose profile had been almost the inverse curve of this Halek female's, and Rydin did not turn out badly.

Perhaps the Ringmasters had assigned this woman to Cinquemain as a sign that he should now develop her potential as he had Rydin's. And maybe he could keep her alive where he had so recently failed with his last partner.

Suddenly Cinquemain, who was virtually ageless himself, felt the need of another memory defrag and resection, because the people he had known were again starting to pile up inside him.

In preparation for the disposition of Rydin's body, Cinquemain took Halek along on the one task that needed no special Jongleur skills but required a strong back and functioning pair of hands: cleaning out Rydin's treehouse. Normally, personal possessions like clothing and what few mementos a Jongleur was allowed to keep were dissolved with the tree. But Rydin had been an amateur biosculptor, with racks of specialized genalysis equipment and samples of current-generation specimens. The former could be salvaged. The latter needed to be exterminated, isolated because of potential contamination from their unlicensed genomes, and then dissolved separately from the surrounding biosphere. As Cinquemain had been Rydin's laboratory assistant and walking notebook, these tasks fell to him.

"What are these?" Halek asked, pointing to a shelf full of green starfish-analogs. As her finger drew near, each one moved away slowly.

"Motile cacti," Cinquemain said.

"Do they bite?" the woman asked.

"Only if you are a species of lichen."

"Did this Rydin ever make anything that was ... useful? I mean, some plant or animal that I would recognize?"

"He was concerned with genetic alternatives."

"And with weirdness," Halek said, frowning.

"Not always a bad thing. It leads to wonder."

At last, after an hour's work, they had rendered the biological samples inert and packaged for disposal, boxed the equipment for transport, and stacked everything else on the side of the chalk path opposite the tree. Cinquemain signaled to Tavia's pilot, Skeezicks, that the ceremony could be scheduled for later that day.

"We might as well stay here. They will come shortly."

"You liked him, didn't you, this Rydin?"

"He was my responsibility."

"I'm sorry for you."

"Why?" he said.

"Because you have to ask that," she replied.

Then the two of them waited in silence. But after a time, Jazdal Halek obviously felt the pressure to talk. She had clearly become curious and, perhaps inspired by the occasion, wanted answers about the life she had chosen—or that chance had chosen for her.

"Do many Jongleurs come back to the here and now to die?" she asked. "Or do they all get killed and buried in the past?"

"Most Jongleurs die of old age, eventually," Cinquemain said. "At the limits of their genetically programmed span," he corrected. "The best of them manage to avoid the dangers of the past."

"It seems like they're training us for all kinds of chaos and murder."

"That is intended to keep you alive, so you *can* come back."

Eventually, Captain Tavia and a disposal team arrived from the compound in an electric surrey. A number of senior Jongleurs followed in a second surrey with a wrapped bundle.

At the same time—and probably alerted by Nexus—Merola Tsverin and Berzher walked up one of the paths from the river together. Cinquemain had not known they were visiting Lune. He had not even known they had come back from their twenty-first century Search, which had been mysteriously delayed and for which Rydin had made the unregistered trip into Cornwall. Cinquemain would have much to ask her, afterward. But for now, he merely saluted her with his right claw.

The second team took the bundle from the surrey and carried it into the treehouse. They laid it in the main room, next to the trunk that supported the whole structure. That way he would be absorbed directly into the spot.

When and how human beings had begun adapting trees and other plant and animal life to their needs was part of a technological history that Cinquemain could reference, if he chose. But why they decided to dispose of both the body's protein husk and the residence's cellulose structure in the same place and time was lost in the maze of human culture and customs. Perhaps it was a measure of respect for the environment, to erase all physical remains, under the rubric of "Leave no trace." And perhaps it was a remnant of superstition, inspired by millennia of ghost stories and spirit sightings, based on some imagined electromagnetic carrier wave that was supposedly given off by the body at the time of death and then tended to become trapped in whatever place the spirit had once occupied. At any rate, the custom of in-situ dissolution was still observed by the Jongleurs, although they had access to all the burial rites carried out by humans in the past.

They left Rydin's shell to his rest against the trunk, exited to the path outside, and withdrew the required distance. Then the disposal team suited up and brought out their canister sprayers. They began dousing the tree with fast-acting, pan-genomic enzymes, moving top to bottom, with extra amounts around the root system. The overlapping leaves of the weather-tight surface turned brown and shriveled. The supporting branches of the structural framework shrank and curled inward. The main trunk began to collapse down into itself. Cinquemain looked among the devolving ruins, expecting to see the wrapped body of his human passenger dissolve into its skeleton, but the layers of melting cellulose had already hidden it.

"Fare you well, Coel Rydin," Captain Tavia said aloud. "You have traveled many pathways. Go safely upon your last voyage."

It was poetic nonsense, of course, because Cinquemain himself had seen Rydin on that voyage. He knew that nothing of Rydin's death had been either tranquil or safe.

Others at the site, including the disposal team, who had now removed their helmets, murmured similar messages of respect, admiration, and human grief.

Cinquemain knew that after the complete dissolution of the tree and its organic contents—a process that would not finish until sometime the next morning—the space where it had stood would be sodded over. The Council of Loving Parents, Lune's civil government, would place a marker on the site, and no one would ever plant there again—probably more of that ghost superstition. In this way, the village maintained a certain amount of open space and expanded slowly outward into the Temz valley. But that space would remain vacant only until someone decided they needed it, removed the deeply weathered marker, and planted and took up residence in a new tree.

This was the human way: to respect no one and nothing for very long. That was unlike the Silicates, whose hard memory cores extended back to the day they were cast in silicon and gold wire. And as a race, the Silicates themselves were immortal.

———

From the shadow of a neighboring tree and partially hidden by its overlapping branches, Glyph watched the time travelers gather around the treehouse belonging to the dead male they thought of as "Rydin." He had followed the red-tinged female, who thought of herself as "Captain," to the site and her thoughts linked the wrapped body inside the treehouse to that of his enemy. Glyph stayed then and watched as the tree collapsed in upon itself.

He understood enough of the processes that were taking place to know the male's body could not now be resurrected. In a few hours, it would not even be recognizable, except through chemical analysis. Already, Glyph could feel the emanations of time and place, the shimmering of past dimensions, evaporate as the body lost its physical structure.

So this human object was truly gone.

Well … there were others of interest.

———

After the treehouse had withered to a clumped of browned-over foliage and a central stump three meters tall, Merola turned away. Coel Rydin had been honored and dissolved. The rest was just memories.

"I guess there's no going back to the twenty-first century now," Berzher said. "No matter what our story might be."

"And there's still the question of who's been living in my house," she said.

Another Silicate approached her on the chalk path. From its configuration and the patina of old scars on its carapace, she recognized Cinquemain. He was accompanied by a young woman unknown to her but probably a newly assigned Jongleur. The Troupe tended to work fast in these matters.

"Hello," Merola said to the robot. "I am saddened for your loss."

Cinquemain dipped his camera stalks. "I was an inadequate pilot."

"Now, you were the best pilot," she told him.

"But still I failed to protect my Jongleur."

"Was it these Ramsays you were chasing?"

"I do not know that name," Cinquemain said.

"Captain Tavia said you and Rydin were tracking down Flüchtlinge in the twenty-first century."

"So she told me. She did mention *telepathic* refugees."

"And armed with what?" she asked. "Magnetic projectiles?"

"So it would appear," he said. "And so the captain would have it."

"And, apparently, I was helping you. And someone called 'Ghost.' "

"So I have been told, but you are here now. You came back early?"

The new Jongleur had been following this conversation closely.

"Are you two even on the same planet?" she asked suddenly.

"I beg your pardon," Cinquemain said to Merola. "This is Jazdal Halek, my new partner and trainee. And this is Merola Tsverin, a former protégé of Coel Rydin's."

"And I'm the lump of metal that carts her around the universe," Berzher said, waving a claw.

Merola and Jazdal exchanged nods. Then Merola noted, "You were saying?"

"Well, it seems as if you and Cinquemain were talking past each other."

"Were we?" Merola asked. "It might appear that way. But it seems to me that somebody has been telling lies." Here she looked hard at Cinquemain.

"The truth is," he replied, "Rydin and I went back in an attempt to protect you. This was after you were late in reporting from your genetic researches in the twenty-first century."

"But I was *never* late," she replied. "I took my samples for two days as planned. Then on the third day I got interrupted by some officious security people. After that, I came home."

"There *was* the business with stealing the baseball," Berzher observed.

"I never had anything to do with a *baseball*," she answered, bewildered.

"Correction. You failed to take your neural imprint. Now the memory is gone."

"That may have been my fault," Cinquemain offered. "Or Rydin's and mine. When you disappeared, we learned that you had dealings with a rich dilettante from Cornwall named Pinkus Boskin. He collects—or once used to collect—twentieth-century sports memorabilia." He turned to Halek. "Close your ears now. These are matters of high policy."

"High crimes, you mean," the trainee suggested impudently.

"A question of interpretation," Cinquemain said. "Anyway, Rydin determined the most direct solution was to eliminate this Boskin's collecting fever. We went a generation upstream in the family and relieved them of their stolen artifacts, the whole collection."

"So I never was approached," Merola said quietly.

"And your reputation and standing are now intact."

"But then ... how and where was Coel Rydin killed?"

"I thought we had settled the security issue with a couple of sight hounds," he said. "But the estate was guarded by magnetic projectors on a delayed setting. The mechanicals obviously confused our leaving with our arrival and took aim."

"I suppose I should thank you," she said, "but I don't know for what."

"Consider it a piece of history that never happened," Cinquemain said.

Still, something was troubling Merola about the whole affair. "Did you happen to visit Rydin's tree before it was liquidated?"

"Jazdal and I tended to his biosculptures."

"Did you notice anything different?"

"The cacti were a bit sluggish."

"But no signs of disturbance? No indication that anyone else had been there?" Merola went on to describe the antique clothing and piece of jewelry she had found in her own tree, sized to her measure but not things she had ever worn herself.

"Is this another lapse in neural imprinting?" Cinquemain suggested.

"They are nothing I ever brought back from the twenty-first century."

"Clearly, we have a mystery on our hands," her pilot said.

————

All the time that Rydin's treehouse was being absorbed, Captain Tavia was conscious of a presence. The ancients had their stories of spirits and ghosts, of course, and they might have described her feeling as the soul of Coel Rydin watching over the service. But this presence was more focused, weighing on her. And it felt … evil.

Once, when her attention drifted from the slow process of the tree melting and collapsing, Tavia thought she saw a figure in the middle distance, watching her from the shadow of another treehouse. At first she assumed it was simply a Divina, because it had that broken-backed shape and the extra set of limbs. But then she noticed that its head was misshapen, its eyes wider set, and its body larger overall than any Divina she had ever encountered. And it was wearing a loose robe of iridescent material that shimmered in the reflected sunlight whenever the creature moved. No Divina of her experience wore such garish clothing, being a modest and unassuming race. And finally, the lurker seemed to be staring right at Tavia, pinning her with its own attention. All the Divina she knew were shy and tended to avoid eye contact.

The entire encounter, distant as it was, troubled her.

After the tree was a molten mess and people were turning away to go about their business, Captain Tavia saw Cinquemain and his trainee approach Merola Tsverin and her pilot Berzher. She had not realized that Tsverin was still in the eleventh millennium, because Cinquemain had said she was now leading the search for the Ramsays back in the twenty-first century, following Rydin's death.

The two Jongleurs and their machines were engaged in a lengthy conversation—probably telling stories about Coel Rydin for Cinquemain's new partner, or so Tavia guessed. In that case, she did not want to intrude. But after a while, she felt an approach might be appropriate.

"It's good to remember a fallen colleague," she told them quietly.

Tsverin hesitated. The two robots went silent. Halek looked alarmed.

"Yes," Merola said. "We were … talking about how Rydin died."

"And you were there?" Captain Tavia was surprised. "I thought you had come back earlier, 'for supplies.' In fact, I thought you would already have left by now. Because Cinquemain told me you were now in charge of finding the Ramsays."

"Ah … There must have been … a disjunction," the Jongleur said. "I must have returned from an earlier—a different—part of the Search. And then Rydin was shot … later."

"By the Ramsays," Tavia suggested.

"We were just working that out now."

"Then you and Berzher will want to be careful to return to the exact point from which you left. You don't want to run into yourselves."

"No … that certainly would be a bad thing."

"And you left *Ghost* there to keep watch?" Tavia asked, suddenly uneasy.

"That—" Tsverin hesitated now. "—seemed to be the logical alternative."

Tavia turned to Cinquemain. "Were you *close* to finding the Ramsays?"

"We must have been," the robot said, "if they managed to shoot him."

"Of course." She nodded. "But you know you cannot go back now."

Cinquemain cocked his camera stalks in confusion. "Why not?"

"You have a new partner to train." Tavia nodded at Halek. "You don't want to take her into a fight, especially not one with projectile weapons. Merola and Berzher can continue the assignment—or their part of it, in their relative future."

"Yes," Tsverin said. "We will—or *ourselves* will—are doing so—or *did*."

"Then you had better gather those supplies and get back to it."

"Yes, ma'am, we will. Or rather, we're *already gone*."

42. Easy Money

WITH THEIR BUSINESS in San Francisco concluded, Genjifer Ramsay decided to return to St. Louis and report to Beckah Courtnay their failure in locating and retrieving her stolen baseball. But first there was the problem of cash flow—or more precisely, its lack of flow. She had spent their available resources on airfare for herself and Gjordge and Giuffre to come west. Before they could return, she needed to replenish their supply.

One source of easy money, readily available to anyone with her and her brothers' mental talents, was the gaming clubs and gambling casinos. St. Louis had a number of them, moored in the waters along the shore of the great river, where they were just beyond the state line and out of reach from the local jurisdictions governing such transactions. Those gaming emporia had been her recourse for pocket money while the Ramsays were attached to the St. Louis coven.

After they left the San Francisco ballpark, Genjifer ordered the taxicab to pause long enough for her to consult the Yellow Pages book in a phone kiosk. And yes, a casino called "Lucky Chances" was located in a town called Colma, and according to the attached map it was just over the city and county border. The casino advertised thirty-one table games and twenty-one poker games, but no slot machines. That was just as well, because Genjifer's mental talents could not affect the mechanism inside such a machine, and if Gjordge tried his invisible hand at it, his interference often had unpredictable results.

There would be nothing "lucky" about her business in the casino. Instead, she would simply work with the minds of the dealers and other players: perceiving for herself the cards they held, skewing their perception of the odds involved, and occasionally pushing into their minds a misread of the face or number cards in their hands. And where those tricks didn't work, she would have her two brothers stationed elsewhere in the room to observe and report telepathically. If she played conservatively, she could parlay the remaining cash in her pocket into anywhere from five to ten thousand dollars, enough to fly them home and live handsomely for a while. And no power on the casino floor could detect or stop her.

But first, she and her brothers had to make an adjustment in their appearance. Dressed as they were in school uniforms, they could easily pass as children in the toy store and at the ballpark. But a casino was a place strictly for adults, and children were not admitted. Although Genjifer could easily have fooled a security guard or concierge into passing her and her brothers, even she was not strong enough to extend the misperception to an entire room full of dealers and players—not and still concentrate on her game. And, if this Lucky Chances Casino was anything like the riverfront casinos along the Mississippi, there would be cameras in the ceiling to observe the action, and she could not know what minds might be watching through their display screens.

The Ramsays were relatively tall for eleventh-millennium adults, although their faces and bodies still presented as prepubescent. And unlike the genetically modified adults of their birth era, the three of them all had full heads of dark hair. So it was a matter of the proper clothing to trick the eye: business suits for the boys, a party or cocktail dress, hose, and heels for her. And Gengifer needed the proper cosmetics for lips and eyes to suggest a more sophisticated look, while the boys needed soot or charcoal to darken their cheeks and chins and suggest a late-day stubble. A bit of jewelry for her—earrings and a necklace, she thought—would also help and could be sold or pawned later.

They could buy these things at any department store, but then her available money would be exhausted and leave nothing for table stakes. She checked another section of the Yellow Pages and found a store called Nordstrom, which was familiar to her from its branches in St. Louis and would have what she needed. This store was located in a shopping center called "Stonestown Galleria," on 20th Avenue in the southwest corner of the city, practically on the way to the casino. She cross-referenced the posted hours of the store, which closed at nine o'clock that night, and the casino, which was open twenty-four hours a day.

The trick now, she decided, was to get them to this Galleria place, bide their time at various inexpensive amusements until early evening, insert themselves and hide inside the Nordstrom store until it officially closed, dress and disguise appropriately, and then find an after-hours cab to take them to the casino.

Genjifer Ramsay wasn't worried about the state of play in the late evening or even after midnight. Experience had taught her that such places had more attendance and were safer for her kind of tricks then than anytime during daylight hours.

She returned to the cab, where Gjordge and Giuffre were waiting passively and the meter was still running. Well, it didn't matter what the meter showed. The driver would accept as payment whatever bill she gave him.

"Take us to the Stonestown Galleria," she instructed.

———

Rydin had thought that the process of tracking the Ramsay siblings toward whatever a "casino" might be would be difficult. As they climbed into the taxicab that Merola had hailed from the curb, he envisioned trying to explain to the driver that they were following another cab, one that was now out of sight, and so they had to rely on the mental powers shared between their Divina friend and their targets of pursuit. Then Piedeleger, from her hiding place in Ghost's pocket, would have to communicate with the Divina by signing with the truncated arms of her stripped-down chassis, receive his signs in return, speak his instructions quietly to Rydin or Merola, and the Jongleurs would then direct the driver. All of this second- and third-hand communication would trace the route that Ghost was supposedly reading, at whatever distance, from the mind of one or the other of the Ramsays.

In actual practice, the process turned out to be much easier. The cab that Merola found was driven by a twenty-first century Divina. It and Ghost carried on a complex greeting and set of directions by signs that Piedeleger tried to follow and report to the two Jongleurs.

"Something about 'the car ahead,' " she said. "Then what appears to be 'her mind,' and that's repeated twice for confirmation. After that, the two of them just stared off into the distance with that dreamy expression they usually wear—almost as if they were sharing a moment of contemplation."

"So?" Merola said. "Do we tell the driver where to go or not?"

But their vehicle was already in motion. It made a one-eighty-degree turn at the corner around the street's central divider and proceeded in the opposite direction.

"I believe the Divina driving us already knows," Rydin said.

They appeared to move about the city aimlessly for almost half an hour. During that time, Rydin caught glimpses of a yellow taxi in the traffic ahead. Once he thought he saw three dark heads through the cab's rear window.

"Tell the driver to hang back a bit," he instructed Piedeleger to repeat to Ghost. "We don't want them to know they're being followed."

The yellow cab they were following stopped for ten minutes in the middle of a block, and their vehicle paused at the corner. Genjifer Ramsay got out of the target vehicle, went to a blue-and-white booth on the adjoining sidewalk, and consulted a thick book there. She returned to the cab, and it sped off. It soon became apparent that the aimless wandering was over, and the ride took them west and south across the city.

"I must warn you," Rydin told Merola, Berzher, and for Piedeleger to relay to Ghost, "in case we close with them, that the Ramsays are armed with pressurized darts or syringes that they can throw or use to stab you. The contents are a fast-acting nerve agent that causes paralysis. In enough quantity, I believe it can shut down the autonomic nervous system and kill you."

"Did Captain Tavia tell you about this?" Merola asked.

"No, it's from when Cinquemain and I met them before."

"But you beat them then."

"Just barely."

The yellow cab turned off a main north-south avenue and entered the vast parking area surrounding a series of low buildings that appeared to have a purely commercial purpose—like the center of downtown but placed out among the trees and open spaces of this residential district. The Ramsay siblings got out and went through one of the many entrances.

The Divina driving their own taxi seemed to understand. It pulled in behind the target vehicle and Ghost opened the door on his side. Rydin leaned forward to negotiate the fare, but the driver waved him away, pointing and nodding at Ghost, smiling dreamily, and still refusing his money.

Rydin shrugged and followed the others into the building.

————

After six hours of trailing the Ramsays through the shopping center and trying to stay out of their sight, Merola Tsverin was becoming thoroughly bored. Rydin insisted that the two Jongleurs and the Divina not move as a group but surround their target—who themselves moved in almost perfect lock step—with leading and trailing observers and always on a different level. When the Ramsays wandered on the second tier, the Jongleur team moved below them on the ground floor. When the three non-children moved down the escalators to the first level, the Jongleurs mounted to stay above them. And they stayed in contact by radio contacts among, and whispered conversations with, their hidden companion Silicates.

The Ramsays did not always wander aimlessly. Sometimes they stayed at one of the food shops for an hour at a time. Then one sibling would eat while the other two kept watch. But after that, more wandering. Unlike the other humans crowding the center, they did not study the displays in store windows or enter any of the shops—except one, the large emporium labeled "Nordstrom" at the far end of the concourse. There they went in, made a circuit of the store on the upper and lower levels, as if familiarizing themselves with the various departments, and then came back out.

Rydin distributed money to Merola and Ghost and sent them in rotation to buy and consume food for themselves. Merola found a shop that sold noodles mixed with chopped vegetables and bits of meat. The dish reminded her of the fare she could get at home in the eleventh millennium. She did not know what Rydin or Ghost ate.

By the sixth hour, it was clear that the Ramsays had a purpose in being here. They were waiting for something or someone. But still, Merola had no clue as to what or whom.

In the eighth hour Merola noticed a change in the pace of the human beings around her. Their step quickened, and more people were heading for the exits than entering. Then a garbled communication over the public address loudspeakers said something about "closing time." One by one, various shops shut and locked their doors or rolled armored screens down across their wide entrances.

Her last view of the Ramsays had been of them once again going into the Nordstrom place, this time on the second level. She kept her station, to see what they would do next, but they never left—even after the store rolled down its own screens.

When the center was almost deserted, except for personnel working in the shops, Berzher received a communication from Rydin and Cinquemain. He gave her directions to a door labeled "Utilities" on her level. The lock mechanism bore the scorch marks of a Silicate's communications laser. As she approached, Rydin opened the door and ushered her inside, where Ghost already waited. The available space was small because the room was crammed with brooms, mops, brushes, waste bins and buckets mounted on rolling castors, and shelves full of cleaning supplies.

"We can't stay here," she told Rydin. "This is the place where janitors come after hours. It's how they keep the public spaces so clean, by working at night."

Rydin did not appear concerned. "We're not staying long. Just until the security staff makes their rounds and closes the outer doors."

"I hope you know what you're doing," she said.

"More important, what are the Ramsays doing?"

———

Genjifer Ramsay had no reason to think that she and her brothers had drawn unwarranted attention, either as they left the toy store or at the ballpark. Now and again, she received flashes of mental interest, mostly linked to the random focusing of eyeballs and attention spans. She dismissed these as the normal background flutter as the trio passed through crowded human spaces.

She knew they tended to attract attention in public: three sober children, two obvious male twins and their nearly matching sister, all dressed alike, and together moving through the world without an accompanying adult. She was also aware that they were *not* children and that some of the people around them might intuitively sense this.

In the cab ride, where they were more isolated and moved more quickly across the city, the feeling of random attention being paid grew less. And yet … and yet she felt a persistent mental presence, like a low hum, sometimes lost in the mental noise of the city, but always there. It was not the focus of a single human mind, or not exactly. She had occasionally tried to probe the minds of the creatures called "Divina," both in St. Louis and again here, and then she had felt something like this hum: distracted, subvocal, radiating in frequencies that no human being possessed. But she had no reason to think that any Divina was now paying attention to her and her brothers. They had other business in this world.

At the Stonestown Galleria, the sense of being observed strengthened. Genjifer sampled each mind as it flashed by and decided that the increase was due to the three of them being on foot again and in a crowded place. None of the mental stares seemed hostile. And that persistent hum remained, although every Divina she could see appeared to be thinking of something else.

According to her plan, the three dawdled through the afternoon and early evening. Once she took her brothers on a trip inside the Nordstrom store. She mentally pointed out the places where the boys could steal appropriate clothing off the rack. Genjifer marked for herself a dress she would like to acquire and the cosmetics and jewelry counters she would need to pilfer before the trip to the Lucky Chances Casino. Then the trio went back to their dawdling.

At ten minutes before the Galleria's official closing time, she led Gjordge and Giuffre back into Nordstrom. She took them to a public lavatory she had noted on the second level. It was a single-use space, designated "unisex" in this culture. She closed the door behind them but did not lock it. She gave the boys sharp mental instructions to stand against the wall and remain perfectly still. She covered the motion sensor on the light switch until the overhead fluorescent went out, and she kept her hand in place after that.

If any of the security personnel decided to check the lavatory during their lockdown sweeps, they would push the door open, see only darkness inside, and move on. Or that was Genjifer's plan, which only required patience and the ability to remain absolutely still and silent.

And those were talents the Ramsay siblings cultivated.

43. A Fight in the Dark

RYDIN SET CINQUEMAIN and his communications laser to cutting the bars of the roll-down screen that blocked the entrance to the Nordstrom store. Because the pilot's stripped chassis, suitable for carrying in a human pocket, had only four legs and those just ten centimeters long, he could only get a good angle on bars less than half a meter above the floor. But that would be enough for the two Jongleurs and the larger Divina to wriggle through.

"You know these bars are not aluminum," Cinquemain said, as the first one fell away. "They *look* like aluminum, but that is just an outer shell. Inside, there is a steel core."

"Do you need help?" Rydin asked.

"We have it," Berzher said, climbing out of Merola's pocket, and Piedeleger immediately followed. In a moment, two more beams were working on the screen.

As the last bar was cut and the section of screen fell away, Cinquemain spoke again. "This truncated chassis is running low on power. I will soon need to reinstall inside a battle chassis or attach to a ship's core."

"Do you have a reserve?" Rydin asked.

"Twenty percent. After that, I go dark."

"Try to maintain for the next half an hour."

"We should carry them," Merola suggested.

Once through the screen, the two Jongleurs and Ghost started down the main aisle of the store. The Silicates in their pockets extended camera stalks above the pocket rims and held communications lasers at the ready.

"Shouldn't we spread out to find the Ramsays?" Merola asked.

"Those three are too dangerous for any of us to handle alone," Rydin said. "Cinquemain and I almost lost the battle at the Windlace house—and that was with the element of surprise."

Merola gestured to the darkened store around them, full of shelves, racks, and display counters. "We have good cover here."

"And yet we don't know where we will find them in all this space," he said.

"I have a pretty good idea," Merola said. "Follow me."

She led the team to a corner of the store's second level that a sign on the back wall identified as "Fashions for Men." All Rydin could see was rack after rack of drab clothing in muted blues and grays. He approached one and felt the sleeve of what appeared to be a jacket, just for covering the upper body. But when he spread the front opening he could see a pair pantaloons, or leg coverings, hanging inside.

"Why would they come here?" he asked.

"Because—" Merola started to reply.

Before she could finish, two dark heads popped out of the shadows at the far end of the aisle. Rydin recognized the brothers, Gjordge and Giuffre. "Take them," he ordered, moving forward. "And watch out for darts."

The heads drew back—and that was a tactical mistake. The cross-aisle where they were standing backed them against a wall with a display of shoes, and that space ended at the inside corner of the building. Rydin ran down one of the boys before he could double back along the far wall. Merola ducked through a gap between the clothing racks to chase the other one trying to escape in the next aisle.

Rydin's Flüchtling was, so far as he could see, nearly naked—wearing only a kind of white loincloth or breechclout and socks, having shed the school uniform that the Ramsays had been wearing as children. He was carrying a pair of pantaloons and obviously had been in the process of changing his appearance.

The fugitive stopped, turned, and pulled loose a piece of white tape across his back. His hand came up with one of the glass darts, throwing it underhand at Rydin's face.

Rydin ducked, and so he did not see exactly what happened next. When he looked again, the Ramsay twin was lying on the floor motionless. Rydin approached and saw a hole through the boy's forehead, weeping a drop of blood.

"Our orders were to bring them back alive," he told Cinquemain.

"That was an impossible shot!" his pilot said. "Check his hand."

Rydin pried open the curled fingers. Inside was a second dart.

"All right," he said. "I'll give you credit for quick thinking."

"That needle pierces your kind of skin, not my metal shell."

Rydin went through the cross aisle to follow Merola's path. He found her standing over the second Ramsay, also half-naked and lying dead on the floor.

"He tried to stab me," she said.

"I drilled him for it," Berzher said.

"That's two down," Rydin concluded. "Now where is Genjifer?"

"Probably getting dressed," Merola said. "For a woman, it takes longer."

———

Genjifer Ramsay had chosen for herself a dress in scarlet-red satin that was flared at the hips and cut low across the chest. Even though her genetically reduced mammary glands could hardly do it justice, she liked the effect. It had taken her but a moment to slip it off the rack, find and open a package of thigh-top hosiery to wear beneath it—after shedding her school shoes and white socks—and select a pair of heeled pumps in black that would coordinate with the new outfit.

She then went to the cosmetics counter on the first level and tried, under the store's reduced security lighting, to locate a lip color that would match the dress. Having succeeded in spreading the liquid gloss around her mouth, Genjifer's next task was to trace dark lines on the edges of her upper and lower eyelids, then daub on the bruising coloration of the lids themselves that indicated a mature woman of the time.

All during this process she kept in mental contact with Gjordge and Giuffre. She had to instruct them at long range in the selection of business suits that would make them appear to be serious adults. And then she had to explain to them, in visually transmitted terms, the difference between hangers marked XS, S, M, L, and XL, and that they would only find what they needed at the lower end of that range. She sighed, thinking about how long it would take the boys to find shirts and ties—although they could probably wear the shoes they had brought with them. No one looked at a man's legs and feet in this century, only woman received that kind of scrutiny.

In the middle of applying the last touches of color to her eyes and hurrying the brothers along in dressing themselves, she suddenly felt their minds register a kind of shock, then panic, and finally, one after the other, go blank. Genjifer called out to them with her full mental force and received nothing in return. Something had gone terribly wrong.

She put down the coloring brush and waited.

She cast her mind wide for nearby threats.

She found them in the presence of two disciplined mental states. They might be human security guards from the twenty-first century, except they resonated with the cool patience of minds genetically designed and trained in the programming of the eleventh millennium. They were either rogue Flüchtlinge, who had somehow followed her from the ballpark to avenge Osip, or Jongleurs, who had arrived in this century for some unknown purpose but perhaps related to the baseball thief.

A third presence among these two displayed the distracted musings of a Divina—and Genjifer knew for certain that such a creature could not be employed as a contemporary guard, nor move freely among the Flüchtlinge, nor travel with the Troupe. So the Divina's presence disturbed her. Still, the other two were the real problem.

Gengifer moved to the other side of the counter, which backed her against the wall of display shelves, where she crouched down and waited.

She slipped two of the pump-action darts from the elastic top of her undergarment, held them in her dominant hand, and unsheathed their needle tips. These two were all she had left with which to defend herself. Because she faced two possible assailants—she could discount the presence of a Divina—Genjifer dared not risk throwing at one and missing. So she would have to deal with the threats individually and at close range—and hope they did not possess weapons that could disable or kill her at a distance. But if she could get to their minds first …

———

Walking down the moving stairway, or "escalator"—which was now stopped for the night—Rydin and Ghost followed Merola in descending to the first level of the store. From the midpoint of the steps he could see almost a hectare of space, all of it devoted to women's clothing, accessories, cosmetics, and jewelry. Rydin opened his eyes wide, engaging his peripheral vision in the semidarkness, and tried to detect the potential movement of a single diminutive female among all that clutter.

"I don't see her," he said quietly.

"Neither do I," Merola replied.

However, with uncharacteristic determination Ghost pushed past them, moved into the store's central aisle, and strode down it with purpose. He stopped in a section where various competing brands of lip glosses, eyeliners and shadows, powders, creams, and herbal treatments were displayed on separate counters. He turned toward one of these, faced the two Jongleurs, who had followed him, and pointed just beyond the counter top, into the narrow place between the counter itself and the wall display.

Rydin and Merola looked at each other. Rydin nodded for her to move around the counter's far end, while he took the near end. He held out three fingers, then two, then one, and stepped into the gap.

The dark-haired Ramsay woman was crouched there, facing in his direction. She wore a startling red dress that left her shoulders and arms bare. She held at least one of the poison darts in her right hand, pointed upward at him.

He felt Cinquemain shift in his pocket, preparing to drill her with his laser.

"Hold your fire," he instructed both of the Silicates. "We need her alive."

Genjifer Ramsay stared at him, with full eye contact and fiercely focused. In the already darkened Nordstrom store, where any color was merely a suggestion rather than a bold statement—except for that brilliant red dress and the woman's jade-green eyes—everything else around Rydin went gray and muted. The world faded except for those eyes boring into him. A voice at the back of his mind, neither male nor female, perhaps the firing of neurons buried deep in his subconscious, began a chant: *"Forget … lose yourself … forget … sleep now … forget …"*

For just an instant, he felt his mind slipping. And then he *remembered*.

"You tried that trick on me before," he said, "and it didn't work then."

Rydin was fully awake when the woman rose, screaming, and lunged at him with a syringe full of nerve toxin. He caught her jab with a sideways, cross-body sweep of his right hand that ended with a tight grip on her wrist. If she held a second syringe in her left hand, then he was dead. But, instead, she tried to pull that trapped hand free, and he saw two steel needles poking beyond the tips of her fingers.

He slid his grip a few centimeters downward, to include that hand, and squeezed. Rydin mentally dismissed the physical inhibitions he had lived with since taking the Simian-ACTN3 treatments, and he *squeezed*.

Genjifer Ramsay howled as he crushed the bones of her hand, shattered the two glass vials against each other, lacerated her palm and fingers with the shards, and forced the silvery liquid into her flesh. He squeezed until her hand was a throbbing mass of tissue under his grip.

She collapsed in an angular heap on the floor, supported only by his right hand.

He dragged her out from behind the counter and arranged her against its front.

Her head lolled and her eyes, still open, stared past him. The chant was gone.

"Is she dead?" Merola asked at his side, looking down on the frozen woman.

"Paralyzed but still breathing," Rydin said. He could still feel a pulse in her.

"Weren't we supposed to bring the three of them back alive?" Merola said.

"We will," he replied. "Just not these three, not from this particular time."

He gathered the Divina and his pilot, Piedeleger, in front of the woman.

"See what you and Ghost can find out from her mind," Rydin said to the Silicate. "I'm betting she is completely relaxed and compliant now. I want to know when and where the three Ramsay siblings arrived in either this century or the last, what they've done since then, who they know, and why they came here now."

"In this truncated state," Piedeleger said, "I am not certain I can communicate all of that with signs."

"Try anyway," he said.

Before he could go on, the Divina faced Rydin, bent over, took him by the shoulders and elbows—just as Ghost had held Merola, briefly, outside the ballpark—and stared into his eyes. Rydin felt a mental pressure, a questing, like the probe that Genjifer Ramsay wielded, and at first he resisted. But where the Ramsay woman had been pushing thoughts into his head,

Ghost was pulling them out, but gently, almost courteously. Perhaps *absorbing* was the better word for what was happening. Rydin relaxed and let his mind simply consider all the things he wanted to know about the three Ramsay siblings.

After a surprisingly short time, seconds rather than minutes, Ghost released him, backed up, and nodded. Then he turned to the slumped woman.

———

Noumisma supported and, at the same time, restrained the fallen woman's shoulders with his lower pair of hands. He took her dark head with a grip on either side using his upper pair of hands. He stared into her fixed and apparently sightless eyes.

There he encountered anger, hatred, resistance, and confusion in a mind that he sensed was stronger than his own and could, with sufficient time and energy, dominate and destroy him. But Noumisma also understood that this mind was locked in a brain that was slowly dying of oxygen starvation. So he had to work fast.

The Jongleur that the others addressed as Rydin—and there was a mind worthy of study in itself—wanted to know the exact place and time and method by which the three Ramsay twins had come into this century from the eleventh millennium, where they, the Jongleurs, and Noumisma himself had all originated.

Noumisma knew how the Jongleurs traversed time, moving up and down the probabilistic path with ease using their flying ships. He was curious what method the Ramsays had employed, and whether it was like the Divina's means of traveling from one probabilistic reality to another—although he had never seen a blending of the two, moving forward and backward in time combined with traversing from one path to another.

To find the Ramsays' secret, he had to scroll far back in the woman's memory, to the place of captivity, first in a Jongleur laboratory, then in a Jongleur prison—scenes and bits of imagery that he understood only from the associations in her own mind—until their moment of escape. This had involved telepathically manipulating their guards and stealing an ordinary liteship. Not much of interest there, as the fugitives' mode of time travel was mechanical after all.

Noumisma gave the Divina equivalent of a shrug and a sigh and moved forward.

The trio had arrived at a place in the moonlight that had no name at this point in the woman's memory. He struggled to find a word associated with it, but came up empty. He did have an image, though, of a modern—for the time—cityscape dominated by two huge broken tusks leaning toward each other. It was as if the city had been visited by a gigantic beast from a different age, an African elephant or Siberian mastodon, that had died and left its teeth on the spot.

Nearby in her memory, Noumisma found another strong image. It was a square building with a portico of four straight columns. High on either side were small, half-circle windows. Above the portico was as square tower with a clock and a spire topped with a small sphere. In the frieze over the columns were four symbols in wrought gold, which Noumisma could not translate, and four golden words in block capitals from the English alphabet, "DEO UNI ET TRINO," which also meant nothing to him.

But the place meant something to Genjifer Ramsay. When he probed further, Noumisma found her and her brothers gathered inside the building, at a table below the figure of a man nailed to, and hanging from, a wooden bar that was supported by a wooden upright. Genjifer was urging her brothers to perform some ceremony or sacrifice, but the meaning of it was lost to him in the woman's fading mind. On either side of her, the two boys each held a long stick or cudgel made of heavy silver. They were using them as mallets to smash a glass sphere against the table's top. Each blow, as the ball skittered around, struck off splinters of glass and bits of gold foil that littered the table's white cloth. One final blow broke the ball into a thousand pieces. In Genjifer's confused mind, the ceremony became clearer: it was both grateful thanksgiving for their escape and gleeful destruction of an animate being, a *living* thing—although how that glass sphere could be considered "alive" was a mystery to Noumisma.

And then, against Genjifer's will, the act had become something else. Out of the air around the three—perhaps through a door, but as likely through the stone and wood of the building itself—a creature or a spirit came to them. It was drawn by their glee and their lust for destruction. The creature's movements were slow and hesitant, silent and curious. Sometimes it stood erect on two legs. Sometimes it dropped to its knees with the support of a lower pair of hands. The figure's head was larger than life size, with bulging eyes. It was draped in a loose robe of iridescent fabric that shimmered as it moved.

Genjifer, in her memory, had been the first to sense the intruder and turn to confront it. In her mind's eye, Noumisma saw the image of his Creator. So this was where the being that the Jongleurs called a Möglich had attached itself to the Ramsays. It happened in a moment of malicious gloating and desecration in a place to which neither they nor it belonged. Noumisma suddenly had a sense of the words above the door, *Deo Uni Et Trino*, Old Latin, "the one and threesome god," an omen that Genjifer had long since studied and pondered.

While Noumisma reflected on this discovery and how he might use it, he sensed a sudden ebbing, a falling through, and then darkness. Genjifer Ramsay had expired.

He backed away from the corpse and stood up.

44. The Broken Teeth

COEL RYDIN WATCHED as Ghost and Piedeleger exchanged signs. The Silicate in her truncated chassis stood on stumpy legs atop the cosmetics counter above the head of the Ramsay woman, who was no longer breathing but still stared off into the distance. The Divina was agitated or excited, signing quickly, sometimes with both sets of hands. His face showed unusual animation and intensity.

"I keep telling him to slow down," Piedeleger said between bursts of movement. "His meanings are getting jumbled."

"Did he find out where and when they arrived in this century?" Rydin asked.

"Yes, so he says. But he does not have a date or place. Nothing I understand."

"What does he tell you? Translate exactly." Rydin ordered.

"He knows how they escaped from the Jongleurs, using their mental powers. He saw in her mind a city, or the outline of one, just the rooftops. It may have been at night. The most remarkable thing, buried in her memory, was two giant teeth, broken teeth, looming over the skyline."

"Giant teeth?" Merola asked.

"He keeps repeating that word."

"What else?" Rydin asked.

"He says he found his 'creator.' He repeats that word several times, along with 'grandfather,' and the sign we've been using for the Möglich."

"We knew the Möglich was following the Ramsays," Rydin said.

"No," Piedeleger said. "Not following. They *called* to him. He came to them in some building made of stone—Ghost had a vision of it, down to the writing above the front door." Piedeleger went on to describe a square structure, with four columns and a steeple, that stood close to—almost in the shadow of—those broken teeth. Ghost had spelled out the golden words above the door with hand signs that shaped the individual letters, and now Piedeleger repeated them, but the inscription meant nothing to either of the Jongleurs.

"Share your exact translation of everything Ghost signed with Cinquemain and Berzher," Rydin instructed. "We might be able to find that building."

"They were performing some kind of rite or ceremony there," Piedeleger said. "They were sacrificing something living, or some kind of animal, and the one Ghost calls the Creator came 'out of the stone'—whatever that means."

"But we still don't know where that is," Merola objected. "What city."

"Or when, within a hundred years," Rydin replied. "Only these 'teeth.' "

"I have an idea," Merola said.

She went behind the counter and came out with a large piece of gray paper, folded in a complex fashion, with two loops of cord attached to one edge. Rydin realized that, when unfolded, it would make a sack for customers to carry off their purchases. Next, she searched among the merchandise scattered on the counter next to Piedeleger and held up a black stick that appeared to be a stylus or pencil. Its tip was sharpened to a point. She put these things into the Divina's hands, where he held them passively.

"Can Ghost draw what he saw of the skyline?" she asked Piedeleger. She pantomimed using the pencil on the flat of her hand.

Piedeleger made signs and Ghost nodded with his vacant smile.

The lower set of hands held the shopping bag level, and the right upper hand began tracing. He made a series of sawtooth lines, one below the other, that might be rooftops. Above them, he drew a pair of curves that, for their smoothness, might be the two sides of an inverted catenary, like a loop of chain suspended from two points, except that these curves extended not downward but up, into the sky, high above the roofline.

And it was not a compete catenary, because the two sides were broken near the top, with jagged edges that Ghost traced in minute detail.

"Those are the teeth he's talking about?" Rydin asked.

"It looks more like a pair of tusks to me," Merola said.

" 'Tooth' and 'tusk' would be the same sign," Piedeleger said.

"That still doesn't help us find the place—or time," she said.

"Not directly," Rydin said. "But I think I recognize the shape."

––––––––

While Rydin stayed to prepare the dead bodies, Merola and Ghost went out into the parking lot to find transportation back to the city, where they had cached their three liteships.

Berzher offered to open the doors of any of the vehicles remaining in the lot, but Merola knew he was functioning on reserve power himself, and neither she nor Ghost knew how to operate twenty-first century automobiles. Instead, she ordered Berzher and Piedeleger to go into suspended mode while she solved the problem.

Merola surmised that, while a taxicab had already worked once in their favor, the vehicle they had flagged with Ghost's help had been passing on a busy street in bright daylight. At this late stage in the evening, however, with all the shops in the Galleria closed, such a conveyance would probably not enter the parking lot. So she led Ghost up the connecting road to the nearest busy thoroughfare, which bore the overhead sign "19th Avenue," and there they waited.

Without Piedeleger's active participation, she had no way to communicate with the Divina, but she tried it anyway. "Get us a taxi?" she suggested. "Like last time?"

Ghost turned toward her with a mystified expression. Then he raised his hand and stepped off the curb. Three cars in a row swerved out of his way. The fourth, which had a rooftop light bearing the word "TAXI," stopped beside him.

The driver was a human being this time. Merola pushed the Divina into the back seat and asked to be taken to San Francisco.

"You're already *in* San Francisco, lady."

"Then take me, us, to Union Square."

She did not want to approach the toy store directly, which she knew from previous experience would by now be cordoned off as an emergency area and perhaps as a crime scene. From Union Square they could walk to the building across the street. Their three liteships, biosuits, and the battle chassis for each of the Silicates were concealed on the roof there, folded into the energy panels so that they would appear, to the untrained eye, as a bundle of plastic scraps.

At the square, she paid the driver with one of the large bills from the wallet Ghost had appropriated earlier that afternoon. When the man protested, "Lady! A hundred is too much," she told him to keep whatever he needed and pulled Ghost off along the sidewalk.

Merola had to wake Berzher up long enough to break into the building, burning through locks on the back entrance, the stairwell, and the exit door to the roof.

Once there, Berzher and Piedeleger installed themselves in fully charged carapaces and began assembling two of the liteships. The components of Rydin's ship, along with his biosuit, helmet, and Cinquemain's chassis, they lashed to the central spar of Merola's ship. Meanwhile, she and Ghost donned their own suits, as they would have no further business in this place.

The trip back to the Galleria took considerably less time and trouble. When they alighted on the darkened roof of the Nordstrom building, Rydin was already waiting for them there with three bundles wrapped in white sheets from the Home Décor department.

Cinquemain scrambled on his stubby legs up the core of Merola's ship, mounted the carapace hanging there, and slid into it with an electronic burble that she interpreted as a sigh of relief. The carapace flexed all eight of its crab legs and both of its claws, then began releasing Rydin's ship and suit.

In five minutes, the third ship was assembled and the three pilots had slung the bodies of the Ramsay siblings beneath all three on cables attached to quick-release joints.

"This will be the same drill as before," Rydin explained.

"They weren't here for 'before,' " Cinquemain said.

"Right," Rydin said. "So we take them well above atmosphere, move westward over the ocean at high speed—but still suborbital—and release the bodies. They burn up and the ashes scatter out of sight of land."

"You don't want to return with them?" Merola asked. "As proof to Captain Tavia that we completed our mission?"

"This mission isn't over," Rydin said. "Not even really begun."

Ten minutes later, above the dark half of the globe covered by the Pacific Ocean, they cut the bodies loose. The three lite-ships hung in space above the release point, to make sure the bundles—which the pilots could track on infrared—indeed entered atmosphere and started burning. Merola strained her eyes and, sure enough, caught sight of three dim, orange trails against the vast dark sea.

"Now," Rydin said over his suit radio, "Merola and Berzher must return to the Jongleur compound in the eleventh millennium and requisition three biosuits."

"Any particular size?" she asked.

"I'd say the Ramsays were a bit taller than average. But I don't mind pinching them—they will probably be unconscious when we bring them home."

"All right," Merola replied. "We obtain suits, and then what?"

"Meet Ghost and me twenty hours from this reference now."

"Meet you here?" she asked. "Hanging over the ocean?"

"No, back in Sane Looie, where this all went wrong.

Dawn was approaching from the far side of the planet as Rydin and Cinquemain flew above the flatlands of the national subdivision called "Missouri," heading toward the big river and the city on its western shore. Rydin and the Jongleurs called the city "Sane Looie," which was a survival of the local rendering, "Saint Louis." The name honored a French king who—as Cinquemain's partial records of the period indicated—had never actually visited the place.

Rydin knew they had arrived when he saw the silhouette of a great steel-plated arch, in the form of an inverted catenary almost two hundred meters tall, rising against the sky brightening in the east.

"Now we need to find a central communications function of the period," Rydin said. "A newspaper office. But where? And how?"

"I remember from the Boskin collection," Cinquemain said, "seeing memorabilia related to the team known as the 'Saint Louis Cardinals.' The collection included an original newspaper with the masthead 'Saint Louis Post-Dispatch.' I would look for their main office."

"How will you find it?" Rydin asked.

"These people were not shy about labeling their buildings," his pilot said. "But for this search I will need more light."

As the sun rose in the sky, Cinquemain disguised the liteship by using the energy of its panels to wring moisture from the air, hiding them in a small cloud that drifted back and forth, north and south, east and west, above the city without regard to the prevailing breezes. The pilot hung below the ship's landing foot, just outside the cloud's perimeter, and made longrange scans of the business district from every angle. Then he retreated up the central core and considered each image from his memory in detail.

"I have a five-story building in brown brick," he finally announced, "on North Tucker Boulevard. That would be the headquarters."

"We should go there," Rydin said.

"Now? With you dressed as a child?"

"All right. Tonight, after they close."

"A newspaper office never really closes," Cinquemain said.

"The part we want won't be open at night," Rydin replied.

They spent the rest of the day hiding among the earthwork domes and pyramids of an ancient city on the other side of the river. Rydin and Cinquemain had visited it once before, when they were flying a crippled ship and needed to stop for repairs. According to records that Rydin had since been able to explore, the place was called "Cahokia" and had been built by a culture that predated Sane Looie's by fifteen hundred years or more. All that was left of it now was an arrangement of grass-covered mounds and a modern museum and gift shop.

After the sun had gone down, they returned to the city and landed on the roof of the building on North Tucker Boulevard.

"What exactly are we looking for?" Cinquemain asked as he folded and cached the ship. He remained in his battle chassis because they didn't plan on meeting anyone inside.

"The records office or library," Rydin said. "Old copies of the newspaper."

"Ah!" Cinquemain said. "You mean the 'morgue.' Probably in the basement."

The entry point on the roof led to an unoccupied stairwell that took them directly to the basement. Rydin carried the pilot under his arm to keep him from jumping down and clattering on the metal steps. The door that was clearly labeled "MORGUE" was locked, but Cinquemain burned that out with one blast of his laser.

Inside, they found an array of machines in booths. Some were obviously digital monitors and keyboards linked to a contemporary computing system; others were some kind of optical image processing linked to spools of analog film base.

"What are we looking for?" Cinquemain asked again, taking control of one of the computing machines.

"The origins of that big arch against the skyline," he said. "Specifically, when it was built. And any photographs of the construction process that match Ghost's drawing."

"Very well. You study the microfilm. I will interface with this computer."

Cinquemain had to show him where the spools of film were stored, based on the little robot's scan of the room. The labeled drawers went back more than a hundred years, to 1878.

"Based on the tensile strength of the steel needed to construct that arch," Cinquemain suggested, "I would not begin my search much before 1950." He pointed to the appropriate drawer.

Rydin took the spool, settled down at a nearby machine, figured out on his own how it worked—including getting the lamp to turn on—and began scrolling through images of the newspaper's front and inside pages, starting with January 1 of that year. After ten minutes of studying the black-and-white images, his eyes were beginning to burn. He still had ten months left in that year alone, plus fifty more spools to bring him up to the present year.

"All done with the computer," Cinquemain announced at his side. "Many references with published images, but they are all current. Nothing historical about the arch's construction. I believe the system must have been converted to digital only recently."

"I'm just getting started here," Rydin admitted.

"You are using your human eyes, of course."

"What else would I be using?" he asked.

Cinquemain motioned for him to get off the chair. Then he hopped up on the console itself, focused his camera stalks on the screen, and began spinning the advance wheel so rapidly that the page images went by in a blur.

"Are you recording all that?" Rydin asked.

"Shut up and get me a dozen more spools."

Within half an hour, the robot had covered the entire history of the city from the middle of the last century. Rydin had no doubt he would retain it all for future reference.

"I can see that I'm still doing the donkey work," Cinquemain said. "Like sorting orchid embryos on the induction plate of your microscope."

"What's a donkey?" Rydin asked.

"Small variant of genus *Equus*."

"Some of us are better at some things than others," Rydin said. "What have you found about building the arch?"

"Construction began in February 1963 and was essentially completed in October 1965. I have seen two dozen publicity photos of the progress between those years."

"And do any of them match the broken curve in Ghost's drawing?"

"Two," the robot said. "One is not quite as complete, from Thursday, September 24, 1964. The second, more advanced than his drawing showed—that is, closer to touching at the tips—from Sunday, October 18, of the same year."

"So," Rydin concluded, "we have a window of just over three weeks in which the Ramsays arrived here."

"Yes, Cinquemain said, "allowing for a lag between the day these pictures were taken and the date they were published, using these primitive technologies."

"Now, what about the building with the columns and the steeple?"

"I had already found that in my page scans. It's the city's old cathedral, now called the Basilica of Saint Louis the King of France. The structure is sited practically under the arch. I even know what the golden words mean: 'God One and Three.' "

"Thirteen?" Rydin guessed.

"Something like that," Cinquemain said. "It is supposed to be a mystery."

"We need to go and meet Merola and Ghost," Rydin said. "We are now overdue."

"Did we set a meeting place?"

"Busch Stadium, where else?"

45. Mistaken Identity

MEROLA TSVERIN, WITH Ghost in tow, landed at the Jongleur compound and went to find Juwana Dyllin, who not only fabricated their exotic materials but maintained the Troupe's supply of unassigned biosuits. Merola found Dyllin in her studio, working on the seams of a suit in pearlescent gray, one that she knew belonged to Captain Tavia.

The young woman looked up and held the heat gun to one side. "Hello, Merola. Need some repairs?"

"Not this time," Merola replied.

Dyllin looked at Ghost, standing in the doorway, and set down the gun. She touched the fingertips of her open right hand to her mouth, then moved the hand to a palm-up position in front of her chest.

Ghost repeated the gesture with his upper hand.

Dyllin next rested the fingers of both hands on her chest and moved them down then up a couple of times. Finally, she held the fingers of her right hand together, rested the little finger against her spread left palm, and slid her right hand straight outward, until its heel rested against the tips of her left fingers. All of these movements were casual and brisk, just flicks of her hands and fingers.

Ghost pinched the skin on the back of his left hand with his right thumb and index finger. Then he bunched his right hand, palm up, and flicked his thumb several times off the second knuckle of his index finger.

Dyllin nodded, bunched her own right hand in front of her chest, palm facing left and holding up her little finger. Then she made a cross on her open left palm with her right index finger.

Seemingly in reply, Ghost held his open right hand, palm facing left, against his right temple and moved the hand forward, as if saluting. He clenched his hands and moved the heel of the right sideways, back and forth, across the back of his left hand.

Dyllin nodded again and made the saluting gesture with her right hand.

Merola watched in fascination. "What was all that about?"

Juwana Dyllin shrugged. "I just asked him how his suit fit. He said it pinched a little. I offered to fix it, and he said later. Apparently, you two are busy."

"Oh, yes. Rydin says we need three biosuits. We're going to try to bring the fugitives back alive."

Dyllin stared at her. "*Rydin* says?"

"Well, yes. He's our team leader."

"I know. But I thought he was … you know …"

"He was *what?*" Merola said, mystified now.

"Never mind. I shouldn't have said anything. It's probably from another part of your mission—a part that hasn't happened yet—or not with you present. Otherwise, you would have come back … afterwards."

"Now you really have me worried about Rydin."

"Just forget it. I'll go get those suits for you now."

"Tell me what's going to happen!" Merola insisted.

"I don't *know* what happened. But watch out for magnetic projectiles."

"Well, yes," Merola said. "But not a lot of those where we're going."

Dyllin touched her arm. "Just take care of yourself. … Be strong."

Then the woman did go into the back room to collect the biosuits.

Merola turned to Ghost—as if *he* might know what she was talking about.

The Divina only looked down at her with a sober gaze and lowered his eyes.

––––––

Berzher to Nexus: "My human wants to know why the Troupe created the Ramsay siblings. What is their purpose?"

Nexus to Berzher: "Genetic modification of the twins was a human project. The Silicates were not involved."

Berzher: "Certainly some of us were. Specific microbiological processes are better left to electromechanical control. Cinquemain, for example, helps his human Rydin in sorting embryos for biosculpting projects."

Nexus: " 'Helped,' past tense. Coel Rydin is no longer among the living."

Berzher: "This is news. I and my human Tsverin left him very much alive in the twenty-first century."

Nexus: "Perhaps he has died since then. Temporal overlaps are also a possibility. Cinquemain brought his body back three days ago. It has since been dissolved and Cinquemain assigned to a new Jongleur human."

Berzher: "Then we must warn Rydin of the danger. How was he killed?"

Nexus: "Cinquemain described the impact from a fifty-millimeter magnetic projectile, and the body's condition confirmed this. Damage to his liteship was also consistent with such an attack."

Berzher: "No weapon firing magnetic projectiles was in use during the period we left."

Nexus: "Whatever the case, Rydin died between that year and his reference now in the eleventh millennium."

Berzher: "I will so inform my human—and Rydin, if we should see him again. But first, did any Silicates assist in creating the Ramsay twins? Search your memory."

Nexus: "There are reports, intercepts of policy and planning documents circulated among the Troupe humans. Probability of actual execution falls below seventy percent."

Berzher: "Summarize anyway."

Nexus: "The humans wanted to create a telepathic variant that would hunt out and destroy Möglichen. Their brains were supposed to resonate in trans-temporal dimensions, offset by twenty to thirty seconds from their own reference now. But the experiment failed. The siblings exhibited telepathic abilities—

one of them is even rumored to be telekinetic—but no temporal abilities. They also expressed severe mental aberrations, extremes of paranoid delusion mixed with sociopathic tendencies. The surviving specimens were ordered to be terminated. However, they escaped before the order could be carried out."

Berzher: "At what stage of development did the Ramsays escape?"

Nexus: "Just past the age of sufficient mental coherence for them to understand moral distinctions and formulate their own intentions and actions. Or seven years, according to the standards of Lune."

Berzher: "Then we are fighting mere children."

Nexus: "Yes. Very dangerous children."

46. A Foretaste of Death

RYDIN HAD THOUGHT that he and Cinquemain would meet with the returning Merola and Ghost on the vacant land beyond the elevated freeways, to the south of Busch Stadium. But when they passed over the ballpark, which was blacked out except for security lights spaced along at the back of the stands, he saw two dark lantern-shapes sitting on the infield grass, glowing faintly with the residual energy at the edge of their panels.

"Land there," he told Cinquemain. "And hope no one else is here to see us."

When his liteship touched down, Merola, Ghost, and their pilots approached.

"Do you want to explain why we came here, to Sane Looie?" Merola asked.

"Because I found your broken teeth, or tusks," Rydin said. He pointed to the Gateway Arch, which glowed in the night sky beyond the right-field bleachers. It was lit by decorative spotlights that shone from below. He then explained about the construction progress photos Cinquemain had found in the newspaper archives, images that matched the drawing Ghost had made and gave a time frame of three weeks late in the year 1964. He also explained how they had identified the building where the three Ramsays attracted the Möglich to themselves.

"They did more than that," Berzher said. "I had a talk with Nexus about the project that spawned these triplets. From what the Silicates have been able to gather, she said the Ramsays' minds were designed to seek out and destroy Möglichen. They were supposed to have temporal as well as telepathic abilities. So they may actually have created the Möglich out of the trans-temporal dimensions."

"And yet they did not destroy him," Rydin suggested.

"They appear to be an imperfect tool," Berzher said.

"So the plan then," Merola said, "is we go back to the beginning of these three weeks in sixty-four, wait by this 'basilica' place until the Ramsays arrive, and take them alive? We just tried that, remember? And we ended up having to kill them."

"Nexus also said they escaped from the Troupe as children," Berzher said. "Seven years or a little older."

"Oh," Merola said. "That should make this easier. Except ..." She turned to face Rydin. "There was talk in the Jongleur compound that something has happened—will happen, from our perspective—to you. It's something bad, but no one would tell me exactly what."

"He dies," Berzher said . "Nexus explained that, too. At some point in this mission, Rydin and his liteship get shot with magnetic projectiles, big ones, fifty millimeters. Cinquemain had already brought his body back for disposal before Merola and I arrived. Somewhere in the transition our individual returns got crossed. But the death is already history in the eleventh millennium."

Rydin heard this announcement without comment. No one liked to contemplate their own death, much less hear about it. It was one thing to know that everyone, everything that lives, eventually dies. His experiences as a Jongleur, spanning millennia, had certainly taught him that. But it was another thing to hear about his death in detail, in the future, confirmed as a fact. And yet ...

"The year in which we will be operating," he told Merola and the Silicates, "hasn't seen magnetic projectors yet, except in people's imaginations. And I doubt that the Ramsays, at the age of seven, would have had the foresight to steal one on their way out of custody. But there are many ways to launch a projectile, and we all should be on the watch for an ambush of some kind."

Rydin paused. He glanced at Piedeleger, who stood beside Ghost and was translating this speech by signing rapidly with both claws. The Silicate was still working through the last bits.

"If we can meet the Ramsays as they arrive back in the twentieth century," Rydin went on, "and capture them before they can create or attract this Möglich to themselves and ultimately to Merola, then we will have changed the world and everything in it—" He waved a hand around, carefully avoiding looking at Ghost. "—back to how life is supposed to be. The Möglich started the process of splitting evolution into competing domains of tetrapods and hexapods. Without him—and we've already killed him once—none of this will exist."

Rydin wondered how much of that Ghost would understand. But then, how much of anything they did got through to the Divina's distracted brain was an open question. Anyway, it was too late to start doubting him how.

"So let's mount up," he finished, "take another neural imprint—because we're going to change our own history yet again—and transit to the year nineteen sixty-four."

———

After she started seeing the misshapen figure at random times and in random places around the Jongleur compound, Captain Tavia started carrying a sidearm. She still was not completely certain that the figure was real—solid flesh completely configured in this temporospatial dimension—rather than a fragment or an afterimage of her overworked imagination. But she could feel the waves of jealousy, anger, and contempt that emanated from it, real or not, and she felt better for being armed.

In the past, as a Proctor with the Lune security service, she had carried an electromagnetic stun stick. The device interrupted nerve impulses in the bodies of transgressors, rendering them temporarily paralyzed without permanent damage. The problem was that, to use the stick, the officer had to get close to the quarry, close enough to touch him with it.

Tavia did not want to get that close to something as malevolent as her stalker.

But during her travels into the past she had become familiar with many different kinds of personal weapons. And she had picked up a souvenir on one of her missions: a Model 1911 Colt point-45 caliber semiautomatic pistol, along with enough ammunition for her to learn to fire it accurately and still have a reserve left over for her own protection.

If the stalker—which she suspected in her private thoughts to be a Möglich that had somehow become attracted to her—was indeed a creature of flesh, she would know how to pierce it. And in case that flesh was tough and resistant to punctures, she spent one evening treating the six bullets she had emptied from the magazine and the seventh taken from the chamber.

Captain Tavia had read up on these guns in the Jongleur archives. She learned that sometimes the tips of bullets were scored or grooved so that, when they hit something solid but not impenetrable, they split open, like a flowering bud, and spread the force of impact. So she had cut the rounded ends of her bullets, through the copper jacket and deep into the lead underneath, with a tiny cross. She then reloaded the weapon and carried it with her in a holster that was another souvenir from the twentieth century.

Her chance came three days later, when she was riding in one of the electric surreys on the road to Lune. Out of the corner of her eye, she saw a shimmering image pass from trunk to trunk in the screen of trees bordering the road.

Tavia slowed the surrey, stepped out on the opposite side, drew her pistol, and waited for the vehicle to pass. When it was clear, she watched the trees and saw the bent-backed figure in the iridescent robe move one more time. She raised the Colt in a steady two-handed grip, took aim, and fired.

The explosion of that first round was loud in the woods.

The figure of the Möglich darted back, and she fired once more.

Captain Tavia advanced and fired a third time at the now scrambling figure.

On the other side of the trunk where she had tracked it, she found the creature. It was crouched down on the four lower limbs, using the upper pair of hands to cover a ragged tear in the robe at its chest where the heart should be. The crooked head with the wide-set, bulging eyes regarded her with hatred but also with open-mouthed horror.

Tavia put two more bullets through the clasped hands, into the sunken chest. Then she fired her last two rounds into the center of the face. Those incredible eyes flicked open one final time and the light inside them died. The thing crumpled into the dirt. But, for every shot, there was no trace of blood, or ichor, or whatever the creature's heart pumped—if it even had such an organ.

This was not done in anger, Tavia told herself. This was temporal pest control, nothing more.

As if to prove it, the misshapen head with the now-blank face started to collapse in on itself and to … fade. The body's exposed limbs became glassy. The robe that was at once no color and all colors together slowly flattened out against the ground. All that was left was a piece of shiny material with three irregular holes in it.

Without this evidence, such as it was, Captain Tavia would have had no proof that the creature had ever existed at all.

Backward

47. The End of the Hunt

Merola Tsverin worked the feet of their first prisoner into one of the three biosuits she had brought back from Lune. The job was made more difficult by the fact that the woman was unconscious and unable to help her navigate the junctures and seams at the suit's crotch, knees, and feet. Fortunately, the prisoner was genetically related to the Jongleurs of Lune, with the same small build and supple limbs; so Merola did not have to contend with emergency patches and field repairs to maintain the suit's integrity.

By the time she had drawn the suit up around the torso and was inserting the limp arms, the woman was starting to rouse from the effects of the blow to her head. Merola considered reinforcing it but feared to do lasting brain damage. As the woman was still groggy, Merola quickly tugged the suit up around her shoulders, sealed the front seam, and snapped the helmet in place.

Before the woman had fully recovered, before the look of surprise and hatred had returned to her eyes, Merola pinned her against the core column of the first liteship that Berzher had erected. It was a matter of two straps that Merola held in her teeth, and a ratchet lock that she closed with her free hand, to secure the prisoner's wrists above her head. With a push of her shoulder, Merola boosted the body off the ground and secured the ankles above the lower struts for the energy panels.

The woman started to struggle. Merola gave the helmet a ringing slap, caught the prisoner's attention inside the face shield with just her eyes, and shook her head.

"Do you have anything that can keep her quiet?" she asked Berzher.

The little robot stopped adjusting the ship's upper struts. "I can set her radio to generate a white noise above the range of human hearing. It will confuse her—maybe even knock her out—"

"Then do it," Merola said.

"It will also open her sphincters."

"Fine. Someone else will take charge of her when we get back. They can clean out the suit."

"Very well then."

Berzher made some adjustment on the inter-suit radio channel, using controls located inside his carapace. The woman's face went slack and her body sagged.

Merola turned to the second prisoner, a young male. He had also started to awaken. She applied arterial pressure under his jawline to put him out again then proceeded to fit him into the second suit. This one was easier to adjust because he was not only of Jongleur stock but also not yet fully grown. In fact, his legs would not quite reach the suit's attached boots nor his hands fit into the gloves. But that was no matter, because he wouldn't be doing any walking or need to grip the ship's handholds for the duration of the flight. How he would get about when they landed him in Lune would be the Troupe's problem.

When she was done and the small male was trussed to the core of the second liteship, she turned to Rydin. "What about the bodies?" she asked.

"Captain Tavia will want them brought back, too," he replied.

"We don't have enough suits for them."

"They are already dead, aren't they?"

"Yes—it's why I asked," she said.

"So, no sense in stinking up a perfectly good suit with the smell of decomposition. Tie them up and suspend them below the landing foot on the other ship. By the time we get above atmosphere, they will be freeze-dried. Not much more can happen to them after that."

Finally, all the pushing, hauling, and tying were done. The three liteships were fully assembled and ready to fly, with the fourth ship bundled and strapped to the core of Ghost's liteship. And Piedeleger had taken charge of the brain-damaged

Silicate. Then Merola and the rest of her party donned their biosuits and stepped aboard. Before she secured her helmet, however, she took one last neural imprint by touching her right forefinger to her left eyelid.

She wanted to remember everything she had done on this mission when they landed in Lune—in a world that had never seen or heard of the invasion of the hexapods. She was going home to her own time and to the life she had always known.

48. A Case of Brain Damage

WHEN THE DAMAGED liteship from the future landed for the third time beside the church under the broken arch, Cinquemain decided to interfere. While Rydin and Merola were taking custody of the last of the Ramsays, an unresisting child who clung to the core's handholds in fright and showed signs of near exhaustion, Cinquemain mounted the ship from the other side. He carefully inserted his carapace between the energy panels, for they were still hot and carried a residual charge. He wanted to see who among the Troupe's complement of Silicates had offered to help these dangerous fugitives and, if possible, take the rogue pilot into custody.

Cinquemain sent the customary recognition signal by telemetry and received in return only the blank hum of a carrier wave.

"Something is wrong here," he sent to Berzher and Piedeleger. "This Silicate is unresponsive."

"We will help," the other two sent back. They stopped what they were doing and came over to the ship.

Cinquemain climbed further into the rigging, positioning himself next to the pilot, who ignored him. The Silicate must have had some awareness, however, because he—or it, or however it might describe itself—was selectively powering down panels and maintaining the ship's equilibrium as the Jongleurs came aboard, took their captive, and left. And he continued to balance the ship when the other two pilots climbed up beside Cinquemain.

"What is the pilot's condition?" Berzher sent.

"Not entirely catatonic," Cinquemain returned.

"Is he aware enough to fly?" Piedeleger asked.

"As nearly as I can tell ..." Cinquemain replied.

But all this time, the pilot still ignored them. His camera stalks did not swivel around to identify the others. His claws gripped their position on the core's external controls. His carapace's umbilicus remained plugged into ship circuitry.

"Help me detach him," Cinquemain sent.

Taking hold of different points on the Silicate's shell and appendages, the three of them tried to pry the pilot from his hold on the central column. He did not actively resist, but his attachment to the ship was stronger at any point than the leverage Cinquemain, Berzher, and Piedeleger together could apply.

In frustration, Cinquemain spoke aloud for the first time. "Detach and unplug!"

The pilot promptly went limp. His claws relaxed. His umbilicus withdrew. His carapace dropped from the column, fell onto one of the bottom energy panels, leaving a glowing circle of blue light where it impacted, and slid through the gap onto the ground. At the same time, the ship automatically powered down—but unevenly, so that the core struck the cobbled surface hard with its landing foot, the uncompensated weight of the three Silicates unbalanced the whole, and the ship rolled onto its side.

When Cinquemain and the others had extracted themselves from the now-dead ship, they went to where the pilot was lying on his back. His claws were splayed out and his eight legs were caught in a halfway clutch. It was the natural pose of a carapace whose brain matrix had been removed.

"Did you kill him?" Berzher sent.

"No, I just … spoke to him aloud," Cinquemain replied. With sudden inspiration, he switched to vocal mode again and directed his words at the carapace. "Get up!"

The claws twitched and began the counter-clockwise rotation that would flip the robot body over. The legs folded on one side and extended on the other to help the process. In a second, the pilot was standing upright with his camera stalks focused on Cinquemain.

"Someone has put this chassis under voice control," Berzher sent.

"How is that possible?" Piedeleger asked. "An empty chassis cannot fly a ship."

"It is not just voice control," Cinquemain sent. "Someone has damaged this Silicate's higher brain functions. How is *that* possible?"

"If you compromised the volition circuits," Berzher sent, "you would get this result."

"Memory, retained skill sets, and logic patterns would probably be unaffected," Piedeleger agreed.

"Poor thing," Berzher sent, with a subtext of dismay and anger.

"We have an active problem," Cinquemain replied. "We will need the pilot to return this fourth ship to Lune in the eleventh millennium."

"He can still fly," Piedeleger observed. "He brought the ship here."

"But how can we give directions when we go above atmosphere?"

"Ah," Berzher said. "Sound in a vacuum. No way to communicate."

"That is a problem," Piedeleger agreed. "We must leave the ship."

"But take his matrix," Berzher sent. "Perhaps we can restore him."

"I would not leave him," Cinquemain sent. "Whoever he might be."

49. Battle Royal

THE BATTLE HAD broken out just as the liteship with its unidentified Silicate pilot came down out of the night sky for the second time. It touched down in the paved space in front of the old stone church with the golden lettering about the One and Three God. At the time, Rydin did not know, and could not tell, what exactly had started the fight—only that the Flüchtling male standing next to him, the boy-shaped man named Nathan, fired his large-bore weapon in the general direction of the ship.

When Rydin had first seen that weapon, he thought it might be some compact version of a magnetic projector. The hole at the end of the tube was certainly wide enough, although not the full fifty millimeters he had been warned about. Besides, the tube was too short and thin-walled for the necessary number of induction rings, and the stock which pressed against the Nathan's shoulder did not appear to have the capacity to store sufficient energy. Or not that Rydin could see, unless these Flüchtlinge had made tremendous technical advances since retreating to the twentieth century.

When Nathan fired, however, the weapon expressed a great deal more flame and smoke than a projector would make. But it did tear a fifty-millimeter-sized hole in one of the ship's upper panels. The panel came apart in tatters with a blaze of blue light that illuminated the whole scene.

In response, the other Flüchtlinge began firing their weapons in all directions. Rydin saw Beckah Courtnay methodically shooting her gas-discharge pistol into the darkness beyond the far side of the church. What she might have seen to shoot at baffled Rydin. She only stopped when the pistol had expended its six cartridges, and then she had to flip open its cylinder and feed in new rounds. Otherwise, her firing was nearly continuous.

Once again, he wondered why the Troupe elected to send Jongleurs into a wild and dangerous past unarmed. True, their Silicate pilots had communications lasers, which made effective small-gauge weapons. And Rydin himself had been treated with Simian-ACTN3 for superior fighting strength. But his muscles were no match against flying projectiles, and his team's Silicates had all been captured by the Flüchtlinge. And yes, Captain Tavia famously carried an antique pistol of her own, but the Troupe considered it an eccentricity arising from her paranoid nature. And Tavia never took it into the past, where she went disguised as a child, as did all Jongleurs, for a time when children were supposed to be helpless, meek, and mild—and never overtly dangerous.

Not so these Flüchtlinge, who all went about heavily armed.

Rydin's clue to the actual nature of the battle that night only appeared when the smoke from the discharge of their weapons, which was thickening in the still air in front of the church, was pierced by a narrow, faintly reddish beam. It cut a semicircular arc across Nathan's chest and dropped him dead. Laser weapons were supposed to be merely theoretical in the twentieth century. And that could only mean the Silicates had somehow freed themselves to follow Rydin, Merola, Ghost, and their Flüchtlinge partners to the rendezvous point.

"Stop shooting!" Rydin shouted. "This is a mistake!"

In all the din, no one heard, and his call had no effect.

But Beckah Courtnay reacted swiftly to his attempted interference, turning her pistol on *him*. But then she hesitated in confusion. And Rydin, with his enhanced musculature, reacted even more quickly. In three long steps he crossed the two meters between them, batted her gun aside—sending it far off into the darkness and breaking her arm—and aimed a punch at her jaw. In mid-flight he regained control of the punch and only gave her a light tap, merely rendering her unconscious and not dead by driving her jawbone and maxilla up into her brain.

"Stop!" he repeated. "Cinquemain! Berzher! Piedeleger! *Power down!*"

With that, the red beams crisscrossing the smoky field winked out.

The Flüchtlinge fired for a second or two more, then stopped.

In the sudden silence, Rydin took stock of the situation. Courtnay lay injured and unconscious on the ground. The remainder of her crew seemed directionless without her. The Ramsay sibling who had been traveling on the liteship—one of the boys, Gjordge or Giuffre—had stripped off his biosuit, hung it on the ship, and stepped away from the core and its tented panels, which offered no protection from gas-propelled projectiles. But he had been killed anyway—once with a ragged bullet hole in his chest, and again by the neat scoring of a laser through his neck.

Their captive from the ship's first landing, the woman Genjifer, whom he had left sitting in restraints on the church's stone steps, was also dead. Whether she had been executed by the Flüchtlinge after the fight started or just caught up in the crossfire was unclear. A bullet to the forehead had cratered her skull and she had fallen backward. In the dim light, Rydin could not study the exposed skin to tell, from potential flash burns and powder residue, whether the shot had been at close range and therefore intentional, or distant and the result of mischance.

The three Silicates stepped out of the shadows beyond the corner of the church. They all appeared to be unmarked. This was hardly surprising, because their carapaces were low-slung and hugged the ground, while the Flüchtlinge had all been firing at human height. Rydin noticed that the Silicates still had their comm lasers exposed and that the lenses busily tracked the Flüchtlinge who remained standing.

"This is a mess," Rydin said. "Did you fire the first shot?"

"Not from us," Piedeleger said. "It came from the coven."

"We thought you were being held captive," Cinquemain said.

"Or that you had escaped and were being ambushed," Berzher said.

"So, once the firing started, you decided to join in," Rydin concluded.

"The liteship's arrival threw in a random variable," Cinquemain explained.

"Machine thinking!" Rydin said. "Fast, complicated, linear—and *wrong*."

50. Where It All Went Wrong

As HER STOLEN spaceship descended out of the night sky, Genjifer Ramsay saw a great river rise up below her. The pilot glided steadily downward and then suddenly had to swing wide, past two huge metal constructions that emerged out of the darkness. They were shaped like giant, broken teeth that leaned toward each other. They were lit from underneath with powerful, white lights, as if the people down on the ground were supposed to see them but pilots in spaceships were meant to fly into them.

She unsnapped and lifted the helmet of the heavy suit that she had needed to fly into space. But with the helmet on, she could not talk to the ship's pilot, a little robot that answered to the funny name "Schnelleziffer." He could only take voice commands, and it was time to tell him what to do next.

"That big, square building down there." She pointed.

"I see it," the robot replied. "What are your orders?"

"Land me in the space in front of it," she directed.

Genjifer liked the look of the place, set in an empty, park-like area that resembled the open spaces around Lune—except that this park was bordered by a wide strip of smooth stone or hardened ground that protected it from the surrounding city. The building itself would be an excellent place to hide while the ship returned for Gjordge and Giuffre.

"Wait for me to take off this suit and put it back aboard, because my brothers will need it. Then go to wherever we left them and bring them, one by one, back here. Can you do that?"

"Same time, same place, three-minute intervals?"

"Yes, I guess. Whatever works. Can you do it?"

"It is not a technical problem," the robot said.

———

Beckah Courtnay and her crew had been following the two Jongleurs and their pet Divina to the old cathedral on the riverfront for three nights now. And each night, from midnight until dawn, while the her people waited in the shadows on either side of the entrance, and the party from the future hid behind the pillars in front of the main doors ... nothing happened.

She suspected that this Rydin had played an elaborate hoax on her and the rest of the coven. In the past, Jongleurs had tried to recapture the free citizens that they called "Flüchtlinge," or fugitives. But Beckah and her people were actually refugees from a punitive cult that maintained iron control of the future. And, from their place of refuge in the distant past, her coven posed no threat to the Troupe des Jongleurs, except as an example to others. They could not even change the time stream leading to that future, or not meaningfully, because well-charted disruptions like the Fire Strike of 2613 AD scrambled the chain of cause and effect that might reach eight thousand years downstream to the Troupe's regime. Her coven only interfered when the Troupe sent its members directly into her era—as it had now.

But here she was, actually helping the Jongleurs, because the fugitives who were supposed to appear one night during the next three weeks posed an even greater threat to both the Troupe and the coven. Even if she still believed that story ...

"The ship is coming," Rydin called in a low voice.

Beckah moved forward, around her corner of the building, and looked into the sky. Beyond the lighted underside of the still uncompleted Gateway Arch, she saw only stars. None of them moved. Nothing indicated a ship was on its way.

She approached the cathedral steps. "How do you know?" she called.

"Ghost senses her mind," Rydin replied. "Now get back out of sight."

Reluctantly, Beckah Courtnay rejoined her group on the north side of the building.

Two minutes later, still looking up at the sky, she saw movement—or rather, the lack of it. Two stars winked out and then reappeared, as if briefly hidden by a shadow. But a shadow of what?

Then a dark shape moved sideways, past the near side of the broken arch. When it became lit by reflection from the city's floodlights, she discerned a pentagonal shape. And when it returned to the darkness beyond the floodlights, she saw that the shape was composed of elongated triangles, like a loosely constructed tent, and that each one glowed blue along its edges. The craft continued descending until it touched the pavement in front of the church.

Beckah expected a team of at least three more Jongleurs, fully armed this time, to storm out of the gaps between the triangles. Then they would join Rydin and Tsverin in taking her and the rest of the coven captive.

Instead, a single person stepped off and stood still for a moment. She was small by the standards of the twentieth century, small even for a genetically streamlined person of the eleventh millennium. She was, in fact, a child of no more than six or seven years.

The child was dressed in one of the Jongleur "biosuits" and carried one of their helmets in her two hands. She reached back into the ship's interior spaces and secured the helmet somehow among its wires and braces—at least, she was not holding it when she backed out again. Next, she unsealed the front of the suit with gloves that barely fit her small hands, while the suit's sleeves bunched up along her arms, as its leggings gathered around the ankles of her boots. She shrugged off the suit, stepped out of the boots, and bundled the whole as compactly as she could. Again she turned and stowed it aboard the ship.

Without a word or gesture, the ship's panels started to glow again, and the flimsy contraption ascended into the night sky. It left behind a little girl in what looked like a hospital gown and slippers, standing on the ground in front of the church.

Why, Beckah Courtnay wondered again, was Rydin so afraid of this child?

———

When the liteship came down for the first time, Merola Tsverin found herself involuntarily stepping back behind the pillar. She had vividly in her mind the fact that, somewhere on this mission, Rydin would be pierced through the body with a fifty-millimeter projectile. And who else would wield such a weapon but fugitives freshly escaped from the future?

But then she remembered the story Cinquemain told back in the eleventh millennium, that he and Rydin had been flying at the time of the ambush, not waiting on the ground. And Cinquemain was not available now to witness any potential attack and compare the circumstances. So the arrival of the Ramsays, under the present conditions, was not likely the case in which Rydin had died, or would die, or whatever.

By the time Merola stepped out from behind the pillar again and into the night, the ship had already landed and its single passenger was stripping off her biosuit. As soon as the little girl—for so she appeared to be—put the folded suit aboard, the liteship took off again. This was proof the Ramsays, even as children, had somehow gained the confidence of a Silicate pilot, which also suggested they had help from inside the Troupe. But that was a problem for later. Curiously, the ship had brought only one passenger—obviously the sub-adolescent Genjifer Ramsay—when it might have carried two or even, given their small size, all three of them.

Rydin had already reached the girl when Merola crossed the open space before the church and stood in the spot where the ship had left. Genjifer faced him with a scowl, obviously not expecting to be taken so quickly. And it was clear from the way Rydin avoided looking at her that he did not want to be drawn into her mental trap.

"You have the restraints," he told Merola.

She produced from her pocket the pair of steel bracelets that the St. Louis coven had provided. The devices closed with a simple ratchet and were connected by three links of chain. But when she took Genjifer's left wrist and closed the first bracelet around it, even with the ratchet pushed all the way to the end, the girl's hand slipped through.

"We should have brought a dart with their paralytic syrup," Merola said.

"If only we had the formula," Rydin replied. "Can you tie her up?"

"With what? We don't have rope."

"Tear out the hem of your jumper."

Merola ravaged her child's disguise, yielding two strips of corduroy cloth about forty-five centimeters long. She pressed Genjifer's hands together—trying not to look into those burning eyes—and bound them with crosswise loops and a knot. Then she knelt and tied the girl's ankles together with the same knot.

"Is that really necessary?" Beckah Courtnay asked. By now, she and her companions had come out of the shadows and gathered in the space where the ship had landed.

"It will keep her from running away," Rydin said.

At his gesture, Merola half-carried, half-dragged the Ramsay girl to the church steps and pushed her down into a sitting position. All this time, the little girl had said nothing at all.

Ghost appeared from his hiding place behind one of the church's pillars. He gestured for Merola's attention, pointed at the girl, then up into the sky. He repeated the upward point twice, as if for emphasis.

"I think the ship's coming back," she called to the group.

Everyone stepped back into the shadows.

———

Cinquemain led Berzher and Piedeleger in their approach to the stone church identified as the Basilica of Saint Louis. Other than the old ballpark, it was the only reference point in the city as of 1964 that their Jongleurs had intended to visit. Therefore, it was the only place that the Jongleurs could be. And the memory that Ghost had drawn from Genjifer Ramsay's mind had shown the three siblings visiting the church at night. Therefore, the Jongleurs would visit it at night.

The Silicates arrived at the west end of the building, opposite the main entrance that faced the river, at two hours and sixteen minutes after local midnight. They crept along the southern wall until they encountered people who waited in the shadows at the corner of the building. Cinquemain scanned them in the infrared range and identified five separate figures with body masses and core temperatures that approximated the coven members who had taken their Jongleurs captive.

"We do not know what the situation is yet," he sent to Berzher and Piedeleger. "I do not see Rydin, Merola, or Ghost."

"I detect weapons," Berzher sent back.

"But held loosely," Piedeleger added.

While they watched, the five coven members suddenly stepped out of the shadows and moved toward the front of the building.

"What is drawing them forward?" Berzher asked.

"I detect a liteship descending," Cinquemain replied.

He signaled to its pilot for an identification code but received only a blank hum. He probed electronically for the radio circuitry of a biosuit, but the passenger had it turned off. This was a curious situation.

"I receive no response from the ship," he sent the others.

"And so, should we move now?" Piedeleger asked.

"Wait until we understand more," he replied.

After a few minutes, the ship rose into the sky, still without acknowledging his calls. He signaled his companions to move forward and wide of the building, so that they might gain perspective on the entrance without being detected.

From that vantage point, the could see Rydin and Merola but with Ghost nowhere in evidence. The two Jongleurs were taking charge of a child, a biological female. She did not resist when Merola bound her hands and feet with strips of cloth. Eleven members of the St. Louis coven had joined them from both corners of the building. As they watched, Merola took the child to the steps and pushed her down. Then Merola called something to the group, and the coven members split, with six returning to the southeast corner. Merola and Rydin retreated to the church steps and hid behind two of the four pillars.

Cinquemain ordered his companions to crouch down, their carapaces resembling stones in the darkness, and did so himself—but with one camera stalk extended to watch what would happen next.

———

Genjifer Ramsay did not try to struggle when the two adults grabbed her after Schnelleziffer took off with her spaceship. The pair, a hard-faced young-old man and a stern-faced young woman, were dressed in funny clothing—loose, floppy, and colorful—like nothing she had seen either in the Jongleur laboratory or the place called Lune.

She tried to probe their minds, first the man's, then the woman's, but they were too strong and disciplined. Or else they had erected blocks against having their thoughts probed and controlled.

Other people came out from around the sides of the building where Schnelleziffer had landed. They, too, wore the same funny kind of clothing. But their minds were more open. Genjifer read questions, doubts, and fear among them. She understood intuitively that they did not like or trust the hard man and the stern woman. But these others were also less sure of themselves—even though they held devices made of metal and wood that, she intuited, were intended to give them strength and dominance.

It was a curious situation.

Genjifer probed more deeply and discovered in random thoughts among the people standing around her what the devices were meant to do. They were *weapons*, instruments of death and destruction, designed to be used against fragile human flesh.

She did not resist when the stern woman tried to shackle her with metal rings and then resorted to tying her wrists and ankles with strips of cloth torn from her clothing. Genjifer did not resist when the woman dragged her to the steps of the building and pushed her down, because she already had a plan for those weapons.

She could see it play out in her mind.

51. Out of the Box

CINQUEMAIN TRIED TO decide whether the human emotion proper to the current situation, if he chose to express one at all, would be humiliation or frustration. Humiliation, because he and his Silicate companions had been captured so easily. Frustration, because there seemed to be little they could do to free themselves.

His two large pincer claws and eight claw-tipped legs were trapped in the bag of tightly-woven jute fibers that the St. Louis coven had used to ensnare and handle him. And, presumably, Berzher and Piedeleger had been taken the same way. Then their captors had placed them in a large iron box or chest, piled one on top of the other in a too-small space. If the Silicates had been the earthly crustaceans they resembled, they would have fought each other for space and dominance until one of them was killed to give the others barely more freedom of movement. Fortunately, they were rational beings and could reason their way out of their predicament.

"Who is on top of this heap?" Cinquemain sent to the other two.

"I detect a flat metal plate above me," Piedeleger answered.

"That is the underside of my carapace," Berzher sent.

"Tap with your legs if you can," Cinquemain sent. "I will drum in numerical sequence. Berzher will alternate four legs on the left side, four on the right. Piedeleger will alternate two fore pairs with the two hind pairs."

For a few seconds the box rattled with the muffled thumps of twenty-four crab legs twitching in their own order.

"I sense four legs in a left and right pattern," Piedeleger sent.

"So I am on top," Berzher sent, "as I cannot feel anything."

"That puts put me at the bottom," Cinquemain finished.

"Excellent!" Berzher replied. "Now what do we do?"

"Obviously, we should cut our way out of the box," Cinquemain replied.

"If only I could get my comm laser free of this bag," Berzher
sent.

"We will have to work together on this," Cinquemain said.
"Rip and tear the front of your own bag with your main pincers. Then we can all push backward with our legs to slide the
bags off ourselves and from the one below us."

"What if we are facing different directions?" Piedeleger
asked.

"Then push in opposite directions," Cinquemain replied.

The jute fibers were strong, and the claws they wielded
had no true cutting edges. But the hydraulics built into their
carapaces were stronger yet. After ten minutes of ripping and
shucking. The three Silicates had a measure of freedom. But
they were still in the dark.

Cinquemain exposed a camera stalk and set his comm laser
as far as possible and on a wide-beam dispersal that the camera sensor could pick up as infrared. The image showed only
two side walls and the bottom plate of the box he was trapped
in, with the rounded underside of Piedeleger's carapace above
him. From the carapace's orientation—and the struggles they
had to make to free themselves from the bags—he concluded
that Piedeleger and he were facing the same direction. Piedeleger informed him that Berzher seemed to be facing in the
opposite direction. Still, two out of three was a start.

"We can burn through the wall of this box," he told the
other two.

"But we do not know how thick the metal is," Piedeleger
sent. "What if we drain our energy reserves before breaking
through?"

"The alternative is to stay boxed in until our reserves run
out," Berzher replied.

"Piedeleger and I will concentrate on the plate in front of
us," Cinquemain sent.

"What if it backs up to a wall or other obstruction?" Piedeleger suggested.

"Then we will concentrate on the plate to our left side," Cinquemain sent.

"Not the one to the right?" Berzher suggested. "Just for sake of asking."

"We have to start somewhere," Cinquemain sent. "Front and then left."

He and Piedeleger fine-tuned their lasers and started cutting. Piedeleger worked along the top, as high as she could aim, and down the right side of the panel. Cinquemain cut the left side and bottom edge. Because no light leaked through their cuts, no matter how deeply they probed, the two Silicates could not know whether they were penetrating the metal or not.

Soon, rivulets of melted iron were running across the floor of the box and scoring the bottom of Cinquemain's main claws and the front edge of his carapace. But the marks did nothing to reduce his function, and nothing hurt in the human sense. Anyway, he could requisition another chassis once they returned to Lune. He continued cutting.

When the cut outlines were completed on all sides, Cinquemain instructed Piedeleger to push against the piece with her claws, and he did the same. The square of metal held in place for a second, then gave way, falling outward into darkness.

Cinquemain and Piedeleger wriggled through the gap and out from under Berzher's chassis. Soon the third Silicate joined them, emerging backward through the square hole.

The three found themselves on a concrete floor in a blacked-out room.

"Now what do we do?" Berzher asked. It was clear that he deferred to Cinquemain, who was pilot to Rydin, the senior Jongleur on Search.

"We find our humans," he sent. "And your Divina," to Piedeleger.

"And where would the humans and Divina be?" Piedeleger asked.

Cinquemain considered. "We have two local reference points …"

"Either at the ballpark or the basilica," Berzher suggested.

"Then do we roll a random number?" asked Piedeleger.

"It is near midnight in this time frame," Cinquemain said. "They will be watching at the basilica. So there we will go."

52. Escape to the Twentieth Century

ONCE HER BROTHER Gjordge had broken the parts of the robot's brain that made it move around and do things of its own accord, like a living creature, it had become much more manageable. Genjifer discovered that the robot would only answer to the odd name "Schnelleziffer"—a name that even Jazdal Halek, who was its Jongleur keeper, could not explain. Because the thing would now only respond to spoken words, and took them all very literally, Genjifer had to think carefully about her instructions and probe Jazdal's mind when she didn't know the right words.

For instance, "Bring me your spaceship" got no response. Genjifer had to ransack the young Jongleur's thoughts, while Giuffre pinned her brain's motor functions against escaping, to retrieve the proper words: *liteship,* for the thing the Jongleurs used to travel in space and time, and *requisition,* as the way these liteships were assigned to the Jongleurs and their robot pilots. It was all very complex.

But still, nothing happened when she spoke the right words.

"What is the mission?" Schnelleziffer asked automatically.

Genjifer probed Jazdal's mind again, and learned that the Troupe des Jongleurs would only assign ships to teams that had a purpose for their travels backward, or upstream, in time.

"Then take us someplace safe," Gengifer said.

"Define 'us,' " the robot said. "Define 'safe,' "

She turned to the Jongleur, who gazed back with tears in her eyes. "Where is the last place you went with this pilot?"

"A training mission," Jazdal said under compulsion. "Just a short hop above the atmosphere. And nowhere in time. ... I'm not ... a real Jongleur yet."

Genjifer considered this. Then she turned to the waiting robot. "Where was the last place *you* went? *In time?*"

"Sane Looie," it replied. "Mid-twentieth century."

"And what was your mission then?"

"Hunting the Flüchtlinge."

Genjifer went again into the Jongleur's mind to find a definition: *fugitive, refugee, saboteur, transient, traveler*. Any of those would describe herself and her brothers.

"Your mission is to find the Flüchtlinge," she told Schnelleziffer.

With that, the little robot hopped off the table and left the treehouse.

"How long will it take to get us a ship?" Genjifer asked Jazdal.

But the young woman was exhausted now. All Genjifer could find when she probed the tired brain was the image of those eight little metal feet picking their way along a roadway of crushed chalk. Traveling thousands and thousands of meters of crushed chalk. And then negotiating with a mechanical being called "Nexus." And such negotiations didn't always go easily. So it was going to take a long time.

Frustrated—but also mindful that she didn't want to damage the Jongleur's mind—Genjifer relaxed her hold and let the brain lapse into sleep.

———

Giuffre Ramsay had been following his sister's dialogue with the crablike little robot. And he understood both sides of the conversation, because he had also been inside the young female Jongleur's brain, right alongside Genjifer. So he shared her dismay when they heard the call from outside the treehouse and went out to see Schnelleziffer arrive back in Lune with the "liteship."

Instead of an enclosed capsule, some kind of saucer, the usual thing that people meant when they said "ship," this was a contraption of sticks, filament, and shiny fabric. The word "flimsy" passed through his sister's mind, along with a trailing flavor of scorn and rising anger.

Genjifer awakened the young woman without asking for Giuffre's restraints and force-walked her out of the treehouse.

"What is this?" his sister demanded aloud.

"It's a ship," Halek replied, and her mind formed *liteship.*

"How do you ride it into space? How do you *breathe?*"

"With a biosuit," the woman replied, and Giuffre saw in her mind a thick garment, like a bag enclosing her whole body, with a heavy helmet covering her head.

"Do we have to requisition that as well?" Genjifer asked, angry now.

"No, I keep my suit here at home. It's ... new."

"Get it for me." And Genjifer added the mental instruction to Giuffre to follow her inside the tree and be ready to lock her limbs if she deviated from the instruction.

He left his sister and brother outside, watching the little robot that clung to the central spar of the huge black kite as it hung over the gravel path and surrounding green lawn.

Inside, Jazdal Halek went into a separate chamber with a vine hammock for sleeping and opened a spacious compartment that grew out of the trunk. She removed the garment and helmet that Giuffre had foreseen and carried them back outside.

"This is my suit," she said in response to a mental probe Genjifer sent. "It is stocked and primed for travel. I was ... awaiting my first assignment."

"One suit," Genjifer said, and Giuffre sensed the complication when her mind reflected, *Three of us.*

"This is a problem," Gjordge said.

"We can requisition two more," Genjifer said. "It will only take time."

"No, you can't," Jazdal Halek spoke up. "The suits are fitted to each Jongleur. You would have to present yourselves to the Troupe in order to have yours made."

"You know that is not going to happen," Genjifer said.

"You have to go in our place," Giuffre told his sister. "Take this suit, go to this Sane Looie. You will be free."

"And what about you and Gjordge?" she asked.

"Send the ship and the suit back for us," he said.

"It will follow repeat instructions," Gjordge said.

His sister hesitated, then took the garment from Halek's unresisting hands. It was too large for Genjifer by half. She had to bunch up the sleeves and legs of the woman's suit to reach into and secure the gloves and boots. She took the helmet in hand and made Halek—under compulsion, with Giuffre's guidance—show her how to climb aboard the liteship and where to place her hands and feet.

"If this time travel is nearly instantaneous, at least from your ... perspective," Genjifer said, and Giuffre could feel her dig the thoughts simultaneously out of the Jongleur's brain, "then this ship should return in just a few minutes. Each of you follow me in turn, and let the robot take you wherever I went."

Yes, sister, Giuffre and Gjordge replied with a single thought.

"And if anything happens ..." She left the thought hanging.

"We will be together in our minds," Gjordge volunteered.

Giuffre echoed the thought, "And in our ... hearts ... our souls."

With that, Genjifer Ramsay fitted the helmet to the suit ring around her neck and rode the black kite up into the sky.

53. Mutual Distrust and Cooperation

COEL RYDIN DID not trust Beckah Courtnay. But the only way to get himself and his team out of their current predicament and proceed with their mission was to *appear* to trust her, and that meant telling her and the St. Louis coven the truth.

"We are seeking three fugitives from the eleventh millennium," he said.

"Escapees from the Jongleur tyranny," the coven leader said. "As are we all."

"No, not like you. Not refugees, but criminals. They will present in the current time frame as children, not just as a disguise, but because they *are* children. Seven years old at most."

"And how have these children, *real* children, attracted the Troupe's attention? What crimes have they committed?" Courtnay asked. "And how then did they manage to escape into the past?"

The first part of that question Rydin knew better than to answer. The second part he did not know. So he told what part of the truth he could tell.

"All I know is that they are dangerous." He shook his head. "Two boys and a girl, all siblings and possibly fraternal triplets. Genjifer, Gjordge, and Giuffre, surnamed Ramsay. They are all telepaths, but with varying psychic abilities. We do know that the girl is the strongest, their leader, and a pure sociopath."

"All at the age of seven?" Courtnay chuckled.

"She can be extremely manipulative," he said.

"And you two have dealt with these children before?"

"Yes," Merola said. "At least twice. And each time we did—"

"—and each time," Rydin cut her off, "we barely managed to escape."

It was no good telling these Flüchtlinge, isolated and trapped in time as they were, that the Jongleurs had already killed the Ramsays. Rydin had personally dispatched Genjifer twice—once in the home of Bill and Emily Windlace, on his first mission to rescue Merola Tsverin, and more recently in the Nordstrom cosmetics department—and each time it had produced no lasting effect.

"So! Now we are warned," Courtnay said. "We will watch out for them. We don't need a pair of Jongleurs to do that."

She nodded to the two men from the coven who stood behind Rydin and Merola with those hammers. Supposedly, it was the signal to strike.

"But telepathic psychopaths are not the worst of it," Rydin said quickly.

"Oh? There is more to your story?" But she signaled again to the men.

"Together, the Ramsays summon a monster. Here, in this time frame."

"And what does this monster do?"

"It changes the world," Rydin said.

———

Beckah Courtnay did not trust the Jongleurs, particularly this Coel Rydin. But the only way out of their current impasse was to *appear* to trust him—that, or kill him and his companions outright. But then there was the possibility that he was telling the truth about these children from the future and the monster they would bring.

"Tell me about this monster," she said.

"The Ramsays give it entry into this world. Soon, perhaps even tonight, because we are now in the window of their arrival. It's a Möglich, a being at the edge of time—"

"We've all heard of your Möggy-things. They are a fantasy."

"No," Rydin said. "An actual creature—in the full sense of that word, *created* out of time's vagaries by human intention. It then persists and does mischief until it can be unmade or killed."

"Another Jongleur fairy tale."

"No," Merola Tsverin said. "I saw this thing myself. We went—I went—back to the Devonian period as part of a scientific tour by the Sindicato della Conoscenza, and the creature had attached itself and was following me. It tried to change the course of evolution and only partially succeeded."

"It decided to poison the water," Rydin explained, "in the place where our evolutionary ancestors, the lobe-finned fishes, first emerged on dry land. The Möglich set loose a virus that created all this." Here Rydin waved toward the Divina that stood next to the Tsverin woman. "I tried to stop it with an antivirus, but the cure was not completely … effective."

"What 'all this'?" Beckah said. "You mean your pet Divina?"

"No, all of them. All of the class of hexapods, the six-limbed variants of the warm-blooded animals you know. This Möglich created them in his own image, because *he* had six limbs."

"Then you are crazy," she said. "The hexapods have always existed."

"Not in our time," Rydin said.

"And what time would that be?"

"A world not very different from yours," Merola Tsverin said. "But everything there walks—or used to walk—on four legs. Or with two legs and just two arms. Or flies with two wings and not four."

"Your future world is like that?" Beckah asked.

"Our world was always like that," Rydin said.

"Until this Möglich changed it," Tsverin said.

"Now we want to change it back," he finished.

———

Rydin watched as Beckah Courtnay considered their story. He knew he was asking her to believe in a world that—for her—had never existed. It was also a world that might seem to be *less*—less complete, less exotic, less interesting—than the world she knew. But it was the world as it was always meant to be, before this particular Möglich came into being and did its dreadful work. It was the *natural* world, the *unaltered* world. And it was the whole reason that he and Merola and Ghost had come to this place in this time.

"I don't care about your world," Courtnay said. "One way or the other."

"But—" Rydin began.

"But these Ramsays, appearing suddenly in Saint Louis, as you say they will, could be a danger to us. To my people here. We exist by keeping a low profile, by blending in, by not calling attention to ourselves. And a trio of telepathic psychopaths would be hard to keep in line. They would stand out."

"Yes," Rydin said.

"So when are these three, the Ramsays, supposed to arrive here?"

"Sometime in the next three weeks. They will come at night."

"And where do you think they will land?" she asked.

"At the old stone cathedral, down by the river."

"I know the place. Not much visited after dark." Courtnay was still considering, and Rydin let her. "Then my people and I will help you catch them. After that, you can take them back where they came from." She paused. "On the condition that you, the Troupe, all the Jongleurs, leave us alone, forever after."

Rydin nodded. "Agreed." And then he paused. "But we have indications that the Ramsays might have brought weapons from the future." There was no need to say that the indication was his own body, punctured and rendered inert, in an ambush.

"We are not exactly defenseless," Courtnay said, holding out her snub-nosed .38 revolver. She nodded at the other gas-discharge weapons her people held. "We can protect you."

"The Ramsays' weapons would be bigger. Magnetic projectiles."

Courtnay aimed at the warehouse floor and fired. The bang was loud. The soft-lead bullet tore a gout out of the concrete.

"These are fifty millimeter scale," he said. "Moving at about Mach five."

"I see," she said. "And what are you proposing?"

"At least return our pilots. They have laser weapons and impeccable aim."

"Ah, that. And they could probably pick off all my men in a second or two."

"The Silicates would have no reason to fire on you," he said. *Unless I ordered it,* he added mentally. "Besides, they are the only ones who can converse with our Divina. They do it by making and interpreting signs."

"One of my group knows that language and can interact with your Divina, if it becomes necessary" she said. "No, the robots stay in the box."

Rydin nodded again, in resignation. And when this mission was done, he decided, he was going to take this difficult woman back to the eleventh millennium for the Troupe to deal with. Either that, or he was going to kill her.

54. The Place of Needles

Genjifer Ramsay knew she had to do something for herself and her brothers. The last time she looked into the mind of the woman who styled herself *Captain Tavia,* she saw only disappointment and dark resolution. The familiar thought that sometimes lingered there, centered on the *wiggly genes from the pale people*—whatever those were and whoever they were—had been slowly fading. Now it was beyond reach.

After that last encounter, the other people in the white place that Tavia thought of as *the lab,* had moved the three siblings to a smaller holding place, which was just *the cell*. This one was still white, but it had no bright cushions, no stimulating toys and games, nothing to do. It was bare tile and a sink-with-toilet-seat, with a grated drain in the center of the floor. After they had been taken there, Gjordge fretted and Giuffre moped. And then both brothers lapsed into silence and stillness, which was worse.

Genjifer schemed. She had to, because when she looked into the mind of the dottore who attended them, she saw only steel needles. These were not the kind that the lab people stuck into her and her brothers' arms to take samples of their red blood or to make them sleep. Instead, these injected a blue-colored *something-not-nice*. And after that, in the mind of the dottore, there was always darkness and a thing she imagined was *death*.

Their first night in this barren cell, Genjifer had invited Gjordge to study the lock on the door. "Locks are made of parts," she told him. "You are good with parts, aren't you?"

He stared at the metal plate below the handle. It was blank on this side, the inside, but she had seen when the door was first opened to admit them, and again whenever it opened to admit the dottore and the keepers, that it had a tongue and a mouth, just like all the other doors she had seen.

And on the outside was a pad with numbered buttons. Gjordge could have pushed them with his mind, except he didn't know which ones and in what order. The lab people always concealed the buttons with their bodies and thought of other things when they pushed them. So her brother had to work on the lock itself.

"Make the tongue draw back," she urged. "Push with your mind."

But after a long time staring, he shook his head. "No parts inside."

"What 'no parts'!" she said. "All doors have parts."

"Not this one. It's got an iron rod and a coil. A magnet."

"So? Work on the magnet," she ordered. "Open that door."

Gjordge stared again. "It's just too strong for me. It won't go."

If Gjordge couldn't move the lock, Genjifer had to dig the keypad sequence out of the minds of the dottore and the keepers. But then she thought of a bigger problem. Once they were out of this cell, where would they go? How would they survive? They only knew this place of the white tiles and, once before, the bright cushions, the games, and the needles. To escape and survive, she and her brothers needed to find someone on the outside who could help.

Genjifer probed for a measure of kindness among the minds that were within easy reach during the day. She found only the dottore, who had the death thoughts, and the attendants, who had no sweetness when she sampled them. To their minds, Genjifer and her brothers were a kind of animal, an *experiment,* and due for *termination.*

But at night, after the lights embedded in the ceiling dimmed from hard white to pale gray, and all the other, clustered minds had wandered out of reach, she found one. This mind registered as neither dottore nor keeper. More like a watcher. And unlike the others, it radiated sunlight, hope, and eagerness— the effect of what the dottore thought of as *endorphins.* But the watcher's brain was also tired, veiled in *fatigue poisons.*

And that made this mind perfect for Genjifer's purpose.

———

As a new recruit to the Troupe des Jongleurs, and not yet trained and tested for traveling in time, Jazdal Halek had to perform her share of menial duties around the compound that, actually, anyone else could do without all that training and testing. In her case, the assignment was to guard the genetics laboratory on the night shift.

She wouldn't mind watching the place during daylight hours, because the work there was supposed to be interesting. The lab's technicians found a purpose for—and made use of—all the genetic samples that full-fledged Jongleurs brought back from earlier millennia and centuries. But during the day there were really no intruders to guard against. Actually, there were not many potential break-ins at night, either, because the compound itself was so heavily defended.

It was a boring job, then, made worse by the fact that she was supposed to stay awake and alert the whole time. And Jazdal still had her full schedule of combat and flight training during the day to qualify her for Jongleur status. Well, it could have been worse. She might have been assigned to garbage detail in the kitchen or cleaning bathrooms in dormitories.

She was sitting at the reception desk outside the laboratory's main entrance and, truthfully, was beginning to nod off when an image appeared in her mind. Three sad-eyed, dark-haired children, two little boys and a little girl who was close to tears. They were being held captive in a cold, white cell inside the laboratory, behind those entry doors. They were properly the Jongleurs' own children, rightful heirs to Troupe status, being held against their will. And they had done nothing wrong! It was all so unfair! They hadn't done anything! And they were being punished anyway!

Nothing in Jazdal's training or instructions for this guard post had suggested that human beings were the subject of genetic experiments. So, if children were being imprisoned in the laboratory—even naughty children—it was a mistake, because the compound had its own detention facilities, and they were not connected with the lab but located on the other side of the quadrangle. And who would put such sweet children in jail in the first place?

Jazdal got up from her chair and, using the special key she had been entrusted with, opened the doors behind her. She had never actually been shown around inside these rooms, but somehow everything seemed familiar. She moved with unerring instinct to a side corridor, down its length, to a glass door at the end.

The sad-eyed little girl was standing right behind it. Her arms hung at her sides. Her mouth bunched up as if she was about to cry. She gave Jazdal a pleading look with her incredibly green eyes.

"You poor thing," Jazdal said, mouthing the words, because she was sure the glass was soundproofed. She peered into the semi-darkness beyond the girl and, sure enough, two boys—dark haired just like her—were huddled in a far corner. Three children exactly as she had imagined.

"I should let you out," Jazdal said aloud, but more to herself. "We can sort this all out with the Troupe administration in the morning." She moved her hand with the key toward the door's lock plate, but there was no keyhole. Instead, the door had a pad with numbered buttons.

"I'm sorry. I don't have the combination," she said, wishing she could do something for the children. And, as if in answer, a string of numbers came into her mind. Almost automatically, she used her forefinger to push the right buttons in sequence on the pad.

The bolt clicked, Jazdal stepped back, and the door swung outward with a little whisper of escaping air pressure. The girl moved out into the corridor, still staring at Jazdal with those amazingly sad eyes, green eyes, which seemed to be growing larger and greener by the minute. Behind her, the two boys appeared to wake up, rose from their crouch, and left the cell.

"What am I going to do with you?" Jazdal said, mostly to herself. "The Ringmasters won't be able to hear your case until the morning."

The little girl, whose name was *Genjifer,* tipped her head.

"I had better take you home for safekeeping," Jazdal said.

———

The Jazdal woman lived in a tree. At least it looked like one of the things called *trees*, which Gengifer Ramsay had sampled from the woman's mind. When they arrived just after dawn in the place the woman thought of as *Lune*, it was filled with many of these stately growing things. And these looked deceptively like the others along the road they had just traveled away from the Jongleur compound.

But inside, the treehouse had rooms with wooden floors and furniture that grew out of the floors and trunk. The walls were made of overlapping green leaves that glowed on the side with the rising sun's light. The rooms on the far side of the trunk and still in shadow were lit by biolume strips—the same lights used at the compound, except that these lined the upper branches instead of a ceiling. As daylight grew, these strips automatically dimmed and went out—which was just the reverse of Genjifer's life at the compound.

For the triplets, it was all new and magical.

And then they discovered that Jazdal Halek had a marvelous toy of her own. It was a mechanical crab that marched out of a hidden closet and greeted the Jongleur woman with spoken words.

"What in the static hells is this?" the toy demanded, waving a claw at Genjifer and her brothers.

"These are my three new friends," Jazdal said obediently.

"I just received an alert from Nexus," the robot replied. "These are escaped prisoners. You have abetted them. This is a serious crime."

"No, I—" Jazdal started to say.

Genjifer increased the hold on her mind.

"—am helping them. They are orphans and need shelter."

"I will have to alert Nexus about this situation," the robot replied.

Genjifer tried to command it with her thoughts, but the machine appeared to be immune to telepathic control—if it even had a mind. So instead, she issued a command to Jazdal's brain.

"Do not … *tell* … anyone," the woman ordered.

"This is a breach of protocol," the robot said.

"It will be my … responsibility," she said.

"The Troupe will expel you for this."

Genjifer tightened her grip again.

"Does not matter," Jazdal said.

———

His sister had given Gjordge a difficult problem to solve. The only way the three of them could be safe forever was for Jazdal Halek to fly them through space and time to a distant past where the Troupe des Jongleurs did not exist. Genjifer could easily enough order Halek to do this, but the trip required the cooperation of her robot, whose name was revealed as "Schnelleziffer." And this mechanical creature, who was the only one who could pilot the Jongleur liteships, was stubborn.

Neither Genjifer nor Giuffre could change its mind. And that meant Gjordge had to work on it mechanically, using his telekinetic fingers. At first, he tried a few gentle touches and probes inside that metal shell. The robot did not seem to notice. But with his mind Gjordge could only see pistons and levers, more of those iron cores wrapped in magnets, some warm blocks of soluble crystals that contained an electric potential, and a glass ball that seemed to have no real purpose. None of it he understood directly. And nothing looked anything like a brain.

When he confessed all this to his sister, she confronted and probed Jazdal Halek's mind to find out what they needed to know. And Genjifer learned that the woman actually knew very little about her mechanical pilot and companion. But she did have a manual, a handbook issued to all Jongleurs in tablet form. It included a description of the so-called "Silicates" and their various functions and capacities.

Gjordge took the square of glass and metal from Halek and turned it this way and that. The woman touched a button in the frame, and the glass surface came alight with black squiggles.

"What is this?" he asked.

"It's writing," she replied.

With all of the tests and training they had received in the Jongleur laboratory, none of the three had been taught how to read, although they understood the concept from the notes the dottore and his attendants took on their progress.

"Have her read it to me," Gjordge told his sister.

So for hours the woman sat cross-legged on the treehouse floor and read aloud from the manual. Gjordge tried to follow along, quietly probing the robot's carapace while the creature sulked in its closet. He quickly learned that the glass ball he had earlier dismissed was the key to its activation. The ball contained many layers of an element called "silicon" that had been doped with atoms of lightweight metals to become a "semiconductor." These layers had then been wound and wrapped in networks of gold foil and wire to carry electric currents in a maze of channels. Gjordge used his tiniest mental fingertips to trace out these pathways in the robot's brain and soon became confused. They were too many, too complex, too interrelated!

"But how does it *think?*" he finally asked Halek.

The woman ran her finger along the edge of the tablet, stopped at a place, and read aloud: "The volition circuit is the core of Silicate intelligence and the motivator of its decisions and actions. In essence, the circuit is a random number generator, which periodically issues an unpredictable single digit from zero to nine. This digit provides a variable that affects the operation of other circuits in the matrix. Generating random numbers approximates the condition that, in a human being, would be called 'free will.' "

"Does this circuit operate all the time?" Gjordge asked.

"I don't know," she replied. "It just says 'periodically.' "

That would have to be good enough. Gjordge would have to take a chance. Of the many bits of foil and wire, only one gave off little bursts of that electrical energy while the robot lay dormant in its closet. These bursts came as regularly as clockwork, and each time they had a slightly different strength. If that wasn't a "random number," Gjordge didn't know what else to look for.

With the tiniest telekinetic pinch, he severed the gold wire exiting that circuit.

55. Into the Box

Beckah Courtnay and her coven were preparing to bed down for the night in the old warehouse attached to an abandoned factory, a dozen blocks from Sportsman's Park, when Nathan came running in.

"They're here! They're here!" the disguised man-child said breathlessly.

"Who's here?" she demanded. "What are you doing out at night alone?"

That stopped him. "Um … I was out at the ballpark."

"There's no game tonight. So what were you doing?"

"I was keeping watch," he said. "In case they come."

"Who is coming? A rival gang of children, perhaps?"

"No!" He snorted. "The Jongleur invasion. It's here."

That stopped her. Once, maybe ten years ago, the Troupe des Jongleurs had sent a party to hunt down the temporal fugitives living in St. Louis. The fear was that these escapees from the far future might do something in the past to upset their precious time stream—as if anything a small group who just wanted to be left alone could do to change history. Not when that history was already upset with civilization collapses and natural disasters that wiped out everyone's day-to-day lives.

But the memory of that hunting party, and the ruthlessness of the Jongleurs in general, made for a good bedtime story. Fear of being captured and returned to servitude was one of the ways Courtnay retained control of the coven. The downside of telling this story, however, was that once or twice a year one of her brood would think they had seen another invasion, and then everyone would be up all night.

"All right," she said. After all, it would hurt her authority if she simply dismissed Nathan's story. "Everyone get ready for battle."

"Should we bring along hammers?" Malvina asked.

Courtnay turned to Nathan. "Did you see spiders?"

"Yes, they were folding up their big black kites."

"Then take your hammers and the burlap bags."

———

The three Silicates had finished caching their liteships in the darkness under bleachers in the old ballpark's outfield, and Merola had just taken her final neural imprint, when two children appeared in the dim light from safety lamps above the dugout along the first-base foul line.

Two was not three, Merola decided, and the Ramsay's always traveled in a group. So perhaps these were just normal human children after all. In any case, she pointed them out to Rydin. By the time he had spotted and focused on them, two had become five, then eight. And more were coming out from the third-base side. Three more followed the Silicates back across the grass from the outfield.

"This looks like a welcoming committee," Rydin said.

"They're just children," she said, and then she noticed.

"Children in this time frame don't go armed," he said.

Every one of them was carrying a weapon of some sort. Most were just baseball bats—which was almost to be expected, given their venue. But some of the things they held were the elongated tubes with wooden stocks that might be toys emulating the gas-discharge ballistics of the period. But, from the self-aware manner in which these seeming children carried them, Merola guessed that the weapons were live and could do real damage.

"They're Flüchtlinge," she whispered.

"I know," Rydin said in a normal voice.

"You two are from the future," said a woman who stepped forward. Unlike the others, she was not dressed as a child but as an older person, in a flowered dress and a shawl against the night air. Her wig was thin and gray instead of childishly thick and curly. "And you have a Divina with you," she said, pointing at Ghost. "That is unusual."

"We are not here for you," Rydin said.

"Except you've brought spiders." She pointed at the three carapaces hurrying along on their crablike legs, trying to rejoin their human counterparts. "Active spiders—which means you are not refugees but Jongleurs."

"Still," Rydin said, "we mean you no harm."

The woman turned and gave a signal to the three Flüchtlinge who had followed the Silicates to the edge of the infield. There the not-children drew from their belts short mallets or hammers and fell on the robots. From ten meters away, Merola heard the *clang-clang* of their blows on the three domed carapaces.

Normally, such a beating couldn't hurt the Silicates' shells, which were battle hardened to begin with. But the surprise attack caused them to draw in their camera stalks and legs, and fold their claws under the upper lip of their chassis, to avoid damaging these more sensitive working parts. As soon as the robots were closed down, the children scooped them into bags of heavy woven fabric and tied them tight. That pinned the robots' extensions in place, including their comm lasers. It rendered them inert—unless the Silicates decided to become indiscriminately violent, and Merola knew they would avoid firing blind and possibly hitting their own party.

"And now you can *do* no harm," the woman replied.

"Neat trick," Rydin said. "I'll have to remember that one."

"My name is Courtnay," she said. "You've come to the wrong place."

"No," Rydin said. "We are exactly where we are meant to be."

"Then you are my prisoners," Courtnay said. "Come."

She and the children with working weapons directed the two Jongleurs and Ghost—and carried the bagged Silicates—out into the street and away from the ballpark. After a long walk, they opened the side door of a brick building that appeared to be abandoned. The inside smelled to Merola of dust and rot and feral humans living under conditions of poverty. It was lit by incandescent bulbs high in the raftered ceiling.

The three who carried Berzher, Cinquemain, and Piedeleger went over to a chest made of black iron with steel cross straps and reinforced at the corners. They dumped the robots in one by one and slammed the lid with a hollow *bang*. Only then did the other Flüchtlinge visibly relax.

"Are you going to put us in a box, too?" Merola asked.

"It might be safer if we did," the Courtnay woman said.

"Or just kill us here," Rydin said. "We are not armed."

"That, too." And the old woman smiled back at him.

56. Why They Were Born

Captain Tavia studied the little green-eyed girl seated before her. Dottore Jensan had offered to put the child in restraints, but that was not necessary. Tavia didn't fear any creature that massed less than thirty kilograms.

"We've had some incidents in the lab," Jensan said.

"What? Disappearances?" Tavia asked. "Predictions of the future?"

"More like ... things we know that no child should—but they do."

"Are you telling me these children exhibit telepathic abilities?"

"Two do. One of the boys instead seems to be telekinetic."

While Tavia and the dottore talked, the girl stared at her intently, boring into her with hostile eyes. Tavia could withstand the hostility, but she wondered what thoughts the girl was taking from her mind right now. Next she wondered what thoughts the girl might be *putting into* her mind. But then, those would have a *flavor*, wouldn't they? A strangeness that would mark them as something coming from the outside. And Tavia did not detect anything like that.

"How strong are they?" she asked.

"How do you mean? Physically?"

"I mean these mental powers."

"That's hard to say. So far we've only had ... indications. Instances strange enough to cause comment. We haven't run organized tests for psi powers, because you said—"

"I know my instructions," Tavia replied.

She wondered if it would be worthwhile to test the children's mental abilities. But then, what would a Jongleur variant gain by being able to read other people's minds? Maybe inserting thoughts into the heads of the people they encountered in the past would be useful, particularly at moments of crisis. But taking thoughts *out*, which was all the dottore had suggested so far, was not worth the effort. Even as a means of translating a foreign speaker's words and meanings—which was problematic, given that most people thought in their birth tongue—the skill did not merit disrupting an entire genome. And besides, mental tricks were not the purpose of this experiment. After all, Jongleurs were *time travelers*—not judges or police interrogators.

"But no proven *temporal* effects?" she probed.

"Nothing we've detected. Not even a glimmer."

His word, *glimmer*, put Tavia in mind of the gene set they had first observed on the Divina's X chromosome. The base pairs themselves had been shimmering, passing in and out of view, as if those sequences were not fixed in place—or in time. The thought among the Troupe's geneticists had been that, if they could capture those genes and attach them to a human sequence, they could then breed a Jongleur able to travel in place and through time without the need of liteships and their pesky robot pilots. They could breed a new race of being, *Homo temporalis*, the human travelers.

But a race of mentalists and mystics was not part of the program.

"Do you *want* us to test for these mental powers?" Jensan asked.

"There would be no point to that," she said. "No, terminate them."

And as she said this, Tavia wondered what a seven-year-old girl would make of this conversation. Would she understand the word "terminate," even if she could put it in context from Tavia's mind? Would she apply that word to herself and her brothers?

From the way the girl stared at her—unwavering, unflinching, not reacting at all—Tavia did not think she understood. And if she did, would it matter?

57. A Muddy Field Downtown

As HIS LITESHIP descended toward the ground, Rydin sensed that something was wrong. The great broken—or rather, still incomplete—metal arch was in the right place on the night skyline. And the space immediately below them was clear of buildings and other obstructions. But the ground itself was not the level grass and graded dirt of a baseball field. Instead, he could see by the light coming from nearby building windows that it was a sea of mud dotted with irregular hummocks of dirt. And the near horizon—which was supposed to be an enclosed ring of small arches that housed the ballpark's grandstands, field lights, and scoreboard—was open to a view of those downtown buildings.

"Where are we?" Rydin asked on the biosuit's radio circuit.

"These coordinates are for Busch Stadium," Cinquemain said.

"This isn't the same place we visited last time," Merola observed.

The radio was silent for a second while the ship continued descending.

"Ah!" Cinquemain said. "My mistake. I just completed a scan of the newspaper files I took from the *Post-Dispatch* morgue. This is the site of *new* Busch Stadium, which is the one we visited in nineteen ninety-eight. It was still under construction in this time frame, thirty-four years earlier."

"So where are the Ramsays supposed to be?" Rydin asked.

"At that funny old church?" Merola suggested. "Can you find that?"

"I don't want them coming down right on top of our cache," Rydin said.

"The Saint Louis Cardinals are currently playing at *old* Busch Stadium," Cinquemain said, "formerly known as Sportsman's Park. However, the schedule shows no game tonight; so that stadium should be empty. It is only five miles northwest of here."

"So take us to the old ballpark," Rydin said. "We can sort things out from there."

———

The boy Nathan, who had chosen "Lopez" for a convenient surname, watched as the sky above Sportsman's Park fluttered, with the stars winking out and coming back in discrete groups. It was as if two, no three, small clouds were moving across the sky—except any clouds flying low should have shown up as gray or white masses in the glow from the city's lights. So these objects were not clouds. And, in fact, they had solid edges that cut off and then revealed the stars quite sharply.

Nathan Lopez had never seen a Jongleur liteship landing in St. Louis. But he remembered them from his time in Lune. That was long ago, or rather eight thousand years from now—living in two worlds got confusing. But he knew the fact that Jongleurs were coming to his city now was important.

He waited in the shadows below the foul pole at the end of the third-base line. He counted three ships touching down just behind the pitcher's mound. He counted two Jongleurs in their space-faring suits and a third that, hard as it was to believe, had to be a Divina. Nathan had never heard of a Divina traveling with members of the Troupe des Jongleurs. He watched the party long enough to see the Silicate pilots start to break down their ships, indicating that they would be staying for a while.

That was enough to know. He had to escape and report all this to Beckah Courtnay.

Sideways

58. Arriving at the Compound

THE THREE LITESHIPS descended through the clouds above the Temz valley. The trip forward eight thousand years in time and six light years across interstellar space had been uneventful—except for the two living captives. The woman, Beckah Courtnay, strapped to the central core of Rydin's ship had awakened and struggled. When Cinquemain turned on her suit radio, all Rydin heard was a stream of curses in the vernacular of the twentieth century. He told Cinquemain to turn off the radio, except for sending a low-frequency hum into her helmet whose modulations were designed to induce sleep on the long voyages where a Jongleur's biosuit needed to conserve internal supplies. Soon the old woman was no longer struggling or moving her mouth under the visor in what would certainly have been more curses.

He checked with Merola and Berzher, whose ship carried the other passenger, one of the Ramsay brothers. He had apparently remained passive for much of the trip. But Berzher reported that, at one point, he had felt a series of tiny interruptions, micro-adjustments, in his own internal circuitry. He had interpreted these as someone—likely the Ramsay boy—trying to modify his cyber matrix. Berzher explained the damage the Ramsays had done to the Silicate who had been piloting their stolen liteship.

"Can you still function?" Rydin asked. "Did he damage you?"

"Not that I am aware. I put him to sleep at the first approach."

"Good thinking. We will warn the Ringmasters when we arrive."

"Or we can arrange a suit accident above atmosphere," Merola suggested.

"It's late for that," Rydin replied. "If the Troupe wants him alive, they can keep him sedated." He paused. "But all three of you Silicates—Piedeleger, too, because we don't know the boy's psionic range—will need to run a diagnostic when we get back."

"And you humans," Cinquemain said, "will need psychiatric evaluation. The girl was more powerful, after all."

"Right after I take a long rest," Rydin said.

As they approached the landing apron of the compound's hangar, Rydin had sent word for assistance with the two frozen and vacuum-dried bodies—those of Genjifer Ramsay and the second brother—that hung below his and Merola's ship. So people were now clustered below to greet them.

As the ships descended within two meters of the ground, these people reached up, detached, and carried away the bodies. They would return to take the captives into custody as soon as the ships touched down.

Rydin—who had been holding his breath for almost the whole trip—took this pause at two meters' elevation to look around. He did not see any six-limbed people. But inside the Jongleur compound that was hardly proof, because Ghost was the only Divina who actually belonged there. Rydin looked quickly across at Piedeleger's ship to make sure Ghost was still with them, distinguished by his modified biosuit. And yes, the Divina still rode complacently across from his Silicate pilot. And no, he had not blinked out of existence just because Rydin and Merola had finally captured the Ramsays, who had drawn to themselves the Möglich, who had followed the original Merola back to the Devonian period, and who had poisoned the waters of the lobe-finned fishes, thereby engendering the evolution of the hexapods and starting this whole crazy cycle.

But Rydin could hope that the breach in time was now sealed. He expected that Ghost himself was no more than an artifact, an oddity, a set of one, something left over from this adventure. It would be difficult to explain him to the Troupe now, because nothing like him had ever been seen in this world. And it would be lonely for him, too—if Divina even *had* feelings of separation and loneliness—because half of the evolutionary creation in which Ghost had grown up, and all of his own kind, were now expunged from the world. But Rydin could spare Ghost only a bit of sympathy, compared to the relief he felt …

Something moving along the base of the wall of a building across from the hangar caught his attention. Although the Troupe maintained a neat and disciplined compound, with proper storage of foodstuffs and disposal of wastes, they still had a rat problem. Three millennia of genetic engineering had been unable to eradicate the pests that infiltrated human habitations. And so the Troupe tolerated a colony of small predators, near-feral cats, that controlled the rat population better than any program of poisoning or eugenic measures. What Rydin saw moving along the wall was one of these cats, stalking something in the grass. And the way the animal moved—two front legs creeping forward, two hind legs crouched to spring, two middle legs arched for balance—told him the whole story.

"Merola," he said through the radio. "Look over there." He pointed at the cat.

She slid around the core of her liteship, her helmet turned in that direction.

"Maybe it's an anomaly?" she said. "A one in a million mutation …?"

Rydin heard pleading in her voice. "Do you think that's the case?"

"Unh, no. But, you know—damn it!"

"Damn it, indeed," he agreed.

————

Cinquemain was in a training session with Jazdal Halek, learning the Old Norse language and customs in anticipation of a mission—one that had already been twice postponed—to the late first millennium. The presumed goal of their travels would be to unravel the strands of a population migration that had left linguistic and genetic clues from Greenland to southern Russia.

"Repeat after me," their Silicate teacher, Languevipère, told the two of them. "*Allir menn eru bornir frjálsir ok jafnir at virðingu ok réttum.*"

Halek began slowly: "All her men err, errooh, born-er fraylzer ..."

All human beings are born free and equal in dignity and rights, Cinquemain repeated mentally, because he could acquire any language through telemetry in a few microseconds. Cinquemain only attended these lessons to offer Jazdal moral support—and to prove to his human passenger that he could be fluent when the time came.

That sample sentence was from the preamble to the "Universal Declaration of Human Rights," a multi-language document that had survived from a thousand years past the period in question and had little to do with the culture he and Halek had been studying. But the thought was a nice and the words were basic and simple.

As she continued struggling with the phrasing, he and Languevipère both received a broadcast from Nexus. It concerned the routine return to the compound of a Jongleur team that had been on assignment.

Cinquemain immediately challenged the embedded intelligence's report. "That is not possible," he sent. "Coel Rydin cannot be leading this team. He is dead."

"This is the message I have," Nexus sent back. "If you do not like it, go see for yourself."

"I must leave," he said aloud to Languevipère and Halek.

"I understand," the teacher replied.

"What's going on?" Halek asked.

"Coel Rydin has returned," he said.

"But you brought Rydin back dead."

"We had proof of that," Cinquemain replied. "We must go and investigate."

"But ..." she said, "this is the mission about the Ramsay triplets, isn't it?"

"That is the official story ..."

"Then I can't go," she replied. "They were my responsibility, four years ago, and I failed the Troupe miserably. And if they are the ones who killed your friend—"

"They did not," Cinquemain said quickly. "You should trust me on that."

"Still," she said. "I don't want to see those horrible children ever again."

"I understand," he said. "You stay here and continue the lesson."

But he had trouble keeping his vocoder chip from vibrating. *Rydin was somehow alive!* Cinquemain had not failed him.

———

Merola Tsverin and Berzher had taken refuge in the ancient hill fort or castle that lay to the west of the Jongleur compound. She thought of their stay in this long-abandoned place as "hiding out" until they could be sure about what exactly was going on.

Merola had told Captain Tavia that she was going back on the mission to the twenty-first century to reconnect with Rydin—the now-dead Rydin—and then she had fled, because she could not reasonably continue a mission that she did not start. Her faith now was that the situation concerning whatever she was supposed to be doing in the past would eventually resolve itself. So she told Berzher to continue monitoring communications with the Troupe but without giving away their own existence or position in the eleventh millennium.

While they waited, Merola lived by snaring rabbits on the castle grounds to avoid draining the reserves in her biosuit, in case they had to fly again. Fortunately, a natural spring under the walls provided all the water she needed. And Berzher attached himself daily to their liteship's core in order to keep up his power levels. Otherwise, they passed the time reminiscing about Rydin and speculating about the future—which was useless.

Her "eventually" arrived three days later, when Berzher intercepted a broadcast message from Nexus.

"Coel Rydin has returned from his mission," he told Merola.

"Nonsense," she replied. "We were there for his dissolution."

"Whatever. Someone calling himself Rydin just landed at the compound."

"Then I'm in big trouble, because I never rejoined him on that mission."

"Actually," Berzher said, "you are also landing at the compound."

"Now that cannot be. I'm right here. You can see me, can't you?"

"Along with someone called 'Ghost,' and his pilot, Piedeleger."

"Captain Tavia mentioned this Ghost person, but I never understood."

"The situation does seem confused," Berzher said. "Or more so than usual."

"I guess we had better go back and face the music," she replied

"Oh? Do you think there will be a band?"

————

When Skeezicks reported Nexus's broadcast, Captain Tavia went down to the hangar to greet the returning team. But she suspected there was some mistake, because Rydin was dead and Cinquemain had already been reassigned to the Halek woman. She expected the confusion was something that could only be resolved face to face.

What she did not expect to see was Rydin stepping down off his own liteship followed closely by his robot pilot. If this was some vagary of time travel—such as Rydin's arriving back downstream in the eleventh millennium sometime before he was killed upstream in the early third millennium—then she was reasonably sure that the Silicates with their internal clocks and their analogue of the human neural imprint could unravel it. But Rydin dead or alive had never been assigned another pilot from the eleventh millennium, and that was a known fact.

"You are looking well, Coel," she said cautiously.

"Yes, it was a near thing," he said. "A firefight with antique gas-discharge weapons. And only two dead—unfortunately, those were the Ramsay sister and one of the brothers. The Troupe just took away their bodies."

"Not a problem. I was going to have them terminated anyway. Who are your captives?" she asked as Jongleurs from the gathering crowd unbound them from the ships' cores and removed their biosuits.

"The boy is the second Ramsay brother," Rydin said. "You want to watch him, though, because he appears to be telekinetic. He tried to rummage about in Berzher's brain matrix, but we put him to sleep. The woman is Beckah Courtnay."

"Courtnay?" Tavia asked. "Why did you bring her?"

"She was the leader of the Sane Looie coven."

"You could have executed her there."

"I thought she had crimes here."

"Before your time and mine," Tavia said, shaking her head. From the lines on Courtnay's face, the woman was old, even for a Jongleur. Of course, she might have lived out her life in the second and third millennia, having left Lune a generation ago—or left sometime in the next month or year. Only a search of Troupe records could tell who she was. In any case, she was an inconvenience, no more.

"And who is your pilot?" Tavia asked. "I don't recognize him."

"I am Cinquemain, of course," the robot said. "You still can't tell us apart?"

"Cinquemain has been—" She wanted to explain about the death but stopped.

"This *is* Cinquemain," Skeezicks said at her side. "His identity is confirmed."

"Then would someone tell me what the hell is going on?"

59. Confronting Other Lives

MEROLA TSVERIN SAT in the Ringmasters' council chamber alongside Rydin and Ghost, with their pilots Berzher, Cinquemain, and Piedeleger squatting on the table in front of each of them—the complete team returning from twentieth-century Sane Looie. They were attended by Captain Tavia but none of the other senior staff, at least not until Tavia was satisfied with their explanations of the current situation.

The captain's main complaint was that Rydin was supposed to be dead, and he wasn't. And that Cinquemain was supposed to have been reassigned to a new Jongleur, and he wasn't. The substance of these notions seemed to be shared by everyone else in this reference now, and Merola had heard something obliquely similar from Juwana Dyllin. So she wanted to get at the truth, too.

Before the inquiry could get under way, however, a young woman walked into the room. As she was hairless, like most Jongleurs, and possessed genetically smoothed features, Merola did not recognize her at first. And even if she had studied that face, she might not have recognized it from the one she saw when she looked in a mirror, which was infrequently, because the image would appear the reverse from what she saw as her "normal" self. But the reaction from around the room was marked.

"Merola?" Captain Tavia asked, looking from the newcomer to Merola herself.

"Yes," she replied—at the same time and in the same voice as the other woman.

"Two of you!" Rydin said quietly.

Accompanying her was a Silicate pilot in a crablike carapace. As they approached, Berzher touched Merola's arm with a claw and whispered, "That one pings as *me!*"

"Where did you come from?" Merola asked the woman. "And why are you and your pilot pretending to be me? Or us?"

"I've been keeping out of sight," the young woman said, "ever since you took up residence in my treehouse. By the way, that yellow wig is hideous, and the shoes will break your feet. And where did *you* come from?"

"We were just in Sane Looie, tracking down the Ramsays."

"I keep hearing that name, but I don't know who they are."

"I think I can clear this up," Rydin said, interrupting them.

"Aren't you dead already?" the other Merola asked calmly.

"That's another mystery here," he replied. "But first, were you last in Safronesco taking genetic samples in the early twenty-first century?"

"Yes, that was my most recent Search mission."

"And you went into a toy store downtown?"

"I went in but never took any samples."

"And did the toy store blow up—in your experience?" he asked.

"Only after I was detained by security, by then I had left the place."

"So you never crossed paths with the genetic triplets, the Ramsays," Rydin concluded. "We were chasing the wrong lead all the time," he added.

"What lead?" Captain Tavia asked, sounding even more mystified.

But Merola had another question: "What about the baseball?"

"I don't know anything about baseball," the woman said.

"We are supposed to have stolen one," Merola told her.

"When was this? I never stole a thing."

"It was in ninety-eight, in Sane Looie."

"I never went there. Not at any time."

"Ah-hah!" Merola replied, satisfied.

That solved at least one mystery.

———

Coel Rydin was watching the exchange between the two Merolas when another Silicate came into the room. Immediately, Cinquemain rose to his full height on the table, eight legs extended, camera stalks pushed forward, and claws lifted—a bristling reaction that combined surprise and outrage.

"You are *not* me!" Cinquemain blared out loud.

"Of course not! I am myself," the other replied.

Captain Tavia rose from her chair. "Explain yourselves!"

"We are both Cinquemain," they said together. "We are … confused."

"You are the one," Rydin said to the version that still stood in the doorway—and he hoped it would not jump up on the table, because then he might lose track of which Cinquemain was originally his own. "You are the pilot who says I was killed."

"I brought back your body," the new one said. "Many here attended your dissolution ceremony. You died."

"Perhaps this was at some point in a future I haven't seen yet," Rydin said.

"No, I think not. We were confiscating the Boskin family baseball collection."

"But … that happened in the past, when I was trying to rescue Merola, before—"

"Exactly! Before Boskin could suborn her to steal the McGwire home-run baseball."

"Yes, and after that, we came back to a changed world, full of six-limbed sea lions."

"I don't remember that," the other Cinquemain said. "This world never changed."

"Maybe you didn't take your neural imprint? Or circuit imprint. Or whatever!"

"That is not the case," the impostor said. "There have *always* been six-limbed mammals, reptiles, and amphibians—probably pinnipeds, too, for all I know. But you and I never saw any sea lions. You were shot as we left the Boskin estate, after removing the baseball collection. Then I flew your body back here directly."

"That is not possible," Rydin said. "We returned immediately to San Francisco and began tracking Merola. We had to find out how she had changed—"

He suddenly had a cold thought: there were *two* of him. One was dead, killed in the middle of his attempt to keep Merola Tsverin from stealing the baseball. And one was still alive, after he had completed that attempt, but by then Merola had gone on to cause other, greater problems by visiting the Devonian period and drawing the Ramsay siblings' Möglich after her, where it had created—and Rydin himself, *this* Rydin, had failed to prevent—the infusion of hexapod animals into the world they both knew.

In the same way, there were now two Merolas—along with two Berzhers and two Cinquemains. One of her had never stolen a baseball, never completed the genetic sampling, and so had gone home unhurt to the eleventh millennium right after the toy store blew up. And so she never traveled to London, never joined with the Sindicato della Conoscenza, and never went back to the Devonian period. And yet, despite that fact, her world was still filled with Divina and other hexapod creatures.

Whereas the other one, *his* Merola, *had* gone back to the beginning of land-based evolution, where Rydin had eventually found and rejoined her. But he failed to prevent the catastrophe that they both had been trying to correct ever since.

And *that* was the difference.

"We don't belong here," Rydin said aloud. "Merola and I—" He touched the arm of the woman seated beside him. "—are not from this time stream.

"But how is that possible?" he went on, still musing. "How did we cross the Wahrschein Punkt—the most important probability nexus in all of human history—and not even know it?"

Such a transference was theoretically impossible. Travelers stayed in their own time stream, navigating up and down but never sideways, never crossing into the other potential multiverses. That was supposed to be a law—or at least a theory, but one with strong empirical underpinnings, like gravity or evolution. Time travel was supposed to be ... *safe*.

———

Captain Tavia listened to this broken, disjointed exchange between the suddenly alive Coel Rydin and the Cinquemain who had brought back the newly dead Rydin until she could stand no more.

"Rydin!" she said. "Explain yourself. What do you mean, you don't belong here?"

"We come from a world—" he began calmly enough.

"This world!" exclaimed the Merola sitting beside him.

"—or time frame, or time stream, that has no hexapods—"

"Except for the insects," that version of Merola supplied. "But nothing warm-blooded. Nothing like six-legged animals or humans."

"—and Merola and I," he continued, "and our pilots Cinquemain and Berzher here—" He pointed to the two Silicates sitting on the table. "—have been trying to turn this world, your world, back into that one, with just tetrapods in the animal kingdom, just humans on the ascended plane, and no Divina."

"That's right," the Merola sitting beside him said. "We wanted to undo the damage that we did—that the Möglich that was following me back to the Devonian did—and ... put things right."

"But things here *are* 'right,' " Tavia said. "And anyway, for all the things you've done—"

"We tried to interrupt this time stream," Rydin said. He then gave the details of his and Merola's—his Merola's—"secret mission," which they conducted under the guise of Ghost's first extended training flight. "We were trying to stop our version of Merola—"

"You mean *our* version!" Tavia reminded him, pointing to the woman still standing in the doorway. "The one originating in *this* world."

"—from going back to the Devonian period," Rydin finished. Then he described their complex travels, when Tavia had sent the pair plus Ghost off to track the Ramsays. "We killed them, twice," he concluded. "Once in San Francisco, and again forty years earlier in Saint Louis, because we learned that they had created the monster who attached itself to Merola in the first place—"

"Hell, the thing even attached itself to me, briefly," Tavia said. And when they looked blankly at her, she went on: "Big head, six limbs, shiny garment, disturbing eyes?" Then the others started nodding. "It must have followed you back when you returned to the compound the first time and found me. And I killed it. It's gone."

"Dead in the eleventh millennium, perhaps," Rydin said. "But that's long after the damage was done."

"And yet, for all your efforts," Tavia said, "the hexapods are still here, in this world that you claim is your own. The Divina still walk among us—and sing, tell fortunes, erase our regrets, and find lost loves for us."

"What do you mean about 'regrets' and 'lost loves'?" asked the other Merola, the one from that alternate world.

"You told us Divina were imbeciles," the Rydin impersonator said. "That they were innate beggars. Unreliable."

"But I never said they weren't useful," Tavia replied. "You know by now that they have a form of telepathy. They can help people … find things, see alternatives, understand their choices. Sometimes, that's a great comfort. And the Divina can … sense different time streams, although we've never been able to figure out how."

"And yet, they don't belong here," Rydin insisted.

"So you keep saying," Captain Tavia replied. "But they've been part of every past you have visited, haven't they?"

"Perhaps …" Rydin said, pausing, "we need to steal another timeship from Tekavade & Son in Lore. Go back to the Devonian again. And try to beat the Möglich there. Again."

"Or," Tavia said, "you might just attract the Möglich to yourself this time—or another one, worse than that—and do even more damage. No, Coel. Consider that a time stream so deeply embedded in human history and choices, this one containing hexapod creatures and the monster who made them, cannot be erased with a single act or acts. They have become part of so many alternatives that they will persist, no matter what you do.

"The early dabblers in time travel believed in what they called 'the Grandfather Paradox,'" she went on. "This notion dictated that you could not go back upstream in time and kill your own grandfather, because then you would never have been born. But we know from experience that you have free will and unlimited movement in time. If you go back and kill your grandfather, someone else will have carried and passed down what are now your genes. A different mother and father will raise you. Your past and future will change accordingly after the murder. That is why we take the neural imprint before entering the past—" She touched the medallion that all Jongleurs wore around their necks. "—so that we will know what's real when we return. There are no paradoxes. Free will rules this universe. Free will and the Wahrschein Punkt, the probabilistic decision point, the place where you change your future."

"Or not," Rydin said gloomily.

"Yes, or in your case, *not*."

Noumisma watched the proceedings in the Troupe compound's place-of-deciding. He could follow the discussion partly from the spoken words that the humans and the machines used, partly from the ideas and images that floated through the humans' brains. But the machine minds—if they possessed minds at all—were opaque to him. And once or twice Noumisma caught the word "Ghost," which he knew was the name the Jongleurs used for him. Otherwise, the subjects under discussion were of no interest to him.

When another human female came into the room, a twin of Merola Tsverin, he started to take notice. This second one had the mind and most of the mental imagery from the woman sitting right beside him, the one he had first approached about joining the Troupe and with whom he had been traveling ever since. And yet this new woman's thoughts were subtly different and her experiences were not the same.

But then, when two other machines entered—one accompanying this Merola twin, the second by itself—nothing changed to Noumisma's way of thinking, and he started to lose interest again. There were simply two more machines in the room. Yet the humans seemed confused, believing that each pair of machines shared a common identity and an already existing, unique, and singular being. That reaction did not really surprise Noumisma, who always had trouble telling the robots apart anyway—even the one called "Piedeleger," who was assigned to him as pilot and companion. They were, after all, just articulated mechanisms made of metal and ceramic.

Noumisma tried to catch up on the discussion by reviewing the words and images these people had been using. He wrestled with Rydin's reference to the "time stream"—until he realized it was just other words for a parallel probabilistic reality, a different probability curve occurring in a concurrent time frame. If so ... then perhaps Rydin could sense these alternatives, too?

If that was the case, Noumisma knew how to fix the situation.

He tapped on Piedeleger's metal shell to get the machine's attention and began signing.

Noumisma put the fingertips of his two upper hands together, then spread them and simultaneously pulled them apart, to indicate "a great amount." He extended his forefingers away from his body with palms up, then flipped those hands to palms down, and repeated the gesture several times, to suggest "events," "happenings," or even "accidents." He made fists, moved them so that the little finger of the right was in line above the forefinger of the left, and twisted his wrists as if grinding them together, for "make." He opened the right hand, palm down, over the left, which was palm up, moved the right in a circle, and slowly closed the fingers and brought them down until they touched a point on the left palm, for "center." And finally, he used the thumb and forefinger of his right hand to pinch skin on the back of his open and downward-facing left hand, rocking it back and forth, then he made a fist of the right hand, raised it to his chin, and dropped it, to indicate the pull of "gravity." After a brief pause, he again made fists with his hands, this time with the palms facing together, right above left, and twisted his wrists to invert their positions, so that they were left above right. He repeated this gesture several times, to suggest "changes." And at last, he raised his right hand near his cheek and pinched together the thumb and forefinger, indicating "small."

He nodded for Piedeleger to translate.

"Something about a lot of happenings making a center of gravity," the machine said. "And then changes are small."

"What does that even mean?" asked the one called Captain Tavia.

"What you were saying about paradoxes," Rydin answered, and Noumisma could see the thoughts developing in his mind. "Once the six-limbed species were introduced on this planet, the time stream was changed and it … accumulated … so many small changes that by now life on Earth should be unrecognizable. Merola and I—"

"And us, too, remember," said one of the machines sitting on the table.

"—we should have come back to a world that none of us recognized. But instead, we found a world that we knew—that we even thought was our own. But there were minor differences—like Jena Gerbus now having a head of hair."

"Or you hating my blonde wig," the Merolas beside him said to the other one.

"All right," the Tavia woman agreed. "So the world—your world—didn't change much. What then?"

"I think it works both ways," Rydin said, "based on your refutation of temporal paradoxes. The existence of the hexapods in this time stream has shifted its 'center of gravity.' That is why we couldn't erase them by killing—or eventually unmaking—the Möglich who was their creator."

Noumisma began signing again. He made a fist of his right hand, extended his little finger, and thumped that hand against his chest, for "I." He opened his left palm, positioned his right hand on top of it with thumb and forefinger spread, then raised that right hand and closed those two digits, as if plucking something from the left hand, for "find." He pointed the forefingers of his two hands in opposite directions, ninety degrees apart, and brought the right hand down sharply on the left, for "right" or "correct." He opened his left hand, palm facing to the right, pressed his right forefinger and thumb together, and moved them in a circle around the left palm, imitating an antique clock face, for "time." And at last, he held his hands parallel, open and facing each other, off to the right side of his body, then moved them downward and to the left, gradually separating them, and repeated the gesture, for "flow" or "stream."

He nodded for Piedeleger to translate.

" 'I find correct time stream,' " the machine said.

The room sat in silence—but Noumisma could feel their minds vibrate with wonder and curiosity.

"Can he do that?" Rydin finally asked.

"They can see, or sense, alternatives," Tavia said slowly.

"Yes, but can they … move them?" Rydin asked, and Noumisma could see the thought form in his mind. "Can they change from one to—"

Noumisma nodded emphatically. He made Vs of his first and second fingers on both hands, held up the left with the fingers steady, then alternately tapped the forefinger and second finger of the right hand on the corresponding fingers of the left, to indicate "alternative." Then he made the finger-pointing and flipping gesture again, for "events."

"Yes," Piedeleger said. " 'Alternate … happenings' … 'alternate reality,' I guess."

"Ask if he can do it now," Rydin said. "Right here." And Noumisma saw the thought and its urgency in his mind.

Noumisma shook his head. But how to express this? He cupped his right hand, palm facing up, made a fist, shook it twice, and moved it quickly across his chest to the left, opening his hand, as if throwing something. Then he extended his left forefinger pointing up, his right forefinger above it, and touched the two fingers together twice, for "point."

"I remember that," said the Merola at his side. "He wants to go to a casino." And her mind was filled with a brightly lit hall, many tables covered in green cloth, and people playing with squares of pasteboard.

Noumisma shook his head.

" 'Gambling' …?" Rydin guessed hesitantly.

Noumisma nodded at the image forming in the human's brain.

" 'Probability,' " Rydin said. And his mind was suddenly filled with memories of a muddy riverbank, a dense forest of spindly trees, and thousands of slimy, stump-finned fishes. "We have to travel to the Wahrschein Punkt—the probability nexus—where the hexapods were first created."

Noumisma nodded and touched his own nose in agreement.

"So we're going back to the Devonian after all," Rydin said.

60. Meeting an Old Friend

JAZDAL HALEK HAD been summoned to the Jongleur compound's maintenance shop by a message from Nexus that was relayed through her pilot Cinquemain. They arrived together and found two other Silicates working on a third whose carapace was mounted on a jig and partially disassembled. The two were pulling components out of the body cavity and setting them aside on a nearby bench.

"What's going on?" she asked, because she knew almost nothing about the internal workings of the robot pilots.

The two who were working on the broken machine swiveled their camera stalks at her, then focused on Cinquemain.

"Did you not tell her?" one of them asked him.

"I did not know what you would find," he said.

"I have the matrix," said the second one, pulling a glass sphere as big as Jazdal's fist out of the shell and holding it aloft in a pincer. It was layered and murky, with glints of gold in its depths.

"Is the bulb visibly damaged?" the first robot asked.

"Not that I can see. And no damage to the cradle, either."

"I should introduce you," Cinquemain said to her. "This is *another* Cinquemain—" Here he pointed to the first speaker. "—but from a different part of the time stream. And the other one is Berzher, who traveled with him on the mission to capture the Ramsay triplets."

"Those are the people I helped to escape," she said.

"Under compulsion and against your will," said the second Cinquemain. "We know, because we have dealt with them before. And our compatriot in pieces on the table here is Schnelleziffer, your old—"

"Is that his *brain?*" Jazdal asked, pointing at the sphere.

"Yes, essentially. That is his central processing matrix. It possesses all of a Silicate's higher functions. This one has been damaged."

"The Ramsay boy fiddled with the overlaid circuitry somehow," said the machine identified as Berzher. "He tried something similar with me as we were coming back from the twentieth century, but I managed to zap him first. Schnelleziffer's autonomous functions appear to have been destroyed."

"Can you repair him?" she asked.

"We will send this matrix to the field-effect transistor specialists of Sheffod, which is our place of origin, north of here," the other Cinquemain said. "They know a thousand times more about Silicate circuitry than Berzher and I do."

"By a factor of one thousand and twenty-four," Berzher said.

"But repairing layered circuits is extremely difficult," her own Cinquemain warned. "I would not want to get your hopes up."

"Can you put him back in his shell, please?" she asked.

"Why would we do that?" her Cinquemain replied.

"I would like to say good-bye," she answered.

Her pilot nodded. Berzher reinserted the glass sphere and closed the carapace.

Schnelleziffer's camera stalks swiveled around without focusing. His two pincers opened and closed randomly. And his eight legs drummed briefly in the jig.

"Schnelle?" she said softly. "Can you hear me?"

The cameras focused. "Jazdal! It is really you!"

"Yes! And you have come back to me at last."

"I am not functioning at capacity," he admitted.

She blinked fast to keep the tears away. "They're going to make you all better."

Out of the corner of her eye, she saw Cinquemain droop at the obvious lie.

"And as soon as you are fixed," she went on, "you can teach me to fly."

"Yes. I know how to fly, Jazdal," the pilot said. "You and I will *fly*."

61. Back to the Beginning

CINQUEMAIN DID NOT have either an accurate time reference or a complete geographic location from his and Rydin's last trip to the Marathid Republic in the ninth millennium *Anno Compradoro*. That was because their liteship had been crippled and had exploded upon landing—or rather, one hundred and four meters above the ground. Still, the forested hillside below him looked like the area around the city of Lore—once "Lahore" in a mythical place on the Indian subcontinent called "the Punjab." He signaled to Berzher and Piedeleger for them to land and began his own descent.

"Are we on the mark?" Rydin asked.

"Generally …" Cinquemain replied.

"And what exactly does that mean?"

"This is the place—although a little closer to the city than the last time we crashed here. And the reference now is certainly the spring of the year 8834. But whether we are arriving before or after the last time we visited, I cannot say. We never had a chance to take an accurate temporal mark then."

"I think I'm still carrying the bruises from that fall," Rydin said.

"The question is whether we will run into ourselves trying to steal another ship."

"I think not," Rydin said. "After all, the versions of you and me from this time stream never got so far in tracking their version of Merola as to arrive here. I never got back from removing the baseball collection."

"That is a point," Cinquemain said.

After the landing, and while Rydin, Merola, and Ghost stripped off their helmets and biosuits, Cinquemain and the other two pilots disassembled and prepared to cache the three liteships.

"Do we bury them?" he asked Rydin.

"Um …" His human seemed to be thinking. "Even though we'll be traveling in a saucer, I don't like leaving our ships and suits behind. They are our only alternative. So just cover them with brush and we'll pick them up once we have a ride."

When the landing spot was presentable to casual observation, the team walked downhill until they intercepted a public tram line. They rode through the outskirts of the city, then through the metropolitan area, to the vast automated shipyards of Tekavade & Son.

As before, the security system's intelligence at the entry gate was no match for Cinquemain, and soon they were walking the yard's empty streets. They quietly stepped aside whenever robot carriers passed up and down, transporting driver cores, pieces of saucer shell, and interior modules from one workshop to the next. As Cinquemain had discovered on their last visit, the whole complex was operated by machines. The only human interaction was that of Arjun Tekavade and his son Abhay—who probably lived miles away and in a state of luxury.

Cinquemain located a shop with the most sophisticated robots and jacked into the enterprise network. Once again, he found the link between Quality Control and Accounting, and from there he tied into the Sales Department and the As-Built Inventory list. The mute intelligences operating all these functions accepted him, because he used the identity of the assembly cyber that was his entry point.

While still plugged into the system, he turned to Rydin. "The last time we stole a ship, we faked a transfer from the account of a family in Old Hong, Cheng 758. Shall I try that again?"

"It won't be 'again' if we never visited from this time stream," Rydin said. "But that was for a medship. This time, we'll be flying into the midst of both the Conoscenza party and our interception of their expedition to the Devonian period. Things are likely to get crowded. So I'd like to be flying something with a little more fire power."

Cinquemain scanned the inventory of ships completed and being prepped for delivery.

"Interesting!" he said aloud to Rydin and the rest. "I have a commerce raider, fully automated but with life support for a boarding party of twelve humans. The specs mention the owner's plans for traveling back to the sixteenth century, during the Spanish colonial period, to locate, sink, and then resurrect treasure galleons lost in the triangle between Cuba, Puerto Rico, and Bermuda."

"We'll be going back a lot farther in time than that," Rydin said. "Three hundred and sixty million years—which means we'll be chasing the Sun halfway around the galaxy in that span. Does your treasure ship have the legs for such a journey?"

"I will call in last-minute modifications to its core capacity."

"And supplies," Merola said. "Make sure the ship is well stocked. Even at supra-light speeds, it's a long trip."

"Of course," Cinquemain said. "I will even put aboard some table games for the two of you to play. It will help to pass the time."

"Thank you," she said.

"But, please," Rydin said, "don't give the ship its own personality this time. Just fly the damn thing yourself."

"To hear is to obey," Cinquemain said.

———

"What is your time on mark?" Rydin asked his pilot as their stolen saucer descended toward the river that flowed sluggishly through the mangrove swamps of ancient Earth.

"Understand, first," Cinquemain began, "that the Devonian period stretches for millions of years."

"Sixty million," Berzher put in.

"And the river system and coastline that the Conoscenza party visited covers hundreds of thousands of hectares," Cinquemain continued.

"Two thousand square kilometers," Berzher said.

Rydin suppressed his agitation. "So, are we *close?*"

"Based on a comparison between Berzher's and my relative timing references," Cinquemain said, "we are now within a day of the Conoscenza party's first landing and a kilometer from their camp. Do you want to make contact, either with them or with yourself when the originals of you and me arrive?"

"Oh, no!" Rydin said. "We're not here to do or change anything."

"We're not?" Merola asked, sounding surprised.

"We want to let the events play out naturally, right up until the Wahrschein Punkt. That will occur at the time the Möglich pours his mutating virus into the river, trying to change the hox gene set of the sarcopterygian fishes, so that they produce six lobe fins instead of the usual four. But before that, and based on what we observed of the mutated fish, the other me concocted my antibody to hook the virus and prevent the transformation. We then all went upstream—both temporally and physically—to inject my serum into as many fish as we could find."

"But that did not stop the virus, did it?" Merola said.

"As I understand what Ghost was saying back at the compound," Rydin replied, with a nod to the Divina, who stood passively by, "that action created three possible outcomes at the probability point. One, the antibody was ineffective, all the fish were changed into the monster's six-limbed forms, and a world dominated by hexapods was created and flourished— the world of six-finned sea lions that Cinquemain and I saw—"

"Or six-legged pug things the Conoscenza party saw in altered London," Merola said.

"Exactly," Rydin said. "A world without recognizable humans or other familiar animals. Or two, the antibody was fully effective, none of the fish were transformed, and the world that we originally inhabited was preserved. And three, my antibody was only partially effective, some of the fish were changed, some not, and—"

"And we got the hybrid time stream we just arrived from," she concluded. "So what do we *do* to get back to that second, unchanged time stream?"

Rydin turned to Piedeleger, who had been listening to the conversation along with the other Silicates. "Can you explain all this to Ghost? About the fist, the virus, and the antibody? And, if he really is sensitive to other time streams—to his 'alternate realities'—can he tell us when this time stream, the one we're inhabiting now, starts to branch? And then, can he do anything about it?"

The little robot absorbed all this, and Rydin saw her camera stalks dip. "I will try," she said.

Piedeleger turned to Ghost, got his attention, and began a long series of signs. From time to time during her transmission, Ghost turned to Rydin—and he had the impression that the Divina was probing his mind for exact meanings and fuller definitions. Well … whatever worked to get the message through. With a final set of corresponding signs from Ghost, the conversation seemed to be over. The Divina turned to him again and nodded gravely.

"Now what?" Merola asked.

"Now we must wait," he said.

"So … another game of chess?"

————

After Merola had beaten Rydin two games out of three—but only because she sensed his mind really wasn't on playing—the Divina's pilot approached and got their attention.

"Ghost says it is almost time," Piedeleger said. "The branching point itself is inexact, because it is also a matter of higher-order probability, among so many of these lobe-finned fishes, which ones are infected, which ones protected. Do you understand?"

"Can he see the Wahrschein Punkt?" Rydin asked.

"He sees it," the robot said. "The change is close."

"What do we do?" Merola asked. "Stand up, or—"

"The two of you are each to take one of his hands."

Ghost approached and reached out his lower arms.

"And then we—?" she started.

"You transition in the stream."

"Through physical contact?"

"Yes, you must touch him."

"But what about our pilots?"

"They remain in this stream."

"But we can't just leave them."

"Physical objects do not transit."

"But we need them to *get home!*" she insisted.

Piedeleger paused, then she turned to Ghost and began rapid signing. The Divina returned another set of signs, and Merola wished she had taken the time to study and read the visual language.

"Open their carapaces," Piedeleger instructed. "Remove their matrices—he calls them 'brain balls'—and hold them tightly in your hands."

"I thought you said," Rydin objected, "that physical objects can't cross over."

"Ghost reminds me that you yourselves are physical objects—as is he. Hurry now, because the probability point is almost here."

Merola and Rydin knelt down to release the catches on the chassis of Berzher and Cinquemain, and the two pilots did not resist, because they had been listening to the exchange. "I'm sorry," she whispered as she extracted Berzher's glass matrix, the essence of his mind and true being.

She clutched it in her left hand and took hold of Ghost's extended fingers with her right. Rydin did the same on the other side.

"Aren't you coming with us?" Rydin asked Piedeleger.

"I belong with my Jongleur," she said, "wherever he goes."

Merola stared at the Divina. "How will you get back?"

With his upper set of hands, Ghost put his two fists together, knuckles to knuckles, and slid the right in a small arc backwards, behind the left. Then he held his right hand with the fingernail of the index finger against the folded thumb and flicked that finger out and forward.

" 'Back,' " Piedeleger translated, "with a query sign."

Before Merola could ask what he meant, the Divina faded from sight. Her right hand was suddenly empty. She and Rydin were still standing on the deck inside the stolen saucer. The opened carapaces of their two pilots were still crouched at their feet. Other than the missing Divina, she did not feel that anything was different.

"Where did Ghost go?" she asked Piedeleger.

The Divina's pilot stood mute, claws raised, camera stalks poised. But there was no response. The machine was frozen as if its own matrix had been removed—or changed.

"Back to a world where he can exist?" Rydin suggested.

"And Piedeleger?" she asked. "What happened to her?"

"She's now in—I don't know—a world where she never existed."

"But are *we* in that world now? The time stream where we belong?"

Rydin bent and reinserted Cinquemain's "brain ball" into his chassis.

"There's only one way to find out," he said.

62. Arriving in Lune

As before, Rydin ordered Cinquemain to land their stolen saucer on a hill outside of town. He wanted to verify the local situation before they committed themselves to reuniting with the Troupe.

"You know we will eventually have to declare this ship as a Troupe asset," Cinquemain advised. "I cannot imagine Captain Tavia would pass up the chance to own and operate a heavily armed raider."

"We'll deal with that eventuality when we come to it," Rydin said.

For now, he ordered the hatch sealed. Then he and Merola, with Cinquemain and Berzher walking alongside, went down the hill. They left the frozen shell of the vacated Piedeleger inside for the Troupe and the community of Silicates to sort out later.

As they went, Rydin kept looking among the clumps of grass on the hillside for signs of animal life and in the sky above for birds. Once, he thought he saw either a small rabbit or a vole, but it was too far away for him to count the legs. When the entered the fringe of natural trees that screened the village itself, he searched the branches for birds. He saw two that were sitting still, wings folded, and indicated them to Merola.

"Look!" she said, pointing. "That one just took off."

As it flew, Rydin tried to count the number of wings, but they blurred with their rapid flapping. It was not until the creature dipped into a glide that Rydin could successfully establish that it had only two wings and two legs.

"That's one bit of evidence," he said.

On the benches along the chalk paths he looked for the Divina who, in the time stream they had just come from, made a small living by singing for modest donations from passersby. But all the benches they saw were either empty or held only human beings with the normal number of limbs.

"Why, hello, Mira Tsverin," a young man on the path said to Merola. "Have a good flight?"

Rydin experienced a savage dose of *déjà vu*.

"Yes, um, thank you," she replied. "Very smooth, Mir Dustin." And after he had gone on, she turned to Rydin. "That was—"

"I know—he worked on your last liteship."

"Yes, as a circuit designer," she finished.

"At least our time on mark is impeccable."

"Should we ask him about the Divina?"

"We don't want to confuse the man."

"Do not bother interrogating the locals," Cinquemain said.

"We have already consulted the network of Silicates," Berzher said.

"None of them report any morphological abnormalities," Cinquemain said.

"This is the original time stream from which we came," Berzher said.

"The breach created by the Möglich has been sealed," Cinquemain finished.

"Then let's go report in," Rydin said.

Before they could find an electric surrey for the ride out to the Jongleur compound, however, they met Captain Tavia on one of her rare visits to the village.

"What are you two doing here together?" she asked. "You—" She pointed at Merola. "—are supposed to be taking genetic samples in the twenty-first century. And *you*—" This was directed at Rydin. "—are due for final checkout with Dottoressa Gerbus on your Simian-ACTN3 treatments before your next assignment."

"Yes, ma'am," Rydin and Merola said together.

"So, where have you been in the meantime?"

"Oh, here and there," Rydin said vaguely.

"Just nowhere, really," Merola added.

"Around and about," Cinquemain said.

"Looking for a baseball," Berzher finished.

Captain Tavia squinted with suspicion. "And does any of you," she asked, crossing her arms, "know anything about the flying saucer parked outside of town?"

"That," Rydin said, "is actually a long story."

"I have ten minutes," Tavia said. "So tell me."

———

From a nearby treetop, the one called Glyph observed this chance reunion in the place by the great river that had more greenery than ever, fewer humans, and none of his own divine children. Glyph parted the branches with two of his four hands, holding himself securely in place with the other pair on alternate branches and with his feet curled around the main trunk. He studied the small group with his bulging, wide-set eyes.

He recognized the human male, "Rydin," who had killed him long ago in this dimension, but only the blink of an eye away, in the manner in which Glyph accounted for time. He also recognized the human female, the one with the red-tinged mind, the "Captain," who had killed him just as surely, but in another dimension that was separated from this one by that same blink.

It might have surprised him that Rydin had returned from the dead, having been pierced through the chest and then bodily dissolved in that other dimension. But that was then, in that place, and this was the here and now.

Glyph had scores to settled with both the male and the female.

He wondered which of them he would follow first.

About the Author

THOMAS T. THOMAS is a writer with a career spanning forty years in book editing, technical writing, public relations, and popular fiction writing. Among his various careers, he has worked at a university press, a tradebook publisher, an engineering and construction company, a public utility, an oil refinery, a pharmaceutical company, and a supplier of biotechnology instruments and reagents. He published eight novels and collaborations in science fiction with Baen Books and is now working on more general and speculative fiction. When he's not working and writing, he may be out riding his motorcycle, practicing karate, or wargaming with friends. Catch up with him at www.thomastthomas.com. *(Photo by Robert L. Thomas)*

Books by Thomas T. Thomas
Medea's Daughter
The House at the Crossroads
ME, Too: Loose in the Network
Coming of Age, Volume 1: Eternal Life
Coming of Age, Volume 2: Endless Conflict
The Children of Possibility
The Professor's Mistress
The Judge's Daughter
Sunflowers
Trojan Horse
The Doomsday Effect (as by "Thomas Wren")
First Citizen
ME: A Novel of Self-Discovery
Crygender

Books in Collaboration
An Honorable Defense (with David Drake)
The Mask of Loki (with Roger Zelazny)
Flare (with Roger Zelazny)
Mars Plus (with Frederik Pohl)
Between the Sheets (with Kate Campbell)

Excerpt from
The Children of Possibility

(Scenes in Backward Chronological Order)

1. Briones Park

"ALL RIGHT, TEAMS," said Mrs. Gorage-Rhymes-With-Porridge as they filed out of the school bus. "Two by two and keep together."

Josie Barnes was paired with Mary Jane, the strange orphan girl who had the beautiful blonde hair. No one else had wanted to team with her, because she was so quiet, so confident, and so … self-possessed. It was almost like having a little adult among them. The other girls respected her, sure, but that didn't mean they *liked* her. Still, Josie figured it might be good to have someone so smart working with her on this assignment.

The class had come out to Briones Park, in the East Bay hills between Richmond and Orinda, to do an ecology count on the first clear and windy day of spring. Basically, that meant Mrs. Gorage and Melanie, her classroom intern, had gone out yesterday, identified a likely field full of weeds and wildflowers, and marked it off in big squares with orange tape. This morning, as they rode the bus over the Bay Bridge and through Oakland, the two teachers had passed out battered Palm Threes with data wands and explained how to use them. The computers were already loaded, they said, with the field grid and entry points. The assignment was to count the plants and animals— well, insects—and then take soil moisture and pH readings. After that, they had to study the data and draw conclusions. This was the hard part for Josie, because she never seemed to know what to think.

But she figured Mary Jane would be really good at that.

Mrs. Gorage had assigned each of the teams their own square, but right away the other girl broke the rules. And that, too, was kind of what Josie expected.

"We're supposed to be doing Square Fourteen," Josie said as Mary Jane walked resolutely over the tapes toward the far side of the field.

"There is more growth over here," she replied.

"That's not the point. We're supposed to count the plants in *our* square."

"This will make a better report."

"But …" Josie had to follow to keep up the conversation. Very shortly, they were a long way from their square and getting farther away all the time. The only good thing was that the teams assigned to this part of the field hadn't reached their squares yet, so nobody was fighting with them, and Mrs. Gorage hadn't noticed anything. Josie still had time to reason with Mary Jane.

Before Josie could get her thoughts together, Mary Jane walked right over the last strip of orange tape and pushed on, into the underbrush.

"I'm sure we're not supposed to go in there," Josie said, raising her voice.

"Be quiet and do what I do," Mary Jane told her, taking Josie's elbow in a hand that was small but very strong for its size. The fingers gripped in a way that didn't exactly hurt, but Josie could feel the side of her arm tingle. She followed as Mary Jane dragged her out of sight.

Under the trees, Mary Jane looked around as if taking her bearings. She studied the twisted, leaning trunks of the live oaks—Josie was proud that she could identify them—and approached first one and then another. She put a tentative hand on the scaly bark, feeling a humped scar where a branch had broken away. Then Mary Jane nodded and plunged deeper into the thicket.

"What are you doing?" Josie asked.

"I have to find something."

As Mary Jane climbed over and slid under the low, tangled branches, she reached into her pocket and took out something small and round. It looked like a big glass-and-metal ball, the size of the balls on her uncle's pool table. It certainly wasn't anything a girl their age ought to be carrying. But Mary Jane held it up, cupped in both hands, right below her chin. Josie thought she might be talking to it.

The ground dropped away in the direction they were traveling. Soon the two girls were standing side by side on the lip of a rocky ravine.

"We're not going down there," Josie said. "Are we?"

"This is the right way. What I want is down there."

Mary Jane put the glass ball away and started down the bank. She went facing forward, looking down and dancing from rock to rock. Josie turned around and used her hands and feet to climb down backward, feeling with her toes for each step. Mary Jane's way was faster, and she reached the bottom first.

"We're going to get in *such* trouble," Josie complained.

Mary Jane nodded absently. She was searching the narrow strip of ground alongside a rushing stream. Fifty feet further on, she stopped beside three rocks that were a very light gray, almost white. She stood in the middle of the triangle, faced the one rock that pointed most closely toward the cliff wall, then stepped over it and walked forward.

Josie, following behind, bent to touch one of the rocks. The surface was glazed white, like it had been burned to ash and then the ash fused to glass. What kind of fire, she wondered, could do that?

The gulch was steeper here and more overgrown. Mary Jane reached into the curtain of hanging branches and pushed them aside. Beneath was the entrance to a low cave. The girl crouched down, ducked her head, and crawled in.

This was where Josie stopped. Who knew what was inside? Maybe bats. Maybe a bear. Certainly squishy things that lived beside streams, like toads and salamanders. If Mary Jane wanted to go in there, let her.

After a minute, Mary Jane's feet reappeared, moving backward, then her rump, shoulders, and head. She was dragging something out of the cave. When the girl had fully emerged, Josie could see it was just a load of trash: two pieces of corrugated cardboard that were torn and bleached almost white, tattered scraps of silver foil that once might have covered them, fluttering bits of black plastic sheeting, a tangle of wire, and some clothes that resembled a pair of child's pajamas, the kind with feet attached. The clothes were grayish, splotched with mildew, and they smelled bad, even from where Josie was standing.

"Ew!" she said. "Why do you want to touch that?"

Mary Jane turned over a piece of the cardboard, and scraps of foil blew away on the breeze. She looked up with tears in her eyes. "It is … my …"

"It's garbage. You'll get germs."

Mary Jane tried to straighten out the clothing, but the fabric was stuck together with crud.

"Leave it," Josie insisted, pulling on the girl's arm.

"They were not like this. We left them in order and packaged against—"

"Well, then someone got to them. A homeless person. Or maybe a bear. My daddy says there are bears in these hills." Now Josie was growing really scared of the cave. She pulled on Mary Jane's arm, more gently this time. "Come on."

Mary Jane stood up slowly. She was still looking down at her trash heap.

"We've got to get back before Mrs. Gorage misses us and sends out a search party," Josie said.

Mary Jane nodded. "You are right."

"Besides, you can always buy more stuff like this."

"No," the girl said with a sigh. "That is one thing I cannot do."

2. In Protective Custody

EMILY WINDLACE LOOKED at her wristwatch. It was eight o'clock. "Time for bed, Mary Jane," she said.

The little girl who had come into her home three days ago from Family & Children Services looked up from the coloring book. "All right."

She put the crayons away in their box. Emily knew without looking that they would be arranged in order by color, like a rainbow, with the browns sorted below the reds and the black above the violet, like a spectrum. Mary Jane closed the book, flattened the binding with the heel of her hand, squared it with the edge of the coffee table, and stood up. She picked up the paperweight which was her only possession, the only thing she seemed to care about. It was a sphere of cloudy, layered glass, mottled greenish-gray with flecks of gold, about as big as a softball. Emily's first impression on seeing the sphere— she never did get a chance to examine it up close, because the girl carried it everywhere, setting it carefully beside her when she sat down, keeping it always in sight—had been that the thing was not pretty enough to be a paperweight. Mary Jane now slid it into the pocket of her corduroy jumper and patted the cloth over the heavy bulge.

"Good night, ma'am," she said with a nod to Emily, like a little adult. She turned to Emily's husband Bill. "Good night, sir."

He barely looked up from his magazine. "Night."

Mary Jane turned and walked down the hall to the guest bedroom.

In her ten years of taking care of foster children, Emily Windlace had never seen anything like this girl. It was like having a maiden aunt in the house.

As soon as the bedroom door closed, Bill got up from his chair and knelt by the coffee table.

"Don't—" Emily started to say, then shut up.

Bill opened the coloring book. Emily could see, even from where she sat, that each page had been meticulously filled in. The colors were bright and glossy, like enamels, with no gaps or scribbles. Emily had watched Mary Jane working the end of each crayon, twisting it in her fingertips to sharpen and soften the wax, so that the colors flowed like paint onto the page. She even added smudges of white to make highlights, undertones of black to make shadows. When Mary Jane was done with them, the line drawings—it was a book full of Disney characters—were beautiful, like a medieval monk's illuminated manuscript.

"Obsessive," Emily said quietly.

"She's had a tough time," Bill offered.

"Do we really know that?"

"Well, the cancer ..."

It hadn't taken them long to discover that Mary Jane's golden curls were a wig. It was a good one, too, probably made with real hair. But underneath, she was totally bald. She also lacked any trace of body hair; so Emily had to use her makeup kit to fill in the girl's eyebrows and supply her with a set of false eyelashes. Being nine years old, according to the best estimate from the report forwarded by the Human Services Agency of San Francisco, Mary Jane wouldn't have to worry about growing hair anywhere else just yet.

The girl's medical condition was still a mystery. She had been found in the street after the explosion of a gas main leveled the toy store, F.A.O. Schwarz, the previous month in San Francisco. Mary Jane had been slightly injured, mostly scrapes and bruises, a mild concussion, but apparently left amnesic, with no recollection of her former life. Even her name, Mary Jane Doe, was just what the nurses at San Francisco General had put on the admitting paperwork. Because the girl fought when they tried to take blood or tissue samples, no one had been able to give her more than a cursory checkup.

Cancer was suspected only because hair loss was the commonest reaction to chemotherapy, but in all other respects

Mary Jane seemed healthy—remarkably so. Almost supernaturally so, because she never complained of a sniffle, an ache, or any of the minor ills to which neglected children were usually subject. The doctors theorized her hair loss might be *alopecia totalis*, an autoimmune disorder possibly caused by stress, which foster parents sometimes saw in the children that came their way—although few arrived with their own high-class wigs. But Mary Jane was the calmest, most reserved and self-contained child the Windlaces had ever taken on. Still, Emily was rooting for the stress thing because, without diagnosis or treatment that the girl would sit still for, a cancer would remain undiagnosed and progress silently to take her before her tenth birthday, whenever that might be.

"Are you sure she's even a little girl?" Bill asked now. "I mean … you've undressed her?"

"She's one hundred percent female," Emily said.

"But weird. Have you talked about women things?"

"She's very well informed. Maybe too much so."

The possibility that Mary Jane had been abused, used for child prostitution or worse, was something they routinely discussed with the agency about all their charges. This girl's physical person, reactions, and temperament indicated no such history. In fact, she seemed to have no history at all. She had been found with no identification, no clothing tags, no latchkey stuff. No jewelry, except for a plain metal locket with no pictures or engraving inside—not even an "inside" that anyone in Family & Children Services could discover after much tweezing and prying. And no one had shown up to claim her. Mary Jane seemed to be the little girl who dropped out of the sky.

"Strange child," Bill said, shaking his head.

"Not the worst we've had," Emily said.

"Count our blessings, I suppose."

————

In the guest bedroom, the girl known as "Mary Jane," whose real name was Merola, took off her clothes and laid them out on the bed. She fished the glass sphere out of the jumper pocket and set it on the nightstand. Then she hung the outer coverings, which were still in Emily's category of "not yet dirty enough to wash," inside the closet room and patted them smooth. She folded her other garments, which were of the category "need to be washed now," by halves and halves again, into neat square packages. She put these inside the rounded box made of dried and woven vegetable fiber, which Emily called a "hamper." That was the designated place for clothing of the latter category.

Life was strange among these people. They made distinctions where none were necessary. Take clothes, for example. The pieces in the hamper were what Emily called "underwear." But the pieces on the hangers could not be called "overwear" or "outerwear," which was reserved for a separate category associated with rain and storms. They actually had weather here!

Underwear was vaguely nasty and had to be cleaned incessantly. The other garments were publicly acceptable and so could be worn with accumulated dirt … even though they were more exposed and so likely to need cleaning more often. Everything else in this culture was the same. Taboos and covenants to the right and left of her.

Standing naked beside the bed again, Merola took off her wig and set it on the bureau. Emily had apologized for not having a proper "wig stand." Instead, she had provided a "cookie jar," which was supposed to keep the scalp net's shape. Merola never mentioned how much the wig had been crushed in transit when she came to this city.

She peeled the false lashes from her eyelids and rubbed Emily's paint off her brow ridges. Merola had used better cosmetics when she first came here, but they were gone now. She rubbed her palms over the dome of her skull and sighed.

Left to her own preferences, Merola would just curl up and sleep, but there were more conventions to be observed. She reached under the pillows and took out the sleeping garments Emily had called "peejays." Storing them among the bedclothes—an entirely new category of clothing—seemed logical enough. However, the garments themselves, sometimes also called "pajamas," were strange lumpy coverings secured with stitched bands of rubberized material and buttoned tabs that tangled, tugged at her skin, and itched. They wholly impeded Merola's sleep habits.

So did the layers of cloth she was supposed to pile on herself after lying down on the bed. This was so much more complicated than simply adjusting the room's climate to begin with. Emily and Bill's house systems were designed to maintain an ambient temperature, of course, but it was fifteen degrees below Merola's normal body temperature. The sheets, blanket, and bedspread were a throwback to living in a cold, damp cave. And the musty construction of springs and fabric called a "mattress" was a throwback to a bunch of dried grasses wadded on the floor of that cave. Merola longed for a pair of field plates, but that was beyond hope.

Seven thousand years of so-called civilization had taught these people nothing.

Once she was installed under the coverings, Merola took the glass sphere from the nightstand and into the bed with her, clutching it under her chin. She had let everyone imagine that the sphere was no more than an ornament, a toy. Children of Merola's assumed age and distressed situation were supposed to fixate on such irrelevant possessions. But the sphere, whose real name was Berzher, was hardly irrelevant. He was her companion in distress, her first officer, her technical assistant, her oldest friend—and her only means of getting home.

They would have to figure out a way to do that, and soon. Of course, Berzher himself was immutable in his current state. Merola could bury him in the yard outside and he would eventually find his way home, by one path or another, with all of his memories intact. Merola herself was relatively immutable, too—and that was the problem.

Emily had already enrolled Merola in the local "grammar school" in a naïve attempt at socializing what Emily half-believed to be a "runaway"—not an actual Flüchtling, but a feral child. Clearly, Emily liked Merola and harbored fantasies of raising her as a daughter. How ironic! Merola had the advantage of thirty years on this woman. Probably more than that.

This house was a good place to hide, to wait for rescue, if any was coming at this late date. But this refuge would not serve for long. In time—one year? two years?—the children in Merola's school class would begin to change around her. These "fourth-graders" would go through puberty, grow breasts and body hair, gain inches in height, and become what Emily would call young women.

But not Merola. Not ever.

So she had to get out of this absurd situation. She must escape this overly protective society, in which she was not even a legal person, much less a citizen. But where could she go, that they would not recover her and return her to this place, or worse?

Merola knew she had made mistakes on this mission. Berzher would catalog them for her, if he could. As she drifted off to sleep, Merola recounted those mistakes ... in order to plan her next move ...

3. Medical Service

On the pediatrics floor of San Francisco General Hospital, Shannon Carter, RN, hesitated outside Room 221A. She moved the hypodermic set in her left hand around behind her back. Maybe if the girl inside didn't see it this time …

"And how are *we* today?" Shannon sang out as she opened the door and entered the room, moving fast and making her best effort to sound cheerful and excited.

In the far bed, the bald little girl with no name was sitting up. Her knees were drawn up under her chin, and her spine curved forward, away from the bed's raised head portion. Her pose was an angular caricature of the fetal position except that, instead of being comatose and withdrawn, the girl was terribly, almost hyperactively, alert. Her head snapped around like a spring-loaded machine. Shannon felt the cold, gray stare of those eyes pass through her like a ghost. There was no other response.

"It's—uh—time for your medicine," Shannon said.

The girl's body tensed. That is, it was already tense and now it started to vibrate.

"This won't hurt a bit," Shannon said, bringing the hypodermic with its pediatric dose of Seconal into view for the first time.

The girl glared at the needle as if it were a knife aimed at her heart. "No!" she said in a deep, hoarse voice that reminded Shannon of all the demonically possessed little girls in films about exorcism.

"This will help you relax," Shannon said as she laid the needle on the tray table and opened a cotton swab saturated with orange antiseptic.

"No!" The girl pushed herself back up the slope of the bed.

"It's on doctor's orders, so it's good for you," Shannon explained carefully.

341

"No!" The girl had her back against the green-painted wall by this time, wedging herself among the instrument fittings and gas outlets.

"Come on now," Shannon reasoned. "It's on your chart. If you don't take the injection, I could get in trouble."

The girl looked to the left and right, seeking a way to escape. Shannon herself was leaning over the near side of the bed, blocking the path back down the mattress. The other side was obstructed by the tray table. If the girl bolted that way, she would have to go over the remains of her lunch and put her weight, however briefly, on the wheeled table—which would probably roll away and dump her. Shannon could read the calculation in the girl's glance.

"Gotcha!" she said to herself.

She moved the swab toward the crook of the girl's arm.

The girl froze, watching as if it were a burning brand.

Shannon touched the saturated tip to the pale skin.

The girl didn't move, although the skin visibly twitched right at the point of contact. Taking such docility as a good sign, Shannon moved the swab in a small circle, painting loops on the skin. The girl stared down, as if fascinated by the sudden coolness of evaporating alcohol.

While she was distracted, Shannon leaned forward—to block the girl's line of sight—and took the syringe from the edge of the tray table. She moved it slowly, almost languidly forward, toward the prepared spot above the vein.

When it came into view, the girl's attention was instantly riveted on the needle.

"That's okay," Shannon crooned. "Nothing there. So tiny you can hardly see it. You won't feel a thing."

When the tip was still six inches from her arm, the girl heaved. With her head and shoulders braced against the wall, her feet against the mattress, she arched her back and shoved Shannon aside with a deft thrust of her stomach. Then she was making a straight run down the bed.

Without a thought for safeguarding the syringe and where the needle might stick, Shannon tackled her.

The girl rolled and kicked, accurately striking Shannon just below the sternum and knocking the wind out of her.

Before Shannon could lift her head, the girl was across the room.

Just at that moment, a Candy-Striper came through the door.

"Don't let her get away!" Shannon ordered breathlessly.

The Candy-Striper bent her legs and spread her arms.

The girl veered toward the bathroom. Shannon let her go in, then signed to the Candy-Striper to close the door. There was no way out except back through the room. And even if there were another exit, the girl's only possession—a skuzzy paperweight made of fused glass and metal—was still perched on the windowsill. She would never stray far from that thing.

"What's all the fuss about?" the Candy-Striper asked.

"She hates needles," Shannon said mildly.

"I *guess*," the younger woman said.

Then Shannon saw that the syringe was sticking out of her own leg at an angle. Luckily, the plunger had only depressed a half-centimeter or so—maybe a third of a child's dose of sedative. Oh well, she was at the end of shift anyway. She withdrew the needle and threw it onto the tray table in disgust.

Outside, at the nurse's station, Shannon met her shift supervisor, Ann Maccles.

"Any luck?" Ann asked.

"Now what do you think?"

"I'm guessing she fought."

"Like a wild animal," Shannon agreed.

"Poor kid, her chemo must have really been bad."

Shannon shook her head. "My experience is that children become inured to the injections, rather than fighting them. For a few cc's of Seconal—compared to what she normally gets—this gal should be putting out her arm with a smile."

"Not all of them become blasé," Ann said. "Some are terrorized. It's just an emotional reaction."

"She was terrorized *before* she saw the needle. She was vibrating like a tuning fork even before I got to the room."

"Well, consider what she's been through: the cancer, the chemo, and now that awful explosion and being abandoned. It's a hard life for a little girl."

"Uh-huh," Shannon said dubiously, rubbing the sore spot below her breastbone. "I'm reserving my sympathy for a patient who doesn't kick like a mule."

4. Essopee for Shocky

MEROLA WOKE UP in a garishly lighted room that was swaying from side to side. She slitted her eyes and, without moving her head, permitted herself a surreptitious look around. This was the cabin of some sort of vehicle, perhaps a small saucer—except for the jolting gravity fluctuations. Facing her were two paired metal panels holding view screens, or was it possible they were actually doors with windows made of fragile, fused silica? The view beyond them showed gray city buildings constructed of steel beams, stonework, and mirrored glass panes—all receding at dizzying speed but still at ground level.

Not a saucer then. And this was not a rescue.

A moment of panic seized her. Whoever had taken her was physically removing her from the scene of ... whatever had happened. And the place where she had been was also her last time on mark. According to Jongleur protocol, if she failed to return from a mission, a rescue team would be sent immediately—perhaps even before the "whatever" happened—but only to her last known location. And she was moving rapidly toward a new and unknown place.

Rydin, her section chief, would be so angry. Merola had allowed herself to be ambushed, trapped like a trainee on her first Search, separated in one stroke from her ship, the resources of her biosuit, her intelligence, and ... nearly killed? That last part was still hazy. She almost hoped the Troupe would not send Rydin after her, because she could not stand the contempt she would see in his face. Rydin was not only her trainer and mentor; he was her friend—and maybe something more than friend, at least in Merola's imagination. But he was also resourceful. Rydin, if anyone, would be able to find her wherever these people might be taking her.

As she watched the world slide away behind the vehicle, the city blocks where she had been picked up were replaced by less substantial dwellings of cream-colored stucco and painted wood. All of this movement was accompanied by dizzying sounds: the roaring of some kind of mechanical engine, the squealing from friction of rubber tires on pavement, and alternating, amplified wails, whoops, and chirps that were meant as warning to other vehicles.

She moved her head a bit more to inspect the insides of this cabin. To her right and left, the wall surfaces displayed oblong hatches secured by simple pressure latches, probably storage compartments—but for what? Merola herself was lying on a thin pad covered with white cloth and attached to some sort of pipework frame.

She was held in place with straps.

A needle and clear tube came out of her arm.

Berzher's naked entity was no longer clutched in her hand.

But everything depended on Berzher now. Merola's fingers moved convulsively and immediately brushed against the glass sphere, which was rolling around on the pad just below her right hip. She scooped it into her palm and held it tightly.

"You thought you'd lost that, I bet," said a voice above her head.

Merola looked up and found a dark-haired man sitting on a low bench opposite her restraining rack. He was letting his body sway easily with the cabin's movements. His hands were sorting supplies into the various hatches, but he was keeping one eye on her. The man wore a white uniform, suggesting a servant or attendant of some kind, but his manner was more watchful—like a jailer's.

"Mine," Merola groaned, tightening her hold on Berzher.

"Wouldn't touch it for the world," he said, raising his hand.

"Where am I?" she asked.

"Ambulance. Going to Esseff General."

Merola digested that, trying to interpret.

"And why am I being restrained?"

"It's essopee for a concussion," he said. "You were knocked out."

"Knocked out?" she said blankly. "How?"

"Oh, I get it. Some short-term memory loss, too," the man said. "Well, it seems a gas main blew up under the toy store. Took out the whole back half of the building and pancaked the rest. Luckily, you were up near the front, actually blown out onto the street."

"What are you doing with my arm?" Merola asked suspiciously, nodding toward the needle and the transparent tube, which attached to a plastic bag hanging from a hook over her head. From what she could see, the bag and tube contained clear fluid—not the red of flowing blood. So, either these people had filters on their sample extractors to block platelets, or the flow was reversed, going *into* her arm rather than out. The position of the bag—high in the air, to let gravity assist the flow—suggested this as well. But Merola waited to hear what the man had to say.

"You looked kind of shocky, so I started a saline drip with norepinephrine." He paused. "That's a—"

"It's a neurotransmitter and vasoconstrictor," Merola said. She felt within herself to confirm the fluid was doing nothing more. As an interrogation technique, giving her salt and hormones would prove ineffective. "Just medicine," she decided.

"Say! How does a little girl like you know such big words?"

"It's essopee." She let her head fall back on the pad.

Pumping twenty-first century nostrums into her bloodstream was a harmless diversion, as Merola's body was adapted to compensate for a wide range of poisons. What she had to guard against was anyone taking samples out, whether by intention or inadvertence. When she left this cabin—this "ambulance"—she must be awake in order to destroy that needle. Even the smallest sample, such as a tissue plug caught on its inner surface, would be enough to type her and reveal far too much about her situation.

As the ambulance careened onward, Merola closed her eyes and prepared for a convulsive thrust that would enable her to destroy the evidence. She was a prisoner now, subject to interrogation. It would take all her strength, all her sense of purpose to remain anonymous and get on with the job of connecting with Rydin or, failing that, finding a way to get herself—and Berzher—home.

5. Something Wicked This Way Comes

GLYPH HAD DISCOVERED that watching over a city was easier and safer in those times and places when the tallest building at the center of affairs was a cathedral. The roofline of the department stores and office buildings around this place, which—as he read in the minds of people passing below—was called "Union Square" at the center of "San Francisco," contained no gargoyles. In fact, these buildings had no decoration at all. How boring and utilitarian!

Not that he needed to worry too much about camouflage and concealment. If any of the inhabitants below should happen to look up and notice him, he could be gone in the blink of an eye. Glyph was an oddity among his own kind—if he had a kind. While other beings like him could only see across the dimensions that separated the various Branching Universes by using sensitive instruments that drew gigawatts of power, Glyph could do it with just his mind. Sometimes, when he really concentrated, and when the stars were in their proper alignment, he could perceive things moving as in a vision. And sometimes, with a frightful expenditure of mental, emotional, and physical energy, he could cross. Briefly.

But as if in compensation for this remarkable talent, Glyph was effectively blind upon entering any new world. It swarmed and swirled around him as a confusion of objects, actions, interactions, and energies, all without purpose or meaning. He could only see and navigate through any new space by locking onto a guide, a mind that was already accustomed to the dimension's intricacies and could show him meanings behind the shapes he perceived. And then, not every mind would work for him. He needed to find an affinity, the right kind of energy, a mind attuned to the same anger, spite, and malice that lay behind his own chaotic creation. A kindred mind could focus him in this dimension, as a beam of light threw up reflections and shadows against the darkness.

Glyph had only come to this boring, gray-toned place above the San Francisco streets because he had found and followed, not one, but three such minds. Small minds, to be sure, but locked in a triangular web of thoughts and emotions that caused them to blaze in his consciousness. Others of their kind—if they had a kind—called them the "Ramsays," or sometimes the "Silent Three," and thought of them as bizarre and dangerous beings. Among the three, however, they whispered the names "Genjifer" and "Gjordge" and "Giuffre," and they thought themselves beautiful—but also dangerous. The strongest of the minds was the one that identified as female, and on her Glyph tended to focus his own thoughts. The two others—brothers? womb mates? some relationship accounting for their linked energies?—were less obvious and not always clear to him.

They had gone into the building across the street and not yet returned. As far as Glyph could see, there was only one entrance and, judging from the movement of people in and out, that was probably the only exit. So he waited patiently. Besides, just as their three minds had passed through the doorway and joined a crowd of other, dimmer lights inside, he had read images of chemical instability, of erupting gases, of fire and destruction. Random death and destruction were thoughts that pleased Glyph immensely, and he sensed these attributes habitually stalked Genjifer Ramsay and her brothers.

When they finally emerged and hurried off down the street, he still had seen no fire, no destruction. Glyph was torn between following them along their further path or waiting here for what might happen next. A sense of mutual expectation, mirrored in their departing minds, told him to wait.

Within a short time, as Glyph counted time, the roof of the building opposite rose up in a great rolling wave that progressed from back toward front. Walls and windows at the various levels along two sides of the building shattered and flew outward in pieces. Yes, there was fire in bright orange streamers. And there was death in many of the dim minds that were caught beneath that roof and the stages of the building as it collapsed. Glyph watched contentedly as the collapse crushed out tens, multiples of ten, more than a hundred of those little minds.

One of them, however, managed to escape. The survivor flew out of a window at mid-level, just ahead of an arching tongue of flame. She—for even in this streaking flight Glyph sensed a female in bodily form and mental structure—landed as a small bundle that continued rolling across the street. This mind was not small, however, like those that had been extinguished, and it was not malicious, like those who had foreshadowed the explosion. This mind was as bright as the Genjifer female's but more orderly and with differently bound energies. Something of this one had been reflected in the minds of the three as they entered the building. Glyph sensed this person had been their target … and they had failed, so far, to kill it.

Glyph focused on this new female mind. He detected about her the shadows of many different dimension sets. He could sense them clinging to her like the various aromas wafting off the clothes of a person who had walked through many kitchens. His heart quickened then, because Glyph sensed she was a human traveler. He could use a traveler.

Strange as her mind was, he force-fit his thoughts into hers. But she was already fading—if not into death then into some lesser darkness. He exerted all his will to pull from that dying mind every image, every secret it might hold. He concentrated so hard that he lost his footing in this reality and … *Blink!*

6. Safronesco

"WHEN THE CLOCK tick-tocks, toys come out to play,
    "And as children gather 'round, we like to say:
    "Welcome to our world! Welcome to our world!
    "Welcome to our WORLD—of TOYS!"

Billy Lane paused at the foot of the escalator, his eyes drawn to the animated figures clustered around and peeking out through doors in the giant clock tower. Each one of them—the strutting toy soldiers, the singing mice, the dancing red shoes, and the rolling eyes of the smiling clock face itself—all moved in time to the music of the song. Billy stared long enough to confirm this notion for himself: that what seemed like separate little stories and bits of action were really all just part of one big, cranked-up machine. Like some ingenious … clockworks! Cool!

Billy climbed the escalator steps two at a time, so that he went up faster than the people around him. The first floor of the store was all girl things—stuffed animals, doll houses, and Barbie accessories—and he wanted to get away from that world as quick as possible. The second floor was for babies—or the things that adults thought babies wanted—brightly colored blocks, jigsaw puzzles with pieces as big as Billy's hand, and animal-shaped music boxes. He raced around the end of the escalator and kept on climbing.

Halfway up the next flight he saw three very odd children—two boys and a girl—riding the opposite escalator. They were standing straight rather than walking down the steps, as Billy or any other child would. All three looked the same: straight, dark hair and solemn, pale faces with deep-set, green eyes. The three were dressed in dark suits, like Billy's mom wanted him to wear at Sunday service, except that the girl wore a pleated skirt instead of trousers. It took Billy just a second to figure out that the boys were actually twins and the girl had to be their sister. She stood in front, on a lower step, with her arms folded across her stomach. Billy could see she was clutching a bundle of folded cloth with something round and hard hanging from her fingertips. He recognized it as a Power Rangers suit—the girl's kind, in pink and white satin—and a matching helmet with black, almond-shaped eye lenses. The boys each held what looked like pieces of a large kite made of shiny black mylar.

When they caught him staring, their three faces turned as one to stare back.

He ducked his head and raced on up the steps.

The store's third floor was Billy's special place, full of robots and action figures, construction sets, and remote-controlled cars—things that worked, that did stuff, that made sense. He stopped first at the Lego display. Billy's set at home was big, almost a thousand pieces, but he could never make the castles and rocket ships and other fantastic shapes that the store people always built. He tried to count the number blocks in the battleship they had made this time, all out of gray blocks. And who had a set of nothing but gray, anyway? He stopped counting at two hundred, and he was not even halfway down the ship's side. He wondered if the thing was hollow, or if there were decks and rooms inside. That would be really neat! But there was no way to tell, because the battleship was hanging by wires from the ceiling. No playing with it allowed.

Billy ran on to the display of robots. There was a wide space in the floor here, between the toy shelves, where the store people had unwrapped the robots and let you play with them, for a little while, as long as you agreed to share. Billy picked up the remote box for a Mech Monster. It wasn't actually a remote, he saw, because a gray wire went from the box to the robot's heel. That wasn't as good as radio control, but maybe it meant the robot could do more things. Billy pushed the buttons and saw the robot swivel its head and swing its arms. Now, if only it could fire some weapons …

A girl was watching him. Billy stopped and stared back at her. Girls didn't play with robots. Girls weren't actually supposed to be in this area, if you asked Billy's opinion. After a minute, she dropped her eyes and went back to playing with her robot—or the store's robot, which she was just using.

Billy squinted at her robot. He had never seen anything like it before. It was twice as big as a Mech Master, more like a Mech Walker. As a toy lover, Billy knew all about the different kinds of plastics: the soft kind you could bend, the hard kind that broke with a snap, and the kind with the silvery surface that was supposed to look like metal but wasn't, not really. Most of this robot was made out of real metal, not as shiny as the plastic stuff, more like a dull gray. And the clear parts were much clearer than plastic, more like glass. And the toy didn't have any wheels, not even concealed in its feet. Billy walked over to where the girl was sitting. And hey, where was the control box?

As he came up, the robot rose from its crouch. It stood on two legs, balanced forward, and swayed slightly, like a basketball player guarding his man. Cool! Billy had seen something like that in movies, where you could do anything with computers, but never in real life. And not in any kind of toy he could remember.

"Where'd you get that?" he asked, pointing.

The girl looked at him, then at the robot. "Around here."

"Can I play with it?"

She shrugged. "Sit down."

Before Billy could move, the robot dropped back into its crouch.

"Not you," the girl said to the robot. "Go and play."

Swiveling its blunt head, which had two red diode eyes and what looked like radar antennas for ears, the robot looked at her. "Won't you introduce me to your friend?" it asked in a voice that wasn't as … cute? cuddly? at least not as babyish as all the talking toys Billy had heard before. This one spoke more like … her kid brother.

She nodded at Billy. "He doesn't want to meet you yet. Go and play."

The robot stood up, looked Billy up and down, pivoted on the balls of its feet, and walked off. Billy followed the thing with his eyes. The robot immediately found another boy, who was playing with a remote-controlled police car, and squatted to watch him intently.

"How'd you do that?" Billy asked the girl.

"Voice control." She looked at him with a pale gray stare, as if daring him to call her a liar.

"I … uh … didn't know they understood English," was all Billy could say.

"It's a newer model." She patted the floor beside her, and he sat down. "So … are you here with your mother or somebody?" she asked.

"Yeah, Mom's downstairs with my little sister. They're looking at doll houses."

The girl made a face, as if she thought such things were as stupid as Billy himself did. "How old are you?" she asked. Not his name, his age.

"I'm ten. And you?"

"I'm ten, too."

"What's your name?" Billy asked.

"Mer—Mary … Jane. Do you live around here?"

"No, in Walnut Creek. But I was born here."

"In the city?" The gray eyes brightened.

"From the time Mom and Dad lived in an apartment out on Hayes Street, before Shelly was born. But I don't remember it too much, because … Ouch!"

The pain in his forearm was intense, like something cold and sharp. Billy looked down and saw a needle embedded deep in the muscle. Instead of a plunger, like the needles a doctor used, this one had a tiny glass bulb. It was turning red, and Billy guessed that was his blood. The girl leaned over and plucked it out of his arm. Her fingers twitched, and the needle disappeared … maybe into her pocket. Billy couldn't follow her movements.

"Why did you do that?" he asked, rubbing the spot. It was sore, but there wasn't any blood coming out.

"It's kind of a game," the girl said.

"It's a really bad game," Billy said. "I'm going to tell—"

"Don't be a baby! It didn't hurt that much, did it?"

At that moment, the metal robot walked back over to where they were sitting. It tugged the hem of her jumper with a clawed hand. "We are not alone, Merola," it said quietly.

"Where?" the girl asked.

"Circuits on all sides." The robot waved a claw around the store. "Just lit up in the last eight seconds."

"Right." The girl stood up and pulled Billy up, too. "Get out of here," she said. "Take your mother and sister, if you can find them. But get out—" She gave him a push toward the escalator. "—now!"

When Berzher said "not alone," Merola knew he wasn't talking about store detectives, local police, or any kind of trouble that the humans inside the store could detect—or understand. He meant the Flüchtlinge. Perhaps even Möglichen. Either would be a deadly threat to Merola and her kind.

They both had been expecting some kind of interruption all morning. You really could not operate in the clear, among people like this, for very long. On a Search, everyone was watching. But she had done well: four marrow samples with a geographic range that might be as wide as ten thousand miles and forty thousand years, given that one of the children matched the phenotype Rydin called "Chinois"—or perhaps even one of the fabled wild-type Nipponiers. The last specimen had been as blonde as Merola's own wig. Rydin would have called him a "Euro," maybe of Scandian stock, or possibly a Roos. Good diversity. A good spread. And the samples were now stabilized in the environment of her special pocket.

As the boy Billy ran for the escalator, Merola turned to Berzher. "Stand and fight?" she suggested.

"Not unless you want to leave streaks," her lieutenant replied. "Besides, I need this chassis."

Merola hesitated for a fraction of a second longer. But then … the others would have all the time in the world. They would know everything about her party: its composition, deployment, weapons, and time on mark. They would be coming in force sufficient to guarantee the outcome of any engagement. "Best to fly," she agreed.

They ran to the back of the store—moving closer, of course, to the building periphery, the enemy's indicated arrival point, but closer still to her ship. They had left it in a storage room that was crowded with boxed and baled merchandise for sale: legions of toy robots, electric wheeled vehicles, some sized to fit a child, gaudy boxes of puzzles and games, dress-up costumes representing a variety of currently admired mythical characters, and a collection of wind-powered flying machines called "kites." While Berzher attended to ship preparation, Merola retrieved her biosuit.

She had left it on an upper shelf, folded with a stack of pink and yellow costumes for females that were labeled "Power Rangers." From the dust in the creases of these garments, Merola had guessed that no one would disturb the pile during her brief time on mark. Now she dug through it, feeling for the peculiar weight of her suit's laminated fabric. It wasn't there! She found plenty of thin nylon garments, some that might even fit her, but none that would sustain her life under the extreme conditions presented by her intended journey. Even her helmet was missing from the line of pink-and-white plastic shells with lozenge-shaped lenses. Someone—some near-sighted clerk with remarkably insensitive fingers—must have sold her biosuit in place of a make-believe superhero outfit.

"One minute, Merola," Berzher warned. From a bin of folded kites—twenty-first century toys made of sticks, paper or plastic film, and string—he had extracted four of the panels of their liteship, unfurled their laminar plies of molecule-thin energy branes, rigged the retaining wires, and released the selvaged singularity that was the liteship's heart.

His carapace froze. "Two panels are missing!"

"I know," she said. "My suit's gone, too."

Berzher gave the mechanical equivalent of a shrug and leapt to his position on the starboard support rod. He clung there with three of his robot claws and jacked his sensorium into the control station. The top and bottom panels were already glowing with charge. "We can make it off planet on four panels," he said.

"My suit's gone!" she repeated, more loudly. "I can't fly!"

"Well—then—you could—I could—"

"No choice. You fly out of here. I stay behind."

"And do what? Fight the Möglichen? *Bargain* with them?"

"You can get a message through. Tell Rydin I messed up. Have a relay team deposit another suit for me. Or leave a note, upstream of our departure, warning me not to be so careless."

Berzher detached himself from the liteship. "Maybe I can find your suit."

"There's no time!" she exclaimed.

And then, from deep in her mind, a cadence began. It welled up, took the shape of words. She closed her eyes, visualized, and whispered aloud: *"I am whole. … I am full of light. … I am perfect. … I am full of light. … The light surges into and through my blood, making of it a fountain of purity, vitality, youth, and beauty."* Followed by the ritual pause for reflection … *"The universe and I are One."*

From down near her hip, Berzher asked, "What are you doing?"

"Preparing my mind for the ultimate translation."

"Good idea. … It's already started."

The back wall of the room bulged inward and exploded in a shower of bits: dust, plaster flakes, cement fragments, and steel needles torn from the wall's reinforcing bars. The liteship disintegrated. Its tiny singularity dissipated with a *buzz* and a *snap!* even before the shock wave fully engulfed it. Berzher's chassis flipped sideways into the opposite wall. The robot's carapace split open, and the glass sphere that was his entity rolled out on the floor.

In reciting the "Prayer to Light," Merola had also been preparing her body, loosening her spine and limbs, to ride the wave wherever it took her. But now the sight of Berzher, naked and helpless, galvanized her. She launched herself ahead of the rippling wall of fire that followed the first shock wave, scooped up Berzher, curled around him to protect the nested glass-and-foil layers against her stomach, and still managed with toes, knees, and elbows to steer her trajectory out through the storeroom door.

The blast threw her across the store's main sales floor, over the heads of people caught in the act of turning toward the still-evolving explosion. She flew past one of the building's structural columns as it, too, disintegrated. She struck a display of brightly colored objects—hollow plastic toys boxed in crushable polystyrene and cardboard—and drove it through a window high in the west wall of the building that faced outward, onto Stockton Street. That saved her life.